D0990963

PRAISE FOR

THE GENERAL'S BRIEFCASE

"Through a highly convincing plot with credible characters and realistic conversations between them, Ray Collins masterfully presents a fast-paced national security threat scenario directed against the United States. Devoid of unexplained acronyms and the hyperbole that sometimes plague stories of this national security nature, this refreshingly readable book delivers highly memorable scenes throughout. (Movie script writers, take note!)

"With sharp prose, terse drama, and short chapters, it's positively evident that Collins has skillfully combined his James Pattersonesque writing style with his several years of service as a US diplomat. I thoroughly enjoyed—and highly recommend—this exceptional high-stakes global thriller!"

—Ralph R. "Rick" Steinke, Award-Winning Author of *Major Jake Fortina and the Tier One Threat* and *Next Mission: US Defense Attaché to France*

"*The General's Briefcase* is a gripping . . . engrossing . . . well-developed book. A terrific read."

—Paul Bailey, Author of *Homecoming* and *Blood Will Tell*

"I loved the fact that both the protagonist and antagonist were dominant females. The extremely fast pace of the story is mind blowing. I couldn't put the book down. The thought processes of both the good and bad guys put me and kept me in the middle of the action of the story."

—Samuel G. Tooma, Author of *Assassin's Revenge* and *The SOOF*

"This is a terrific book, much in sync with current events. It is edgy. The characters are real. I rooted for the protagonists Alex and Jolene, found the villainous al-Sadi the soul of deception and detached cruelty. The book moves quickly. The plot is smart, thoroughly engaging. Plenty of twists and turns. It felt like Nelson DeMille *The Lion's Game* in tempo, suspense, and nerve-wracking anticipation."

—John Nicolay, PhD, Professor University of Maryland, Author, Managing Editor of the Virginia Writers Project

The General's Briefcase
by Ray Collins

ISBN 979-8-88824-023-6

Published by

köehlerbooks™

3705 Shore Drive
Virginia Beach, VA 23455
800-435-4811
www.koehlerbooks.com

THE GENERAL'S BRIEFCASE

RAY COLLINS

VIRGINIA BEACH
CAPE CHARLES

For my wife Betty Ann—my first reader and constant cheerleader, and my children Jim, Ann, Nori, and Susan.

CHAPTER 1

Near midnight Saturday, Dana Hussein al-Sadi stepped down from the limousine and strolled into the Hyatt Regency Hotel in Fairfax County, Virginia. Glancing at her watch, she was right on time—twenty minutes on the dot since the general left her at a nearby bar in Tysons.

She brushed past the bellman, who stared at her. Dana saw her image reflected in a mirrored wall. Tall and model thin, she was cloaked in a knee-length black silk coat, deliberately chosen, although it was too warm for the middle of summer. An enormous gray and black hat swooped down to hide her face and ebony hair like the outrageous headpieces worn on Ladies Day at Royal Ascot in England.

Bypassing the elevators to prevent the bellman from knowing where she was going, Dana took the escalator to the conference level. There she detoured to the nearest elevator. She pressed the button for the eleventh floor where the Plaza Suites were located. Exiting when the elevator doors swooshed wide, she turned right. On reaching the target suite, she buzzed. The door swung open.

"Good evening, general. I see you've gotten comfortable," she observed.

The gray-haired man wore a hotel robe.

When he'd met her at the bar, he'd worn the smart blue uniform of an Air Force officer with two silver stars designating his rank as a major general. Imposing rather than handsome, his air of command dominated the room.

"Come in, Helen."

Surprised he remembered her pseudonym, Dana strode into the room, taking in the surroundings at a glance. Her future would be decided in the next few minutes.

"You're more lovely than I remember. Let me take your coat." He moved to assist in removing her chic outer garment.

She pirouetted out of his groping embrace, leaving him holding an empty coat.

Sweeping off her hat, she flipped it like a Frisbee to land in a nearby easy chair. She kicked off her low-heeled pumps, sending them flying to the foot of the chair on which her extravagant hat lay. Bare feet tested the plush carpet, as if on a judo mat.

Retreating from the too-hasty pass, the general pointed to his glass resting on the coffee table in front of a pillowed couch. "How about a drink?"

"Scotch and soda." A highball readily available in four-star hotel minibars.

While the general was mixing the drink, she cased the room, looking for what she'd come to steal.

He handed her the highball.

Nodding in acknowledgment, she cast her eye around to complete her survey of the room.

She took a token sip and carefully positioned her glass adjacent to his on the coffee table.

"I need to use your bathroom to freshen up."

"Of course. There's a robe on the bed if you'd like to get comfortable."

She entered the bedroom, welcoming the excuse to extend her search. What she was looking for was not visible in the sitting room.

Looking around the bedroom and under the bed, she noted the partially opened suitcase with a change of underwear, uniform, and a shaving kit. The latest Tom Clancy novel and an empty highball glass rested on the bedside table.

She checked the closet and spied the general's briefcase, quietly removing it. The briefcase was a Zero Halliburton model, like the one containing the "football" carried by a military aide to the president, ever ready if it were necessary to launch nuclear weapons. Her informant's information was accurate.

After a cursory examination to confirm there was no easy way to access the contents, she returned the unopened briefcase to the closet.

Dana grimaced. There was no alternative to stealing the case. But to do so, she'd have to kill the general.

Growing anxious with the passage of time, she yanked off her dress. Shrugging at the inevitable denouement of the scenario she'd initiated in the bar, she slipped off her bra and panties. Donning the robe, she belted it loosely around her waist, the dangling sash an unspoken invitation.

Mindful of her expressed interest in the bathroom, she stepped in, flushed the toilet, and ran water in the sink long enough to appear convincing.

Before leaving the bedroom, she opened her purse and removed a Glock 26. The so-called Baby Glock was loaded with ten 9 mm cartridges and would do a big gun's damage to the human body. Having confirmed the pistol was ready to fire, Dana replaced it and carried the purse with her into the sitting area.

Perched on the edge of the couch, the general stared at her robe's open neckline and barely tied sash like an eagle eyeing a mouse.

She noticed the general's glass, half-full when she left for the bedroom, was nearly filled to the brim. Hardly a shock to confirm he was a heavy drinker.

Moving to the couch, she placed her purse on the floor and snuggled into the pillows on the general's right. His arm moved toward her waist. She leaned forward and picked up her highball. Leaning back, she took a sip of her drink and breathed a deep sigh of contentment. She relaxed as the general's arm completed its encircling maneuver.

Dana watched silently as he grasped her robe's sash and tugged.

The robe fell open, revealing shapely breasts with erect nipples. The general bent forward and continued his seduction.

She feigned a moan of sexual pleasure. She felt his hand feathering its way down her stomach, caressing her inner thighs, moving inexorably toward its goal.

Determined to take control of the sexual action, she brushed his hands away, slid off the couch, leaned over, and kissed the general on the lips.

He eyed her angrily at the altered rhythm. "What are you doing?"

"Lie back. Close your eyes."

Dana's plan was a simple one. Once his eyes shut, she would open her purse, remove the Glock, use a pillow to muffle the sound, and fire a bullet into the general's brain. The briefcase would be there for the taking.

It was her turn to be surprised. He sprang to his feet and ripped off his robe. Flinging the coffee table and drinks aside, he threw her down on the couch, standing for a moment with a still limp member swaying. He swung his left hand against her cheek with such force she was nearly knocked unconscious. She raised her arms to defend herself, but he pushed them away. Before she could react, his right hand slapped her other cheek, driving her back against the pillows.

Trapping her on the couch, his closed fists hit her repeatedly about the head. She could feel the spray of blood as her nose was struck. Though dazed, she noticed he was now fully erect. The rumors were true. *The general was able to perform only in the aftermath of beating his sexual partner.*

Accustomed to hand-to-hand combat, she knew it was impossible to resist such a frenzied attack for long. She twisted her body sideways and hurled herself against his knees, driving him backwards and causing him to topple over. Quick to capitalize on the momentary reprieve, she launched a snap kick into the general's exposed crotch, eliciting a blood curdling scream.

Grabbing her purse, she removed the Glock. Belatedly more

aware of the danger posed by the general than worried about the risk of undue noise triggering an alarm, she pointed at center body mass and fired. The bullet entered midway between her target's nipples. The general attempted to push himself up. Taking time to aim, she placed the kill shot between his eyes.

Hurrying to the outer door, Glock in hand, she listened for any indication the two shots had been heard. After a minute she came away convinced no one was raising the alarm. Dana glanced at the naked corpse framed between the couch and the overturned coffee table, hopeful the appearance of an orgy would distract attention from the real cause of the murder.

She raced to the bathroom and washed blood off her face. She grabbed a hand towel and hustled around the suite, wiping her highball glass and anything else she had touched. Nothing could be done about DNA from her nasal blood spatter or other bodily evidence, but no official record was available that could identify her. Fingerprints were another matter. No need to make it easy for intelligence agencies or Fairfax County CSI to track her down.

Dana dressed, ignoring the temptation to use an ice compress to ease her facial pain. She collected the general's briefcase from the bedroom closet and left the suite. Departing the hotel, she noticed the young bellman staring at her, just as he had on her arrival.

CHAPTER 2

Jolene Martin eyed the bright sunrise burning through the morning haze, promising a pleasant summer day. She felt free of the pressures of the past six months and the anguish of the late-night incident at the end of her workweek. She strode into the stable, eager for her morning ride on Regret. The young woman stroked the horse.

"You're a wonderful filly."

After saddling the two-year-old, Jolene trotted out to the training racetrack, a holdover from the days when Virginia had a rich tradition of horses and horse racing. Now the Gold Cup, the steeplechase race held each October in The Plains, less than an hour's drive from her ninety-acre farm near Leesburg, was virtually the only vestige of live horse racing in the state.

On the track, she put Regret through the filly's paces, working gradually from a trot to a gallop. Jolene's pulse was beating in keeping with the faster tempo. Beginning to relax, she thought back six months, a fragile time in her life. She'd bought the filly, attracted as much by the name as by the horse's pedigree. Regret's lineage flowed from the first thoroughbred filly to win the Kentucky Derby over a hundred years before.

The filly's acquisition was a reminder of how triumph could emerge from regret.

Jolene was going through a rough patch, having been fired after a promising year as a CIA recruit at a time when a combination of hard-nosed assessment, hope, and wishful thinking convinced her she was on the fast track to a position as a CIA operations officer.

Accusing Rick Birmingham, a senior official in charge of training at The Farm, of attempted rape cut short her CIA career and had sent Jolene into an emotional tailspin.

During the first day at Camp Peary, her roommate Valerie Dalton cautioned Jolene about Birmingham's reputation as a cocksman. A Southern belle from a prominent Atlanta family, Valerie's blunt and sometimes vulgar speech earned her the reputation of telling it like it was.

"A friend of mine, who shall remain nameless, graduated from last year's training class." She said Rick the Dick—her favorite name for him—made passes at all the attractive women in her class. The seducer's overtures started with sexually explicit jokes and innuendo and progressed to actual groping if the opportunity arose. Her advice was, "Don't ever allow him to get you alone in a room."

Toward the end of her training program, Jolene let down her guard and Birmingham cornered her in the self-defense dojo where she'd returned to practice some falls. She tried to get past him, but he blocked her movement toward the exit. He stepped so close she could hear his heavy breathing.

"You've been evading me for weeks, but I'm going to show you what you've been missing."

He grabbed her arm, pulled her to him, and reached inside her judo jacket to stroke her breasts. She countered by seizing his wrist, twisting his arm to push him off balance, and throwing him onto his back.

Determined to thwart this and any future attempts at sexual assault, Jolene struck him in the throat with a karate chop, her fingers stiff and extended.

Birmingham collapsed, held his neck, and gasped for air.

Jolene fled to her room. After calming down, she went to security and reported the attempted rape. By the time investigators arrived at the dojo, Birmingham had gone. When contacted, he denied the incident occurred. She had no proof.

A bittersweet smile crossed Jolene's face. She *had* been the object of amorous congress last summer at The Farm, just not by Birmingham. George Southern—a sexy Black scholar athlete—was her major competition for the title of number one CIA trainee. He'd also been her partner in a clandestine love affair conducted without the knowledge of The Farm's staff. After she was kicked out of the CIA, George won the number one award by default.

• • •

Jolene's circuit of the track was interrupted by a teenager running from the stable waving her western straw hat frantically in the air and screaming something indecipherable. Jolene curbed Regret and began riding toward the hyperactive newcomer.

"Stephanie, what's going on?"

"Call. This guy says they need you to come in for some emergency, but he won't tell me anything."

For the umpteenth time, Jolene second-guessed her penchant for leaving her mobile phone in the farmhouse to minimize distractions likely to interfere with the rhythm of riding Regret to relieve pressures of her job.

Knowing any urgent call from her workplace could carry life or death stakes, she prodded the filly toward the stable, jumped off at the door, and yelled, "Take care of Regret for me."

Jolene felt comfortable leaving the energetic seventeen-year-old in charge. Stephanie, who looked after the stable every day, had proven she was as fond of the thoroughbreds as Jolene herself and even more skilled in working with them.

After a quick change of clothes, Jolene hurried to her car. She pushed her BMW 440i Gran Coupe's six-cylinder engine to the maximum as she raced from her farmhouse east on Route 7 toward Tysons. She glanced at the speedometer and confirmed her Midnight Blue bullet car was burning pavement at over one hundred miles per hour. The air conditioner hummed at its coldest setting, protecting her from what the morning news warned was the onset of a record heat wave for mid-July.

Her watch revealed it had only been fifteen minutes since she'd received the urgent call to attend a nine o'clock top-secret Sunday meeting at the National Counterterrorism Center. The NCTC was in Liberty Crossing, just a short drive from the Hyatt Regency Hotel at Tysons and four miles south of CIA headquarters on Route 123.

She knew the meeting concerned whatever happened over Saturday night to General Bartholomew Winston, who chaired her NCTC work group. She would not soon forget the general was staying at the Hyatt. The memory of their Friday evening confrontation in his suite was seared into her brain, an unwelcome echo of Rick Birmingham.

Unscathed by the police, she scooted through Loudoun County. If she weren't stopped by a Fairfax County cruiser, she'd arrive at Tysons in another ten minutes and, depending on lights and local traffic, reach the NCTC soon after.

CHAPTER 3

Jolene arrived at NCTC to discover the security complement had doubled. Even Horace, who could be counted on for a flirty look and an occasional off-color joke, was unusually somber as he waved her through. She parked in her assigned space and hurried to the meeting room, relieved she'd beaten the deadline by a few minutes. Apart from the elaborate security arrangements inside and outside the building, NCTC had a generic bureaucratic look, indistinguishable from a thousand locations scattered throughout the Washington, DC area.

Spotting her favorite colleague, Amal al-Askari, at the coffee bar, she hurried over. Amal was an FBI special agent, nearly forty, whom Jolene had come to regard as a mentor.

"Do you know what's going on?" They blurted out the question at the same time and, laughing at their shared anxiety, shook their heads.

The two women sat down at the far end of the huge oval table, away from where the bigwigs dominated the meeting. The seats around the perimeter of the room were mostly occupied.

At nine o'clock sharp, a door at the rear of the room opened and Director of National Intelligence Frank Mansfield marched in, flanked by the directors of NCTC and the CIA. A beanpole of a man with a bald head, Mansfield towered over the accompanying intelligence gurus.

Jolene knew things had to be serious to bring out Mansfield, who, when not advising the president on intelligence matters, spent a lot of time with the media and attending ceremonial events. Most days, the various parts of the intelligence community ran their own show and were not in fact "directed" by anybody.

With no wasted motion, Mansfield headed to the table, sat in the throne of power, brushed at an imaginary wrinkle in his suit coat, cleared his throat, and began speaking.

"Last night, General Bartholomew Winston was shot to death in his suite at the Hyatt Regency Hotel in Tysons, just a couple of miles from here. He was found this morning when a waiter showed up with his standing room service breakfast order. You may hear bizarre rumors hinting at a sexual motive for the murder. Ignore those stories. The reality is far more serious. Most of you are aware General Winston headed an interagency work group that just completed a pioneering report on terrorism. The general's briefcase containing the report is missing, presumably stolen by whoever killed him."

Jolene was shocked at the news—both the general's murder and the terrorism report, which had been the focus of her labors for the past six months, stolen. Her memory flashed back to her disastrous Friday evening visit to the general's suite. She knew her meeting with the general was a matter of record. Was she a suspect in his killing?

She had to admit the general's sexual advances triggered such a rage in her that she was tempted to kill him herself. Instead, she'd kneed him in the balls and fled the hotel. To bury the memory of the incident, she'd sought refuge in the sanctuary of her farm and a midnight ride on her filly Regret.

Mansfield paused, unsure for the first time. He looked over the room, eyes flickering from person to person around the perimeter. "Is Jolene Martin present?"

Jolene half stood and raised her hand. At her appearance, the DNI visibly relaxed.

"Ms. Martin, I understand you are the executive secretary of the Anti-Terrorist Work Group, and you wrote the final report. Is that correct?"

"Yes, sir." She strove to appear calm, relieved Mansfield's tone was not accusatory.

"The report was approved by General Winston on Friday," she continued. "I transmitted copies to work group members and to NCTC affiliated agencies. That evening, accompanied by two armed guards, I delivered the original to the general in a secure Zero Halliburton briefcase."

"Please give us a summary of the report."

Jolene stood and scanned the room. A forest of eyes stared back at her from faces: some concerned, some curious, but none bored as in the typical bureaucratic get-together.

"The report is a comprehensive analysis of terrorism, assessing the pros and cons of major terrorist strategies. At one end of the spectrum is the 'lone wolf,'" she said, making air quotes with her fingers, "who is easy to incite through ISIS social media, but who in most cases will kill comparatively few people. At the other end is the suitcase bomb, which could utilize a nuclear device. In addition to those who would die in the explosion, more would be contaminated by radiation. A successful attack would be a far more serious blow to the United States than 9/11."

She glanced at Mansfield to check if her comments mirrored his expectations. A brusque wave of his hand indicated approval but encouraged her to wrap up her remarks.

"Part one of the report outlined each strategy, spelling out a detailed 'how-to' as well as pluses and minuses from the terrorists' point of view. Part two set forth actions to counter each strategy."

Mansfield nodded. "Thank you for a succinct summary, Ms. Martin. I must emphasize that the report represents a blueprint for disaster. We will spare no effort to recover the general's briefcase, and to destroy whoever is responsible for his assassination. I've assigned the task of tracking down the culprits to Alex Werth. I expect every member of the intelligence community to extend him their full cooperation."

He gestured to the man who had quietly entered the room. Alex moved to the table and took the seat at Mansfield's right just vacated by the director of NCTC.

Jolene's initial reaction was to be underwhelmed. This was hardly the Jack Reacher goliath she'd expect for an assignment so momentous. She guessed Alex Werth was barely six feet tall and tipped the scales shy of two hundred pounds. His sandy hair was clipped short and brushed to the side. *Was that a bald spot visible when he bent down?*

Dressed in a rumpled outfit of gray slacks and a blue blazer, with a blue button-down shirt sporting narrow red stripes and no tie, he could pass for middle management in the CIA or any of the agencies represented on her NCTC work group. Not quite a loser, but hardly one you'd count on to bring home the gold medal.

Alex looked over those assembled and waited for the room to settle down.

"The terrorists have a head start." His low voice resonated throughout the room. "Possession of the report moves their threat to the front burner. My first task is to select the team who will recover the briefcase and punish the terrorists who killed General Winston."

He gestured to Jolene. "Ms. Martin, I'd like you to come with me to a private office where we can talk. You will assist me in deciding who will be on the team."

Addressing the rest of the room. "Once we've selected the team, we'll return. I'd like everyone who was involved with the NCTC work group in any capacity to remain in this room. The rest of you are dismissed."

He nodded to Mansfield and the directors of CIA and NCTC to make it clear he was in charge, and they were free to go.

CHAPTER 4

Jolene led the way to her office, aware of Alex's quick step behind her. *Why the hell was she chosen for this team?* She was no more Wonder Woman than Alex was Superman. Her ego boost at being selected for what earlier in her career she would have regarded as a dream job was offset by annoyance at the offhanded way he'd gone about picking her.

She sat in the leather executive chair behind her desk and waved Alex to one of the two matching maple hardwood captain's chairs, with the Yale coat of arms prominently emblazoned. The chairs represented a rare gift from her annoyingly remote dad. She thought of the chairs as a consolation prize for getting fired last year from the CIA. She wondered whether her dad—who always seemed to be playing some role at the fringes of the intelligence community—was behind her landing a plum job at the NCTC, just as her brief career was about to crash and burn.

Alex raised his eyebrows when he spotted the university seal. "*Lux et veritas*, light and truth. Is that what you believe in, Jo?"

"I prefer to be called Jolene," she said stiffly.

"Jo suits you," he said in a tone that suggested the matter was settled.

Annoyed at his taking liberties, she decided to bite her tongue and dive into more important questions. "Why'd you pick me to help select the team? What role do you expect me to play? I'm hardly a trained Special Forces operative, which seems to be what this situation requires."

"I picked you because you're an expert on the terrorist bible you folks created. It was a damn fool thing to do, but since it's done, we need to anticipate how the bad guys are going to use it—or rather bad *gals*, since it was a woman who shot the general and stole his briefcase. As for your role, we'll play it by ear for a while. But I'm assuming we'll partner in running the team. That'll be our secret, until I'm satisfied you can hold up your end of the log."

Jolene—now officially Jo—opened her mouth to object to her labors of recent months being ridiculed as "a damn fool thing to do." She compressed her lips, determined to stick to the high road considering the crisis they faced.

Alex waved his hand dismissively. "You're wrong to think this incident calls for Special Forces. Brains, not brawn, is what's needed. I'll include a few Special Forces guys I've worked with in the past to ensure they can mobilize the cavalry when necessary. But the priority is to track down the perpetrators. We need someone who understands how the perps think and how they're likely to act now that they have a blueprint of strategies to conduct jihad in America."

Jolene shifted impatiently in her seat.

Alex shook his head to forestall any interruption.

"The key to our success will be a brain trust who are expert on terrorists and terrorism. Jo, you're going to help select the brain trust. And you're going to be their leader."

Jolene let her frustrations explode, her face flaming. "You son of a bitch. You don't know anything about me. I've never led anything in my life. The sum total of my short career in intelligence is that I left the CIA after one year and I wrote a 'damn fool' report that got stolen before anyone could read it."

She was torn between the impulse to hit Alex and trying to keep from bursting into tears.

"Calm down, Jo. I know *everything* about you. You're the daughter of a backstage intelligence guru and a Lebanon-born French American woman who's a noted surgeon in the Big Apple.

Growing up, you spent years in Lebanon and France, interspersed with your dad's tours in various secret capacities with government agencies abroad and in Virginia."

Upon hearing mention of her dad and mom, Jolene absently fingered the heart-shaped gold locket hanging around her neck and dangling between her breasts. The locket, a present from her mom on her sixteenth birthday, contained pictures of her parents. "To remind you," her mom told her, "that even when your dad and I seem remote at times, we love you very much."

When Jolene returned her attention to Alex, he said, "You were an all-state soccer star in high school and a tennis champion in college. The CIA recruited you out of Yale where you had the highest grades of anyone in Middle Eastern Studies. The CIA fired you to cover up a scandal when you blew the whistle on an attempted rape after you finished second in your training class at The Farm."

Jolene grew irritated listening to her abbreviated biography. She leaned forward to interrupt his recital, but Alex made a shushing gesture with his index finger on his lips. She leaned back after lasering him with an angry look.

"I suspect, but can't confirm, General Winston attempted to seduce or rape you when you delivered the briefcase to his Hyatt suite Friday night."

Jolene's eyes bugged wide. No way Alex could know what happened after her armed escort left her at the door to the general's suite.

He ignored her reaction.

"The general figured he was safe to come on to you because of your CIA fiasco. His nature would be to gamble that you wouldn't risk being fired for yet another unproven rape accusation."

Where does he get this stuff? She was determined to slip in her rebuttal as soon as he shut up. But what could she say? His guesswork was spot on.

"When visiting the crime scene, my initial reaction was to assume you'd killed the general and hidden the briefcase. Retribution for an attempted rape. Understandable, if not justified, by what happened to you at The Farm."

Hurrying to forestall her movement to leap from her chair, Alex said, "I realized you weren't guilty when I saw you today."

Jolene halted her attack in midstride, collapsed into the executive chair and leaned forward with her elbows on the desk.

"Why'd you change your mind? Because I have an innocent face?"

Alex smiled. "I wouldn't accuse you of that. Murder maybe, but never innocence. No. You're not guilty because your nose hadn't been bloodied or broken."

"Is that your rule of thumb? A murderess must have a bent nose. I thought that stereotype went out with bad noir mysteries."

His smile broadened. "In fact, the general's murderer did have a bloody, possibly broken, nose. We assume she got it when the general struck her in the face. Forensics tell us it was her blood spattered all over him, the couch, and the carpet. She washed up in the bathroom and used a hand towel to erase her fingerprints throughout the suite."

Alex ignored her look of astonishment.

"According to a young bellman on duty after midnight, she looked unhurt and gorgeous when leaving the Hyatt. Unfortunately, his description was clouded by a romanticized version of what he saw. I doubt we'll get anything useful from security cameras throughout the hotel."

Deflated, Jolene was beginning to believe there was more to Alex than she'd given him credit for. No Jack Reacher, but someone to reckon with.

Struggling to analyze the situation dispassionately, despite her lingering anger at Alex, she had to acknowledge that she *was* the most qualified person to assume the role he'd outlined. Not only had she written the report in the general's briefcase, but she'd also mastered every nuance of terrorist operations and strategies to combat them. Sure, she'd been thrown out of the CIA, albeit for the wrong reasons, but not before learning the ropes of how to function in covert operations. She was, by God, rightfully first in her training class at The Farm. Even her dad's obscure influence, operating in the shadows, could be counted as a plus.

Reacting to her change of demeanor, Alex said, "It's time to focus on stopping the terrorists. That's the challenge facing our team."

CHAPTER 5

Dana Hussein al-Sadi held the briefcase aloft for a moment so it could be admired by the quintet crowded around the table. She laid it ceremoniously on the tabletop. Conscious of the need to mask the pain of her throbbing nose where she'd been struck by the general, she controlled her body movements on the pretext nothing was amiss. At all costs, she must preserve the myth of invincibility to hold tight the reins of command.

"Tell us," said Jaber Sadiq, the youngest and most impetuous member of the terrorist cell, each of whom looked to her for leadership and of whom she demanded total allegiance "tell us again how you killed the general and stole his briefcase."

"Give it a rest," said Zaha Nashashibi, apart from Dana the only female member of the cell. In her midtwenties and lushly attractive, she readily confessed to an overactive imagination when it came to things sexual. "You just want Dana to describe how she got naked and grabbed the general's cock so you can jerk off to the story tonight."

"Jaber wouldn't have to pleasure himself if you'd come to his bed," said Omar Aziz, oldest of the terrorists and prone to play the jokester.

"I'll come to *you* tonight, Omar, but I'll bring my dagger. Would you like that?" Zaha said, flipping him the bird.

"Only if you promise to perform the dance of the daggers."

"I'll take my dagger to both of you, if you keep up these foolish games," Nour Sayed said. The cell's enforcer—whose sheer bulk at six-four and two hundred thirty pounds brought an end to most arguments—was plainly anxious to learn about the report, which remained hidden in the briefcase.

Dana knew Nour had no patience with colleagues whose behavior was a distraction, even though he was smart enough to know this was their way of releasing the built-up nervous tension they'd shared in recent weeks and months.

"All of you, out of here," said Majid ibn Ishak, the cell's engineer. "It's time to open the briefcase."

Dana nodded. "Clear out and let Majid discover if we possess the weapon to unleash jihad on the Great Satan." She pointed to the door and Nour led the procession outside.

While members of the cell were filing out, Dana congratulated herself on her recruitment strategy in assembling a high caliber group of terrorists. Born in America to wealth and privilege, when she decided to embark on a violent jihadist campaign, she thought carefully how to gather a team of helpers.

Above all, she was pleased with her selection of Majid as her second-in-command. Barrel-chested, almost portly but with bulky shoulders and arms, he was nearly Dana's height. Wearing a rumpled suit and scuffed loafers, he would not elicit a second glance except for his characteristic Middle Eastern appearance: brown eyes and hair and a dark cast to his complexion.

In picking followers, she analyzed the experience of terrorists in the United States and Europe to distill elements essential to success. She decided each member chosen for her cell must come with the temperament to withstand the pressures of operating as a hated outsider.

The recruitment criteria based on her analysis proved successful in building her cell. First and foremost, she settled on a small, close-knit cadre, five followers proved to be the magic number; only American citizens—native-born or naturalized; well-educated and possessing special skills; no criminal record—Nour Sayed being the sole exception, having been arrested for beating up three men who accosted him in a bar in Silver Spring—and no history of attracting the attention of the FBI, TSA, or intelligence agencies.

Dana was determined *her* efforts would strike a decisive blow in the jihadist struggle. Her near-religious commitment was driven by the conviction America had betrayed her family.

• • •

"You too, Dana. Out. I must confirm the briefcase is not booby trapped."

After his compatriots left, Majid strode to the door and secured the lock. He opened the room's closet and took out a black bag—the very bag his physician father carried for twenty-two years before being killed by an American drone strike at a village on the outskirts of Baghdad.

"An unfortunate case of collateral damage," the US military spokesman had said to rationalize the deaths of fifteen medical personnel working at a hospital far from Iraqi forces.

From that day, the only son of a martyred Sunni pledged his life to terrorism against the Great Satan, the United States of America.

Majid removed a magnifying glass from the profusion of esoteric tools stored meticulously in the black bag. He examined every inch of the briefcase with care, turning it this way and that, devoting special attention to the combination locks. Nothing appeared to differ from the half-dozen similar Zero Halliburton briefcases he'd studied after learning that was the model in which the Anti-Terrorist Work Group's report was to be delivered to the general.

Once other tests were completed, Majid decided it was time to use his special tools to force the combination locks. From the outset, he believed if anyone wanted to boobytrap the briefcase, manipulating the locks would trigger the bomb. An expert on all types of explosive devices, he knew there was no other way to access the documents inside without disturbing the locks.

He'd tried cutting the sides, top, and bottom of the cases he'd studied with various tools and all methods disturbed the locks.

Majid credited his adversaries for being as smart as he was, and he was confident in his brilliance. That assumption was a safeguard against underestimating the enemy. There was no doubt the locks were the key, even though they were combination locks.

Having tried several methods of circumventing the locks, all of which failed, he decided to resort to brute force. He was sweating from the intensity of his labors, tension, and the soft whisper of fear. The summer heat outside was not a factor since the terrorists' house was air conditioned.

In frustration, he grabbed the suitcase, held it in the air and shook it. Suddenly, his fingers slipped, and he dropped the case. It hit the floor with a loud bang. He froze in fear.

He had no wish to die. In the privacy of his room at night, he scorned the fools who believed in a paradise depicted in the Quran where they would have eternal erections and make love to seventy-two virgins who flaunted pear-shaped breasts.

A simple tool—his largest screwdriver—did the trick. The locks opened with a scary *POP*. Holding his breath, he shut his eyes, lifted the lid, and counted to five.

At five, he opened his eyes, a bit stunned to be alive. He took comfort in the thought that sometimes a briefcase is just a briefcase.

He probed and removed a thick manila envelope. Inside was the expected treasure—the work group's report that Jolene Martin had delivered to General Winston Friday evening at the Hyatt.

Majid unlocked the door to the room, summoned Dana, and handed her the report.

CHAPTER 6

Annoyed with Alex at the highhanded way he was forcing a leadership role on her—a role she would otherwise be proud to assume—Jolene tried to concentrate on who should be on the team. Names came to mind without conscious awareness. She decided to test whether Alex was serious about her heading the so-called brain trust.

"Amal al-Askari is a must. She's the best-informed person about Islamic State terrorism I know. After 9/11, she was in the first wave of Middle Eastern experts who became FBI special agents and spearheaded the agency's shift in focus under Director Robert Mueller from crime to counterterrorism."

"Done. Who else?"

Jolene eyed Alex skeptically. Although pleased to have her first pick ratified, she wondered if he was convinced or merely humoring her.

After a brief hesitation, she said, "Major Steve Randall saw action in Iraq and Afghanistan. Unlike many military in the intelligence field, he refutes the saying that military intelligence is an oxymoron. He's picked up a practical understanding of Middle Eastern terrorism and how to combat it. Even though he only recently joined the NCTC team, he's caught on to things amazingly well. He's an Army Ranger, so he also qualifies as Special Forces."

"Okay. What about Navy Commander John Moore?"

Jolene blinked. She saw no basis for considering Moore fit for the challenges of tracking down terrorists. "What makes you ask about him?"

"Never mind that. Give me your assessment."

"John Paul is an empty suit. He would add nothing to the *brain trust,* as you call it. He's not that bright, but more important, he's always against whatever course of action the group favors."

Unable to read Alex's reaction to her brusque dismissal of the Navy commander, Jolene wondered if their fearless leader was influenced by the pull of John Paul's admiral father who, according to office gossip, had gotten him assigned to NCTC in the first place.

She relaxed when she heard: "Forget him. Who else?"

"Captain Courtney Gonzalez . . . she's the first female officer to meet the stringent physical standards of the Marine Infantry Training Course. A true team player, she has an intuitive understanding of Islamic terrorism. An Olympic medal winner in judo and pistol shooting, she would qualify as Special Forces."

Jolene was reluctant to give up her belief in the importance of Special Forces in dealing with those who stole the general's briefcase. *Brain trust* indeed—that sounded like typical Washington bullshit.

"Agreed," Alex said, in a tone Joleen interpreted as reluctance, but he nodded for her to continue.

"Hans Jensen is a White CIA analyst in his early thirties. He was recruited out of Yale a few years before me, with a better record than mine in Middle Eastern Studies. An Army brat, his parents dragged him from Turkey to Syria to Egypt. While his dad served as a military attaché at various embassies, Hans picked up a working knowledge of local languages and cultures."

"Okay. Give me one more."

"Felix Goldblatt was recruited from Israel by the NSA. He's an all-around genius who knows or can figure out anything of a scientific nature. I've watched him shoot at the range, and he's an expert with most weapons. But I don't buy the rumors he was a hit man for Mossad, not that such skills would be a bad thing on our *brain trust.*"

Alex ignored her zinger. "Seven, including you and me. I'll add a couple of military officers I know and trust—Mike Sato who's Delta

Force and Luke Worthington who's a Navy SEAL. Both served in the Middle East. They're the kind of men you'd want standing beside you when things go to shit and bullets start flying. Nine is a workable number for an action-oriented think tank."

He wondered what Jo was thinking. His chosen partner both intrigued and annoyed him. He sensed a similar ambivalence on her part. Under other circumstances, he would have found her attractive—a candidate for a dinner out, perhaps taking in a play, or a romantic weekend in Annapolis. In her assigned role, she just made him uneasy.

CHAPTER 7

Cradling the NCTC document reverently in her hands, Dana Hussein al-Sadi whispered to Majid ibn Ishak, "Stay in the room with me. Keep the others out. I must confirm the information we need is in the report."

Majid nodded, closed, and locked the door. Physically and emotionally spent, he retired to the rear of the room and collapsed onto the house's only couch.

Throbbing nose forgotten for the moment, Dana began skimming the NCTC work group's product. She said a silent prayer of thanks for Jolene Martin's thoughtful organization and craftsmanship. The report was a model government report of the old school. Simply written, it led the reader from a presentation of facts to the conclusion of what actions must be taken in light of the story told by the facts.

She quickly found the principal section of interest: how to obtain a suitcase nuke and the pros and cons of various means of deploying the nuclear weapon. The report confirmed her expectation that portable nukes were expensive, costing in the millions. While she was able to front the half million dollars necessary to learn what she needed to know to steal the general's briefcase, the cost of the bombs themselves were beyond her means.

However, she was confident she could access unlimited funds from sources in Saudi Arabia once aligned with Osama bin Laden. The NCTC report provided the means to realize ISIS's dream—the ability to deal the US a crippling blow, far more powerful than 9/11. She was certain the how-to detail in the report would persuade the Saudis to hand over the money Majid assured her they were anxious to donate. If her efforts were successful, she would become the recognized leader of jihad against America.

Her next step was to meet in Geneva with representatives of the hardliners who had yet to commit to her side. Dana's bargaining position was enhanced because her father was related, albeit distantly, to the Saudi royal family, notwithstanding his reputation as a bit of a black sheep.

While Majid had worked to facilitate the Saudi connection, he wasn't aware of her backup plan. Relatives and friends on her American mother's side of the family were wealthy. She could obtain millions from Wall Street tycoons who were so disaffected from both the president and old-line conservatism they were willing to buy the populist revolution poppycock she'd been feeding them.

She would be the one to light the fire that burned across America—Dana Hussein al-Sadi, a woman.

What the Saudis could not know—indeed, what neither her followers nor anyone else could suspect—was the web of circumstances that motivated her to assume the mantle of a terrorist.

She was confident a close examination of her background would fail to arouse suspicion of any terrorist links. She'd led a privileged life, born in Northern Virginia, the offspring of a wealthy Italian American mother, Dorothea Hamilton Di-Longhi, in a second marriage to Jousef al-Sadi, a distinguished Iraqi soldier-diplomat. Dana boasted deep roots in America, proven by a BA from the University of Virginia and a Master of Fine Arts and a PhD from Harvard. Those diplomas were supplemented by study in the Middle East and at Sorbonne University in Paris. She was a professor of the History of Art at George Mason University, currently on sabbatical.

What only the most intimate scrutiny would reveal, however, was a close relationship with her older brother Jacob al-Sadi. Dana and Jacob—or "Jake" as family and friends called him—were virtually inseparable until Jake entered West Point when Dana was a junior at James Madison High School in Vienna, Virginia. When she was a child, Jake taught her to swim at the beach near the family estate in East Hampton, Long Island. When she was older, he showed her how to hunt and to live off the land during hiking trips over the mountains in Colorado.

Brought up as Muslims (despite the best efforts of Dorothea to introduce them to Catholicism), the youngsters frequent visits to a mosque in Falls Church labeled them as "different" to their Vienna neighbors, before prosperity and population influx made diversity fashionable in Northern Virginia.

Overall, she was confident any security check—US or foreign—would give her a pass as a patriotic American, albeit with a Muslim coloration.

Losing Jake to West Point brought a shock of loneliness, offset by pride in his accomplishments. Quick to be singled out as a future star, Jake moved from one prime assignment to another, eventually distinguishing himself in Special Forces. He saw repeated tours of duty in Iraq and Afghanistan. He was stationed in Kandahar Province in Southern Afghanistan when disaster struck. Despite the best efforts of the Pentagon to cover up what happened, Dana probed until one of Jake's buddies confided the truth.

Jake was the victim of an IED explosion, set, not by the Taliban, but by a fellow GI, who was outspoken in his hatred of Muslims. The military chain of command reported the death as occurring at the hands of the Taliban, anxious to quash any story likely to remind the American public of Vietnam-era scandals, when murders or "fragging" of officers by irate enlisted men were common.

From the day she learned the true story, Dana determined to exact revenge on the Pentagon and an America that had betrayed her beloved brother.

CHAPTER 8

Members of the team hurried one by one into the meeting room at the National Counterterrorism Center. Alex arrived first, followed shortly after by Jo. Some Good Samaritan who'd been assigned the chore of coordinating logistics for the lunchtime meeting arranged for hot and cold drinks and assorted sandwiches. Cookies for those with a sweet tooth and apples for the health conscious.

Quick to get nonessentials out of the way, Alex grabbed his favorite combination of Coke and roast beef. He took the seat of command at an oval cherrywood table, which was surrounded by a dozen leather executive chairs. He waved Jo toward the seat at his right.

He munched away, mentally ticking off each of the team who entered the room, picked up their lunch, and made their seat selection. He and Jo were the leaders, so their seating was preordained.

Felix Goldblatt, true to his rumored past as a Mossad hitman, sat at the far end of the table, his back against the wall, directly opposite Alex. Alex believed a lot could be learned about a person from their choice of seating in an important meeting. Perhaps Felix's seat location was intended to cast him in a counter-leadership role. Or maybe he just had a deep-seated aversion to being shot in the back. Felix sat motionless, conserving energy.

Mike Sato and Luke Worthington, Delta Force and Navy SEAL, respectively, took the seats bracketing Alex and Jo. From those locations, the team's attack dogs—as Alex thought of them—could watch everyone, at the same time keeping an eye on the only entrance to the meeting room. In their midtwenties, the two men were a study in contrast. Mike, a Japanese American, born in Hawaii from a traditional family, was slight in stature, but with the stern yet strangely appealing visage of a samurai warrior. Luke was football player big, formerly a star linebacker on the Midshipmen's team at the Naval Academy.

Alex had instructed each of the team members to come to the meeting armed and to remain armed until the crisis was over. Mike and Luke carried his instruction to the next level. Partially concealed beneath stylish blue blazers, they wore the latest type of ballistic vest, designed to protect against both small arms fire and knife thrusts, and carried Heckler & Koch MP5 9 mm submachine guns. Popular with the FBI and Special Forces, the weapons had the capability of switching among single shot, three round bursts, or fully automatic fire.

Amal al-Askari sat two seats over from Jo's right, ratifying Alex's expectation Jo and the FBI special agent would be the de facto leaders of the brain trust phase of the team's work. Amal ignored Mike at her left elbow while he stared at her openly. She moved restlessly in her chair, eagerness for the meeting to get under way causing her leg to vibrate rhythmically.

Alex realized Amal and Jo were both breathtakingly attractive women, though neither seemed aware of the fact. Amal's skin reflected the luster of the desert sand, and dark hair hung in ringlets to her shoulders. He found it hard to believe she was nearly forty.

Jo's face was deeply tanned, the freckles on her nose testimony to too many hours in the sun on tennis courts worldwide. Her deep burgundy hair was the product of a recessive chromosome or the result of natural inheritance, given a multiethnic family history. Alex wondered if growing up Jo was called Scarlett or Freckles.

Courtney Gonzalez, Olympic medal winner and Marine expert on devising damaging terrorist strategies, settled in next to Luke. She was a close runner-up in the beauty department, with golden locks cropped close in a mannish cut. He wondered if her choice of seating was an affirmation of her ability to compete with anyone, Navy SEAL or not. His scrutiny took in the warmth of Courtney's get-acquainted handshake, which caught the taciturn Luke off guard.

Steve Randall took his time making lunch selections, seemingly using the opportunity to study the layout of the group. Deciding, he sat near Courtney, but left an empty seat in-between.

Alex caught Steve casting surreptitious glances at Jo, leading to speculation the Army Ranger had designs on her. The team leader felt annoyed but dismissed the thought it could be jealousy. Why would he desire Jo when he'd just met her?

The final member to arrive, CIA analyst and Middle East expert Hans Jensen, faced off with Steve, and nodded to Amal in the adjacent seat. It was obvious he knew her, and, despite the brevity of their exchange, Alex wondered if their background had been limited to the strictly professional.

Alex smiled inwardly. The brain trust grouped themselves to his right on Jo's side of the table. The attack dog contingent was amassed on his left. Felix Goldblatt was a self-identified loner, with one empty chair between himself and Hans on his left and Steve on his right. On further reflection, he wondered if a truer characterization of Felix would be that he saw himself a part of each faction.

Despite his core of self-confidence, Alex wondered how the team members perceived him, since he'd parachuted into prominence at NCTC without a word from Mansfield about his background or credentials for leading the team's search for terrorists.

Having finished gobbling down his lunch, and with little patience for the amenities of a typical meeting, Alex cleared his throat and rapped the table to get the group's attention.

"You all know why we're here. I'd like you to take one minute and give the team a quick overview of your background. Those of you who are new to the group will get better acquainted while we're doing our job."

Once the obligatory icebreaker was completed, Alex pointed to the electronic whiteboard on which he'd already input information.

"I want us to focus on a few initial questions:

- What are we dealing with? Is it one woman acting alone, or a terrorist cell?
- Assuming it's a cell, do they have an inside source at NCTC? Is there a traitor? Perhaps someone around this table?
- Will they immediately pass on the report to ISIS or keep it secret for the glory of orchestrating a 9/11-type disaster?
- How much time do we have before the first catastrophic attack?"

Jo shrugged impatiently. "We don't need to waste time on the first two questions. There's no doubt; this is the work of a terrorist cell. This cell has an inside source at NCTC. The traitor could be me or one of you, but he's probably someone else whom we'd least suspect."

"Everyone agree?" Alex asked, mildly annoyed to have questions he'd considered pivotal summarily dismissed as of no importance.

Affirmative nods provided a unanimous answer.

Jo turned to the next query. "Whether the cell keeps the report secret for their own use or immediately passes it up the chain of command is the sixty-four-million-dollar question. If they intend to forward the report or have already done so, it's game, set, and match. The damage is done so far as who stole the briefcase and killed the general. None of that will matter, and it's not worth our time. We should immediately turn to Part Two of the report and plan for actions specific US agencies must implement to safeguard against each strategy, together with follow-up in the event of a successful terrorist incident."

"It's our job to track down the cell." Amal said. "There's no way terrorists with the nerve and skills to carry out what they did at the Hyatt would miss the chance to make history in the Muslim world. They'll try to pull off a major coup, like a suitcase nuke or some event that could kill thousands—screwing with water supplies, electrical grids, or air controller systems at major airports. Paradise with seventy-two virgins is compelling to many Muslim men. Allah only knows what motivates the woman who seduced and killed the general."

"Whoa, Hoss!" Steve revealed his Texas roots in his reaction to Amal's pronouncement. "We're forgetting this cell is under the direct control of an ISIS higher-up. The cell depends on the Islamic State for money and other resources to pull off any act of terrorism."

Hans waved his hand impatiently. "It's a mistake to think of the Islamic State as having a well-defined chain of command. The overseas cohort is even more loosely organized. Motivation is personal and situational. *This terrorist cell will act on its own.*"

Alex moved to cut off debate. "Jo and Amal are right. If the cell passes on the report, our job is easy. We close up shop and turn over the problem of protecting the United States to someone else. Our only course of action is to pursue the cell as if they are the prime movers out to create a high-impact terrorist disaster." He pointed at the whiteboard.

"The next question is: How much time do we have before the first attack?"

All eyes turned to Amal.

"Here's the good news," Amal said. "We have two to six weeks to track down the bad guys."

Steve guffawed. "How the hell could you possibly know?"

Alex sized up the dissension in the group and decided to let the argument play out.

Showing no anger at the tone of Steve's question, Amal said, "My assumption is the terrorists will try to hit a home run. In other words, attempt to pull off one or more of the strategies outlined in the report that would inflict the maximum number of casualties. No lone wolf gambits for them. Other cells are as well or better equipped to carry out smaller scale attacks, since those mainly depend on one or two individuals, usually young American citizens, who've been inspired by ISIS's social media. They may have no direct contact with Middle Eastern terrorists."

"Suppose you're right," Steve countered. "Where'd you come up with a precise two- to six-week time window?"

"If you recall, we listed the pros and cons of each terrorist strategy. Two weeks was the minimum time for *any* of the high impact options. In a best-case scenario (from the bad guys' perspective), we calculated a suitcase nuke could be procured and detonated in six weeks."

"That's a pipe dream," Steve said.

"Read the report," Jo countered. "I agree with Amal. *The terrorists will attempt to do their worst in two to six weeks.*"

As the team was leaving, Felix, who'd remained silent during the discussion, pulled Alex aside. "Amal and Jolene are wrong. The terrorist cell will already have an incident planned. We should expect a strike at any moment. One designed to paralyze our leaders and scare the hell out of the general public. Time will tell how it will compare with 9/11. US authorities will be caught off guard. Our team will be discredited, and the responsibility for tracking down the cell will be turned over to another group. The terrorist cell will have room to maneuver to carry out the ultimate attack."

CHAPTER 9

Kandahar Province, Afghanistan—Three Years Earlier

"Sarge, I don't want to hear any more. We've got a job to do. And your job is to follow orders."

Captain Jacob al-Sadi, or "Jake" as he was known by soldiers in his unit, had lost patience with Sergeant Reid Berkowitz. For his part, the sergeant looked ready to take a punch at the captain.

The two men were physically evenly matched. Jake was tall, with broad shoulders and slim hips—what his swim coach at West Point had described as an ideal build for a champion, long arms and a powerful torso. Berkowitz matched Jake in height—large-boned, with well-muscled arms and shoulders, a winner of several Special Forces heavyweight boxing matches.

Recognizing the flared nostrils and heavy breathing that foreshadowed aggression, Jake said, "Sarge, simmer down. Unless you want to spend time in the stockade."

Long-standing tension between the two men had come to a crisis over their dealings with local Afghans. Berkowitz had refused to take a meeting with the village chieftain that Jake had needed to miss because he'd been summoned to a briefing with Colonel Wendell "Buck" Stewart.

Jake's Muslim heritage, coupled with an ear for languages, opened him to a variety of assignments interacting with the Afghan National Army, the Afghan police force, private Afghan militias, and village leaders—all of whom were instrumental in helping NATO curb Taliban encroachment. To a unique extent among US officers, Jake could make himself understood in spoken Pashto and, being fluent in Arabic, he could read and write Pashto and Dari, the dominant languages among Pashtuns in Kandahar Province.

Berkowitz had none of Jake's language skills, but he could pass on a written message to Abdul Khan, a former Afghan general.

Many GIs resented the need to work closely with the Afghans, believing, with some justification, their effectiveness as allies was undermined by corruption and incompetence. A few transferred that resentment to Jake, since he was the officer in command who gave the orders. Sergeant Berkowitz was the most outspoken in voicing his disdain for the Afghans, Muslims in general, and for any assignment that called for cooperation with Afghan officialdom.

The two men had frequent disagreements over the nature of whatever was the assignment of the day—army, police, militia, or civilian authorities.

After the confrontation, Jake allowed Berkowitz to stalk away, deciding there would be better opportunities to settle the pissing contest.

• • •

That day's argument was the last straw for Berkowitz. He resolved to get even with Captain al-Sadi. He mumbled to himself, "What kind of a name is al-Sadi for an American anyway?"

Corporal Lou Hardee looked up from his bunk when he overheard the comment. "That you bitchin' about the captain again? You hate his ass so much, why don't you request a transfer?"

"Why should I have to transfer? He's the Muslim son of a bitch who doesn't belong in the Army."

"Whether he belongs or not, you better pray he doesn't find out about your nightly trips into the village and what you do to the teenage girls who won't fuck you."

Berkowitz grabbed Hardee by the front of his jacket and jerked him to his feet, drawing his fist back. "If you ever say anything like that again, I'll beat you within an inch of your life."

"Okay. I'm just saying. The captain's got more clout than we have, whether he's Muslim or not."

• • •

Afghanistan was a hazard-rich environment. Every day brought a new story about military or civilian deaths from improvised explosive devices (IEDs), bombings, crossfire, night raids, and day-to-day combat.

Berkowitz considered ways the captain could succumb to one of those risks. He decided death by IED was the most certain, and the one least likely to leave his fingerprints as the assassin. Unlike fragging during the Vietnam war, when a military grenade was used by a fellow soldier to kill a superior officer, an IED had no link to the US military. It was a common threat from the Taliban and easy to come by, since troops performing clearing operations stored the explosive devices in a temporary warehousing area.

Around midnight one cloud-filled night, Berkowitz broke into the warehouse and stole an IED. He chose a simple device that relied on military munitions for explosive power and could be detonated by a cell phone call to initiate the firing sequence.

He relished the irony that al-Sadi, in a sense, would be responsible for his own death. The bastard captain awoke early, before the crack of dawn. Known for iron discipline and regular habits, the West Pointer followed the same trail for each day's morning run.

Leaving himself ample time, Berkowitz began digging a hole to plant the explosive device at four o'clock in a dark area beside an ammunition supply depot. He had a moment's concern the IED's detonation might set off the explosives stored in the depot, but he shrugged his shoulders, deciding his chosen observation post was sufficiently distant that he'd be okay no matter what happened.

Satisfied the bomb's location would not be spotted by the captain during the run, the sergeant hid behind a metal storage outbuilding a safe distance away. He wore a Kevlar vest and helmet and lay stretched out on his belly. His cell phone was primed to send a fatal signal with the final push of a button.

After what seemed like an interminable wait, Captain al-Sadi came into view, running at a steady pace. Berkowitz imagined he could hear the runner's footfalls, although at one level, he knew that was a fantasy. No sound ruptured the unaccustomed quiet of the base.

No sound, that is, until he unleashed hell with the push of a button. Even with earplugs, his head was ringing like he was in the belfry at Saint Patrick's Cathedral in his native New York.

To his shame, Berkowitz hid his face when he fired the IED, so he failed to witness the climactic explosion as it tore the captain's body to shreds. He was relieved no echoing detonation occurred in the ammunition depot. Shakily, he rose and hurried to the site of the blast.

As he observed the carnage wrought by his assassination, with bloody body parts everywhere, Berkowitz threw up, soiling his boots and MultiCam pants.

• • •

Colonel Buck Stewart scowled at the shavetail lieutenant standing rigidly at attention who was elaborating on the news of Captain al-Sadi's death.

"Repeat what you just said, Masters."

Second Lieutenant Adam Masters blinked nervously. But he responded in a strong voice.

"Responsibility for the captain's killing rests clearly on the shoulders of Sergeant Reid Berkowitz."

"What's your evidence for that accusation?"

"Security cameras recorded the sergeant stealing an IED from the warehouse, digging a hole, and planting the device on the path Captain al-Sadi is known to run every morning."

"Masters, who gave you authority to investigate the captain's killing by an IED?"

"You did, sir. When I first arrived, you said it was my responsibility to investigate any suspicious events."

Angry with having to deal with this can of worms, the colonel mumbled curses under his breath.

"What did you say, sir? I couldn't hear you."

"Never mind, Masters. You're confident the evidence you've compiled proves Sergeant Berkowitz's guilt?"

"Yes, sir. Without a doubt."

"Listen to me carefully, Lieutenant. And, when this conversation is finished, you will forget everything that's been said in these quarters. Is that understood?"

His nervousness palpable, the lieutenant said, "Yes, sir."

Colonel Stewart wagged his finger for emphasis. "You will destroy the evidence and any related records or reports. You will tell no one about your investigation. The official record, which I shall write myself, will show Captain al-Sadi was killed by an IED planted by the Taliban."

"But what about Sergeant Berkowitz? Does this mean he gets off scot-free?" The lieutenant looked shocked at the apparent injustice of what the colonel had just said.

"You leave him to me. Berkowitz will be taken care of. The less you know about details, the better."

After Masters left his quarters, the colonel summoned two of the captain's closest officer friends, both of whom were present when al-Sadi had won a Silver Star for valor in combat. He briefed the men on the manner of the captain's death.

"Are we agreed Berkowitz can't be allowed to get away with it?"

They both nodded grimly.

The colonel continued. "The kicker is top brass in the Pentagon have made it clear we can't have incidents in Afghanistan that remind the media of the fragging of officers during Vietnam."

Reading the expected agreement on their faces, the colonel went on to outline a plan for Berkowitz to be sent on a hazardous assignment with the two of them.

"You will return. The sergeant will not."

CHAPTER 10

Wedged into Jo's office, seated behind her desk, Alex faced Amal and Jo in the two captain's chairs. Her tight-lipped frown telegraphed annoyance at his having usurped her rightful seat.

He briefed them on Felix Goldblatt's theory the terrorists planned to strike immediately, keeping US intelligence sources off balance while they prepared a massive assault based upon the report stolen with the general's briefcase.

Although he had full faith in Jo and Amal's abilities, he realized after talking with Felix, they may have miscalculated. The glib confidence with which they'd touted their belief the next act of the terrorists would be to launch a major assault employing a nuclear weapon or some other devastating strategy—hence, giving the Americans a two- to six-week window to prevent the tragedy—glossed over the possibility the cell had already planned their next move to catch the intelligence community by surprise.

"In short, based on Felix's input, we should take seriously the possibility of an imminent terrorist attack."

Amal, nonplussed, sat back in her chair. After a few moments, she hit her forehead with the heel of her hand.

"Of course. To play it safe, we need to accept Felix's theory. If we gamble on a longer time window and the terrorists strike, we're discredited since we don't know what the fuck's going on. Another team is given the ball, and we're sent to the showers."

Jo reached over and clasped Amal's hand. "Let's face it. The bitch may be smarter than both of us."

Alex said, "So are the terrorists pulling a bait and switch? Threatening a big strike but settling for less devastating hits. Or is the tactic to distract us and buy time for the Big One?"

"They've been planning this caper for months," Amal said. "Whatever happens next could be a gambit to buy time. I repeat—if I haven't already squandered whatever credibility I had—they'll seek to acquire a suitcase nuke."

"I agree," Jo said. "But today's question is, if they're planning a first strike, how do we stop that?"

"I'll inform Mansfield of our current assessment," Alex said. "He has the responsibility to advise the president and affected agencies to prepare for an imminent terrorist attack." He shrugged. "Even though we have no idea what target to protect."

CHAPTER 11

Imoh Objekwu had been driving a taxi for five years, ever since he had immigrated to Fairfax County, Virginia from Nigeria, with the help of his sister and brother-in-law. For the past year, he'd owned his cab, an almost-brand-new white Toyota Camry. He guessed this must be about the hundredth time he'd pulled up in the departure lane outside the United ticket counter at Dulles International Airport. He glanced at his watch and congratulated himself on making good time from Vienna. It was one minute to four o'clock.

His passenger, a well-spoken Korean—who said he was a software engineer, whatever that was—had just paid the fare from his McMansion in Vienna, including a ten-dollar tip for the half hour ride. Imoh watched the husky Asian drag two suitcases into the United concourse.

Imoh checked out the rear seat prior to pulling back into traffic and noticed a package his passenger had forgotten. Mindful of good will and the generous tip, he jumped into the back, retrieved the package, and hurried toward the entrance to intercept the Korean before he was lost in the four o'clock crush of passengers eager to "Fly the Friendly Skies."

Lumbering ahead of him was a young Muslim woman wearing a hijab, who had just gotten out of a beige Honda Civic that had seen better days. Imoh was not puzzled at the garment that covered her head and chest—a hijab was ubiquitous among the numerous Muslims in Nigeria and was growing increasingly common in Fairfax—but he was astonished her entire body was cloaked in a voluminous raincoat. He looked up to remind himself the sky was blue and cloudless, and the temperature was over ninety degrees, a typical July afternoon. To his surprise, he realized he was sweating.

The woman crossed the concourse and was partway to the counter by the time Imoh entered the departures/ticketing area. Alarmed, he saw a pistol appear in her hand. She commenced firing at passengers clustered nearby. An elderly man in a wheelchair was the first casualty. Next was a mother carrying a small boy. Imoh's Korean passenger grabbed for her hijab in a clumsy attempt to intervene. She shot him in the face.

Imoh stopped watching and fled to the supposed safety of his taxi.

He opened the door and was about to slide behind the wheel when a tremendous explosion shut down his hearing. A million particles of glass shrapnel bombarded his Camry, some of the smaller pieces embedding themselves in his head and face. Nearly blind from blood streaming into his eyes, he forced himself to climb into his Toyota and drive away.

He narrowly missed a red Escalade that raced past and sideswiped a black Hyundai with a Lyft sign in the window. Barely conscious, he steered his still functioning vehicle onto the Dulles Toll Road. He hurried to escape the Dante's Inferno the terminal had become.

Thanks to the communications network Jo arranged, Alex was able to keep up with fast breaking events in real time. That was the good news. The bad news was that all the news was bad. Worse than bad, catastrophic.

The first accounts Alex received were from Dulles, around four thirty. Transportation Security Administration and Fairfax County Police Department officers at the airport reported one or more terrorists had opened fire in the United ticket area of the main concourse. A female terrorist, wearing a hijab and a dark raincoat, detonated a suicide vest. Nearly two hundred people of all ages, nationalities, and both sexes were killed or wounded.

Paramedics were putting the most serious cases of those still living in ambulances and rushing them to emergency rooms as far away as Prince William and Loudoun counties in Virginia, Montgomery County in Maryland, and Washington, DC.

CNN reported, "TSA and local police are combing the Dulles airport as a precaution in case other assailants are still at large. Getting an accurate head count of the deceased is impossible because so many bodies have been torn apart by the blast. Matching body parts can only be done by the medical examiner's staff. And they're overwhelmed."

Fairfax police had an all points "be on the lookout" for a beige Honda Civic. The BOLO was in response to a report called in by an officer who interviewed a taxi driver in Fair Oaks Hospital's Emergency Room who was being treated for extensive lacerations from glass shrapnel he'd experienced on the outskirts of the Dulles explosion. The driver reported seeing a young Muslim woman as she was getting out of the Honda before entering the concourse, opening fire with a handgun, and detonating a suicide vest concealed beneath her raincoat.

Needing a break, Jo and Amal had taken off in midafternoon for the Hyatt Regency. Amal was helping her move into a room Jo had rented for the duration of the crisis, being unwilling to face the trek back to the Leesburg farm each night.

Alex's concentration on the Dulles incident was interrupted when Jo and Amal burst into the conference room Alex had turned into his makeshift office.

"Dulles is the tip of the iceberg," Jo said. "At four thirty, a similar attack took place at the Smithsonian Air and Space Museum, with over a hundred casualties reported."

Talking over Jo, Amal said, "About the same time, there were copycat terrorist attacks at Union Station, Metro Center, and Tysons Shopping Center. No reports yet of the extent of casualties at any of these locations. If Jolene and I hadn't left the hotel upon hearing the news from Dulles, we might have been caught in the Tysons explosion."

Trying to calm his two lead analysts and get a handle on events, Alex said, "Is there any evidence to suggest more attacks?"

Jo showed Alex her watch, 4:53 p.m. "We'll know in the next ten minutes if there are more attacks. These four incidents were obviously timed to catch us unaware—Dulles at four o'clock sharp, and the other attacks at four-thirty. The Bitch Queen terrorist has a timetable with a rhythm. If there's another incident, she'll trigger it at five o'clock."

Amal nodded agreement.

"By now, the entire Washington area is being closed down," Jo continued. "The FAA will shut down airline travel, just as happened during 9/11. Amtrak and other rail operations will be stopped along the Eastern Seaboard. The metro will quit operating if they haven't already. Shopping centers will close."

The trio sat around the room, looking dejected, watching the minutes tick by until five o'clock.

Tommy Lee—the team's communications guru—rushed in with more disaster reports, which simply amplified what Jo and Amal had already conveyed. Casualties were in the hundreds. Panic was widespread. The rush hour, normally congested around five o'clock on a Tuesday, was impassible, with cars in bumper-to-bumper gridlock. Workers were fleeing government offices in DC and streaming out of business centers, such as the Tysons hub, in the suburbs.

The mission of Alex's team appeared to have been forgotten by leaders in the intelligence community while they scrambled to implement established disaster plans. No one had contemplated multiple catastrophes on the scale being experienced.

Alex's phone rang. Frank Mansfield, Director of National Intelligence, was on the line.

"Thanks for alerting me to the imminent risk of a major terrorist incident. I passed the word to the president and agencies affected. Not that it did any good. No one knew what to look for. None of us could imagine the scale of today's loss of life. Let me know what resources you need: more people, protection for your team, whatever. Right now, it's urgent we brief the president. Head for the White House. Bring whoever you need."

Alex interrupted. "But sir, I'm told traffic is impassible. We have no way to get to the White House."

"Not a problem. A CIA helicopter is on the way to pick you up. The bird should be there by the time I hang up."

Alex ran to the nearest window and looked out at the whirlybird moving in for a landing on the NCTC helipad. As he raced from the room, he thought, *9/11 in July*. This was one of the darkest days in American history.

CHAPTER 12

President Ralph Scofield, ever the gracious politician, welcomed the new arrivals into the Oval Office. DNI Frank Mansfield wasted no time introducing the NCTC team. He gave the highlights of their role in tracking down the terrorist cell believed to be guilty of killing General Winston, stealing the secret report, and the prime suspect in the day's atrocities.

Alex Werth, Jo Martin, and Amal al-Askari solemnly shook the president's hand and took the designated seats on the sofa and chairs around a large coffee table, on which were arrayed cups, saucers, and the makings for coffee and tea. Everyone accepted the proffered drinks, except for Elmer Farnsworth, assistant to the president for the National Security Council, the sole White House staffer in the room.

Stiffly erect and facing the newcomers, the president said, "You're aware of the threat we're up against. I want each of you to speak your mind. We've accomplished a lot since last year's election, but events of the last twenty-four hours have been a rude wake-up call. We've neglected terrorism. I understand each of you is an expert on such threats and what we can expect next."

Staring at Alex, he said, "Frank tells me you're in charge. Brief me. What's the background on the report stolen when General Winston was killed? Why is the report critical in the context of today's incidents? Finally, what attacks can we anticipate and what actions should we take to deal with them?"

Alex set his coffee cup carefully on the saucer.

"Mr. President, these two people are best qualified to answer your questions. Jo, please lead off."

Leaning forward in her seat, Jo took a swig of coffee.

"Some months ago, the prevalent view in the intelligence community focused on a lone wolf scenario concerning foreign terrorist attacks in the United States—that is, if we set aside white supremacists and other domestic terrorists in line with the January 6 insurrection at the Capitol. One or two terrorist wannabes, most likely American citizens by birth or naturalization, radicalized by jihadist social media, would foment an incident. Several people, perhaps a few dozen, would be killed and wounded. While lone wolf attacks attract media attention, the stakes are not high. The United States is a big country. Terrorist incidents are infrequent. The average citizen doesn't feel threatened. No massive commitment of law enforcement or intelligence resources is called for, and none has been forthcoming. Over two decades have passed—9/11 has faded from the public's consciousness."

Jo paused to assess the president's reaction to what was at risk of turning into a lecture. Scofield seemed mesmerized. Encouraged by his rapt attention, she continued.

"Washington is an echo chamber. The more experts touted the lone wolf theory, the more it came to be repeated by the media and accepted. A few of us asked the 'what if' questions. *What if* the terrorists found ways to launch massive attacks? *What if* the terrorists were able to get their hands on a suitcase nuke—a portable nuclear weapon or a dirty bomb contaminated with cobalt-60 or other lethal radioactive material?"

Coming to the punch line, she returned the president's intense look.

"General Winston chaired a work group charged with creating a report that would identify *all* major types of attacks, spell out the pros and cons of each from the terrorists' perspective, and recommend countermeasures to prevent or deal with such incidents. I was responsible for drafting the report. Over the weekend, I delivered a copy to the general in his suite at the Tysons Hyatt."

The president's nod confirmed he was familiar with the nature of her report.

Jo wrapped up her narrative: "When they killed General Winston, the terrorists stole his briefcase containing our report. We believe this terrorist cell had been planning today's attacks for weeks or months, waiting for the day when they had the blueprint and the ability to commit even more horrendous crimes."

"Hold on," the president said. "If they stole the report Saturday, there's no way they could have used it to arrange for attacks on the scale we've seen today."

"Correct, Mr. President," Jo said. "They didn't use the report. Rather, they perfected a variant of the lone wolf strategy outlined in the report with suicide bombers carrying out a wave of terrorist strikes, possibly with ISIS operatives in the United States orchestrating events. Serious as they are, these attacks are a red herring. They're designed to draw our attention away from even more devastating terrorist incidents, such as a suitcase nuke, that could kill thousands and panic the entire country."

Elmer Farnsworth stood and raised his voice. "Today's suicide bombers have killed hundreds and panicked everyone. Why should we take our eye off the ball and focus on the hypothetical threats hidden in the general's briefcase?"

CHAPTER 13

After praising the members of her cell for carrying out a series of successful attacks, Dana Hussein al-Sadi said, "Let's have a situation report from each of you. Jaber, start us off with Dulles. Begin with how you recruited your suicide bomber."

Jaber Sadiq leaned forward in his seat. "In April, I met Reem Fahmi at the Dar Al-Hijrah Islamic Center in Falls Church. She talked about the Islamic State in a sympathetic way, but she told me she avoided the internet and social media. We became friends and, after a few weeks, more than friends."

"You mean you fucked her," Zaha Nashashibi said.

Dana frowned at Zaha. The situation was too serious to engage in sexual banter which was the young woman's forte.

"She would have claimed we were in love," Jaber said. "I encouraged her to believe marriage was in our future. She was easy to radicalize. The hardest thing was to convince her to wear a suicide vest."

"I said, 'If you really love me, you will sacrifice yourself.' Together, we read accounts of female Muslims who detonated vests. After each reading, we had passionate sex."

Jaber paused and sighed.

"Finally, she agreed to wear the vest that Majid designed. Once Dana set the date and time, I drove her to Dulles in the Honda I'd stolen the night before. I waited three minutes from the time she entered the United ticket concourse to detonate the bomb with my cell phone. Reem never suspected the trigger she held in her hand was not capable of exploding the vest. I could hear the boom as I drove away."

"You did well, Jaber," Dana said. "The reaction to the Dulles bombing surpassed our expectations. Some bystanders took videos of the shootings and explosion. These images and tales of the disaster were rebroadcast on TV and through Facebook, Twitter, and other social media. ISIS has spread graphic pictures of the suicide bombings throughout the world. The terror is palpable."

She turned to the cell's only female terrorist.

"Zaha, tell us about Tysons."

"Hassan Pasha came on to me in the food court outside the Tysons movie complex. One thing led to another, and we began having sex. He was easy to radicalize. I think he saw pledging loyalty to the Islamic State as a way to ensure we would continue our lovemaking. Not a problem for me because he was the best Egyptian I've ever been with at pleasuring a woman. When I buzzed my cell phone, he probably died dreaming of making love."

"Thank you, Zaha." Even though she tried to rein in Zaha's exuberant sexual language and conduct, at one level Dana envied the young woman's tendency to flout convention. She was beginning to understand why men, and even women, were attracted to Zaha.

She nodded to Nour Sayed to go next.

The cell's enforcer said, "I met Ahmad Hattar at the gym. He was Jordanian, lived alone in a rooming house, and worked at 7-Eleven. All he cared about was weightlifting. He became a follower of the Islamic State to be closer to me—but as a friend, not a lover. When I dropped him off in front of the Union Station, he walked about one hundred feet and began shooting. I drove off, and detonated his suicide vest as planned. I left the car in the parking lot of the JW Marriott on Pennsylvania Avenue near the White House."

"Excellent, Nour. A textbook operation. Omar, if you please."

"I found my coconspirator, Usama Saba, in a comedy club, one that catered to the Gay/LGBT community." Not usually outspoken, Omar Aziz seemed to relish the chance to testify.

"He was a middle-aged Iraqi homosexual, rather an ugly man.

We struck up a friendship, and I led him to believe about me what he wanted, even though we never consummated a sexual liaison. I dropped him off in front of the Air and Space Museum. He pranced in like he was going to put on a show. Once he was inside, I detonated his suicide vest."

"Well done, Omar. It's thrilling to hear each of you tell how you took our basic blueprint for a terrorist escapade and improvised a brilliant approach. Majid . . ."

Clearly disgruntled at having to wait his turn, Majid ibn Ishak said, "I heard Huda Khousraf speaking about cancer research at the Library of Congress. She was a famous Yemeni scientist, although I knew nothing about her up to that time. After the meeting, I escorted her back to her hotel. She was on a Fulbright scholarship, touring throughout the United States. We became friendly and spent time together. After a couple of weeks, she agreed to my proposal that we bomb Metro Center. The idea of disrupting with one blow the mixing bowl for the Orange, Silver, Blue, and Red lines appealed to her sense of scientific efficiency. I dropped her off, gave her five minutes, and detonated the bomb. I was amazed at the sorrow I felt at her loss, even though she sacrificed herself for the future of the Islamic State."

CHAPTER 14

"Elmer, you've raised the right question," President Scofield said. "Given the chaos five suicide bombers created today, why should we invest scarce resources on future threats that may never materialize? Perhaps the lone wolf strategy is what we should fear, and our only mistake was a lack of imagination in forecasting how much worse it would be if the lone wolves became puppets in the hands of Islamic State masterminds who have infiltrated our borders and hidden among us."

The president eyed the assembled group. "Would someone like to address that issue?"

Amal put down her coffee cup with a clatter, splattering a few drops on the silver serving tray and coffee table. The seasoned intelligence specialist looked not at all dismayed at creating a mess in the otherwise pristine Oval Office.

"Mr. President, Jolene Martin and I, with our colleagues, spent half a year thinking about the threats posed by ISIS. Leaders of the terrorist cell who orchestrated today's disaster are brilliant and more skilled than we anticipated. We underestimated them, just as the intelligence community did the Al Qaeda team who pulled off the 9/11 disaster."

Amal paused to confirm she had the president's attention. "As you implied, the terrorists had plans to strike at five targets in the DC area for some time. Why then did they run the considerable risk of killing General Winston and stealing his briefcase? The missing report put us on an alert status for two days. That knowledge was not sufficient for us to change the outcome. But there was no way they could have been certain their luck would hold. They valued the report highly because it contained vital information needed to carry out even more horrendous terrorist acts."

She cleared her throat. "Ask yourself, what's more horrendous than what they just did. There's no doubt in my mind the cell has the financial resources to acquire one or more suitcase nukes. That's the paramount threat and," she pointedly stared at Elmer Farnsworth, "that's the ball we should focus on."

Jolene chimed in. "What the cell lacked was the step-by-step knowledge of where and how to acquire a portable nuclear weapon and how to detonate it to maximum effect. We saw what just an *atomic* blast did in Hiroshima and Nagasaki. Imagine what a *nuclear* blast could do in Times Square or the Financial District in New York, Michigan Avenue in Chicago, the White House area, or Capitol Hill in Washington."

Amal picked up her coffee cup and began to pour, ostentatiously confident they'd addressed the issue raised by the president.

Moving to clinch the argument, Jolene cleared her throat. "Consider worst case scenarios. If we're *wrong*, the downside is our NCTC team will 'waste' time attempting to block the cell from obtaining suitcase nukes. Unfortunate, but a cost the intelligence community can easily afford. But, if we're *right*, and our advice is ignored, successful strikes with nuclear weapons could cause more damage to US national interests than any attack we've ever known."

"An impressive point. You've heard their reasoning, Elmer, what would you advise?" The tone in which the president asked the question made clear the answer he expected.

Elmer was no fool. "The proper course of action is to authorize Alex Werth and his team to track down the terrorist cell and take all possible steps—no holds barred—to prevent them from obtaining suitcase nukes. Whatever resources are required should be at their disposal. At the same time, Mansfield should focus law enforcement and intelligence resources on apprehending the terrorists responsible for today's suicide bombings."

Looking squarely at Mansfield, the president said, "Frank you're authorized to proceed along those lines."

Elmer, who had scraped through the meeting with only minor loss of face, stood. "Thank you, Mr. President."

CHAPTER 15

"Success has exceeded our most optimistic projections," Dana said. "The United States experienced a series of tragedies certain to reverberate across the country and around the world, to the honor of the Islamic State. A battle won, but not the war. It's time to turn our energies to the next steps in this epic struggle." She gestured toward the door.

"All of you, out of here. Majid and I need to talk. Remain in the house, or close by, where we can reach you. Sleep if you can."

After the others filed out, Majid said, "It's time to plan your trip to Geneva. We will leak to our friends in Saudi Arabia *you* were the one who orchestrated today's suicide bombings. When they learn you have the NCTC report with detailed plans to acquire a suitcase nuke, they'll offer you *carte blanche.*

Dana permitted herself a self-congratulatory smile. "You deserve equal credit for what we've accomplished. Above all, the suicide vests you designed worked to perfection."

Majid chopped the air in a gesture of denial. "That statement is untrue, worse yet, it's foolish. Credit for me means nothing. Credit for you is power. Never share power. My reward is to be by your side when you achieve our goal of bringing down the Great Satan."

She inclined her head in acknowledgment of his dedication.

• • •

This moment was a reminder of her greatest achievement in recruiting the cell: finding Majid. She recalled the fall morning a year before when she had visited the September 11 Memorial and Museum. The visit was a whim that struck when she was in New York to tour the Metropolitan Museum of Art in connection with a project for her Art History course at George Mason University.

Her presence at the site of 9/11 flew in the face of a firm intention to avoid any actions that could attract unwanted attention from the authorities. She was hypercautious, having decided a few months earlier to transform herself into America's worst nightmare in retaliation for Jake's murder and what she believed to be the Pentagon's betrayal of her family.

While listening to a boring museum docent reciting the events that had shattered New York's peace and America's complacency around nine o'clock that fateful September morning, she noticed a fellow tourist whose reactions seemed out of sync. Other onlookers were awestruck or openly sobbing. Possibly Middle Eastern, he appeared attentive, but unmoved, almost as though he were a movie script writer researching his next documentary. She realized with a shock, his reaction was remarkably like her own.

A too-clean face made her wonder if he had shaved his beard prior to paying homage to 9/11.

Curious, she followed him throughout the museum and into the spacious grounds of the memorial. He meandered past the enormous waterfalls and reflecting pools and took a seat at one of the concrete picnic tables. She and the closely shaved man had the area to themselves.

Seemingly admiring the panorama of amber leaves on the forest of white oak trees, she walked up and sat across from him.

He turned to face her. "Why have you been following me?"

"Your behavior in the museum was unusual. It caught my eye. Why did you fail to show empathy at the suffering of the victims?"

"Perhaps I'm a normally stoic individual."

"Really . . .?"

He laughed, although the situation was far from amusing.

Quickly, he reached across the table and seized her purse. Without warning, he dumped the contents onto the table.

Furious at the affront, she started to react by launching an attack. The warning look on his face froze her movements.

He pawed through the typical detritus of a woman's handbag: lipstick, makeup, Kleenex, and a ring of keys attached to a Lexus key fob. The latter signaled she had money, which he'd probably figured out by scrutiny of the gold necklace with an emerald pendant dangling around her neck. The necklace was a gift from her mother she often wore on trips to New York, as a form of penance for not being a more conventional daughter.

He took time to flip through a small notebook, but the scribblings held no interest. Her wallet and ID cards captured his attention. All in all, rather humdrum. The one exception that stood out like a turd in a punchbowl was a Glock 26, together with an extra magazine for the 9-millimeter Baby Glock.

Slipping the weapon back into the purse, he looked at her curiously. "You're not FBI. Who are you, mystery woman? And why were you tailing me?"

She decided it was time to lay her cards on the table. "I'm a terrorist. Just like you."

The ensuing dialogue led to Majid's recruitment as the first member of her cell, which came to number five followers.

Dana said, "The next step is for you to arrange a meeting in Geneva with our Saudi sponsors. Once that's done, make my air and hotel reservations."

"How will you travel?" Majid asked. "We can't risk that your real identity may be on the No Fly List, the Terrorist Screening List, and Allah only knows what other lists maintained by the FBI, NSA, TSA, CIA, and Washington's whole alphabet soup."

"Not a problem. I'll use my mother's US passport. With a little make up, gray wig, and the proper clothing, I can pass for her."

In the cell, only Majid was privy to the knowledge that Dana's mother—the plastic heiress Dorothea Hamilton Di-Longhi—was safely ensconced in a swank private hospital in upstate New York, under an assumed name, suffering from early onset Alzheimer's. A classically lovely woman in her own right, even in her fifties, she and her daughter closely resembled one another in skin tone and chiseled beauty. The difference in names made it unlikely the authorities would have restricted her mother's travel.

She was convinced a combination of the proper hair style, make up, clothing, and posture would be sufficient to enable her to pose as her fifty something look-alike mother. Since Dorothea had been something of a recluse for some time before her hospitalization, there was little likelihood Dana would encounter anyone who could unmask her charade.

It had been several weeks since Dana's last visit to Dorothea. That memory compounded her guilt at exploiting her patriotic mother's identity in the interests of terrorism.

"The first thing my Saudi contact will ask is the price tag to acquire a suitcase nuke," Majid said. "They'll want to transfer funds to their Swiss bank in Geneva before you and their emissaries arrive."

"Tell him I intend to obtain two nukes. I'll need five million dollars."

Majid glanced up, startled. "So much? I'd have thought you could obtain two suitcase bombs for less money."

Dana looked at him scornfully. "Best you leave financial matters to me."

Rebuked, Majid said, "Of course. I'll contact the Saudis." He stalked from the room, not bothering to hide his injured feelings.

She felt bad dismissing Majid's understandable skepticism at the quoted cost. In fact, their best information was that even a pair of portable nukes could be obtained for less than five million. The explosive secret she'd kept from her followers was the intent to fake her death and retire from the terrorism game after triggering two headline-grabbing nuclear explosions. She would "die" a hero of the Islamic State, having avenged Jake's dishonor at the hands of the US.

A related secret was her plan to obtain an additional five million dollars from the Wall Street tycoons who were her mother's friends. All her life, she'd vacillated between resenting and taking advantage of her Italian American mother's wealth, which had paved the way for her travel and studies abroad, as well as graduate degrees in art history from Harvard University.

Dorothea's money, protected by a trust, would not come to Dana until her mother's death, and, quite likely, not then. Dana knew she could count on nothing from her father, who had taken to a life of dissipation in the sin capitals of the Mediterranean.

She was rich in her own right, but the half million spent to acquire the general's briefcase took a substantial bite out of her wealth.

Her original intent had been to turn to American sponsors for money as a fallback in case the Saudi connection fell through. But contemplating retirement, she reasoned, *"Why not?"* Another five million would make for an even more luxurious lifestyle, with enhanced security.

She began fantasizing about the freedom of a wealthy retirement and how she would be able to indulge herself in the many ways she'd forsworn in the struggle for a lifetime of accomplishment. She pictured life on a sandy beach on the French Riviera, basking in sunshine after a refreshing swim in the ocean, while enjoying the admiration of men and women as she tried out the European freedom of going topless.

CHAPTER 16

Jo and Amal, after making their case to President Scofield, hurried to a meeting at NCTC. Alex called the team together to brainstorm next steps.

"Jo, Amal, and I met with the president," Alex said. "He gave us a free hand to track down the terrorists responsible for yesterday's devastation. But our main job is to stop them from obtaining and deploying a suitcase nuke. In the event they have some other mode of attack in mind, we'll address that when we have hard information." He lowered his voice for emphasis. "Our next step is to think through how best to accomplish our mission. The White House has promised to supply any resources we need. For now, let's concentrate on steps we must take on our own. Jo, start us off."

Jo, struggling to deal with the dramatic developments over the past four days, paused a moment to reflect before speaking. "Our main goal is to block any effort by the terrorists to obtain portable nuclear weapons. We need to know where the nukes are located, who controls them, and the circumstances in which the 'owners' will turn them over to the terrorists. Courtney?"

Captain Courtney Gonzalez straightened in her seat, her Marine spine visibly stiffening. She rose to her feet and crossed to the whiteboard. She sketched a rough map of the United States, Russia, and the Middle East. She drew several circles around Russia.

"Apart from the United States, nuclear weapons in general and suitcase or backpack nukes are concentrated in Russia. At the end of the Cold War, the Russians had enormous stockpiles, which US efforts at nuclear disarmament have whittled down a bit over the years. Nuclear weapons were stored in a haphazard fashion in the economic and political turmoil following the dissolution of the Soviet Union. Suitcase nukes, and often more formidable weaponry, were kept in ramshackle warehouses and poorly guarded."

She wrote on the whiteboard: *MAFIA BLACK MARKET.*

"Ever since the nineties, the Russian mafia has flourished—with Vladimir Putin's protection in recent years. Media attention has showcased oligarchs and the actions of Russian hackers, especially the attempt to disrupt American national elections. But little-noticed action by Russian organized crime is even more ominous. This includes the effort to stockpile suitcase nukes with the aim of creating a black market." She wrote *NUKES FOR SALE.*

"It's no secret terrorists, previously including Osama bin Laden, have attempted to acquire nuclear weapons. This hasn't worked, primarily because of the high degree of technological expertise necessary to maintain a small nuclear weapon in a state of readiness over time. But the Russian mafia are businessmen. They've identified suitcase nukes as a product with a potentially large and growing market. The price is forecast to skyrocket in the next few years. The mafia has begun recruiting scientists and technicians able to support small-scale nuclear weapons. In short, Russia is the likely origin of the suitcase nuke—or nukes—we're seeking. And the mafia are the suppliers."

"What about Russian oligarchs?" Felix Goldblatt asked. "They've been caught meddling in US politics."

Courtney nodded. "That's true, but the oligarchs try to maintain an air of respectability. The mafia do not." She sat down and looked around the room for reactions.

Hans Jensen, CIA's guru on the Middle East, said, "We should mention the Russian mafia who've taken root in various cities throughout the United States, especially in Brighton Beach, New York. Our own backyard would be an easier place for the terrorists to shop."

Courtney shook her head in dismissal. "There's no evidence the Russian mafia in the US have access to any type of nuclear weapons. Keep in mind, the mafia are not a monolithic group. Don't get distracted. Focus on the mafia in Russia as the source."

Jo said, "If the Russians have a corner on the small nuke market, what's the going rate? Where will the terrorists get the money?"

Amal stood. "The price tag for a suitcase nuke could be one to two million dollars, although the Russian mafia will charge whatever the market will bear. More important factors than price are the logistics of getting the nuke from Russia to the US and keeping the weapon viable over time."

She ignored Hans's raised eyebrows at the high price tag for acquiring the nukes from the Russians.

Amal cleared her throat. "Going back to the origins of Al Qaeda, Saudi Arabia has been the principal source of funding for terrorism. Not to underestimate the diverse sources of money flowing to terrorists in the Middle East, but disaffected wealthy Arabs in Saudi Arabia are the ones most likely to bankroll the terrorist cell who stole the general's briefcase."

"Maybe, if we tighten our surveillance, we can pick them up when they travel to Saudi Arabia," Hans said.

Growing impatient with Hans's input, Courtney countered, "It's unlikely members of the cell would travel to Saudi Arabia to receive the money. Any international bank could supply the funds. If I had to guess, I'd say the Swiss banking system would be the first choice."

Jo jumped in to defuse the friction between Hans and Courtney. "If Saudi money could be collected at any big Swiss bank, how do we decide whether to focus on Zurich, Bern, Geneva, or wherever? Would the Saudis use Switzerland's largest banks—UBS and Credit Suisse—or some less conspicuous bank? We don't have the resources to go on a fishing expedition."

"We'll hedge our bets," Alex said. "We can send a team to each of the major Swiss financial centers. US intelligence agencies monitor large currency flows in Switzerland. They may be able to pick up clues to indicate which bank is targeted. If we're on site, we can zero in."

Felix spoke up. "Mossad also monitors the flow of funds from Saudi Arabia to terrorists. They're sensitive to the risk that suitcase nukes might be used to attack Israel. A request from the White House could enlist their help. Mossad is reputed to have excellent sources within the Swiss banking hierarchy."

• • •

Jo thought, *Reputed, my ass. Felix probably is on a first name basis with the Mossad agents who monitor terrorist financing.*

Alex rapped the table for attention. "I'll ask Mansfield to enlist the help of Mossad and US intelligence resources. Sending teams to the three major Swiss financial centers is a prudent way to establish an early alert system. That's the next step in our action plan."

• • •

Mike Sato and Luke Worthington sat quietly in the back of the room and listened to the discussion. Mike's stoic demeanor conveyed nothing of the turmoil of his thoughts as he watched the main actors play out the drama of the terrorist threat.

Mike was obsessed with watching Amal. He'd felt a deep kinship with Amal from the first team meeting he and Luke attended. While he knew his role as one of Alex's "attack dogs" was to protect her and other members of the team, he secretly harbored a desire for a more intimate relationship.

Having worked up his courage—not normally a problem for the combat decorated Special Forces officer— as Amal got up to leave the room, he touched her on the arm.

"Could I talk with you for a second?"

Surprise fracturing her calm demeanor, Amal stared at him.

After a beat, she said, "What about?"

Mike could feel his cheeks blush in embarrassment. He struggled to maintain his composure, determined to complete this mission even if it killed him.

"I'd like you to have a drink with me tonight."

"A drink?" The tone of the question implied a Herculean challenge. Taking pity on her nervous suitor, she said, "Are you inviting me to go on a date?"

His first instinct was to hope she regretted her apparent dismissal of what, after all, was a common enough social foray. He decided to press on.

"Maybe we could just go for pie and coffee. That wouldn't really count as a date."

Mike knew his voice sounded desperate. He couldn't believe, as a combat-tested Special Forces officer, he'd so quickly retreated from a drink to pie and coffee.

He didn't know how to get out of the hole he'd dug. He remembered his dad's advice: *When you're in a hole, quit digging.*

Amal's expression softened. "On second thought, I'd be honored to have a drink with you. Let's meet in the Barrel and Bushel at the Hyatt. Seven tonight." With that as an exit line, she left the room.

Mike sat back in his chair, unable to believe his good fortune. Maybe tonight he'd realize the dream of developing a relationship with the dusky beauty. He was unconcerned about the age difference between them.

CHAPTER 17

Majid sauntered into the Peking Gourmet restaurant in Bailey's Crossroads. While he would never admit it to his Middle Eastern collaborators, he had grown inordinately fond of Chinese food. Peking Gourmet was his favorite restaurant on the Virginia side of the Potomac River. The establishment was an ideal locale for a clandestine meeting with his Saudi contact.

Since the era when this was among George H. W. Bush's dining preferences—to the extent the Secret Service had bulletproofed one room, complete with a large round table topped by a Lazy Susan—Peking Gourmet had become a Northern Virginia meeting ground for politicians, diplomats, and people of all professions, nationalities, and ethnicities. To enter was to wear a cloak of anonymity.

Although Majid took the precaution of arriving twenty minutes before the agreed meeting time, he found Kamal Al-Outaibi waiting for him in a booth tucked away in a quiet corner where they could talk in private.

Majid remembered that Dana's father was the one who had briefed him on how to contact the Saudis. At his daughter's urgings, Jousef al-Sadi occasionally interrupted his debauchery, or however he was spending his time and Dorothea's money, to meet with Dana's emissary in Monaco at the Monte Carlo Casino.

Although Jousef's political ties were with the Kingdom's leadership, he had relatives and go-betweens in the camp that had supported Osama bin Laden and continued to offer financial assistance to Islamic State terrorists. He'd put Majid in touch with

Kamal Al-Outaibi, assuring him any overtures would be welcome.

"You said it was time for us to talk," Kamal said, getting down to business with unaccustomed alacrity.

"Yes. I have the information we discussed. I'm passing an envelope under the table that explains everything. My group knows where and how to obtain the product. The only thing needed is to meet the seller's price. We're counting on your friends to help us."

Kamal made an unsuccessful effort to hide his enthusiasm. "*Allahu Akbar*," he whispered.

The waiter arrived and the two men ordered.

Once they were alone, Majid said, "We discussed the possibility of receiving the funds in Geneva. Does that still meet with your approval?"

Adopting a businesslike manner, Kamal said, "Geneva is best. It's an international city and foreigners—Americans, Saudis, whoever—are invisible. What I need to know is, how much?"

"Dana Hussein al-Sadi says she requires five million dollars."

"*What?* I understand it's possible to obtain a suitcase nuke for less than half that amount." Kamal blanched when he realized in his excitement he used the forbidden words.

Majid frowned and kept silent. After a pause, he said, "Dana intends to acquire *two* of the items. Moreover, the Russians have gotten greedy since you and I last spoke. We're not haggling. Contact your principals and receive instructions if they wish to proceed."

Drawing himself erect in the booth as if offended at the implication his negotiating powers were not equal to the task, the Saudi said, "I have full authority to authorize five million. You have my assurance it will be forthcoming. Let's set the time and place for the meeting in Geneva."

CHAPTER 18

Amal strolled into the Barrel and Bushel at the Hyatt Regency Hotel, nervously wondering why she'd agreed to have a drink with Mike Sato. Was she so flattered at being asked out by a virile, handsome young man, she couldn't bring herself to decline the invitation? Or had it been so long since her last sexual assignation that she was desperately seeking romance? Neither of those explanations rang true. Perhaps she was just anxious to experience the companionship of a man outside her usual social circle.

She glimpsed Mike standing at the corner of the crowded bar, shifting uncomfortably from one foot to another. He waved when he spotted her.

Stepping quickly, he moved to join her. Trying to put him at ease, she leaned over and kissed him on the cheek. At that gesture, suddenly her disquiet about the evening disappeared. The date, if a date it was, seemed like the right move.

She placed her fingers on his lips before he could speak.

"I have an idea. Instead of having our drink here, I'd like you to come to my condo at the Rotunda, which is only a few minutes away. We can relax there without the distraction of the Hyatt's mob scene. Are you willing?"

When she removed her fingers, his broad smile told her all she needed to know.

• • •

Jolene waited restlessly in her old office where Alex insisted they meet, since, as he put it, the place was "off the beaten track" of the team's new digs in the basement of NCTC. She glanced up as he rushed in and rose from her desk chair in a confrontational stance.

"Why did you insist we meet here?"

"Never mind that," he said. "We need to firm up plans for you to go to Geneva."

"Why Geneva? More to the point, why me?"

"Let's not replay that old song. Remember, I told you at the first meeting, you're the head of the brain trust. I'm counting on you to sniff out the woman who killed General Winston and stole his briefcase. In Geneva, she's going to meet with the Saudis she's counting on to finance the purchase of the nukes. From the Swiss bank where she receives the funding, she's going directly to the Russians to swap dollars for weapons."

Her face flushed with anger. "How the hell do you know that?"

"Goddammit, Jo. I don't *know* a fucking thing. We need to trust our instincts. Mine tell me, the general's killer is leading the terrorist cell. We've agreed the Saudis are the most likely source of financing to buy nukes from the Russians. Geneva is my best guess at the location of the Swiss bank for the exchange of funds. Foreigners make up almost half the population of Geneva; they can move around with anonymity."

He stared at Jo, trying to read her reaction. "She'll be a needle in a haystack. You're the one with the best instincts to find the goddamned needle. Stop jerking me around, and let's talk about your trip to Geneva." Out of breath and red faced, Alex shut up.

Jolene sat back in her chair and fought to regain her composure. Despite her initial reservations about Alex, she was growing to trust him as the head of their team. It was still too much of a stretch to think of him as Jack Reacher, but he was a leader who had proven he could get things done, most recently in the Oval Office meeting at the White House.

"Okay," she said.

"Okay, what?"

"Okay, about Geneva. Who's going with me? And when do we leave?"

Alex fought to conceal his sigh of relief at Jo's willingness to go along with the action plan.

"Courtney and Luke will accompany you."

"Why those two? Why not Amal and Mike? I told you Amal is the best informed of anyone on Islamic State terrorism." She didn't explain why she'd paired Mike with Amal.

"I don't doubt that. But you've convinced me Courtney is the quickest to size up tactical situations and anticipate terrorist threats. Besides, she and Luke have few equals with weapons and hand to hand combat. They can protect you."

"We won't have weapons in Geneva."

"You will," Alex said. "Arrangements are being made."

"When do we leave?"

"You have reservations for later today. There's a van waiting outside to take you to your farm in Leesburg. Courtney and Luke will join you at Reagan Airport."

CHAPTER 19

Commander John Paul Moore was scared. More than scared, he was terrified. Sweat beaded on his forehead. He could feel the damp collecting under his armpits and at the back of his neck.

He knew what scared felt like. He'd been scared throughout his life. Mostly of his dad, Rear Admiral David Farragut Moore, who'd been named after the first four-star admiral in the US Navy by a granddad who was a frustrated junior naval officer. Apparently, the gene to succeed by progeny was passed on from generation to generation in his family.

His dad's cry to "run faster" when he was a child playing sports haunted John Paul's dreams. Even his name—John Paul, after the naval hero of the American Revolution, John Paul Jones—was a pathetic plea for greatness, too often denied in practice. He was scared of flunking out of the Naval Academy, taking pride in passing, even in the lowest quarter of his class—a pride that was denied by his dad and granddad.

He'd been scared when the destroyer he commanded was confronted by Iranian ships in the Strait of Hormuz. That day, he'd earned a medal for his actions, ordering warning shots be fired on the Iranian vessels. But recognition by the upper echelons of the Navy counted for nothing in earning kudos in the family. No matter what he did, he was always a day late and a dollar short.

Today, he was terrified. After striving a lifetime for recognition, he would give anything to avoid the spotlight. He was aware his dad's manipulation had won him a place on the task force that had created the report stolen by the terrorists. What seemed like a career blessing, he now knew was a curse.

That bastard Alex Werth initiated the search for the traitor who had leaked information about the top-secret report to the terrorists, including when and where Jolene Martin would deliver the Zero Halliburton briefcase containing the explosive document to General Winston. The first time he met Alex, he had sensed Frank Mansfield's protégé suspected him of being the traitor. His misgivings were confirmed when Alex had assigned Major Steve Randall the thankless task of tracking down the Judas. Steve hated the Navy and went out of his way to show contempt for Commander John Paul Moore. John Paul imagined he could feel the Army Ranger's breath on his back.

John Paul cursed the night he'd met the lovely, mysterious Samira Hart, as she called herself. Why had he let himself be lured to that bar in Georgetown? How had she known he could be so easily seduced? And how could she sense his real weakness was more than an addiction to sex? Although God knows, sex with Samira was mind blowing.

No, his real weakness was vanity.

Thirty-five years of yearning for praise, denied by his family, was made up for by a few nights of flattery from the seductive Samira.

He rationalized that it had taken more than sexual desire or vanity to cause him to betray his country. He preferred to believe money—the root of all evil—was the primary motivator.

Despair over lack of money was what had driven him to the Georgetown bar. He couldn't face the never-ending anger and contempt of his wife Constance for his inability to come up with the half million dollars required to fund the experimental medical treatment that would give Kevin, their seven-year-old son, a fighting chance to survive a rare strain of leukemia. The standard care provided in military hospitals had repeatedly failed to arrest the disease.

Days stretched into weeks, while Constance and John Paul watched their only child suffer the ravages of a seemingly incurable illness. Doctors in Germany claimed to have come up with a cure. Dr. Heinrich Klinkmann of the University of Göttingen reported better than a 70 percent recovery rate.

Constance couldn't accept what she screamed was John Paul's willful denial of her son's lifesaving treatment.

"You bastard. If you really wanted to, you'd find a way to save Kevin. What kind of a fucking naval officer are you? How do you expect to protect your country when you can't even protect your own son?"

He couldn't bear her scorn at his futility. The latest episode in a lifetime of falling short.

Samira was his savior.

"I can get you the half million." She told him what he had to do to earn the price of Kevin's life. He did it. And the money was forthcoming.

Constance and Kevin were on a plane to Frankfurt, Germany. From Frankfurt, a ninety-minute train ride would bring them to Göttingen.

Meanwhile, Commander John Paul Moore sat ashamed and terrified at his desk at NCTC waiting for Major Steve Randall, his nemesis, to come through the door. John Paul pulled his pistol from its holster, racked the slide to ensure there was a round in the chamber, and laid the weapon in the middle of his desk.

CHAPTER 20

Dana Hussein al-Sadi smiled to herself as she remembered the subterfuge of traveling on her mother's passport. According to official records, Dorothea Hamilton Di-Longhi arrived in Cointrin Airport at 6:05 p.m. Dana was certain her mother was not on any intelligence agency's no-fly list. Her best guess was the name differences prevented the authorities from making the connection between mother and daughter, assuming she herself was under suspicion.

When she strode into the arrival area, Dana was met by a burly Frenchman, Joffrey Gobert, dressed in a dark blue bespoke suit, who helped her complete the formalities. She'd used Joffrey's services in the past, but never for an operation as sensitive as tomorrow's rendezvous with the hoped-for financiers of her terrorist plans. Even though Joffrey carried himself like a gentleman, she knew he had a criminal background and was not reluctant to use violence. She detected the outline of the pistol even his well-tailored costume failed to conceal. On an impulse, she decided to brief him on the purpose of the meeting and, if all went well, to invite him to accompany her on the journey to buy the nukes from the Russians.

Joffrey expedited inspection of her luggage at customs and escorted her through the airport exit into Geneva. Dana admired the way her escort handled himself. His rough-hewn face bordered on handsome. If her plans to meet with the Saudis were not so crucial to her mission, she would have toyed with the chance for an interlude, despite her resolve to avoid an affair with anyone on her terrorist team.

Having traveled to Geneva in the past, Dana was aware Cointrin

Airport had the unusual feature of facing two countries, northeast into France or southwest, where she was headed, toward the posh hotels on Lac Léman (Lake Geneva) in Switzerland. After she succeeded in obtaining the five million dollars from a Swiss bank, she planned to escape into France and head north.

Dana said scarcely a word since debarking from the plane until she was helped into the back seat of a spacious Mercedes-Maybach Pullman S600, where she mouthed *merci*. From her year at the Sorbonne in Paris, she was fluent in French—the predominant language of Geneva and one of four official languages of Switzerland—but in the airport she refrained from speaking French. Her Italian American mother, whose identity she had stolen, was known to detest the French and never spoke the language, even though it was one of the handful of languages commonly spoken at home.

The ultra-luxury limousine had made its debut at a Geneva auto show the previous year and cost two hundred thousand dollars. It was all the rage among the multimillionaires who flaunted their wealth around the Swiss city by the lake. Dana arranged to be met by the limo as a not-so-subtle way of impressing her Saudi financiers, whom she guessed were having her followed.

To complete her ostentatious display of wealth, she was booked into the presidential suite at the Four Seasons Hotel des Bergues on Lac Léman, near the Mont Blanc Bridge. She reasoned the best disguise for a terrorist being hunted worldwide was to hide in plain sight in a five-star hotel. Accordingly, she waltzed into the hotel lobby on Joffrey's arm, and waited haughtily while he checked them into their suite.

As expected, the desk clerk did not question why they would be staying in the same suite. After all, the suite had two bedrooms, in the event the guests preferred to sleep separately. If not, it was Europe, and no five-star hotel blinked at any but the most outlandish behavior.

Once they'd gotten situated in the suite, Dana sat on the couch next to Joffrey and told him the purpose of the next day's meeting with the Saudis. She didn't gloss over her intent to obtain several million dollars to bankroll terrorist attacks in the United States.

Joffrey remained poker-faced as she concluded her briefing.

"Well?" she asked. "What's your reaction?"

"I pledged my loyalty to you when we first met in Paris. Nothing has changed. Just tell me what you want me to do."

Growing tired, Dana retired to the master bedroom. Preferring solitude, she gave Joffrey no signal she wanted company. She imagined he looked disappointed as he headed for the other bedroom.

After breakfast, as her preparation for the meeting neared completion, Dana was acutely aware she was at risk. Although Joffrey was carrying a pistol, she declined his offer of a SIG Sauer P229. Even though it was one of her favorite weapons (after the Baby Glock)—compact, reliable, and deadly—she believed the SIG would indicate a lack of confidence to the Saudis if she were to show up at the meeting armed. She also turned down the dagger he suggested as an alternative more suited to a woman.

In contrast to her splashy arrival, the morning's meeting with her Saudi bankrollers was cloaked in secrecy. She slipped out the rear entrance of the Four Seasons where Joffrey was waiting with a nondescript Renault sedan. They drove in silence to a small private home in the suburbs of Geneva.

The door to the residence was opened by a swarthy male less than five feet in height but whose shoulders and girth were gargantuan. Dana relaxed a bit when she saw the man—whose name she had never learned—because he was often present when she was a teenager prowling in the shadows at times as her father had met with leaders of the Kingdom of Saudi Arabia.

"Sayeeda Dana Hussein al-Sadi," the man began addressing her in Arabic, bowing as he did so.

Dana responded quietly in Arabic, making a shushing signal with her finger on her lips. "It's good to see you after all these years. But I'm traveling under a different name. We must be discreet. I'm here for the meeting, otherwise Dana Hussein al-Sadi is not in Geneva."

Chastened, having understood the gist of her message, the man bowed once again and pointed the way as he led the visitors deeper into the residence.

Four men in business suits stood when Dana swept into the room. After the amenities were observed, and everyone was seated, Bandar Kamel, the designated spokesman for the group, said, "Majid shared with us the information you stole from the briefcase of General Winston. We are persuaded you have the know-how to obtain small nuclear weapons and use them to destroy important targets in the United States on behalf of the Islamic State."

He frowned to emphasize the seriousness of his remarks.

"What we demand is your assurance you will dedicate yourself and your followers to this task, even if it means all of you must die in the attempt."

Dana stood and looked deeply into Bandar Kamel's eyes. She knew he was not a man who would be impressed by words, no matter how sincerely uttered. None of the sons of the desert who came to Geneva representing that faction in the Saudi hierarchy who supported ISIS would respect an oath taken lightly.

She turned to Joffrey Gobert. "Give me your dagger."

She took the blade and set it on the table in front of her. Then she took off her light gray Armani suit jacket and hung it carefully on a nearby chair.

Other than those in their family, Saudi men were unaccustomed to watching women disrobe. Two of the men present gave an audible gasp as Dana began to undo the pearl buttons on her ivory blouse. Both grew positively bug-eyed when she dropped the blouse on the chair and stood with her breasts covered only by a filmy ivory brassiere. Bandar Kamal and the fourth man were struggling to maintain their composure.

Dana snatched up the dagger and positioned it midway between her breasts and naval.

"No," Bandar screamed, watching the crimson spray when the blade sliced the surface of Dana's midsection.

Reacting with blinding speed, Joffrey pulled a white handkerchief from his pants pocket and pressed it against the wound, staunching the flow of blood.

"Do not be alarmed, gentlemen. Although a dramatic display, this is not a mortal wound. Merely a symbolic cut on my abdomen. I wanted to demonstrate to you my commitment, and that of my cell, to our cause. We will succeed or we will die. If the Americans do not kill me, I will take a dagger like this one and commit *seppuku*, the classic Japanese form of suicide. This is my pledge to you."

Breathing a sigh of relief, Bandar said, "On behalf of all Saudis who support ISIS, we herald your dedication. This envelope which I am giving you contains the codes and authorization for you to obtain five million dollars from the Swiss bank listed herein. These funds will ensure your success."

"*Inshallah*."

• • •

Joffrey took charge, guiding a rapidly fading Dana from the residence to the Renault. The effects of the self-inflicted wound on her stomach were triggering a mild shock reaction.

With a quick stop at the Pharmacie Internationale to pick up first aid supplies, he sped to the Four Seasons and turned the nondescript Renault over to valet parking. He hustled Dana onto the elevator and held her as they rose to the top floor. Supporting her with his left arm around her waist, he slid the hotel key card into the slot and opened the double doors, which he quickly locked after alerting housekeeping with a *ne pas déranger* sign. He was determined they not be disturbed for the remainder of the day and overnight.

Cradling Dana in his arms, he carried her into the bedroom and laid her on the ornate bedspread. He stripped off her blood-spattered clothes, including her bra and panties, and replaced them with a Four

Seasons beige velour kimono robe. He propped her feet up with two of the larger decorative pillows on the bed. Then he held a water bottle to her lips and coaxed her to drink to offset any risk of dehydration.

Having taken the recommended steps to minimize adverse effects of a mild shock, he turned his attention to the cut on her stomach. He opened the robe to view his handkerchief which was still tied in place as a makeshift bandage. The first aid supplies were scattered on the bed.

Groans from the patient greeted his efforts to clean the wound with an antiseptic solution. Dana opened her eyes and gaped at the image of Joffrey leaning over her nearly nude torso with a gauze compress in his hand swabbing her midsection.

"What do you think you're doing?"

"Cleaning your wound before I bandage it. The next time you plan to cut yourself, let me know in advance so I can have first aid supplies on hand."

"Trust me, that was not planned. I acted on instinct, deciding direct action would motivate the Saudis where mere words would have no effect."

"Well, you were right. They couldn't give you the money fast enough."

"Now we've got to go to the bank," she said, attempting to rise from the bed.

Joffrey pushed her gently back. She struggled briefly, but realized, in her weakened state, it was a losing battle.

"Tomorrow will be time enough. Now you must lie still so I can finish bandaging your wound."

She grumbled, but complied. As his fingers gently stroked her stomach, he grew aware his ministrations were beginning to excite her. His fingers were within inches of the junction of her thighs. He continued to stroke her even after the bandage was securely taped. His fingers ran gently down her body.

"You seem to have recovered."

"I have an excellent doctor. Your touch is gentle. In fact, arousing."

Responding to the implied invitation, Joffrey kissed her tenderly on the lips.

"I think you're starting to feel better," he said.

He pulled the sheet chastely up to her neck.

"Bonne nuit."

CHAPTER 21

Commander John Paul Moore's eyes were focused on the door facing his desk. He expected Major Steve Randall to walk through at any moment. Having convinced himself Steve suspected him to be the traitor who had sold information about the secret report contained in General Winston's briefcase, John Paul decided to end the suspense. He summoned his nemesis to his office.

John Paul saw the doorknob turn. He picked up his pistol and pointed it at the entrance. Steve entered the room and flinched at being confronted with a weapon aimed at his chest.

"What's this about, John Paul? You asked me to come. Why are you threatening me?"

For the first time in his life, John Paul relaxed. No longer terrified, he was not even scared. No more sweating. Events were under his control, and nothing he did required praise or recognition from his dad or grandad.

He still cared deeply about Constance's opinion of him, but that boat had sailed when Samira Hart came up with the half million to fund Kevin's treatment in Germany. No matter what else happened, he'd earned his wife's undying love and respect.

"Steve, your assignment is to find the traitor who enabled the terrorist Samira Hart to steal the NCTC report from the general's briefcase. I asked you here to help you find Samira *herself*."

"How do you know the name of General Winston's killer?" Steve's hands were clenched at his sides.

"Sit down," John Paul said, pointing at the chair in front of his desk. "Put your hands behind your neck. I'm going to tell you a story."

Steve did as directed.

"A few weeks ago, I was approached by a woman calling herself Samira Hart. Probably not her real name. She's tall, at least five nine, and willowy, perhaps a hundred twenty-five. Her breasts are not voluptuous, but perfectly shaped. Hair black and cut in a midlength bob. I'd guess her age at thirty-two, perhaps older, poised and in control. She speaks perfect English. I'd say brought up in New York or New England, maybe even the Washington area. But there's the hint of a foreign lilt at times. She's of mixed parentage—maybe American or European with a bit of Middle Eastern blood. Her skin tone is bronze, Italian or Mediterranean. The smartest woman I ever met. She could read me like a book."

John Paul paused as though girding himself to continue this painful confessional. He knew it would not end with a dispensation to "go forth and sin no more."

"She seduced me and bribed me with a half million dollars. In exchange, I told her everything she wanted to know about our report. Of particular interest were disaster scenarios—nuclear and chemical weapons, how to kill hundreds or thousands by disrupting electrical grids or water supplies. You know the drill. I briefed her on General Winston and when Jolene would be delivering our NCTC report to him at the Hyatt."

"Why are you telling me this?"

"Because I'm a patriot."

Steve growled and half rose from the chair. "You call yourself a patriot one more time, you son of a bitch, and I'll come across this desk and rip your throat out. You may cause the death of thousands of Americans. You're already responsible for the massacre of hundreds."

"NO," John Paul screamed. "I didn't know about those attacks. Besides, she didn't use any of the information I gave her to carry out the suicide bombings."

"Perhaps not. But if you'd given us the description of Samira Hart, or whatever the fuck she's really called, we might have prevented those deaths. Do you know anything else that might help us catch Samira or her fellow terrorists? It's not too late to stop the next wave of attacks."

"I don't. The only contact I've had is with Samira. And the description I just gave you is the best I can do in helping you catch her."

John Paul could read the effort it was causing Steve to rein in his anger, desperate for any clue that would help to track down the terrorists,

"Why?"

"The why no longer matters, Steve. What you must focus on is how you survive the next few moments to get out of this room so you can use what I've shared in the hunt for Samira. We're going to have a contest, you and I. Sort of an O.K. Corral gunfight. I'm going to holster my weapon. When I do, you're free to draw and fire. Whoever shoots first gets to walk out that door. Fair warning, I've been practicing."

John Paul rapidly holstered his pistol. Even more rapidly, he drew and leveled the weapon at Steve.

Steve fired three rounds into his opponent's center body mass in textbook fashion.

John Paul's pistol never discharged. His last thoughts were to wonder whether "death by cop" qualified Constance to collect on his naval officer's hefty insurance policy.

CHAPTER 22

George Southern strode impatiently around the VIP area of Cointrin Airport. He looked over the arrival screen for what he told himself was the final check. The flight from Reagan Airport was due to arrive in Geneva on time at precisely 6:05 p.m.

Greeting VIPs was not George's customary duty and, despite assurances of its importance—that he only half-believed—he resented the assignment. He feared it was likely to jeopardize his covert role of tracking illegal currency movements while stationed at the American Embassy in Bern for the Central Intelligence Agency. He recalled his argument with the CIA Chief of Station Bernard Livingstone, citing the numerous ways he was unsuited as a VIP meet and greeter.

"Bernie, the Embassy never sends a Black agent to do the VIP routine in Switzerland. I'm six two and two hundred twenty pounds. I'll stand out like a lump of coal in a snowbank. Besides, since I'm on covert duty, I don't even have a diplomatic passport."

Livingstone had brushed away his arguments as though shooing a fly. "I'm afraid your briefers were less than candid with you. This assignment is of vital importance to the security of the United States."

George fought to conceal his skepticism.

The two men stood silently, facing one another, ignoring the comfort and informality of the easy chairs decorating the CIA chief's office in the Embassy basement.

After a pause, Livingston said, "You recall the suicide bombings that killed and wounded hundreds in the DC area this week?"

The young CIA operative nodded in response to the rhetorical question, wondering where his boss was going with this.

"The terrorists who carried out those strikes are believed to be in Switzerland to obtain funds for even more devastating attacks, possibly with portable nuclear weapons. The NCTC group responsible for apprehending the terrorists is sending teams to Geneva, Zurich, and Bern in the belief the bad guys are coming here to collect funds provided by the Saudis."

"Holy shit."

Livingston ignored the outburst. "You've been selected to meet the Geneva contingent for two reasons: you're the resident expert on the Swiss banking system and you can recognize Jolene Martin on sight."

George fought to control his shock at the news. He knew Jolene, intimately in fact. Not only was she his chief competition in winning recognition as the top CIA trainee, the two were secret lovers for several weeks back then, carrying on an affair as intense as the training regimen at The Farm.

Noting the suppressed reaction, Livingston said, "Ms. Martin is the leader of the team targeting Geneva. I want you to meet her to ensure she's the real deal and not an imposter. You're to stick with the team and assist, particularly with any issues regarding Swiss banking or ways the Saudis transfer funds to terrorists."

Surprised at the news, but pleased at the opportunity to renew his acquaintance with Jolene, George nodded.

"Check in with Denise, my administrative assistant, to pick up your diplomatic passport. She'll give you a voucher for the armory to collect firearms for yourself and the NCTC arrivals. You'll be riding in an Embassy limo. Leave the guns in the chauffeured limo while you're in the airport."

• • •

Jolene couldn't believe her eyes when she spotted George waiting in the VIP arrival area. She hadn't seen her former lover since she'd been ushered unceremoniously off the Camp Peary premises of The Farm following her unsuccessful attempt to nail Rick Birmingham with the charge of attempted rape. Rumors George was assigned to Bern upon graduating from The Farm had slipped her mind. She was still angry he'd departed the country without saying goodbye, even though she suspected he and her fellow CIA trainees were warned not to contact her.

"George, it's good to see you. I'd forgotten you were in Switzerland." She walked up and shook his hand, trying not to give Courtney Gonzalez or Luke Worthington any hint of their special relationship.

Clearing his throat, George held Jolene's hand a beat longer than necessary before releasing it. "I'm your liaison."

Glancing at Courtney and Luke, he said, "I'm George Southern. My expertise is financial systems. The Embassy thought I might be able to help with Swiss banks and Saudi funding strategies."

When they shook hands, Jolene noted Courtney and Luke glance at each other. They'd sensed the vibrations she and George transmitted.

En route to the CIA safe house through a quiet wooded neighborhood in suburban Geneva, George briefed the visitors on the weapons he handed out and other arrangements for their stay. In turn, Jolene filled him in on the theory behind their trip.

"We believe the terrorists are seeking to acquire one or more suitcase nukes from the Russian mafia. Saudi dissidents are the suspected financiers. Switzerland is our best guess for the money transfer. My team is targeting Geneva. Other teams are heading for Zurich and Bern."

Grouped around a kitchen table in the safe house, everyone fortified with a mug of coffee, Jolene stared back at three pairs of eyes.

"What do we do now?" was the unspoken query.

"We need answers to several questions. First, do we have video of the terrorists arriving at Cointrin Airport?"

"When?" George asked.

"Yesterday. Our prime suspect is a woman. She's probably a day ahead of us. She may have arrived on the 6:05 flight like we did."

"She?"

"Our assumption is that the woman who killed General Winston in the Hyatt Regency at Tysons last Saturday around midnight is the leader of the terrorist cell. If not the leader, certainly an influential member. She's sophisticated, beautiful, and able to look at home in any setting. Courtney, show George the CCTV footage from the Hyatt lobby that depicts her arriving and departing around midnight. We've just received a description of the suspect that matches the Hyatt image."

Courtney opened her laptop and played the designated footage. The mysterious figure strode majestically across the screen, tall and thin, sporting a knee length black coat, with an enormous gray and black hat hiding her face and hair from view.

George nodded. "A woman who looked and moved like that would fit in perfectly anywhere in Geneva. Leave it to me. I can get a set of the videos showing yesterday's airport arrivals in a couple of hours."

He glanced at Jolene. "What else?"

"Where's she likely to be staying?"

George shrugged. "Hard to say. Could be a luxury hotel. They're plentiful, especially around Lac Leman. She'd blend in without question, although the visibility would be risky. She could be a guest at a private residence. In which case, she'd be virtually invisible. We can only guess at her ethnicity. Even if we knew more about her, Geneva is a melting pot of the rich, famous, and diplomatically connected. Sophisticated, beautiful women are as common as sand on the beach."

"We have to play the odds," Jolene said. "It depends on whether we have video footage from the airport that matches the Hyatt images. George, can you get a crew checking out the major hotels?"

"Of course."

"Which bank is she most likely to use?" Courtney asked.

"Assuming she visits a local bank, which is only one of the ways she could access the funds, the RGS is the one most used by the Saudis. Other leading Swiss banks are UBS and Credit Suisse."

"Can we have watchers at all of those branches in Geneva?"

"Absolutely," George said. "The ambassador is giving your mission top priority. The directive is backed by the White House. Dozens of operatives are arriving tomorrow."

"They won't be in place until the next day," Jolene said. "Could be too late."

"If we need warm bodies, the Embassy will provide them. Several are arriving tonight. Manpower is not our problem. Deciding where to station them and telling them what to watch for are the critical issues."

CHAPTER 23

Jolene scrutinized the crowd George had assembled to assist her team in tracking down the terrorists. In the early morning hour, several dozen foreign service officers and staff were grouped in the Rive Gauche room of the Hotel de la Paix. Jolene, Courtney, and Luke had checked into a suite in the hotel the previous evening, leaving their safe house for more convenient quarters.

George told Jolene he selected the Hotel de la Paix because he had a weakness for the Ritz-Carlton chain of hotels. Also, he favored the central location facing Lac Leman and Mont Blanc. The clincher was that the hotel was offering rock bottom prices for a five-star establishment since they were in the final stages of a year-long renovation.

Jolene told him she "didn't give a shit" so long as it was an efficient base of operations. She wasn't over being pissed at George for leaving the States without saying goodbye, ignoring the fact she'd been fired from the CIA after an assault. What hurt the most was memory of the time they'd been lovers at the Farm. She was determined to let him know her displeasure at every opportunity.

She introduced herself and encouraged the attendees to move around the room freely. "Help yourself to food, coffee, and other refreshments," she said, pointing to a table in the back of the meeting room. The normal buzz of conversation, when many but not all know each other, was accompanied by curious glances at Jolene from officials wondering about her and about why they'd been summoned to this command performance on such short notice.

After giving a sanitized version of the NCTC search for terrorists, Jolene said, "George will divide you into three teams. Team One will investigate hotels to find a woman who matches the description you've been given. Team Two will investigate banks the woman is expected to visit to collect Saudi cash. Team Three will review CCTV footage taken in Cointrin Airport to identify the woman we suspect is the leader of the terrorists." She eyed George, who roamed restlessly around the perimeter of the room.

"Keep in mind, this operation is classified at the highest level. We're operating under the direction of President Scofield. Discuss what you see and hear with no one—including colleagues or spouses, lovers, whomever—not today, not ever. Anyone who breaches confidentiality will not only be fired, I'll also personally see they go to prison."

An overdressed woman in the front row stood and raised her hand, asking permission to speak.

Jolene nodded.

"I don't understand why I have to be here. I have important work to do back at the Embassy."

"That's not a problem. Leave immediately." Jolene pointed at the exit. "Forget everything you've heard or seen."

She looked over the assembled officials. "Anyone else think their regular job is *more important* than a priority assignment from President Scofield? If so, please raise your hand."

The eyes staring back told her the consensus: to leave was a career kiss of death.

Seeing no takers, she resumed her briefing. "We'll watch a video containing information about the woman. George, play the video taken at the Hyatt in Tysons, Virginia the night General Winston was killed."

After the participants watched the video, eliciting admiring comments about the unknown woman's appearance, George passed out assignments. Billy Merriweather, who boasted two years' experience as a concierge at a five-star hotel in London before becoming a foreign service officer, was the hotel team leader. Tonia Hinch, who had a pilot's license and four years as a flight attendant with Air France before qualifying as an FSO, was primary at Cointrin Airport. George and Jolene took joint responsibility for the bank team.

The hotel and airport teams departed, absent the usual grumbling by bureaucrats dragged out of their day-to-day work environment to undertake a special operation.

Jolene gathered Courtney, Luke, and George around a table in a corner overlooking Lac Leman. The two women wore pantsuits to provide maximum freedom of motion and to facilitate easy access to handguns. Jolene's Glock 19 was nestled in a shoulder holder close to her left breast. Courtney holstered the same 9 mm weapon over her right hip. George and Luke each carried a Beretta M9A3, the latest military 9 mm pistol in standard use.

Jolene gestured to her former lover. "George, we need to focus our search of Geneva banks on those likely to be chosen by the Saudis to fund the terrorists."

When he started to shake his head at the enormity of her request, she grabbed his arm. "You're about to say, 'there's no way to know.' I don't want to hear it. Put yourself in the mind of a Saudi financier trying to fund a female terrorist who's the object of an international manhunt. Some banks would be dismissed out of hand. Others would be possible, but unlikely. Which banks are best suited?"

George cast his eyes toward the ceiling, as though seeking divine inspiration. "If I had to pick one, it'd be RGS on Rue de Lausanne."

"Let's focus on that branch," Jolene said. "You and I will station ourselves there."

She leaned forward, staring intently. "What's your second choice?"

George began to get into the spirit of the high stakes guessing game. "The RGS branch on Place de Bel-Air."

"Okay. Courtney and Luke, RGS Place de Bel-Air is your target. George, go find someone who knows Geneva to accompany them.

Preferably, an FSO assigned to the Economic Section or anyone who's dealt with world class bankers."

Waiting for George to return, Jolene, deep in thought, sipped her coffee, nibbled on a chocolate croissant, and stared unseeing at the gorgeous view of Lac Leman.

• • •

Courtney gestured to Luke to move to another table to give Jolene the space she seemed to need.

"The banks should open in a half hour," Courtney said. "Let's use that time to scout out the area around Place de Bel-Air."

Never one to waste words, Luke nodded agreement.

Looking concerned, she said, "Can we travel around Geneva armed? And what about the bank, will we have to undergo a security inspection?"

"We should be okay carrying weapons," Luke said. "The diplomatic passports Alex sent arrived last night, so we all have protected status in case anything goes south."

Courtney blinked in wonder. Luke had just spoken more in the last few moments than in the entire time since she'd met him at NCTC.

"Okay. That makes me feel better . . . here comes George with our guide. He looks like a diplomat straight out of Hollywood central casting."

George introduced Spencer Wallingford, an FSO in his third year with the Embassy's Economic Section. Blond, six-one, wearing a double-breasted gray suit, a white shirt, and a blue and gold striped tie. He could have been a model for a poster proclaiming *JOIN THE STATE DEPARTMENT AND BE ALL YOU CAN BE.*

After introductions, Courtney led her team to the black Toyota Camry they'd been issued. She slipped into the driver's seat and headed out, hoping Spencer was good at giving directions to Place de Bel-Air.

CHAPTER 24

Dana, in the persona of her mother, ordered a large breakfast for two from Four Seasons room service at 6:45 a.m., with the instruction it must be delivered before 7:15.

"Why so much food?" Joffrey asked. "You've ordered enough for three people."

"We're going to have a visitor. But you won't be around to meet her. I want you to come with me when I travel to France later today. If you agree, you need to get ready. Pack, collect your passport, whatever. If you don't agree, this is goodbye."

Joffrey's face broadcast puzzlement on several levels. Dana knew the invitation to accompany her was a stunner. She'd told him the suite at the Four Seasons was reserved for two more days.

"Why are you asking me to travel with you? What role would I play? Here I was your driver and bodyguard. Is that it?"

"I need a bodyguard. What I must do over the coming days and weeks involves great danger, possibly leading to a violent death. Geneva is a walk in the park. The Saudis posed no threat, at least not to life and limb. The next group I will be dealing with is a different story. Killing me would mean no more to them than swatting a fly." She pointed dramatically at Joffrey. "Do you still want to be with me and share the risk?"

"Nothing would please me more."

"*D'accord*! Now get out of here and get ready. Bring your pistol, dagger, the SIG, and any other weapons you have on hand. After we've collected the Saudi monies from the bank, we'll slip out of

Geneva. From Geneva, we'll travel to Besançon, France. We'll escape no later than early afternoon."

She grabbed Joffrey by the arm as he turned to leave. "One more thing. Do you have clothes that look less formal than the suit you wore yesterday?"

"*Bien sûr.*"

"Wear them. We can expect to deal with all kinds of people, including the worst sort of thugs."

Joffrey raced into the bedroom and collected his belongings. "À bientôt," he said to her and left.

• • •

The food arrived and Dana, wearing her beige kimono robe, directed the gangly waiter to put it on the spacious dining table, signed for the order, and shooed the nervous young man out of the suite.

On the dot of 7:20, Dana heard the buzzer and hurried to open the door. Zaha Nashashibi entered, vibrant despite the early hour and the wear and tear of her long flight from Washington. She wore a stylish light-green wool suit, carried an oversize makeup case, and dragged in a dark gray hard-sided suitcase.

Dana embraced her only female follower.

Visibly flustered by the unexpected warmth of the greeting, Zaha burst into tears, the tension of their secret rendezvous erupting in an emotional outburst. Dana held her close until she regained her composure.

"I'm so sorry, Dana. Believe it or not, I've stayed calm throughout the trip. But I've been so afraid you might be in danger, I could no longer contain my feelings of relief and happiness. Your welcome sent me over the edge."

Smiling, Dana hugged Zaha even harder. "If you hadn't come today, I would be in even greater danger. You're the fox who's going to lure the hounds away from my trail."

"How will I do that?"

Dana tapped the makeup case.

"We're going to swap identities, courtesy of the magic of costumes, makeup, and a little playacting. I will become Zaha. You will be transformed into my mother, Dorothea Hamilton Di-Longhi, a wealthy Italian American woman in her fifties."

She laughed at Zaha's look of bewilderment.

"But first, I'm going to feed you." She steered her alter ego toward the dining table laden with oatmeal, pancakes, eggs benedict, a basket of sweet rolls, orange juice, and coffee."

"*Allahu Akbar*, I'm starved and you've provided a feast."

After Zaha polished off a sumptuous breakfast, Dana guided her into the bedroom, where she began to disrobe.

"Take off your clothes."

After raising her eyebrows at the bandage on Dana's midriff, Zaha got into the spirit of the masquerade. The young woman commenced a striptease, removing her clothes slowly and sensuously, accompanied by suggestive burlesque bumps and grinds.

Both women fell on the bed laughing.

"We need to commence the process of making you over into your new identity," Dana said. She took Zaha's hand, pulled her from the bed, and led her into the master bathroom.

Returning to the bedroom, she opened her suitcase and took out a gray wig she'd purloined from her mother's boudoir. Before departing on the trip to Geneva, she'd taken the precaution of wearing an identical wig.

She strolled back into the bathroom and showed Zaha the wig.

Dana removed her gray wig and restored her long black hair to its original look.

Zaha handed her a bath towel.

"Wrap this over your shoulders. I'm going to cut your hair so anyone looking at my passport photo would swear you are Zaha Nashashibi."

With impressive artistry, she trimmed away excess hair until a pixie cut emerged. Staring into the broad expanse of mirrors covering the wall above the sinks, Dana realized she resembled Halle Berry in movie roles where the actress sported short hair.

Finally satisfied with her creation, Zaha shook the hair from the bath towel and flushed it down the toilet.

"Sit on the edge of the tub," Dana said. She carefully fitted the gray wig and saw a Zaha emerge who looked several decades older.

"We wear the same size, so the clothes I've worn to Geneva will fit you. They're tailor made for a woman in her fifties."

After satisfying herself Zaha's looks would get her through the airport, Dana said, "Another hint. Affect a slight limp. When people, men especially, see a woman limp, that's all they tend to notice. Better that than have them admiring the shape of your ass or your breasts. Although even attracting sexual notice would be preferable to having officials spend too much time staring at your face."

When the transformation of both women was complete, she sent Zaha on her way to Cointrin Airport, with reservations under the name Dorothea Hamilton Di-Longhi on Air France. Destination: Paris. Flight time: one hour and ten minutes.

CHAPTER 25

Jolene and George cruised by the RGS bank and continued up Rue de Lausanne. Despite the early morning traffic, George had no trouble driving near the speed limit. Cars were parked on both sides of the wide thoroughfare. A handful of pedestrians marched toward their destinations with determined steps.

A few blocks past the RGS building, he circled the block and drove by heading west. Continuing this routine, back and forth along the road, the investigators mapped the route anyone trying to enter the bank would have to pass.

While driving around in circles, rather than admiring the beautiful scenery of Geneva, Jolene's thoughts turned to George and their tour at Camp Peary. From the outset of their time at The Farm, the two had vied for supremacy in their CIA training cohort. They came from different worlds.

Jolene was the daughter of a gray eminence who had long operated behind the scenes in the intelligence community and a mother who was a surgeon to the rich and famous in New York City. She was a graduate of Yale, which had been a prime source of CIA recruitment since the agency's inception, an expert on the Middle East with a command of Arabic and other esoteric languages, with many years living and studying abroad. To top it off, she was a champion tennis player and all-around athlete. The CIA expected her to excel from the first day of training camp.

George was a diamond in the rough. He came out of the projects in Chicago, won an athletic scholarship for prowess in football and basketball to Notre Dame where he majored in finance, joined the Army serving as an intelligence officer in Afghanistan, and, after returning to the States, earned his law degree at Howard University. George exceeded the trainers' expectations and graduated first in his class. He'd edged out Jolene, who lost any chance of finishing first after she'd accused the head of CIA training of attempting to rape her.

Neither trainee would have been in the running for first place if they hadn't succeeded in keeping their affair secret. Perhaps it was the attraction of opposites that initially drew them together, but they quickly discovered they liked the same things—not only sports, but music, books, art, and travel. They also shared an affinity for clandestine sex.

Their favorite spot for a secret rendezvous was a wooded lake three miles from The Farm's dormitories. On the pretext it was a routine destination for their daily run, they arranged to meet at the lake.

Jolene's thoughts lingered on their sexual escapades. She grew annoyed with herself when she remembered how much she'd enjoyed the affair. She firmly resolved not to renew her romantic liaison with George.

"The bank's about to open," Jolene said, "Here's a good space. Let's park and walk the rest of the way."

They entered the bank, and George asked the attendant to direct them to the manager's office. The manager introduced himself. Jolene pretended she didn't know French to ensure they would have the advantage of conducting the session in English.

After they shook hands, George passed over the ambassador's letter and waited wordlessly while Monsieur Daniel Dujardin read it.

Stammering, Dujardin said, "According to this, you believe a woman will come to the bank today and attempt to withdraw a large sum of money that's been deposited by a Saudi. Do you really expect me to identify this woman?"

Impatient at playing second fiddle, Jolene interrupted. "We insist you identify her. This woman is a terrorist. She's the one responsible for the recent wave of suicide bombings in the Washington area that killed and wounded hundreds. She must be stopped."

"But the confidentiality of the Swiss banking system is sacrosanct."

Jolene nodded as though in agreement. "And we respect your discretion. Under normal circumstances, we would not dream of asking you to compromise your time-honored practice. However, the national security of the United States is at stake. We have ironclad intelligence that proves the woman who perpetrated the latest atrocity is planning even more devastation."

George pressed. "Swiss banks have close ties with financial interests in America. I'm sure you wish to nurture those relationships. Take care to refrain from doing anything that would jeopardize our mutually beneficial partnership."

Dujardin was not a fool. His face was a portrait of a man aware he was being simultaneously threatened and blackmailed.

"What do you expect me to do?"

George smiled. "Simply detain the woman with some excuse about red tape that must be complied with before you can release her funds. We'll wait here in your office or wherever you suggest so we won't be spotted. You point out the woman to us. We'll do the rest."

"I must have your word there will no violence while she is inside the bank."

"You can be sure we will act with the utmost discretion."

"Very well. It's not possible for you to remain in my office, but we have a comfortable VIP waiting room."

Dujardin pushed a silent button on his desk. In a few moments, a chic young woman wearing a chartreuse silk dress with a matching Hermès scarf wrapped discreetly around her neck entered the room. The manager introduced the Americans to Audrey.

Audrey led the way. George and Jolene followed on her heels. In Jolene's opinion, George devoted far too much attention to eyeing Audrey's sexy silhouette. She was honest enough to own up to feelings of jealousy. *Why do I she care whether he ogles this attractive woman?* she thought.

Once settled in the VIP room, Jolene saw a sign indicating a broad range of beverages and food was available upon request. She and George were content to order coffee. Audrey brought them a large decanter, cups, and the accoutrements. They sipped their beverage and settled down to wait, hoping their quarry would show sooner rather than later.

• • •

Dana was dressed and packed when Joffrey returned to the presidential suite at the Four Seasons.

All business, she said, "It's time to leave for the bank. But, before we do, I must make a call."

She dialed for an outside line and entered the bank manager's direct number at the RGS branch on the Rue de Lausanne.

When he answered, she said, "Monsieur Dujardin, I am the woman you are expecting to make a rather large withdrawal."

Hearing a gasp at the other end of the line, she hesitated, then recited the necessary information to identify herself and the account in question.

Obviously nervous, the manager said, "What can I do to assist you?"

"You seem anxious, Monsieur. Has something happened? My sponsors would be seriously disturbed if anything were to prevent me from obtaining the promised funds. I could not be responsible for their reaction if you were to disappoint us."

She made no attempt to disguise the threat in her voice. "You've undoubtedly been following the news out of Washington where tragic events have transpired. You're fortunate to live in Geneva where everyday life is so peaceful. I'm sure you rejoice every day that your wife and children are safe."

The manager babbled, "Two Americans are here. I put them in

the VIP room. They're waiting to arrest you."

"That won't do at all."

"What is it you want me to do? I would prefer it be something that could be done without their knowledge."

"Not a problem," Dana said. She went on to explain how Monsieur Dujardin should transfer the Saudi account to another specified RGS branch.

"If you transfer the funds before ten o'clock this morning and take care the Americans learn nothing, I guarantee you and your family will come to no harm. My sponsors will be grateful."

Upon gaining his assurances, she hung up.

CHAPTER 26

George called Billy Merriweather, who was assigned to the team investigating hotels.

"Billy, where are you now?"

"At the Four Seasons Hotel des Bergues. We might have something."

George switched to speaker phone so Jolene could hear the conversation. "What do you have?"

"There's a woman staying here who resembles our target, but we can't be sure."

"What makes you think she's the one?" Jolene said.

"One of the front desk clerks noticed the likeness, but the woman in question is in her fifties. So, it's probably not her. We reviewed CCTV footage of Dorothea Hamilton Di-Longhi—that's the woman—checking in. There's a definite similarity. But the Di-Longhi woman has gray hair, walks with a slight limp, is filthy rich, and travels on an American passport. The suspect in the video you showed us is much younger. She seemed to stride rapidly when she crossed the lobby of the Hyatt Regency. I'm only calling because you said we should follow any leads, no matter how slim."

Jolene addressed her comments to George. "Our terrorist is super smart. She might well be traveling on a false passport and be wearing a disguise. Tell Billy to follow the lead and let us know when Madame Di-Longhi returns to her suite."

"I'm hearing you, Jolene. The Di-Longhi woman has gone out. We don't know where. She'll be returning because she has reservations for the next couple of days. She must have a pile of money; she's staying in the presidential suite."

"Di-Longhi sounds pretty far-fetched to me," George said.

"On the contrary," Jolene said. "We're chasing an astute operative. She's following the time-honored technique of hiding in plain sight. She could manipulate her appearance, fake her age, and pretend to limp. We know she has money because John Paul told Steve she'd bribed him with a half million dollars. The terrorists have experience with fake passports. Maybe she's carrying a high-end fake."

"Okay. Let's say Di-Longhi is the real deal. What do we tell Billy?"

"Billy, listen. There's a chance Madame Di-Longhi might come back to the Four Seasons. You should play that hand. Stay at the hotel and wait for her. Be careful. Our suspect is a deadly black widow. She wouldn't hesitate to kill you and dozens more. George will send armed reinforcements. Forward the Four Seasons video of Di-Longhi to all teams just in case she shows up at one of the banks or at Cointrin Airport. We'll call the airport team and ask them to compare your video with CCTV camera footage of her arrival. George, can you think of anything else?"

"No. That covers the precautions we should take if Di-Longhi is our suspect."

Billy heaved a sigh of relief. "I'll follow up and touch all the bases."

Growing apprehensive, Jolene glanced at her watch. It was ten o'clock sharp.

"Whether she's Di-Longhi or not, our suspect has managed to stay one step ahead of us at every turn. I wouldn't put it past her to anticipate what we're doing to track her down at this bank. We've been here an hour, and nothing has happened. I don't think our suspect would wait this late to pick up her money. Monsieur Dujardin is stringing us along."

"Let's pay him a visit," George said.

They returned to the bank manager's office and knocked on the door.

Dujardin's nervousness was obvious.

He stuttered when he said, "Wh-wh-what do you want now? Is the room c-c-comfortable? C-c-can we get you something else to eat?"

"Never mind that," Jolene said. "You've been stalling us. When was the last time you talked with the account holder?"

Dujardin blanched. His face broadcast guilt.

George said, "We warned you of the consequences if you didn't assist us in blocking her obtaining access to those funds. When did she contact you?"

Dujardin slumped in his chair. "This is Switzerland, not the United States. You have no rights here."

George's face hardened.

The manager began to beg. "Have mercy. I have a family. A wife and two young children."

Jolene touched him gently on the shoulder. "We'll spare you if you tell us what you did for her."

Dujardin blurted out, "I only followed instructions and transferred five million dollars to another of the bank's branches."

He gave them the address and, at George's insistence, drew a map to show the shortest route to Rue François-Versonnex.

George and Jolene ran from the bank to their parked car. He drove. She called for reinforcements to concentrate on the target branch.

CHAPTER 27

Joffrey sat in the driver's seat and Dana in the passenger seat. He stopped in front of the RGS branch on Rue François-Versonnex. She leapt from the car and sprinted to the front door of the bank, slowing her pace to a casual stroll as she entered.

She asked for Madame Camille Bruni, the contact given her by Monsieur Dujardin. Once ushered into the bank manager's office, she introduced herself and mentioned she had been sent by her colleague in the Rue de Lausanne branch.

Madame Bruni bowed respectfully. "May I have your account information and password, *S'il vous plaît*."

Dana gave her the required information.

Ten minutes later, she exited the bank five million dollars richer. The funds had been safely transferred to a bank in the Bahamas.

Joffrey had been circling the block in search of a convenient parking space, but he had no luck. When he saw Dana step out into the sunshine, a glow on her face, he double-parked.

She yanked the Renault's door open and jumped in.

"Drive *mon cher*. Head for Besançon."

"Did you get it?"

"*Bien sûr*. We have all the money we need for the next stage of our journey."

He headed for the frontier, driving cautiously, being careful to stay within the legal speed limit and observe all traffic signals.

When the adrenaline's heightened arousal began to wear off, Dana started to feel drowsy.

"I'm going to sleep now. Wake me when we get near our destination."

Bonne nuit ma belle.

CHAPTER 28

George pulled up in front of the RGS branch on Rue François-Versonnex. Seeing no parking space nearby, he double-parked. He and Jolene bounded from the Camry and ran into the bank.

Their abrupt arrival startled bank staff and customers.

"*Excusez-moi*," Jolene said. Where's the bank manager? We have an urgent problem and need his immediate assistance."

Attracted by the excitement, Madame Camille Bruni called out. "*I* am the bank manager. How can I help?"

Jolene stepped up to the manager. "We have an urgent situation and need to speak with you privately."

"Come to my office."

After closing the door, Madame Bruni spread her hands as if to calm her visitors. "Now, what is so urgent?"

Deciding it was best to come right to the point, Jolene said, "We were told by Monsieur Dujardin that this morning he transferred five million dollars to your branch to be collected by a female terrorist. Did the woman arrive? Did you turn over the funds?"

Open-mouthed, the bank manager was unable to speak for a few seconds. Finally, she said, "We observe strict confidentiality about bank transactions. I have no idea what Monsieur Dujardin may have told you. But I will tell you nothing."

Jolene showed her the ambassador's letter.

"We have firm intelligence this woman was responsible for the suicide bombings that resulted in the death and injury of hundreds in the Washington area in the last few days," Jolene said. "She plans to use the funds you gave her to commit even more horrific disasters. Are you willing to be an accessory to her crimes and to taint the reputation of the RGS bank? At best, you'll be fired. If the US government has any influence, you'll spend the rest of your life in prison."

Madame Bruni collapsed into the chair behind her desk. "I only did my job."

Jolene walked up behind the woman and began stroking her back. "Of course, you did what you had to do. There was no way you could have known she was a terrorist." Her voice hardened. "But now you know. You must tell us so we can stop her."

"I don't know her name or anything about her. We only require someone to provide the necessary coded information to withdraw sums of any amount. But I can describe her for you. Also, I can provide you with a video that will give you a perfect image."

Once the torrent of explanations began, the bank manager was unable to stop talking. "She's a beautiful young woman in her thirties, black hair with a pixie cut, a Grecian nose, and full lips like Angelina Jolie. Slightly taller than me—I'm five seven the way you Americans measure height. I learned that when I got my driver's license while I was studying finance at Boston University. She's wearing a light-green wool suit, very trendy, and stylish black flats. She's athletic. I studied ballet for several years; she moves like a dancer."

"That's extremely helpful," Jolene said, cutting off the outpouring. "How much did she withdraw?"

"We transferred five million dollars."

Madame Bruni gave George the details. He immediately called the Embassy to set the wheels in motion to track the funds.

Jolene expected the monies would have been transferred to yet another bank before the American authorities traced it.

By this point, Madame Bruni was falling over herself to be ever more cooperative. She called for a clerk to bring in a copy of the video showing the woman in question. George used the manager's computer to forward the video to all teams participating in the search.

Once they siphoned the information from the bank manager, George and Jolene hurried to the Camry. They arrived just as a *gendarme* was walking toward their vehicle, taking out his notebook. George flashed his diplomatic passport, and the official nodded as they climbed into the car and drove away.

"Where do we go?" he said.

"Head for the French border just past Cointrin Airport. That's the quickest way out of Switzerland."

CHAPTER 29

Zaha Nashashibi stepped out of the taxi, limping slightly. Dragging a dark gray hardcase suitcase and carrying a makeup case, she walked slowly toward the Air France ticket concourse at Cointrin Airport. Focused on the role she was about to play, she ignored the balmy morning breeze and aqua skies that signaled the start of another perfect day in Geneva.

Confident in the persona of Dorothea Hamilton Di-Longhi, Zaha entered the restricted area and presented her passport at the first-class counter. The portly male agent glanced first at the passport and then scrutinized the countenance of the fifty something, gray haired, elegantly clad woman standing regally before him.

He nodded deferentially.

Zaha experienced a thrill knowing the first hurdle in her masquerade had been safely cleared.

"You must hurry to security," the agent said in French. "Your flight will be departing soon."

In a scolding tone, he added, as if to underscore his authority, "If you were not flying first class, I would not be allowed to clear you."

"*Merci*," Zaha said, then flushed with embarrassment remembering Dana's caution her mother hated the French and never spoke the language.

She boarded the eleven o'clock flight from Geneva to Paris. On arrival, she exited the Charles de Gaulle airport and hurried to a taxi, no longer feeling the imperative to limp. The weather in France was a carbon copy of what she had left behind in Switzerland. She inhaled deeply, aware she was safe and could enjoy the bright sunshine and pillowy clouds floating across a blue sky. She directed the driver to take her to Gare du Nord, one of the largest train stations in Paris.

At the station, she entered the ladies' room and locked herself in a stall where she obliterated her identity as Dana's mother and once again became Zaha—a young Zaha with black hair in a pixie cut. She traded the classy formal suit she'd worn from Geneva for a short skirt and a sexy blouse. No one, especially no man, looking at this outfit would connect her with the fifty something woman with gray hair who entered Gare du Nord a few minutes ago. Before leaving the station, she intended to purchase a red beret, which would compound the misdirection. The Di-Longhi clothes and wig were packed in her suitcase for later disposal in a different location.

Once the reincarnation of Zaha was complete, she proceeded to the metro and traveled to Madeleine, where she checked into a small hotel on Place de la Madeleine. For identification, she used one of the false passports she'd brought with her from Washington, which had been secreted in the bottom of the makeup case.

Her plan was to remain in Paris for two days. Since she spoke both English and French fluently, she was confident of her ability to blend in, either as an American tourist or a Parisian resident. Even if she were suspected of being Muslim, she would not stand out, since one person out of ten in the Paris population was Muslim.

She began making a mental list of the things she would do while in Paris: far from a strict Muslim, she planned to eat a *croque monsieur,* the French version of a ham and cheese sandwich, at a sidewalk café on the Champs-Élysées; shop in *Le Bon Marché;* and ascend to the highest observation deck of the Eiffel Tower at night to gaze out over the City of Lights.

Later in the week, she would travel to London via Eurostar on their high-speed train under the English Channel. Similarly, in London she could play the role of an American tourist or one of the numerous Muslim residents of the ancient city.

CHAPTER 30

Tanya Hinch and her team watched hours of CCTV footage of passengers arriving at Cointrin Airport. Tanya was having increasing trouble focusing when a middle-aged woman entering the screen caught her eye. The woman looked not at all like the video of the prime suspect taken at the Hyatt in Tysons, but there was something about her. She blinked and backed up the video to view the image again. Then she compared the picture with the video Billy Merriweather had sent from the Four Seasons Hotel des Bergues.

Bingo. The images matched.

Tanya called George. "CCTV footage shows Madame Di-Longhi entering Geneva the night before last on the 6:05 flight. She was met at the airport by a big man who looked European, wearing a well-tailored blue suit."

Jolene, listening on speaker phone, said, "Good work. Another puzzle piece falls into place."

After a quiet pause, Jolene said, "Now that we've identified her, examine departure videos, starting yesterday."

"Departure to where, do we have a destination?" Tanya said.

"Any destination, any time."

After a lengthy search, one of her group rushed up to Tanya. "Come look."

She followed her colleague and examined another batch of CCTV images captured that morning. She saw the familiar picture of the gray-haired woman in her fifties wearing a stylish light-gray pant suit and walking with a slight limp.

A few minutes later, Tanya dialed George.

"The good news is we got her," she said.

Jolene and George together shouted, "What's the bad news?"

"The bad news is she departed on Air France at eleven o'clock, bound for Paris."

"I can have her picked up at Charles de Gaulle airport," George said.

Tanya said, "I'm afraid that's not possible."

"Why not?"

Jolene interrupted. "Because the flight to Paris takes just over an hour. It's now twelve thirty."

Tanya cleared her throat. "I checked. The flight arrived in Paris on time. By now, Madame Di-Longhi is out of the airport and hiding somewhere in the city. That's a trip I've made myself many times. You'll have to mount a major manhunt to track her down in an urban area of over ten million people, the largest in Europe. Paris has a huge Muslim population—if she's Muslim, she's a grain of sand on the beach."

As an afterthought, Tanya said, "The man who met her on arrival was not with her on departure. I checked the manifest, Madame Di-Longhi was flying first class. No man was in the seat next to her. And, as far as we can tell, no one matching his description entered the airport this morning. It appears she's traveling alone."

CHAPTER 31

Jolene turned to face George in the Camry. "It's time to touch base with Alex and pool our information."

"Okay," he said. "But right now, I'm confused about what we actually know and why we're doing what we're doing."

"How's that?"

"Well, you told me to drive into France in pursuit of the woman who collected the five million dollars from the RGS branch on Rue François-Versonnex. Her video footage at the bank and Madame Bruni's description matched the video image captured of the woman in the lobby of the Hyatt Regency who murdered General Winston."

"That's right," Jolene said.

"But Tanya informed us Madame Di-Longhi—whom we earlier thought was our suspect in disguise as a fifty something woman with gray hair at the Four Seasons—arrived in Paris a half hour ago. The timing of her departure makes it likely *she's* our suspect. She collected the Saudi money, traveled to the airport after changing her appearance, and escaped safely to Paris.

George scratched his head. "Why am I still driving blindly on a road in France when I have no idea who I'm chasing or where she might be going? Our suspect is in Paris."

In his frustration, George took his eyes off the road and turned to face Jolene in the passenger seat.

Mildly alarmed, she said, "George, watch the road."

Glancing back at oncoming traffic, he discovered he had swerved onto the left side of the highway, confronting an oncoming truck less than two hundred feet away. Quickly correcting the error, he looked a bit embarrassed.

Jolene knew Alex would have to coordinate the search for Madame Di-Longhi in Paris. But she didn't share George's belief their Paris suspect escaped with the five million dollars. Her hunch was she and George were in hot pursuit of a different woman in Southeast France who had actually received the money. But that belief was based on several shaky assumptions.

"Let me tell you what I think," she said.

"Madame Di-Longhi, Samira Hart, or whoever she calls herself in her various identities, is our suspect. She's the woman who seduced General Winston and killed him before stealing his briefcase."

Unable to contain himself, George said, "But Di-Longhi looks nothing like the mysterious woman crossing the lobby of the Hyatt, and she certainly isn't the beautiful woman in her thirties who just collected five million dollars of Saudi money in Geneva from the RGS branch on Rue François-Versonnex. Madame Bruni gave us a perfect description, which matched the video image of her in the bank lobby. Besides, Tanya confirmed Madame Di-Longhi just flew to Paris with the money."

"No, George, that's where you're wrong. Let's separate what we know and what we don't know."

She continued in a lecturing tone.

"We know there are two identities for our suspect, but we don't know if these separate identities are one woman or two women. If a one-woman scenario is correct, our suspect fled to Paris with the necessary funds to buy one or more suitcase nukes. If a two-woman scenario is correct, a second person is the one who killed the general and absconded with the Saudi money. We can only guess where she may have gone."

"I'm confused," George said. "Why are we driving into Southeast France if the suspect with the money is in Paris?"

Jolene paused to collect her thoughts, growing more convinced her theory of events was correct. "Let's suppose, the original Madame Di-Longhi arrived in Geneva night before last. She was met by a big man in a blue suit. He drove her to the Four Seasons, and she checked into the presidential suite. At some point yesterday, she met with the Saudis, and they gave her the access codes to five million dollars at the RGS bank."

George still looked puzzled, but he listened attentively as she continued.

"Sometime, perhaps this morning, she was joined by a confederate. The women switched identities. Or rather, the accomplice altered her appearance and 'became' Madame Di-Longhi. The body double traveled to Cointrin Airport and flew to Paris. The original reverted to the appearance she assumed at the Hyatt, now with a pixie haircut, and wore a green wool suit to visit the RGS bank. The original then disappeared, having acquired the Saudi money. My hunch is the original fled into France. She's the one we're chasing."

"Holy shit, Jolene. How do you dream up this stuff? Why do you think she crossed over into France?"

"Because, from Geneva, this is the fastest, most direct, route to Germany."

"I'll bite. Why Germany?" George said.

"More hunches. How hard would it be to travel from Geneva to Russia to collect suitcase nukes?"

George frowned. "Well, it wouldn't be easy. There would be a lot of chances for our team to locate our suspect's tracks."

"Exactly. And how easy would it be to travel from Southeast France into Germany by car?"

Playing straight man, George said, "Not difficult at all. Crossing borders in Europe poses no problems, particularly for travelers with even perfunctory ID."

Jolene nodded. "That's the basis for my hunch about our suspect's whereabouts. She asked the Russian mafia sellers to meet her with the nukes in Germany. It's less trouble for them to get out of Russia than for her to enter. The mafia would have myriad ways of crossing the border into Germany. They could travel through Poland or the Czech Republic."

"My God. Your theories are starting to make sense unless I'm getting dizzy trying to follow the bouncing ball. But if she's going to pick up the nukes in Germany, how do we find out where?"

Jolene shrugged her shoulders. "The location of the meet in Germany is one problem we're going to need Alex's assistance on. Another is tracking down the confederate in Paris. She may have information about where our original suspect is headed. Also, Alex will need to launch the manhunt for the other members of the terrorist cell in the DC area. Those left behind may know something about the overall scheme."

She picked up her satellite phone and dialed Alex.

Alex glanced at caller ID, punched the green answer button, and said, "It's about time you checked in. I'm getting sitreps from everyone but you. What's the situation? Why haven't you reported? And where the hell are you? Courtney told me you've been out of touch."

"George Southern and I are in a Camry about thirty minutes out of Geneva in Southeast France," Jolene proceeded to outline her theory of the two suspects and why she was following the trail of the original woman who had collected the five million dollars. "Alex, we need your help in finding her destination in Germany, assuming I'm right about where she's headed."

There was a long silence while Alex digested what he'd been told.

"I said you were the one with the best instincts to find the goddamned needle. I still believe that. I've been talking with some experts on the Russian mafia in the intelligence community. They believe the gang most likely to sell suitcase nukes to terrorists is headed by Besik Kasayeva. We're trying to confirm his whereabouts. It might be easier to follow him to the meeting place in Germany—if that's what's going on—than to try and pick up her trail."

"Okay," Jo said.

Alex continued. "I'll check out the Paris and DC angles."

"One other thing. Courtney and Luke can help corner our suspect in Germany," Jo said. "Send them to Berlin."

"Affirmative. Anything else?"

"Yes. Can you send Amal and Mike to Dresden?"

"Done. Where are you and George headed?"

"Besançon, France. From there, we'll go to Nuremberg, Germany."

Sounding more relaxed, Alex said, "Well, if the theory of a meet in Germany is accurate, at least we'll be able to cover some of the logical routes from Russia. Try a little harder to keep me up to date."

CHAPTER 32

Majid ibn Ishak called together the members of the terrorist cell. "I have good news to report. Dana called to tell me she successfully obtained the funds provided by friends in Saudi Arabia who support our cause."

Those assembled broke out in cheers. Majid waved his hands for quiet.

"Zaha joined her, adopted Dana's false identity, and led pursuers on a wild goose chase to Paris."

"Is Zaha safe?" Omar Aziz asked. Oldest of the terrorists, and prone to tease Zaha about her sexual hijinks, he was fond of the young woman.

"Yes. Zaha is staying at a small hotel on Place de la Madeleine. In a couple of days, she'll travel to London. There's a large Muslim community in both cities. Zaha will be a drop of water in the ocean. She's fluent in French and English, so she can fit in easily as tourist or resident in either place."

Satisfied, Omar smiled.

"The next move in our plan is to collect two portable nuclear bombs from sellers in the Russian mafia," Majid said. "This could be the act of greatest danger. Dana asked me to join her in Germany. My role will be as a scientist or technician to care for the weapons and ensure they remain viable. She wants you, Nour, to accompany me. You will be our bodyguard."

Majid avoided mentioning Dana told him about Joffrey Gobert who was accompanying her and would also serve as a bodyguard.

Nour Sayed's mouth twitched in a scary smile. The cell's enforcer's sheer size would frighten most adversaries. Expertise with a wide variety of weapons guaranteed his threat of violence could be carried out with confidence.

Nour said, "Will we be armed in Europe?"

"Of course. Dana is acquiring guns from our friends in Germany. She assured me we will have pistols and automatic weapons."

"When do we leave?"

"Later tonight. Pack and be sure to bring your passport."

Majid gestured to Jaber Sadiq, "Dana wants you to remain in America and continue to collect information about the targets she discussed with us."

Jaber, the youngest member of the cell, indicated his assent. But he made no effort to hide his unhappiness at being denied the opportunity to participate in the main action in Europe.

"Omar, you and Jaber must work together. He's the lead and will decide which locations each of you will visit. Dana will want a complete report, with pictures. You've had more experience, since you did the bulk of the work scouting the targets for the suicide bombings.

"Jaber, get together each evening with Omar, review the day's activities, and plan the schedule for the next day. You're young, so you should not hesitate to tap Omar's greater experience."

Majid pulled Jaber aside to impart some confidential information for his ears only.

CHAPTER 33

Felix Goldblatt congratulated himself for navigating heavy traffic during the trip from the NCTC to the Red Fox Inn in Middleburg, Virginia in forty-five minutes. He pulled into the Inn's rear parking lot and inspected the cars already parked for an early lunch. He had an appointment to meet with a former colleague in the Mossad, Yael Ravitz, and was curious if he could guess which was her vehicle. The black Land Rover, which looked as if it could use a trip through the car wash, was the most likely choice. Yael was always casual about the outward appearance of things, in sharp contrast to her meticulous attention to their functionality.

He entered the tavern and spotted Yael seated in the far corner, well removed from the nearest customer. As usual, he'd arrived early, but she was even earlier. She gave a slight wave and rose to kiss him on the cheek.

A glass of white wine was positioned at his plate setting. A half-full glass was on her side of the table. This was a familiar ritual any time they met in a restaurant. Yael always arrived first, and she invariably ordered white wine for both and finished drinking her glass before he did. They made it a practice never to order a second serving of wine, to keep a clear head whenever they were in a danger zone, which for practical purposes was all of the time.

"Yael, you're as gorgeous as ever." With shoulder-length brown hair and dark hazel eyes, she could have been a professional model, although he never forgot her deadly capabilities. At five ten, she was just three inches shorter than him, and she looked as fit as when they had served in the same paratroop brigade in the Israel Defense Forces before both were recruited into the Mossad Collections Department. For years, they were lovers when not on separate intelligence assignments. Eventually, Felix left Mossad to pursue a scientific career path, but he'd been lured back to the agency and detailed to the Americans in a gesture of Israeli-US cooperation. They hadn't seen each other in the past two years.

She ignored the compliment.

"I have vital information about the terrorist cell you've been pursuing," she said. Unspoken was the acknowledgment that official sharing of information was compromised due to periodic jousting between the president of the United States and the prime minister of Israel over Israel-Palestine relations.

At that moment, a waiter walked toward their table.

"I'll tell you the details after we order." Having finished his wine, he ordered coffee. Felix chose fried chicken and Yael trout.

When they had their quiet corner once again to themselves, she said, "An operation I was heading uncovered a Saudi, Kamal Al-Outaibi. We'll skip the gory details, but Kamal confessed he was the go-between who arranged for the transfer of five million dollars from Saudis who were formerly sympathetic to Al-Qaeda."

Listening intently, Felix swigged his coffee.

Yael said, "This week, the funds were collected in Geneva by the terrorist cell headed by Dana Hussein al-Sadi. Dana's father, Yousef al-Sadi, is a distant relative of the Saudi royal family. Her mother is the wealthy heiress, Dorothea Hamilton Di-Longhi. Dana was traveling on her mother's passport."

Felix grunted assent. "We didn't know Dana's identity or background, but we knew she had picked up the five million. Our belief is she intends to use the funds to purchase suitcase nukes from the Russian mafia. The likelihood is she's dealing with a gang headed by Besik Kasayeva. Our best guess is that the transaction will take place in Germany."

Yael paused to take a sip of wine. "Kamal indicated his Saudi backers believe Germany is where the exchange will occur, although he had no specific information about who, when, or where."

Conversation was inhibited since the room was beginning to fill up with diners. After a few moments of silence, she told Felix the location in Northern Virginia of Dana's terrorist cell.

The food arrived and the couple busied themselves with eating.

After Felix paid the bill, Yael leaned across the table and whispered in his ear. "I reserved a room upstairs in the inn. I hope you share my belief terrorists can wait while we renew our acquaintance. It's been a long time, and I've been lonely."

He weighed the downside of delay for an hour, or more, before returning to share the information with his colleagues. For him too, it had been a long time between lovers.

"Let's see how rooms at the Red Fox Inn compare with the George V in Paris."

Yael smiled coyly at the reminder of their romantic weekend spent at the historic hotel and exploring cafés and elegant shops on the Champs-Élysées.

CHAPTER 34

Alex Werth brought in Hans Jensen and Steve Randall to hear the intelligence Felix Goldblatt had obtained from his source in Mossad.

Felix summarized the information Yael had provided at the Red Fox Inn.

"We know the location of the terrorist cell," Hans said. What we don't know is how many are here in Virginia. Jolene accounted for two who were in Geneva, alternately taking on the identity of Madame Di-Longhi. Both female terrorists we believe to be in France."

"What does it matter how many terrorists in the Di-Longhi cell are still in Virginia?" Steve said. "We know from Felix's source the cell is small. We'll overwhelm them with a superior force."

Alex had a clear notion what Steve's experience as an Army Ranger would lead him to consider a superior force. Given endorsement of their enterprise from the president himself, mounting a large-scale attack would not pose a problem. However, he didn't concur such an initiative was the wisest course.

"In order to muster overwhelming force, we'd have to involve other elements of the intelligence community. Best to avoid that. The more people informed, the more likely a leak will give away our plans to Dana Hussein al-Sadi."

"You certainly don't imagine the four of us could pull off the attack," Hans said.

"Why not?" Felix said. "Think back to the suicide bombings at Dulles, Tysons, the Air and Space Museum, Union Station, and

Metro Center. Five attacks. We can assume one terrorist orchestrated each incident. That accounts for five terrorists. In addition, there's the leader, Dana, who presumably wouldn't play a direct role in any of the bombings. That starts with six in the cell. Perhaps more, but if there were a lot more, don't you imagine she'd have ordered more attacks? Two of the six are in France, which leaves a minimum of four terrorists unaccounted for. Even if there were twice that number still in Virginia, which I'd say is unlikely, the four of us should still be able to overpower them with the element of surprise."

"I don't fault your math or your logic," Alex said. "It's reasonable to assume we're dealing with an opposing force of four to eight terrorists. But there are two things we need to consider. First, we need to take one—preferably all—alive. Our main goal is to gain actionable intelligence from the survivors that will enable us to track down Dana's location to prevent her from acquiring any suitcase nukes. Second, we'll be attacking the terrorists in their home base. Who knows what sorts of defensive measures they have that could derail our attack?"

After further discussion, Alex concluded the risks of adding outsiders to their group outweighed the risks of proceeding with the four of them. However, he'd fine-tuned his thinking after recalling blueprints of the house Tommy Lee Weaver, their communications guru, had obtained.

"Six men are needed for the assault—two for the ground floor, two upstairs, and two for the basement. I've decided to add two Navy SEALs to our attack force, Bob Xavier and Fred Jefferson. They're part of Luke Worthington's SEAL team. I sounded them out about joining us at some point. They're experienced in scenarios we're likely to face. Navy SEALs specialize in firefights where they have to extract hostiles without unnecessary killing."

After the decision was made, they hurried to the armory and began selecting weapons.

Each of them was already carrying a handgun—Steve had replaced the pistol he'd used to shoot John Paul after his gun was confiscated as a routine step in any investigation of an official killing by firearm. Alex, Felix, and Steve selected the Heckler & Koch MP5 submachine gun because of its versatility and ready concealability. Hans opted for a combat shotgun. They donned lightweight ballistic vests that would fit under regular clothing.

At Alex's urging, they each picked up a few stun grenades. He said, "The flash bangs will be our first line of attack. They're nonlethal, but the explosions will blind our opponents for a few seconds and the loud noise will disorient them. If we're lucky, we may not have to fire a shot."

CHAPTER 35

Alex drove a black sedan, accompanied by Felix. Steve drove a dark gray SUV, accompanied by Hans and the two Navy SEALs, Bob and Fred. All were professionals who'd trained in this type of operation before. There was no conversation. Both vehicles parked on a residential street, just two doors on either side of the target house.

The Northern Virginia neighborhood was well chosen by the terrorists. It lay midway between the concentration of Muslim homes surrounding the Dar Al-Hijrah Islamic Center in Falls Church and the Tysons shopping and business complex, a magnet for Muslims and persons of all ages, sexes, ethnicities, and backgrounds. Any Muslim noticed in the area would appear right at home.

All of the attackers wore dark clothing and black camouflage face makeup to obscure visibility. The men, like the vehicles, were virtually invisible in the pitch blackness at three fifteen in the morning.

Each man knew his assignment. Alex briefed them, considering blueprints of the residence Tommy Lee obtained. Once front and back doors were breached by the mini-ram collision entry tools, Alex and Felix would head for the second floor, where the bulk of terrorists were expected to be sleeping in the four bedrooms. Steve and Hans would clear the first floor—living room, study, kitchen/eating area, bathrooms, assorted closets, and access to a two-car garage. Bob and Fred would clear the basement—rec room, laundry and utility room, bathroom, and storage areas. No one would hazard a guess how many (if any) of the four to eight estimated terrorists might be found on the first floor or in the basement.

Tommy Lee, who'd driven his own car and parked on an adjoining block, was responsible for cutting off electric power to the house at the appointed time of 3:30 a.m. Each member of the attack team was equipped with night vision goggles, having been cautioned to close their eyes when flash bangs were exploding to avoid being blinded by the intense illumination. Everyone wore acoustic earmuffs to muffle the noise and disorientation from the stun grenades.

Tommy Lee cut the power. The few lights that were on in the house blinked out.

Alex's eyes quickly adjusted to the sudden darkness. He could hear Fred demolishing the door leading into the kitchen, en route to the basement. Felix slammed the miniram into the front door, knocking it off its hinges.

A quiet night was quiet no longer. Alex hoped no neighbors would call the police on hearing the ruckus.

Steve, Hans, Alex, and Felix charged through the wide entrance. They considered shouting "POLICE!" on entry, much as might occur during a no-knock warrant incursion, but decided the combination of confusion stemming from forcible entry and stun grenades, accompanied by silence of the attack team, would be more effective in disorienting the terrorists.

Alex and Felix rushed up a flight of stairs. He threw a flash bang near the open bedroom door, closing his eyes briefly to avoid being blinded. The sound of a pistol being racked to insert a round in the chamber alerted him to the perils of entering a house without knowing who or what was inside.

• • •

Awakened by the flash and explosion, Jaber threw aside the bedclothes and jumped to his feet, wearing only boxer shorts and a tie-dyed T-shirt. He grabbed the tactical flashlight and pistol he kept on his bedside table and racked the slide to ensure the weapon was ready to fire.

Proud of having been placed in charge, Jaber was shocked to realize it was his responsibility to mount a defense. Since Majid and Nour had left for Reagan Airport yesterday evening, any counterattack was up to him and Omar, who was apparently sound asleep in the bedroom across the hall.

Creeping across the room, the young terrorist propped one hand on the door frame. He knew the attack must come up the staircase. Since he was right-handed and the staircase was to his right, the only way to fire at an oncoming attacker was to lean past the door frame and point his pistol down the stairs. That was an awkward position as it exposed his head and the left side of his torso to counterfire.

Why was there was no indication Omar was awake? Knowing Omar would have a safer angle to fire at any attacker coming up the stairs, Jaber counted to five to give his colleague a chance to appear.

When nothing happened, he mumbled, "Fuck it."

Leaning out and pointing blindly toward the staircase, Jaber began firing his pistol rapidly hoping the fusillade would at least startle the enemy.

Suddenly, his left side exploded with pain from a gunshot wound. There was no longer any feeling in his left arm and shoulder. Hydrostatic shock overwhelmed an otherwise healthy nervous system. The flashlight and pistol dropped from limp fingers. He slumped to his knees and stared at the hellacious figure striding forward, illuminated by the halo of his flashlight. A second image passed in a combat crouch headed toward Omar's room.

"I'm dying."

The dark figure bent over as Jaber lay crumpled onto his side.

"You're *not* dying. I shot you in the shoulder. What you're feeling is pain from the bullet wound and shock from blood loss. You're about to pass out, but when you come to, you'll be fine. Tell me where in Germany is Dana Hussein al-Sadi?"

"Dana?" Jaber said, as though he were hearing the name for the first time.

"Yes, Dana. She's going to be in great danger in Germany. You must tell me where she and your friends are going to meet Besik Kasayeva. He plans to murder her and steal the five million dollars she's hoping to use to trade with him. We can protect her if you tell us where she's headed."

Jaber was confused. *What should I believe? Why* is this man saying Dana is in danger? *Is the man the threat or do the Russian mafia really plan to kill her?*

He heard the explosion of a flash bang grenade and shots fired coming from Omar's bedroom. He tried to get up to go to his friend's aid, but his body betrayed him.

His eyes closed and hallucinations battled with common sense. At one level he knew Dana was at risk in Germany. What could he do to save her? Before consciousness faded, he uttered one word.

"Hamburg."

CHAPTER 36

Jolene recognized Alex from caller ID on her satellite phone.

"Alex, what happened? Are you all okay?"

"Everything went off smoothly, Jo. We got some information, although I can't attest to its validity."

Jolene switched to speaker phone so George could hear.

"George and I are listening. What'd you learn?"

Alex described the firefight, highlighting Felix's capture of the older terrorist unharmed, even though so far they'd learned nothing from the man known as Omar Aziz. He recapped the talk with the young terrorist, Jaber Sadiq, he'd tried to persuade to give up Dana's rendezvous with the Russian gang in Germany.

"Before he lapsed into unconsciousness, Sadiq said: 'Hamburg.' He was groggy at the time. It's impossible to know if he intended to tell us Dana's destination in response to my promise to protect her from Kasayeva or to send us on a wild goose chase."

"Hamburg, huh?" Jolene glanced at George as though asking for his opinion.

"Hamburg is plausible. The city has deep terrorist roots, starting with Mohammad Atta and the 9/11 crew that flew the planes into the twin towers of the World Trade Center. Hamburg's the third largest port in Europe, which gives Dana the option of getting the nukes out by ship. She'd be hard to track down in a city that big with tens of thousands of Muslims."

"We could make a strong case for Hamburg as her destination," Jolene said. "On the other hand, Hamburg is more in the western part of Germany than I would have predicted for the meet. Don't forget, we're assuming the Russian gang will be bringing the nukes to Dana. Kasayeva won't be happy passing through more German territory than essential. I doubt he would want to spend too much time vulnerable to the GSG 9 Counterterrorism unit of the German federal police."

Alex asked impatiently, "Jo, do you believe Dana's headed to Hamburg, or not?"

"Not. I'm still inclined to gamble on Berlin, Dresden, and Nuremberg. Berlin has a huge Russian population, and the Russian language is commonly spoken. Since the days when Berlin was a divided city, the Russians have acted as though they're part owners. Dresden is close to the eastern border of Germany, and it's a quick trip from the Czech Republic. Nuremberg's also near the eastern border. The city's a six-hour ride from Geneva, which is why I picked it. And why it would be attractive to Dana."

Jolene laughed ruefully. "My guess is your young terrorist was trying to con you about Hamburg, Alex."

"Perhaps. But I'm unwilling to overlook Hamburg, even if it's a long shot. I'm traveling there and bringing Felix, Steve, and Hans with me. I've added two Navy SEALs, Bob Xavier and Fred Jefferson, to our little band. They'll accompany us to Hamburg. We're headed for Andrews now. Mansfield's arranged for us to take military flights to save time and make it easier to carry weapons."

"Great," Jolene said. "What do you think about sending Steve and Hans to Paris to track down the stand-in Madame Di-Longhi, whom we believe to be Zaha Nashashibi? They can always join us in Germany if that doesn't pan out."

A moment of silence signaled he was considering the suggestion.

"Okay. Zaha might be easier to find since we know what city she's in. How long will it take you to arrive in Nuremberg?"

"Four hours, give or take."

CHAPTER 37

Dana awoke from her nap refreshed. She no longer felt any discomfort from the surface wound to her stomach. She glanced at Joffrey at the steering wheel. He looked as though he was on a leisurely drive in the country. No tension. No fear.

She reached over and stroked Joffrey's face.

"Did you sleep well?" he said.

"Superbly. Coming in possession of five million dollars will do more to relax you than a lifetime supply of Ambien."

He smiled at the lame joke. "Why do I feel you're not going to spend your newfound wealth in one of the high fashion boutiques on the Kurfürstendamm in Berlin?"

"No, *mon cher*. The five million is for a shopping trip of a different kind. And we're not heading for Berlin. Are you sure you want to know what I intend to buy or where we're headed? Your life will be at risk once you know. I'm grateful for what you've done up to this moment. It's not too late for us to say goodbye. You can get off at the nearest train station, and I'll take the Renault."

"But you need a bodyguard."

"And I'll have one. Friends are joining me from America."

Joffrey slowed the car, turned into a motorway rest area on the outskirts of Besançon, and parked. He twisted in his seat to face Dana.

"Did you decide you no longer need me?"

She shook her head in denial.

"It's because I've come to realize how much I need you, even care for you, that I hesitate to ask you to share the danger I'll face in spending the five million. All my life I've been focused on *my* desires, *my* goals. I've never allowed myself the luxury of thinking about what my success costs the others who help me. But I can't bear the thought of you paying the ultimate price for what is likely to come."

She saw he was stunned by the raw emotion revealed in her outburst.

"That you care for me is enough. I'll not hesitate to pay any price to protect you. Tell me now. Where is our destination and what are you buying with the fortune you acquired from the Saudis?"

She nodded soberly.

"Very well. Head for Nuremberg. There we'll be joined by Majid ibn Ishak, a scientist and engineer, and Nour Sayed, a bodyguard. They are loyal to me and willing to risk death. We'll rendezvous with a Russian mafia leader named Besik Kasayeva. He's bringing two suitcase nukes from Moscow for which I'll pay him a large share of the five million dollars. The remainder I plan to keep to fund my retirement in case I survive events of the next few weeks."

Joffrey blanched and stared at her unbelieving. "Are you serious? Portable nuclear weapons?"

"You heard right. Are you surprised to learn I'm a terrorist? Surely, you must have suspected."

He pointed at her accusingly. "The wave of suicide bombings in Washington. That was you. Hundreds died."

"True. And with the suitcase nukes, I'll be responsible for chaos on a scale that'll dwarf those events. Many thousands will die. Perhaps hundreds of thousands."

Saying nothing, Joffrey stared off at a grove of trees at the far end of the rest area.

For the first time anxiety crept into her voice. "Do you still want to be with me now that you know the enormity of my crimes?"

"The enormity of your crimes is nothing matched against the enormity of my feelings for you."

He embraced Dana and they clung to each other.

The tender moment was shattered by the sound of doors on both sides of the Renault opening.

Leering at them were two young men, barely in their twenties. One was tall with strands of dark hair hanging over his pockmarked forehead and a deep scar on his left cheek. The other was short with blond hair and fat lips. Both looked like they'd fallen off the ugly truck from Marseille.

Waving an elegant switchblade, the tall one, standing by Joffrey's door, said, in a voice clearly imitating dialogue heard in a Hollywood film of an earlier era, "Your money or your life."

Dana and Joffrey looked at each other and guffawed.

The short one said, "*Ils sont fou ces Americains.*"

Dana laughed even harder. "He thinks *we're* crazy."

Without warning, she pulled the SIG Sauer from her purse and thrust the barrel of the pistol against the throat of the short robber.

"Hear me good, asshole. Drop your knife and run like the hounds of hell are chasing you. Then maybe I won't kill you."

The tall robber found himself staring into the business end of Joffrey's pistol. Without needing to be told, he threw his switchblade away from the Renault and followed his partner, who was fleeing toward the picturesque grove of trees.

Joffrey stepped out of the car, collected the knives, broke the blades with a sharp stomp of his foot, and dropped the useless weapons in a nearby trash bin.

He climbed back into the car.

"Next stop, Nuremberg."

CHAPTER 38

Fighting fatigue from the long drive and tension of the chase, Jolene said, "We'll stop in Strasbourg and get a bite to eat. It's the last major city in France en route to Nuremberg."

She spotted the inn she'd been searching for—a converted chateau nestled in a cluster of walnut trees—and gestured for George to turn into the driveway.

Shaking his head, he said, "If we press ahead, we can be in Nuremberg in two hours."

"Pull over. We need to eat and take a break. There's no point in arriving an hour earlier if we're exhausted."

At the last minute, George turned sharply and pulled into the long driveway leading to the Strasbourg Inn. He stretched, groaned, and said, "You're right. I'm beat. A sandwich and coffee would hit the spot."

At his sudden shift of mood, Jolene was reminded of one of George's endearing qualities: he seldom dug in on an opinion and refused to budge. Despite his competitive streak, he was always willing to meet the other person halfway.

Once they'd ordered, Jolene said, "Let's take stock of where our crew is located."

During the drive, with time to reflect on the challenges in blocking Besik Kasayeva and his gang from trading nukes for dollars with Dana and her terrorist cell, Jolene had grown increasingly concerned about the shortage of American manpower at each of the sites she'd chosen as the most likely spots for the exchange.

"Alex is traveling to Hamburg, accompanied by Felix and the Navy SEALs he added to the team, Bob Xavier and Fred Jefferson.

"Amal and Mike are en route to Dresden.

"Courtney and Luke are headed for Berlin.

"Steve and Hans are going to Paris to track down the confederate Madame Di-Longhi." The original she now knew was Dana Hussein al-Sadi, the daughter of the real Dorothea Hamilton Di-Longhi who the NCTC had located in a private hospital in upstate New York.

George turned the place mat over and began sketching a rough map of Germany, with the target cities marked with an X. "We've covered three of the major cities in Eastern Germany Kasayeva might visit to deliver Dana the nukes. Hamburg is an outlier whose value depends on how much trust we place in the near unconscious ramblings of the young terrorist Jaber Sadiq."

Jolene took a thoughtful sip of coffee. Uneasy about Alex's hasty decision to bring a contingent with him to Hamburg, she was convinced they were needed in the East.

"I think Jaber was pulling a fast one, but at least with Alex's crew, we'll have four more guns in Germany. Once they arrive in Hamburg, I'll try to persuade him to send a few of them our way."

George said, "One each to Berlin, Dresden, and Nuremberg would even our forces."

Jolene laughed. "In your dreams that Alex would agree to play solitaire. But not knowing which eastern city is Dana's likely destination, dividing our troops by the numbers would be a reasonable rule of thumb."

By any assessment, three Americans trying to defend against the combined forces of Dana and Kasayeva smacked too much of David fighting Goliath without stones for his slingshot. Her original premise in suggesting they stake out a few cities was that those on site would confirm the locale where the exchange was taking place and then Alex would spring the trap with overwhelming force. More exposure to Dana's aptitude in anticipating the American team's every move had persuaded Jolene such an approach was doomed to failure. Overwhelming force, even if available, would not arrive in time.

They had to be prepared to act at once if they were able to obtain the intelligence on the exchange. To do so, sufficient manpower must be capable of being mobilized immediately. She racked her brain to contrive an argument to concentrate their troops that would be persuasive to Alex.

She activated Alex's number and called him on her satellite phone.

He answered immediately.

"I was about to call you. Change of plans. My informant, who's tracking Kasayeva, tells me the Russians are headed for Prague in a black SUV big enough to hold six men and the nukes. They're expected to arrive later today. It seems Kasayeva has a girl in Prague named Gabriela, with whom he's sexually involved. It's a bit more complicated. Gabriela has a twin sister Olga. When he visits, the threesome makes a night of it, often two nights. His sexual proclivities should buy us some time. Knowing he's traveling from Moscow through the Czech Republic rather than Poland, gives us a clue to his destination."

Excited, Jolene interrupted. "Dana's meeting him in Dresden or Nuremberg. We can forget Berlin . . ." She paused, waiting for Alex to say the obvious.

"We can also forget Hamburg. You're right, Jo. The meet is in Nuremberg, which is closer to Dana, or Dresden, which is closer to Kasayeva."

She said, "My hunch is Nuremberg. Dana's the buyer. She'll insist on calling the shots."

"I don't disagree. But we can't afford to gamble. I'll join you and George in Nuremberg with the two Navy SEALs. Felix will hook up with Amal and Mike in Dresden and lead that team, to which we'll add Courtney and Luke. We'll have five searchers in each city seeking to apprehend Dana and/or Kasayeva's gang.

"I'll see you tomorrow at the Nuremberg Sheraton. We'll take the train and taxi to the hotel from the Nürnberg Hauptbahnhof."

CHAPTER 39

Zaha was feeling guilty. With the best of intentions to remain in Paris only two days, she was having so much fun, she'd extended her stay. She had successfully checked off her bucket list of must-do activities.

She had no illusions that the longer she remained in Paris, the more she put herself at risk. She vowed to flee to the somewhat safer sanctuary of England as soon as she'd checked off one final addition to her bucket list.

A dashing young French salesman had caught her eye. He was a fellow resident at her small hotel on Place de la Madeleine. She'd flirted with him in the dining room, and he'd responded in kind. Perhaps tonight she would succeed in luring him to her bed. Once that conquest was accomplished, she was off to London on the Eurostar train through the Channel Tunnel.

• • •

Major Steve Randall and Hans Jensen met at the American Embassy in Paris with CIA chief of station Henry MacArthur, better known as Big Mac from his starring role as a running back in professional football. Big Mac made their day by providing information shared from DGSI (*Direction générale de la sécurité intérieure*), the French agency responsible for internal security. DGSI had succeeded in tracking down Zaha Nashashibi at her hotel on the right bank of the River Seine in the eighth *arrondissement*.

Steve reluctantly agreed with Big Mac's proposal to coordinate her apprehension with a unit of the French National Police. Hans and Steve briefed their police liaison Philippe Cadot about the key role Zaha had played in the recent terrorist killings in Washington, DC. They stressed the importance of taking her alive because she had vital information about a future terrorist incident, without mentioning the expected purchase of suitcase nukes in Germany. With painstaking care, Steve negotiated an understanding he and Hans could lead the attack, attempting to capture their prey unhurt.

The operation that night turned to shit. Cadot dashed up the hotel steps ahead of the Americans and knocked loudly on the target's door. When there was no answer, Cadot and one other officer broke down the door and charged into the room. Steve and Hans were hot on their heels.

Apparently in retaliation for their commands being ignored, the French police commenced firing at the body under the covers on the bed. Steve glimpsed the woman rise on the far side of the mattress and calmly discharge her pistol to kill Cadot and the other policeman.

Steve headed to the left of the room. Hans headed right.

Steve shouted, "Hands up or I'll shoot."

Ignoring the command, she leveled her pistol and commenced firing.

Winged in the arm and seeing no alternative, Steve fired three times. Two bullets struck the young woman between her breasts. The third smashed her nose and splattered brains, blood, and gore against the wall.

Other police crowded into the room. They uncovered the corpse of a young French salesman on the bed, unarmed and drenched in blood. One police officer lifted the woman's head by her hair and, shuddering with disgust, let her body fall to the floor.

Steve scanned the room for Hans but failed to spot his partner. Concerned, he pushed through the crowd of police to the corner where he'd seen Hans standing before the final fusillade.

Hans was slumped against the wall, one hand trying to stem the flow of blood from his chest.

"Quick. Get an ambulance. My partner's gravely wounded."

His pleas were ignored by the French police who were preoccupied with preparing to remove the two bodies of their colleagues.

Steve grabbed a pillow off the bed and knelt by Hans. He held the makeshift pressure bandage to the center of the bleeding chest.

Hans's eyes began to close.

"Hang in there, buddy. We're getting help."

Yelling loudly, Steve tried once again to attract the attention of the police who were milling around the room.

A female officer came over and knelt beside Hans, quickly grasping the seriousness of the situation. She called for urgent medical support.

Hans gave a final shudder and was still.

Steve stared at Cadot's body as the dead police officer was carried from the room.

"Damn the French."

CHAPTER 40

Besik Kasayeva pulled the SUV into an empty parking space in front of an attractive town house fronting Stromovka Park, situated just a block from Prague's City Ring Road. He knew the space would be available because he was faithful in remitting monthly payments to the local police, assuring their services would protect his lover Gabriela and her sister Olga.

Vitaly Albegov came around the SUV and walked up to Kasayeva. The giant of a man said, "Do you want me to keep the SUV here while you're inside? What if the police come by?"

"Stay here," the mafia boss said. "The police won't bother you. They're well paid. If anything, they'd protect the SUV from anyone who might hijack it. Take turns sending the men to get something to eat and drink. Warn them not to drink too much. Anyone who gets drunk on this trip will wake up dead in the morning. Too much is at stake. I'm holding you responsible to make sure there are no mistakes. Everyone should sleep in the SUV, but send two men in for three hour shifts to rest in the town house. Make sure they remain on the ground floor. I'll shoot anyone who climbs the stairs."

Albegov nodded understanding. The instructions were the same for each of their previous trips to Prague. The only difference was the gang usually arrived in separate cars and without the baggage of two nuclear weapons.

Kasayeva took great satisfaction in having purchased the town house a year earlier for the sisters. The dwelling was situated less than a mile from a neighborhood of villas and embassies, including the historic residence of the American ambassador.

In addition to supporting the girls' living expenses, he paid for their studies at the University of Economics where they majored in information technology. Both were bright and conscientious students, with Gabriela making straight A's and her sister nearly matching her academic performance. He was proud of their accomplishments, even though he took greater pride in having risen to the top of his chosen profession—leader of the gang with the most ruthless reputation in all of Moscow—without benefit of a college education.

He was about to translate his gang know-how into a multimillion-dollar windfall. He'd set a trap, and Dana was driving from Geneva to spring it. Until then, he planned to spend two nights in lovemaking with the hypersexed twins.

He'd begun a relationship with Gabriela nearly two years earlier, intending to marry her. Then one night, a nude Olga had burst into their bedroom when they were making love. She jumped onto the covers and began playfully interposing herself between the two lovers. The following night, foreplay began as a threesome while drinking in the den and culminated in an orgy in the bedroom. The girls showed themselves equally engrossed in sexual hijinks with each other as they were with him. He had no complaints.

Without looking back, Kasayeva mounted the steps to the town house and pranced through the ornate front door. While he ambled around the house, he imagined the evening of lovemaking to come. Would he commence with Gabriela or Olga, or perhaps the two together? No, he decided. For a change of pace, he would let them choose. He thought of himself as a modern man and believed today's women were entitled to greater freedom.

CHAPTER 41

Majid and Nour were seated at a table when Dana and Joffrey hurried into the dining room of the Charles Hotel. The travelers arrived in a pouring rain, checked into their luxury suite, changed out of wet clothes, and lost no time getting to the meeting.

Her comrades at arms jumped up from their seats to welcome Dana. After introductions, she ordered champagne for a celebratory drink—being one of the Muslims who believed the Quran revealed Muhammad drank wine. All toasted Dana's success in obtaining the necessary funds in Geneva to support jihad.

Majid took the lead. "The Russians are bringing our product by SUV. Besik Kasayeva will drive here from Prague two nights from now. Until then, I'm told he likes to enjoy a romantic interlude with his girlfriend Gabriela and her twin sister." Majid looked embarrassed referring to the mafia boss's sexual adventures.

"Do we know where the meet is to take place?" Dana said.

"He's going to inform us of the locale at the last minute. My suspicion is that he will come to Nuremberg, stake out the rendezvous, and then notify us. Kasayeva is said to trust no one, for fear of being betrayed."

Joffrey guffawed. "He's the type of crime boss who's *most likely* to betray his associates." He glanced at Dana. "Beware of a trap. Kasayeva knows you're coming with ample funds. The temptation to steal the money will be great. He may not even have brought the 'product' you're expecting. The promise of delivering the dream you are wishing for could be the bait. His gang will almost certainly outnumber the four of us. This transaction is fraught with danger."

"Anything is possible," Majid said. "But Kasayeva has a reputation in Russia for honoring his contracts. That's a hard market. The penalty for swindling is death. No one would survive to the age of forty-five, as he has done, if they cheated their business partners."

Since she had assigned Majid responsibility for arranging purchase of the nukes, Dana sensed he was sensitive to the argument the transaction might be a fraud. She watched him eye Joffrey suspiciously as though the newcomer were determined to undermine him.

Dana raised a hand to calm everyone.

"You're both right. And you're both wrong. Kasayeva has a fine reputation; however, that's no guarantee he won't try to betray us. We're not Russian. We're Muslim terrorists. The Mafia would be praised, not condemned, for double-crossing us. He could walk away with a small fortune and pay no price for the deception."

She neglected to mention she received the five million electronically from the RGS bank, rather than in cash, complicating any betrayal. Currently, her riches—having bounced around the Caribbean—were hidden in the Cayman Islands.

"None of that matters. We'd do nothing different if we trusted Kasayeva or if we mistrusted him. In either case, we must go to the rendezvous prepared for violence. Keep in mind the possibility of a wild card—a third party who's gotten wind of this transaction, and who will attempt to rob both us and the Mafia."

Her voice took on an edge of command authority.

"Here's what we'll do. Majid, you and Joffrey will search for a location in Nuremberg that'll work to our benefit. We'll stake out the terrain. I'll insist the exchange take place there. We'll have the advantage of the high ground. It'll be *our* meeting place. That'll offset any greater numbers the Russians may bring."

Majid nodded. He stared at Joffrey a few moments, then extended his hand. The two men shook, a pledge both would honor to the death.

CHAPTER 42

Jolene checked into the Sheraton Carlton Hotel Nuernberg in the late afternoon. She booked two adjacent suites on the top floor. The weary travelers settled into one of the suites and called down for room service.

She was having a hard time absorbing the news from Alex that Hans Jensen had been killed, and Steve Randall wounded in their unsuccessful operation to apprehend Zaha Nashashibi.

Talking while putting away her sparse wardrobe, she explained to George why they would prevail if the Americans encountered either Dana's terrorists or Kasayeva's gang.

"We'll be the aggressors, not the defenders. We have the element of surprise, because neither of our opposing teams has any way of knowing we've tracked them to Nuremberg, assuming the meet is to take place here rather than in Dresden."

George nodded his head in agreement. "Dana may believe in a worst-case scenario we would tail her from Geneva into France, but she'd never suspect we could follow her here."

"That's what we're gambling on," Jolene said. "But the real questions are: where in the city is she hiding, and where will the exchange of dollars for nukes take place? We must have answers before tomorrow or the next day at the latest, depending on the staying power of Kasayeva's sexual tryst."

Walking restlessly around the suite, George said, "When can we expect Alex and the two SEALs to arrive?"

"Soon. Alex arranged for them to fly into Frankfurt, rather than travel directly to Hamburg. It's only a three-hour train ride, so they should be part way here by now."

The room service waitress rolled in a serving cart heaped with food. George directed her to leave it on the cart, since the dining room table was littered with maps and travel guides of Nuremberg.

Not knowing German, Jolene asked the waitress in English, "Where are you from?"

"I was born in Nuremberg. I've lived here all my life."

"What's the largest park in the city?"

The waitress smiled at the question. "Volkspark Marienberg." Eager to show off her knowledge, she added, "The park's over one hundred years old."

"Have you been there?"

"Many times."

George observed the interplay with the long-legged blonde who was more perky than beautiful. Apparently in response to Jolene ignoring the meal on the serving cart, he poured a cup of coffee and carried it to her.

Addressing the attentive waitress, he asked, "Would you like a cup?"

Startled, she replied, "No, *Mein Herr*. It is not permitted."

Looking reproachfully at George for interrupting the interrogation, Jolene said, "What time does the park close?"

The girl glanced at her watch. "Nine or ten, depending on the day."

"Do lovers sometimes sneak into the park after it closes?"

The waitress nodded. Her deep flush signaled she'd been guilty of trespass in pursuit of romance.

"How strict are the park police in enforcing the curfew?"

"The *polizei* patrol from time to time throughout the night, but they turn a blind eye to trespassers unless they are noisy or causing damage."

"Is the park far from the hotel?"

"No. Would you go by car?"

"Yes."

"Fifteen minutes or less, depending on traffic."

"Show me the best route." She led the waitress to the maps spread out on the dining room table.

George added a generous tip to the bill and thanked the departing waitress.

"What was that all about?" he said.

"Dana is always one jump ahead of us, anticipating our every move. We can only assume she will do the same to Kasayeva. What's his most likely ploy in setting up a meet?"

"He's Russian mafia," George said, as though the answer was obvious. "The mafia are famous for double-dealing. He'll try to control the terrain. Possibly force her to give up the money without handing over the suitcase nukes."

"Dana will anticipate that's how Kasayeva will act. If she holds true to form, she'll insist on choosing the locale. What better place than a city park where she can station sharpshooters at a distance and pick off the Russian gang one by one? If I were thinking like Dana, I'd pick Volkspark Marienberg."

"Damn, Jolene. More mind games. What's our next move?"

"We reconnoiter the park."

CHAPTER 43

Majid stared at the stein of beer he'd ordered, but which he had no intention of drinking. He glanced around the bar and wondered why the Russian he was supposed to meet hadn't shown up. He looked at his watch—7:08 p.m. Two minutes since his last check. Every bone in his body ached with fatigue from lingering jet lag compounded by the stress of continuous travel since he'd left Reagan Airport.

The boisterous enjoyment and hearty drinking of revelers throughout the bar was getting under his skin. Why did Germans enjoy singing in bars so much?

He was still annoyed at Joffrey for questioning arrangements he'd orchestrated for exchanging dollars for portable nuclear weapons. His discontent was stoked by this envoy of Kasayeva's delay in showing up. Most of all, he was angry at beginning to doubt his own judgment because of the Russian mafia's failure to honor the letter and spirit of the agreed to scheduling.

Just as his bad mood was breeding thoughts of leaving, he saw a man enter the bar who matched the description of Vitaly Albegov for whom he was waiting—a giant over six-five and three hundred pounds with long, dark hair, craggy eyebrows, and a swarthy beard.

He watched anxiously as Albegov spotted him and swaggered to the corner table where he was seated.

"Majid?"

"Yes."

The two men stood, face to face, taking the measure of each other.

"You're late," Majid said.

Albegov grunted, unwilling to acknowledge any shortcoming.

Majid waited, reluctant to let the Russian off the hook.

After a lengthy pause, Albegov said, "There was a delay in Prague. But that's not important. I've come to tell you where and when we'll do the exchange."

He pulled out a map of Nuremberg and unfolded it on the table.

He pointed to an X.

"This X is where we are now, in this bar."

He traced his finger across the map to the River Pegnitz. A row of buildings was clustered on the riverbank.

He pointed to a Y.

"This Y is the warehouse where we will make the exchange. Warehouses in this area are old and deserted. No one will bother us."

Albegov tapped the Y for emphasis. He handed Majid a plain manila envelope.

"Instructions about the transfer are contained in this envelope. Follow them to the letter. Any failure to do so and all members of your party will be killed. Our men are armed."

"No." Majid shook his head and returned the envelope.

"You dare tell me no?" Albegov drew his massive fist back as though he intended to strike the smaller Muslim.

Majid pulled his jacket aside to reveal a pistol held in his right hand. The weapon was pointed at the Russian's groin.

"Take your hand and scratch the back of your head. Move slowly or you will never make love to a woman again."

Albegov complied, glaring at Majid in a way that would have terrified a lesser man.

"Now sit in the chair across from me and keep your hands flat on the table."

Noticing the waiter heading over to take the new arrival's order, Majid ordered a stein of beer for his companion. He waited silently until the beer was served.

Keeping the pistol out of sight, Majid used his left hand to fold Albegov's map and drop it on the floor. He removed another map from an inside pocket of his jacket and spread it on the table. An X was marked on Volkspark Marienberg. Like a magician pulling rabbits out of a hat, he produced a manila envelope like the one the Russian had used and laid it between Albegov's spread-eagled hands.

"The exchange will take place at Volkspark Marienberg. The arrangements are spelled out in detail."

"Never. Kasayeva will take the product back to Moscow."

"In that case, he can forget about the money. Smile when you tell him you cancelled the deal. I'm told he always rewards members of his gang who fail to do their job."

Abregov blanched, unable to repress a shudder.

"Wait. I will talk to Kasayeva. Stay here and I'll return with his answer."

"You hurry and confer with your boss. I'll not remain here. I don't like this bar. It's too noisy. If your gang decides to proceed, call the number in the envelope. If not, we'll go back to America and continue to shop. Perhaps another Russian gang might be easier to deal with."

"Bastard."

"Not really," Majid said. "But believe that if it pleases you."

CHAPTER 44

Jolene opened the door to her suite and waved in Alex, accompanied by two Navy SEALs, each of whom was carrying military style duffel bags slung over both shoulders. Her heart fluttered on seeing Alex, pleasure at his presence and relief he could assume the burden of command which was growing heavier with each twist of events.

Once the newcomers were inside, she double-checked the privacy reminder hanging on the door and secured the lock.

Alex introduced Bob Xavier and Fred Jefferson to Jolene and George.

Looking at Alex, she said, "We can use this suite as a command post if you're comfortable with that. Your suite is next door. So far, this floor of the Sheraton has been quiet. I've asked the hotel staff to give us as much privacy as possible."

She gestured to the four duffel bags. "Show us what you got."

Bob began opening the bags and laying out weapons and other combat gear on the rug. Jolene's gaze focused on the Barrett M82 sniper rifle—.50 caliber.

She asked Bob, "Isn't that overkill? We're not likely to shoot anyone who's a mile away."

Bob's smile reflected the confidence of a true expert. "If the need arises, I can do it. Also, if we want to stop Kasayeva's SUV, this baby will blow apart the engine. But the real attraction is that the Barrett has a sniper scope that'll work during day or night."

Concluding she still had a lot to learn about the capability of modern weapons, she kept silent while inventorying the array of

M4 carbines, MP5 submachine guns, pistols, flash bang grenades, ballistic vests, and communications gear.

Finally, she said, "We've got enough weaponry to take on Dana and Kasayeva's armies." Glancing at Alex, she added, "The big question is: do we have enough warm bodies?"

Alex, who'd busied himself with the coffee maker while Jolene inspected their equipment, grinned broadly. "I've got good news. Our spy, who was following Kasayeva from Prague, lost him for a while. When he caught up, he spotted the gang's SUV on the road to Nuremberg. The Russian mafia are coming to us."

"That means . . ." Jolene exclaimed, then hesitated to speak the obvious.

"Felix and the crew in Dresden have been en route for nearly forty-five minutes and should be here in a couple of hours," Alex finished for her.

Jolene did the math in her head. Felix Goldblatt, Amal al-Askari, Courtney Gonzalez, Mike Sato, and Luke Worthington, plus the five in her suite gave them ten guns. Counting on the element of surprise, that would be more than enough to counter Kasayeva's six mafia plus the handful of terrorists accompanying Dana. With any luck, it wouldn't be necessary to encounter all their enemies at the same time.

She explained her strategy of mounting an ambush for Dana in Volkspark Marienberg, the largest park in Nuremberg. "George and I scouted the terrain earlier today. The sticking point is that the park's so goddamned huge. There are several places the exchange could take place. I'd like you to go over there with me and decide whether we make a best guess and focus on one location or split our forces and stake out the two most likely sites."

"We can check out the park now," Alex said. "Do we have vehicles?"

George shifted in his chair. "I rented two Mercedes-Benz GLS SUVs, each of which can seat seven."

Alex nodded appreciatively. "Let's get started. Fred, you stay in the suite. Keep the hotel staff out. Call Felix and tell him to bring his team here. Jo will reserve a third suite when we get back, because she's the face of our team in dealing with the hotel. Jo, Amal, and Courtney will bunk here. You, Bob, George, and I will bunk next door. Felix, Mike, and Luke will take the third suite when that becomes available."

Radiating confidence, Alex looked over the team.

"Explain to Felix that our best guess is the meeting between Dana and Kasayeva will take place tonight or tomorrow night. We may know more after we've reconnoitered Volkspark Marienberg. Have the new arrivals pick out their weapons. If time permits, suggest they get some sleep. It promises to be a long night."

CHAPTER 45

Besik Kasayeva was furious when he listened to Vitaly Albegov's report of the meeting with Majid in the bar. He drew some small measure of satisfaction seeing the giant Russian cringe in the face of his anger.

"How dare she defy me? I should return to Moscow and wait for her to beg me to sell her the nukes." He continued to rant a few more minutes, until the futility of the temper tantrum began to sink in.

"Let me see the map of Volkspark Marienberg." He studied the map and reviewed Dana's plan for the exchange.

Kasayeva frowned and threw the map and envelope to the floor.

"The bitch has decided to betray me. She plans to ambush us in the park and steal the nukes without paying."

Albegov shook his head. "I don't think so. My reading of Majid is they're simply being careful, probably suspecting we'd try to rip off the money, rather than sell her the nukes."

"Never. I've always dealt honestly," Kasayeva said, even though earlier in the day, he'd confided to Albegov that double dealing was precisely his intent.

"But you're my witness, Vitaly. Now that she's shown her true colors, we no longer must honor our contract. We're justified in using brute force to take her money. Even if we rape and kill her, no one will doubt we were within our rights."

Albegov gave a resigned shrug. "Whatever you say, boss. But how do we turn the tables? By now, she'll have staked out the meeting area. She'll have shooters stationed where we can't see them in the dark."

Kasayeva looked thoughtful, pondering the dilemma.

Lacking his usual swagger, Albegov said, "Our mafia soldiers are competent killers, but they're not *Spetsnaz* Special Forces, able to sneak silently up to a victim and slit his throat. The way Majid handled his pistol, he's had combat experience. Don't forget, their suicide bombers killed or wounded hundreds of Americans just a few days ago. They wouldn't hesitate to massacre us. We can't afford to underestimate them."

"Do you think the bitch is the only one who knows how to set a trap?" Kasayeva said. "Here's what you'll do. Rent an SUV the same model as ours, only with tinted windows so no one can see inside—buy one if you must.

Albegov listened attentively.

"Go back to the bar where you met with Majid. Hire a driver. Promise him a lot of money and give him a little in advance. Lead him to believe we want him to drive the getaway vehicle in a big robbery. Give him a pistol, but first remove the firing pin or otherwise render the weapon inoperative."

Albegov began to smile at the prospect of a double cross.

Kasayeva continued. "The driver's actual job is to serve as a decoy by heading to the rendezvous point in Volkspark Marienberg. He should stop the car there, turn off the engine, and blink the headlights three times. He must wait silently in the SUV no matter what happens."

"I get it, Albegov said. "The Muslims will get nervous, see the decoy as a threat from us, and open fire."

"Exactly. Once they start shooting, we can detect their positions. Our men can sneak up and kill them. Then we capture the bitch, steal her money, gang rape her, and—" Kasayeva stopped midthought. His mouth twisted into an evil smile. "No. A quick death would be too easy. Instead, we cut out her tongue, blind both eyes, shatter her kneecaps, and leave her in the park to suffer."

The mafia boss was red-faced and breathing hard as he concluded his tirade.

CHAPTER 46

Jolene and Alex studied the map of Volkspark Marienberg and selected the two most likely places the Muslim terrorists and the Russian mafia would choose for exchanging dollars for suitcase nukes. Once they'd made their decision, they summoned the other members of the crew back to the hotel.

Pointing to the map laid out on the dining room table, Alex said, "We'll divide our forces equally between these two locations. I'll lead Team Alpha, headed for location A. Alpha includes Jo, George, Bob, and Fred. Bob will take the Barrett sniper rifle, and Fred will use an M4 carbine as a sniper rifle."

Jolene pointed to roads leading to location A. "These are the best access routes. If any hostiles arrive in vehicles, Bob can put them out of commission with the Barrett."

When no further points were raised about Team Alpha, Alex continued. "Felix will lead Team Bravo, headed for location B. Bravo includes Courtney, Amal, Mike, and Luke. Mike and Luke will be the snipers. They should immobilize hostile vehicles."

Indicating two places on the map, Alex said, "Team Alpha will set up around A, and Bravo will set up around B. Our best guess for where Dana and Kasayeva will come on the scene is indicated by a *D* and *K*, marked in both locations."

Jolene interrupted. "Keep in mind, our assumption is either the terrorists or the Russians will attempt to double-cross the other. Therefore, either group may try to arrive early and arrange an ambush. That's why Alpha and Bravo teams will assemble just after the park closes to ensure we're in place before the action starts."

"Let's synchronize our watches," Alex said. "The time is 3:06 p.m. Our best guess is that nothing will happen before midnight, but we could be wrong. Plan for a long night and be ready for anything. Unless you're fired upon, don't start shooting until the terrorists show up on the scene. We accomplish nothing if we stop Kasayeva, but the elusive Dana escapes. She'll only seek another seller of suitcase nukes. Our main goal tonight is to kill her."

"What about the other terrorists?" Courtney said. "If any of them escape, won't they try to obtain nukes and conduct an attack back in the States."

"Of course," Jolene said. "But she's the driving force. If we eliminate her, the risk of attack diminishes."

"Killing them all should be the goal," Courtney said.

"Agreed," Jolene said. "None of the terrorists can escape alive."

• • •

Kasayeva and Albegov watched from a small hill at the edge of a woods when the patsy whom they'd lured as a driver pulled the SUV into the middle of a paved parking lot, stopped, turned off the engine, and blinked the headlights three times.

For several minutes, nothing happened. The night was silent, except for the hooting of an owl in the distance. A sliver of moon shone through dark clouds leaking dim light onto the scene.

Finally, a male voice sounded, fracturing the quiet. "Follow the protocol in the envelope or we'll shoot."

The panicked driver began honking the horn. At the first blare of noise, shots rang out. The vehicle's windshield shattered. The driver screamed, threw open the door, and tried to run. He barely made three paces when he dropped to his knees clutching his chest. Falling forward on his face, his final screams were barely audible to Kasayeva.

Silence once again descended, except for the screeching of the owl.

Albegov crept close to Kasayeva and whispered, "Our men

should be closing in on the shooters soon."

The mafia boss nodded. "Things are going according to plan."

Three shots rang out from the woods on the far right of the parking lot.

Recognizing the characteristic crack of a Makarov pistol, Albegov said, "That's one fewer Muslim the Americans have to worry about."

A burst of gunfire emanated from the left side of the woods, accompanied by garbled shouts in Russian and English.

A nervous Kasayeva said, "Vitaly, what's happening?"

"I think Alexei was hurt. That sounded like him yelling. But it could have been Stephan. Maybe it was both. Perhaps our gang is losing. We should go help."

"We'll go together. Run to the woods behind us and we'll circle around to where we heard the shots."

Once under cover of the woods, the two mafioso crept toward the sound of the latest gunfire.

Moving forward, Kasayeva realized he was scared for the first time in his life. He always preached to his gang that they were the ones to inspire terror and had no reason to fear anyone. That mantra always worked for him in the past. But it had lost resonance. The bitch was getting to him.

Kasayeva came to the edge of the woods. He stared into a cluster of bushes and saw bodies lying on the ground.

"Go over there and see who's been killed," he said.

Moving hesitantly, Albegov crouched, still looking like a man mountain in the dark, and inched forward stealthily. At the explosion of a weapon, he spun around and fell to the ground. Even in the dim light, Kasayeva could see blood flowing from the hole in his lieutenant's forehead.

Enraged, the gang boss charged in the direction from which the bullet had been fired. He had taken no more than two steps when the sound of gunfire was accompanied by excruciating pain. He realized he'd been wounded in the stomach and left leg. He drew his Makarov and started to crawl forward.

"You bitch. I'll beat and rape you. Then I'll kill you slowly. You'll suffer for hours and wish you were dead." Another shot rang out and he fell on his face. His last conscious thought was despair that he'd never be able to deliver on those threats.

• • •

Dana roamed the battlefield. *So many dead.* Nour, her bodyguard, and Joffrey, bodyguard, and would-be lover, were among the first killed by Kasayeva's henchmen. She realized the mafia boss had anticipated her trap, sending two of his shooters to either side of her forces while she was distracted by the driver of the SUV.

Fortunately, Majid was too clever for the pair who circled to his side of the woods and mousetrapped them. She and Majid finished off Kasayeva and Albegov. She saw her loyal follower holding his arm.

"Are you hurt, Majid?"

"No. A mere bullet graze. I've done more damage shaving in the morning."

She examined him closely to determine if he was telling the truth or trying to make light of a more serious wound. Eventually, she decided it didn't matter. They couldn't afford to spend time on first aid. The immediate task was to find Kasayeva's SUV and retrieve the suitcase nukes. Then they would return to the hotel and leave Nuremberg as fast as possible. By now, the *polizei* would be alerted.

• • •

Jolene heard the first shots and knew immediately she and Alex had made a serious mistake in positioning their forces. Neither location they'd selected was where the action was taking place. She could hear Alex talking with Felix, directing Team Bravo to head toward the scene of the fighting.

She ran toward their SUVs and saw Teams Alpha and Bravo converging on the vehicles. As soon as Team Alpha settled into one of the SUVs, she gunned it toward where she guessed Kasayeva was likely to have parked.

Entering the sought after parking area, she saw the Russian mafia's vehicle with all its doors hanging open. She and Alex raced to check out the storage area in the rear. As she feared, the nukes were gone. Indentations in the carpet confirmed the terrorists had acquired two bombs.

"Shit. Dana has outmaneuvered us again. By the looks of this carpet, the nukes are larger and heavier than we'd been led to believe."

Alex struck the side of the van with his fist. "Now we have to stop Dana before she flees Germany with portable nuclear weapons."

Watching Team Bravo drive up, she yelled to Felix, "Take George and reconnoiter this area. Leave your weapons in our SUV in case you're stopped by the *polizei*. George has diplomatic immunity so he may be able to talk you out of any difficulty with German officialdom. Everyone else can return with us to the Sheraton and we'll think through next steps."

CHAPTER 47

Dana was torn between despair and elation. Despair she'd lost beloved followers and elation she'd achieved her goal of obtaining two portable nuclear weapons.

A special cause to celebrate was that she'd gained her cherished prize without having to part with a penny of the five million dollars the Saudis had donated to her terrorist cause. An unexpected bonus for her retirement fund.

She turned to Majid and asked, not for the first time, "Are you sure we don't need to go back to the hotel to care for your wound?"

The irritation in his voice ringing clear, he said, "Stop fussing. The wound is just a scratch. It's stopped bleeding. After we pick up our next car, I'll take care of it."

At one level, Dana knew her concern was only in part motivated by misgivings about Majid's wellbeing. In larger measure, it reflected grieving over lost comrades. She was also worried because she hadn't heard from Zaha in several days and wondered if the young woman had successfully transited from Paris to London.

Seemingly out of context, she blurted, "If anything's happened to Zaha, you and I are the only survivors of our cell."

Majid's shocked look at the unexpected outburst was a stark reminder of the extent to which her remark was out of character. She remembered the older man counseling the importance of a leader keeping up the charade of equanimity in a crisis.

Turning her attention to the task at hand, she drove up to one of the warehouses on the bank of the Pegnitz River. Majid hurried to open the warehouse's massive door. She drove in.

It had been Majid's idea to use the warehouse Kasayeva had designated for the exchange. He argued it was a safe place to station the SUV they planned to use when fleeing Nuremberg. The simple rationale was that the Russian mafia would pay no attention to the abandoned warehouse once it was decided the exchange of dollars for nukes was to occur in Volkspark Marienberg.

They hurriedly transferred the nukes, weapons, and luggage to the virgin SUV they'd purchased for their escape. Once that was done, Majid began pouring the contents of two cans of gasoline they'd stored in the warehouse onto the vehicle they decided to leave behind. After Dana drove the getaway SUV onto the dock, he torched the abandoned vehicle, rushed outside, slammed the warehouse door, and jumped in beside her.

Beginning to relax, Dana smiled at Majid. "Now we begin our journey to America to wage the most important battle of the jihad. We will destroy the Great Satan."

"*Inshallah.*"

CHAPTER 48

Once the others had assembled in her hotel suite, Jolene stared at Alex and other members of the NCTC team. Her shoulders sagged with exhaustion. It barely registered that everyone else was red eyed with fatigue and struggling to look alert.

Alex sat on the couch and waved the team into seats. "Our imperative is to block Dana from fleeing Germany with the two suitcase nukes. Jo, what's your best guess how she'll try to get out of the country?"

Jolene stood by the window, passively accepting a proffered cup of coffee from Courtney. She stared blankly at the towers of Nuremberg Castle in the distance, slowly sipping the lukewarm beverage.

After listening to her silence a few moments, Alex stirred impatiently. "Well? The more time passes, the less chance we have of intercepting her."

"I don't have a damn clue," Jolene said. Holding the tasteless cup to her lips, she continued to stare at the historic castle.

The weight of failure was smothering her. Alex had counted on her to win the battle of wits with Dana, and she'd lost once again. She'd come close: betting on Geneva and winning, and choosing Nuremberg and being proven right. Even her guess about Volkspark Marienberg was on the money. But, when it really counted, she picked the wrong spot in the park and Teams Alpha and Bravo arrived after their prey had flown. All was for naught. Dana had won the gold medal. Worst of all, portable nuclear weapons were en route to the United States.

The room was quiet for a time, reflecting the emotions of the leader of the *brain trust.*

Courtney visited the coffee bar and came to the window with a fresh cup. She pried the stale coffee from Jolene's hand and traded her for a refill. "It's time we quit looking back and focus on the future. Dana's ahead on points, but the game's not over. Let's get down to basics. How many ways are there to get out of Germany with two suitcase nukes?"

Felix slammed his hand down on the coffee table for attention. "We have to think outside the box. The best bet is that Dana will ship the nukes, either by air or sea, rather than attempt to travel with them. If she does that, her escape would be much easier."

Energized, Amal jumped to her feet. "If I were Dana, I'd arrange to transport the bombs on a military aircraft or ship, assuming we'd be expecting her to use commercial transportation."

From her pose at the window, where she'd been gazing blankly at Nuremberg's historic landscape, with the drone of passing traffic unheard, Jolene snapped back to life. Her team's comments sparked the realization that she didn't have to do everything herself. Others had ideas and were not as worn down as she felt. She was part of a team, and, as Alex told her at the outset, it was imperative she behave as the team leader.

She sat down in a nearby chair and plunked down her coffee cup on a side table. "Let's consider the military option." She looked expectantly at Bob, Fred, and Luke.

"You Navy SEALs are familiar with air and sea transportation."

Luke, despite his reputation for saying little, was the first to speak up. "There are no US Naval installations in Germany. So military ships are not available to Dana. But military air transport is a possibility. Ramstein Air Base is the base with most activity for all branches of the service. I'd say check out *any* major military base, especially those within reasonable driving distance of Nuremberg. Ramstein, Frankfurt, Berlin, and Stuttgart are all less than four hours from here. "

Bob and Fred nodded in agreement.

Mike stepped forward. "Stuttgart has Kelly Barracks and Panzer Kaseme, with extensive military air traffic."

Courtney demurred. "I'd focus on commercial transport. It's easier to bypass the security arrangements, even in a country with tight controls like Germany. Lots of ground personnel who can be bribed at airports. If I were Dana, I'd head for Frankfurt. Who knows, she may already have made arrangements to get her nuclear cargo out by air."

Alex shook his head. "We can't forget Hamburg. Sadiq saying 'Hamburg' is the only clue we have from anyone in Dana's terrorist cell. Security at ports is always a headache for the authorities, and Hamburg's one of the biggest ports in Europe. As far as the city is from Nuremberg, Dana may prefer the risk of being tracked by the GSG 9 Counterterrorism police to have greater assurance of eventually getting the nukes to the States."

Without knowing quite why, Jolene was irritated at Alex's continued obsession with Hamburg. *Damn Jaber Sadiq for breathing "Hamburg" before falling unconscious at the terrorists' hideout in Fairfax.*

"Let's face it," Felix said. "This conversation proves how many options Dana has. And we've probably missed some logical choices. We'd be better off concentrating our resources on stopping the terrorist attack back home, rather than guessing how we can track her down in Germany."

Jolene looked around the room and realized no one had a clue how to proceed in stopping Dana's nuclear threat.

CHAPTER 49

Dana stayed in the right lane on the autobahn and kept her speed hovering near 100 kilometers per hour. She knew the *Autobahnpolizei* were most likely to pursue those daredevils zooming past on her left who were traveling faster than she was. Struggling to stay alert and concentrate on her driving, she paid no attention to the scenery, even after sunrise lit up the landscape.

Belatedly realizing she was reaching the limits of her endurance, Dana shook Majid awake and asked, "Does your arm feel well enough for you to drive?"

He growled. Fatigue mixed with tension enhanced his irritability. He was unwilling to admit how fiercely his arm pained. She could tell he was annoyed with himself for pretending he wasn't hurt.

"As I've said a dozen times, forget about the scratch on my arm."

She sighed. "Fuck your arm. I'm pulling into the rest area. You need to take the wheel after we get a bite to eat."

They locked the van and walked into the dining area of the *Raststätte*. They ordered and ate in silence. Dana swigged her third cup of coffee and stared out the window, angry with herself for losing her temper with the only member of her cell she could count on to complete her mission, but too proud to apologize. Moreover, she was in no mood for another condescending lecture from Majid pointing out that leaders never say they're sorry.

When they climbed back into the van, she said, "I'm exhausted. I got us past Berlin. Follow the autobahn to Hamburg. Wake me when we get to the outskirts of the city."

Majid hatched the plan to pursue a circuitous route to Hamburg, guessing the authorities would assume they would try to get out of Germany as quickly as possible to avoid scrutiny of the GSG 9 Counterterrorism police. Although following the route from Nuremberg to Berlin to Hamburg was a gamble, once they reached their destination, it would be easy to disappear into the Muslim melting pot as so many terrorists had in the past.

After suffering through his stint at the wheel, he nudged Dana. "We're nearing Hamburg's port area. Time for you to wake up."

Stretching, she began to complain. "I told you to wake me when we entered Hamburg. Why did you wait?"

"Because you were wiped out. We need to be alert when we meet Dr. Klostermann."

"Don't call him doctor. Don't even think of him as a physician. Remember, to us, he's Max Klostermann, a criminal who's agreed to ship our nukes to the States along with some of his so-called medical equipment."

Majid protested. "His company is legitimate. His medical equipment is real enough. That's why he provides a safe way for us to get our bombs out of Germany. He *is* a respected physician turned businessman. What sets him apart are his side dealings smuggling high-cost contraband mixed with routine medical commerce."

Now thoroughly awake, she said, "He's agreed to package and ship our goods for the tidy sum of fifty thousand dollars. What should we do if he tries to up the ante?"

"That would be no surprise. German criminals of that sort are not to be trusted."

Dana blinked, surprised to learn Majid was prejudiced against Germans. Or maybe that was his way of getting back at the heightened anti-Muslim discrimination stirred up by right wing nationalist groups in Germany. "I repeat. What should we do?"

"We have four choices: Pay him whatever he asks. Haggle over the price. Refuse to pay and tell him we'll take our business elsewhere.

Threaten to kill him and his family."

"None of those are good options. But paying him whatever he asks is the only choice where we control the next move on the board. An ironic smile lit up her face. "Fortunately, we have ample funds since it ended up costing us nothing for two suitcase nukes." Her glib good humor evaporated in an instant as the thought of her dead comrades reminded her of the real price of the Russian's betrayal.

• • •

Concentrating on Klostermann's directions to his warehouse a few blocks from the St. Pauli Piers, Majid tuned out Dana's chatter and changes of mood. He pulled up in front of the gray steel industrial door on the building and, as instructed, sounded his horn, waited one minute, and blinked his lights twice. The huge door slowly slid open. He drove into the cavernous warehouse.

A two-man welcoming committee approached from either side of the van. Majid could see they were armed with pistols, holstered outside their stained coveralls. The men were alert, but showed no signs of hostility. Apparently, Klostermann got the message clients were arriving this morning with cargo to ship.

The man on the left side of the vehicle was tall with broad shoulders, blond hair in a buzz cut, and a military bearing. The man on the right was short and fat with bushy black hair and a walrus mustache. The military type waved them toward the rear of the warehouse where two high-end Mercedes sedans were parked.

Majid got out of the van and drew his pistol, holding it out of sight under his jacket. He had no doubt Dana was similarly armed and ready in the event she sensed danger.

Looking bored, the man with military bearing said, "You're safe here. You won't need those weapons. Keep in mind our friends are watching."

He gestured toward elevated catwalks on either side of the warehouse. On each of the catwalks, Majid saw two men with rifles standing at ease, but watching the visitors with keen attention. He holstered his pistol and smiled grimly at the visiting foreigners.

• • •

Dana followed the man with military bearing up a steel staircase into a roomy office area. Their guide moved to a corner of the office beside a window overlooking the warehouse floor and stood ramrod straight with his arms at his sides.

Max Klostermann, MD rose from behind a mammoth rosewood desk, smiled, and walked toward the newcomers with his hand extended. Wearing a dark blue business suit, complete with white shirt and tie, he was dressed too formally for the setting.

"*Guten morgen*."

"Speak English, please. Neither of us understands German," she said, more curtly than intended. She reminded herself not to fall into the trap of looking down on or underestimating the German physician-turned-criminal.

Klostermann's smile lost none of its wattage.

"Good morning. I'm pleased to see you've arrived safely."

Majid and Dana took turns shaking the proffered hand.

Klostermann waved them toward a group of club chairs.

When they declined his offer of coffee and other refreshments, he said, "Have you brought with you the medical supplies you wish us to ship to New York?"

"The shipment is in the rear of the van," Majid said. According to the script she and Majid worked out during the drive from Nuremberg, he was to take the lead in discussing logistics of the shipment. She was to address payment issues.

Majid continued. "The shipment needs to be packaged and handled the way we discussed."

"I understand perfectly," Klostermann said.

Dana wondered if the physician knew or suspected his cargo was nuclear explosives. Or if he even cared since the shipment was bound for the United States. Perhaps he thought it was a radioactive or "dirty" bomb. That would account for the elaborate instructions about shielding the packaging with lead or other materials to frustrate detection from casual screening on arrival in the port of New York.

Klostermann said, "Unless there are other instructions you would like to add concerning the shipping, I'd like to reopen the matter of payment."

Pretending to look shocked, Dana said, "I thought that was settled. We agreed on fifty thousand."

"You're correct, my dear. We did. But since the initial arrangements, I've heard some things from our contacts in Moscow . . ." He paused to eye Dana for her reaction to the statement.

"You heard some things . . ." She kept her expression impassive.

"Yes. What we heard led me to believe the shipment is far more hazardous than I'd understood."

"Hazardous? What do you mean?" Dana asked, with faked innocence.

"Hazardous, indeed," Klostermann said. "And in many ways. The GSG 9 police paid me a visit the other day, claiming they were following up on an informant's tip we were shipping contraband for terrorists. They've come sniffing around before, but just on fishing expeditions. They suspect us of smuggling drugs, but that's not really their bailiwick . . ." He paused. "'Bailiwick,' is that the right word? My American slang has suffered in the two dozen years since I practiced medicine in Detroit."

Dana nodded, determined not to get distracted, as the dialogue was apparently nearing a climax.

Klostermann continued, with a smile that could have passed for a smirk. "This visit, however, was obviously inspired by hard information, which I have reason to believe came from US intelligence sources." He spread his hands as if to show he was laying all his cards on the table. "If I am to ship cargo that may be subject to scrutiny by the German terrorist police, I expect to be compensated for the risk. The new fee for shipping your goods is one hundred thousand dollars."

"That's double," Dana protested, half raising from her chair. Out of the corner of her eye, she saw the blond sentry reach his hand toward the pistol at his side.

"Take it or leave it," Klostermann said.

Recognizing defeat when it stared her in the face, she said, "We'll take it." She rose all the way to her feet. "When will the shipment leave Hamburg?"

"Tomorrow."

"And when will it be unloaded on the dock in New York?"

"Two weeks."

CHAPTER 50

Jolene was angry with herself for being unable to shake off Dana's absconding with the nuclear weapons, leaving behind members of her terrorist cell who'd been killed by the Russian mafia in Volkspark Marienberg. The bodies of Kasayeva's gang also remained in the park to be discovered by the Nuremberg *polizei.*

She'd assigned George the thankless task of liaison with the *polizei* and the GSG 9 Counterterrorism police. She harbored little hope the German authorities would be more successful than Alex's team—she'd come to think of them as *her* team—in apprehending Dana or finding the two bombs before the weapons were spirited out of Germany en route to America.

Bone-tired and frustrated, she said, "I can't think. I'm going for a walk to clear my head."

With every fiber of her being, she wished there were a magic carpet she could climb on and fly to her farm in Leesburg. She fantasized saddling Regret and riding until the filly's rhythm helped her gain perspective on the futile chase to stop Dana from escaping with the nukes. Her own escapism denied by harsh reality, strolling through Nuremberg's busy thoroughfares was the best she could do.

"I'll go along," Courtney said, slipping on a jacket to conceal the MP5 with which she'd armed herself.

"Me too," Luke said. The Navy SEAL donned a sport coat to hide his MP5 submachine gun, which was never out of reach.

Although she was not anxious for company, Jolene nodded assent. She suspected Luke was mostly inspired by the opportunity to be close to Courtney. She saw the necessity for the Americans to be prepared to always defend themselves. Who knew what perils lurked on the mean streets of Nuremberg?

Without conscious thought or dialogue, Jolene set off in the direction of Volkspark Marienberg, drawn irrevocably toward the scene of their latest fiasco. Each of the walkers was in peak physical condition, so they covered several blocks quickly and without speaking. The weather was mild and the sky blue, with pillowy clouds floating in the distance.

Finally, Jolene broke the silence. "Courtney, I need the benefit of your insight. If you were Dana, how would you use the suitcase nukes?"

Courtney glanced sideways at her hiking companion. She flashed a surprised smile that Jolene had broken out of her semi-depressed state.

"Several possibilities. She might follow the blueprint in our report. We invested a great deal of effort to identify strategies with which terrorists could cause the most loss of life and damage to property, detailing specific steps they might take. No imagination or innovation is required. Simply paint by the numbers."

Shaking her head, Jolene said, "But she's aware we would consider such an approach and could focus our defensive actions accordingly."

"Sure, but if I were Dana, I might bluff, and switch to a different approach. On the other hand, since the Dana we know is ultrasmart, I might attempt a double bluff and actually use the strategies in the NCTC report."

Their hike was interrupted by the ringtone of Jolene's phone.

Before she could speak, she heard Alex's excited voice. "Jo, we've got critical new information about Dana. Tommy Lee and Sally have been investigating her background. She had a brother, Jake. When they were young children swimming off the beach at East Hampton, Long Island, Dana was at risk of drowning. Jake rescued her. From that day on, Dana and Jake were extremely close. It's fair to say, she idolized her brother—"

Jolene interrupted. "What's the punch line?"

"Jake was an Army captain serving in Kandahar Province in Afghanistan when he was murdered by an enlisted man. The military covered up the crime. The official record shows Jake was killed by an IED planted by the Taliban. The Pentagon was trying to avoid any hint of the problem of GIs fragging officers that was a common occurrence during the Vietnam War. Official subterfuge was the stimulus that prompted Dana to self-radicalize. It's why she became a terrorist. The US betrayed her beloved brother. She's determined to exact revenge."

Jolene stared at the picture-perfect sky. "Now we have the motive for why the child of a wealthy family, educated at the University of Virginia and Harvard, who's a professor at George Mason University, became an assassin and master terrorist."

"I'll keep you posted if Tommy Lee and Sally come up with anything new." Alex hung up.

Jolene gestured for Courtney and Luke to sit down on a bench at an empty bus stop. They brainstormed the pivotal information she'd just received from Alex.

Courtney said, "If I were Dana, I'd be tempted to explode a nuclear weapon on the bastards who lied about how my beloved brother was murdered."

Jolene nodded agreement.

"The Pentagon, housing over twenty-five thousand personnel, just became Ground Zero for one of Dana's bombs."

CHAPTER 51

Elmer Farnsworth put down the telephone in his office in the West Wing of the White House. He leaned back in his leather executive chair and looked out the window as morning sunshine put a special glow on the bushes in the Rose Garden. He felt a reflected glow of self-satisfaction over having just made a luncheon appointment to meet at an out-of-the-way restaurant in Virginia with Rick Birmingham of the Central Intelligence Agency.

He'd tracked Birmingham's career from the time Jolene Martin had accused the then director of CIA training at The Farm of attempted rape. Birmingham weathered the accusation unscathed, succeeding in getting Jolene fired when she couldn't prove the charge. Rather than harming his career, CIA brass felt compelled to justify their handling of the case by promoting the accused to a position in charge of Western Europe in the Directorate of Operations stationed at Langley headquarters.

Pissed at the way Alex's team had outmaneuvered him in the Oval Office meeting with President Scofield, Farnsworth was in search of allies who could help him exact revenge. Birmingham was an ideal candidate because of his vendetta against Jolene. Moreover, his central role in intelligence focused on Europe put him at the crossroads of information about what Alex, Jolene, and their team were up to in searching for the terrorist known as Dana Hussein al-Sadi.

• • •

Rick Birmingham parked in front of the Spring Moon Chinese

restaurant in Arlington, Virginia. He considered himself to be a connoisseur of Chinese food, and he was invariably skeptical of any establishment where he had not previously dined. He decided to suspend judgment until he tasted the food. Maybe the White House guy knew Chinese cuisine. He'd researched Farnsworth's background after getting the call to get together for lunch and was aware the national security adviser had done a tour in Beijing early in his career before he left the foreign service to make a fortune in international business, which was his route to politics and, ultimately, to leadership of the National Security Council.

Once Farnsworth arrived, the men ordered, and, sipping fragrant tea, bantered about the state of Washington sports. They shared the dream the Washington Nationals baseball team would muster another winning streak and make it to the World Series, and hope the Washington Commanders, Wizards, and Capitals would have a better year next season than last.

When Peking duck and sesame shrimp arrived, Birmingham sought to show off his skill with chopsticks and was astonished Farnsworth matched him bite for bite. Much to his delight, the food was delicious, and he resolved to return to the restaurant as often as possible. After all, the web of secrecy at the CIA made it easy to justify mysterious absences, which could be used for a luncheon meeting or, if a female partner were available, something much tastier.

At length, Farnsworth said, "You're probably wondering why I asked that we meet."

"I'm sure you're about to clue me in."

"What's the latest information about Alex Werth and Jolene Martin's efforts to prevent Dana Hussein al-Sadi from acquiring portable nuclear bombs in Germany?"

Birmingham manipulated his chopsticks and put a bite of shrimp in his mouth. He chewed slowly, reflecting on the implications of the question. After all, the NSC received the same high-level intelligence reports as the CIA, even though the agencies usually got the raw information first and processed it.

"Alex's team failed. Dana escaped Nuremberg with two suitcase nukes she acquired from the Russian mafia."

"And what was Jolene's role in the debacle?" Farnsworth asked with a tone suggesting he was not upset at the news.

"She was the brains of the team, and Alex made her a coleader." Birmingham took a bite of shrimp, chewing slowly while he considered how to play Farnsworth's gambit.

"Jolene guessed right—Nuremberg was where Dana would rendezvous with the Russians. She even deduced Volkspark Marienberg was the location where the swap of money for bombs was to take place. But she set a trap for the terrorists at the wrong place in the park. By the time Alex's team got to the scene, all six Russians were dead as well as two terrorists. Dana fled with the nukes. Jolene hasn't been able to figure out her destination or how she plans to get the bombs to the US. We have asked the German Counterterrorism police for help, but so far, nothing."

Birmingham cleared his throat. "The nukes pose a serious threat to the United States, and Dana must be stopped. But I'm not unhappy Jolene's team blew it. They chose to pursue Dana with only token involvement of the CIA. In my opinion, the White House should have assigned the Agency the lead role. The president can rectify that error now that the stakes are the highest possible. Do you agree?"

"Yes," Farnsworth said. "If I raise this issue with the president, can you give assurances the CIA will back me up?"

"Absolutely." He watched Farnsworth reflecting while he folded the last piece of duck in a mandarin pancake after doctoring it liberally with bean paste dipping sauce.

The national security adviser said, "In the interests of our country's defense, Alex and Jolene must be sidelined. Because the CIA can only operate legally overseas, you're precluded from conducting operations in this country."

"But I'm sure you can persuade President Scofield to make

an exception in light of the extreme danger posed by the nuclear weapons under Dana's control."

Farnsworth grimaced. "Consider a compromise. Since the nukes are presumably still in Germany, I can make a case for the CIA taking the lead in the investigation. It would be self-evident for the investigators to follow the weapons when the search leads to the States."

"That's not a compromise. That's half a loaf."

"Hear me out," Farnsworth said, holding up his hand as though halting traffic. "Dana and the terrorists will need to be tracked down in the States. While this might normally have been the purview of the FBI, Scofield saw fit to assign it to Alex's team, as recommended by DNI Mansfield. A partial rationale is that the team includes Amal al-Askari, who's an FBI special agent, so, technically, the Bureau has been part of the action from the outset. How would you feel if Alex's team continues to pursue Dana and whoever remains of her terrorist cell, while the CIA takes the lead on the portable weapons? If your investigation should somehow spill over to encompass Dana and her coconspirators, that would be understandable."

Birmingham sensed the national security adviser's proposal was the best deal he was likely to get, so he reluctantly agreed.

The two men shook hands, neither willing to acknowledge that antipathy toward Alex and Jolene provided the underlying rationale for the position they intended to advocate to the president.

CHAPTER 52

Despite extreme fatigue, accentuated by the dissipation of her adrenalin rush after having arranged safe passage of the nukes to New York harbor, Dana chose not to risk taking a break in Hamburg. She and Majid drove from Klostermann's warehouse to a parking garage near the main train station. Dana abandoned the SUV on the top floor in a far corner of the garage. They wiped away fingerprints and took everything that could be used by the GSG 9 federal police to identify them. The keys were dropped down a sewer grate a block away.

The fugitives ducked into an alley behind a McDonald's. They took the pistols and rifles from their carrying cases and bundled them into garbage bags and buried them in dumpsters at the rear of the restaurant.

Majid said, "The smell of rotting food should discourage even the most nosy or hungry scavengers from stumbling across the weapons."

"I'm too tired to care. Besides, if anyone finds the weapons, they're more likely to sell them than to turn them in to the *polizei*. If they are found, we'll be far from here."

The pair wound their weary way to the Hamburg Hauptbahnhof, where they bought one way sleeping-car tickets on the Inter-City Express to Brussels, Belgium. Dana ached with anticipation at the thought of getting some much-needed rest during the twelve-hour ride.

The train trip was uneventful, although they experienced a few anxious moments under the curious gaze of the train conductor and border officials who were openly suspicious of a Muslim man and a seemingly European woman sharing the compartment. Since Dana and Majid's fake passports looked genuine, the extra scrutiny caused nothing more than momentary inconvenience.

Rested, Dana and Majid exited the train at *Bruxelles-Central* and took the five-minute walk to the Brussels metro. They rode the metro to the station near the historic Hotel Steigenberger Wiltcher's. She preferred to stay in or pass through hotels with a rich pedigree because the staff were invariably trained and experienced in discretion regarding all clientele.

They walked to the hotel, where they flagged a taxi to Brussels Airport. Dana noticed that the destruction caused by the terrorist bomb blasts of 2016 had been repaired and the concourse was fully restored and operating at capacity.

While Majid relaxed over a cup of coffee in the restaurant, Dana checked departure times for flights to Scandinavia, finally settling on Sweden, which was one of the European countries with the most passengers traveling to the States. She chose to fly SAS to Stockholm because it was the next flight out.

After a brief diversionary tour of Stockholm, she planned to fly Icelandair to Orlando, Florida, for the simple reason that flight stopped over in Reykjavik, rather than Frankfurt, which would subject them to further scrutiny in Germany, or New York City, which posed the risk of heightened exposure.

When she traveled to New York to retrieve the suitcase bombs, it would not be by air, since airline travel was subject to the innumerable security measures instituted since 9/11.

From Orlando, she would drive by van or truck to New York, heading north on I-95, adopting further maneuvers to throw any pursuers off her trail.

She was confident her convoluted itinerary, taken together with the fake travel documents she and Majid carried, and the disguises they'd crafted during the ICE train ride to Brussels, should suffice to keep them safe.

Once in New York City, she had some business that required her attention, so she planned to send Majid back to Washington. He would recruit additional terrorists to fill the empty ranks in their cell and to finalize plans governing use of the first of the nuclear bombs to wreak vengeance on Pentagon generals. She had yet to decide on the target for the second bomb.

CHAPTER 53

After the pilot announced their safe arrival at Orlando International Airport, Dana said, "My whole life, I've wanted to visit Disney World. My mother always made excuses why *this year*, we couldn't go, but *next year* we would go for sure. By the time I was a teenager, I realized we would *never* travel to the Magic Kingdom. The true reason was that my mother suffered from a mild case of agoraphobia, and she would have been terrified by the crowds of children and adults in Walt Disney World."

With a curious expression on his face, Majid said, "What about your father? Why didn't he take you?"

"My father was brought up in the Middle East. He came to the States as an Iraqi diplomat assigned to the Embassy. He could never relate to sports and entertainment in America. His focus was on high-stakes espionage and jockeying for political influence in Saudi Arabia, Iraq, and other desert kingdoms. While he generally supported my interests, he couldn't resist making fun of my desire to see Mickey and friends. Now that we're here, and we have the balance of two weeks to kill before our shipment arrives in New York harbor, I plan for us to spend two days in Disney World."

"As you wish. How do we get to Disney World from the airport?"

"We'll buy a used SUV. A Toyota 4Runner is as common as dirt on the highway. But any SUV in good condition will meet our needs. When we leave the Orlando area, we'll take turns driving. In about twelve hours, we should be in Richmond, Virginia. We'll stay overnight in Richmond and rest up. Then, we'll push on to DC. That will leave us plenty of time to prepare for the next steps in our crusade."

Majid did the negotiating at the Toyota dealer since the salesperson assigned, Ali Salah, was a Sunni who had come to the States on a special visa as a reward for having been an interpreter for the US military during the Iraq War. After looking at several SUVs, Majid selected a 2015 black Sequoia.

On the pretext of needing a cup of coffee, Dana pulled him aside. "Why did you pick the most expensive of the SUV models?"

He said, "You always emphasize price is no object when important goals are at stake."

"I believe that, but what are the goals?"

"The Sequoia will meet all of our needs. The SUV has plenty of capacity to store our cargo once we pick it up. The Toyota engine is sufficiently powerful to keep pace with virtually any car on the road, except for a police cruiser, and if it comes to that, we'll already be in deep trouble. The vehicle is heavy enough it can survive a collision with anything other than a big truck. Most important, anyone who sees us driving such a high-end vehicle will assume we're rich eccentrics, which should cut off embarrassing questions about our ethnicity of the sort we encountered on our train trip to Brussels."

His answer gave her pause. Majid was thinking more strategically than she had been. He was correct. The cost of the Sequoia was, if not irrelevant, a potential asset.

"Instruct Salah to have the Sequoia prepped and available two days from now in the early morning. From here, we'll take a taxi to Disney World. We won't need a car there; everyone travels by monorail."

When they arrived at Disney World, they took the precaution of checking into separate hotels. Dana chose the Grand Floridian Resort because the hotel showcased a magnificent view of the Magic Kingdom from her suite. She urged Majid to choose a hotel at the next stop on the monorail. They agreed on a restaurant where they would meet for breakfast the next morning before beginning their tour.

During the night, Dana's dreams were crowded with images of Mickey and other Disney characters. Awakening, she was unusually anxious, agonizing whether her experiences as an adult would match her expectations as a child.

She needn't have worried. The next day, she and Majid walked from one bustling theme park to another, basking in the wonder. She was amazed when her lieutenant confided he had a secret urge to see the Indiana Jones enactment, and they hurried to make the next showing at Hollywood Studios.

After two days of frolicking, nearly forgetting they were wanted terrorists who planned to destroy thousands of lives later in the month, they returned to the Toyota dealership, picked up their Sequoia, and said goodbye to Ali Salah.

After an hour's driving, Dana reached I-95 and headed north to her destiny.

CHAPTER 54

Alex stopped the taxi outside Brandenberg Gate. He was furious at being summoned to a nine o'clock meeting with Arnold Weber, American ambassador to Germany. His entreaties to the ambassador's secretary about the importance of his mission to the security of the United States fell on deaf ears. She insisted he come to the Embassy and bring his entire crew to a nearby hotel in Berlin, which she specified. Only after she mentioned the meeting was at the orders of President Scofield did he acquiesce in the appointment.

He decided to walk to the Embassy across the cobblestone pedestrian area on Pariser Platz. His intent was to calm down during the leisurely stroll through the historic square. The gambit wasn't working.

His eyes firmly fixed on the entrance to the Embassy, he noticed neither the Holocaust Museum, the Reichstag building housing the Bundestag Parliament, nor any of the famous attractions surrounding him. What started as a casual stroll increased in pace until he had to remind himself to slow down what was bordering on an angry charge lest he draw unwanted attention from the Marine guard contingent who formed the nucleus of the enhanced security in place at all embassies since 9/11.

Once inside the Embassy, security checked his pistol, and two Marines escorted him to the ambassador's suite. The ambassador's secretary, Arabella Lawrence, an imperious woman who was taller than Alex, welcomed him graciously and ushered him into the ambassador's inner office. She pointed to an easy chair by a window with a beautiful view. He sat, but refrained from looking outside, puzzled and annoyed the ambassador was not present. Arabella offered him coffee, which he declined. With a lift of her eyebrows to signal he was a hopeless cause, she left him alone, surrounded by the trappings of international political power.

After several moments, a door to the rear of the room opened. Alex turned toward the sound and was astonished to see Director of National Intelligence Frank Mansfield enter. He rose to greet his boss and mentor, who strode across the room and shook hands.

"Frank, I thought my meeting was with the ambassador."

"The president asked me to come to Berlin to convey his new orders personally. I won't beat around the bush. Your team has been removed from the search for the suitcase nukes."

Stunned by the news, Alex sat back in the chair.

"Why?"

"The CIA is the lead on finding the nuclear weapons."

"How the hell did that happen?" He struck the arm of the chair violently. Despite his best efforts to stay calm, Alex was losing his temper.

"I'm not sure of the details. But my sources tell me Elmer Farnsworth is conniving with Rick Birmingham at the Agency. Scofield tends to listen to his National Security Adviser, and Farnsworth was upstaged by you and your team at the meeting in the Oval Office. This is his way of getting even."

Mansfield waved his hand to minimize the significance of this latest development.

"The president changed his position because the bombs are in Germany. The CIA would normally have the lead role on intelligence operations of this magnitude. Instead, the president gave you the ball. But Farnsworth and Birmingham convinced him you blew it in Nuremberg when Dana escaped with the nukes."

"Despite all odds, we got close," Alex said defensively.

Mansfield kept silent, not rubbing it in that close only counts in horseshoes.

"Does this mean we're out of the game?" Alex asked.

"No. You have the lead role in finding Dana and any of her terrorist cell who are still alive. After all, she's responsible for the wave of suicide bombings in the Washington area. I have no doubt the CIA under Birmingham's personal direction will also mount an intensive manhunt in the States even though the Agency's only authorized to be operational overseas. The president made it clear he's prepared to turn a blind eye if Birmingham colors outside the lines. You can expect competition from the Agency in the search. Be prepared. It could get dangerous."

"Birmingham and Farnsworth are both dangerous," Alex said.

"I don't disagree. The word is, Birmingham is assembling a team that includes several assassins. He makes no secret of his hatred for Jolene, and he's not too fond of you, or me for that matter."

"What can I do?"

"Get your team back to the States immediately and intensify the manhunt. Except for the CIA, where you can expect nothing but obstructionism, all the resources of the intelligence community are at your disposal. I've spoken to FBI Director Burt Robinson. In addition to Amal al-Askari, in whom he has total confidence, he's assigning a second special agent, Randy Colfax, as liaison. The Bureau wants to be fully involved in the pursuit of Dana, and they're batting for your team."

Alex shook Frank's hand. He welcomed the DNI's support, which he guessed must have cost him some points with the president. Despite the CIA's White House endorsement, Alex remained determined that his team, with Jolene as the reluctant, but effective, head of the brain trust, would be the one to apprehend Dana and prevent the bombs from exploding.

The time had come to join his team back at the Grand Hyatt Berlin and tell them the bad news about how and why they'd been demoted. He hoped Jolene or someone on the team could come up with a strategy for next steps, because he felt discouraged and barren of ideas.

• • •

Lounging in a hotel robe, Jolene was resting on the couch, staring aimlessly out the window, wondering why Marlene-Dietrich-Platz lacked the charm of the actress herself, when her phone rang. Alex was calling, presumably to tell her how his meeting had gone with Ambassador Weber.

"Alex, how'd it—" She was annoyed when he abruptly cut her off.

"Never mind that. Meet me in the lounge. I'll be there in five. Tell no one." After that cryptic message, he hung up.

She hurried to the bedroom, took off her robe and flung it on floor. Not knowing what was up, she donned a pant suit, adjusting the jacket to conceal her pistol.

Due to the midmorning hour, the lounge was more than half-empty, except for a diverse crowd of mostly Europeans, Americans, and Asians enjoying a leisurely breakfast. According to her custom, she sat in a back booth. Anxious to blend in, she ordered two coffees, orange juice, and a pastry basket, explaining to the waitress her business partner would be joining her in a few minutes.

Alex rushed in, sat opposite her, and wasted no time on preliminaries. "I've got bad news." He proceeded to summarize what he'd heard from Mansfield, not attempting to sugarcoat the president's decision. The one hopeful point was the close alliance with the FBI.

Jolene hadn't sorted out in her mind what to expect from the failure to intercept Dana in Nuremberg, but Alex's news was worse than anything she'd imagined.

"Alex, I'm sorry. You put your trust in me, and I let you down."

He frowned. "Don't give me that bullshit. The failure to apprehend Dana was mine as much or more than yours."

"What about all that business with me as the 'leader' of the brain trust? Did you mean it, or was that just a snow job?"

"You *are* the leader of the brain trust. Ask anyone on the team and they'll say that's the way they see you. But I'm still the head of the NCTC team. Success or failure is ultimately my responsibility. But pointing the finger gets us no place. Let's leave that to the clowns in the White House and the CIA. We have to decide our next steps and a strategy to track down Dana."

She nodded and sat back in her seat. She took a bite of bran muffin, chewed thoughtfully, and washed it down with a swig of coffee.

"Next steps are easy. We head back to the Washington area. Courtney and I are convinced the Pentagon is Dana's target for one of the suitcase nukes. Knowing that may give us an edge to help trap her."

"What about her second target?"

"No clue."

"Maybe she'll use the report in the general's briefcase she stole as a blueprint," Alex said.

"Maybe. But let me share some thoughts about that possibility." Jolene outlined Courtney's speculation Dana might use the step-by-step strategies outlined in the report, bluff as though using them while trying something different, or double bluff and end up using the NCTC how-to."

"So where does that leave us?"

Staring into her coffee cup, Jolene smiled.

"Most of the members of her terrorist cell are captured or dead. You caught Omar Aziz and Jaber Sadiq in Fairfax. Steve shot Zaha Nashashibi in Paris. Two terrorists were killed in the firefight with the Russian mafia in Nuremberg. Whatever strategy she employs or wherever she decides to detonate the nuclear bombs, she's going to need to recruit new blood for her cell. That may be one of the best ways to track her down. If FBI Director Robinson wants to be involved, helping to identify potential recruits would be a good place to start."

CHAPTER 55

Waking from a sound sleep to echoes of pounding on her door at the Richmond motel, Dana rolled over and looked at her watch. *Dammit.* It was five in morning. What had Majid learned at this hour that couldn't wait until breakfast to share?

She hurried to the door while slipping on her robe, not out of any sense of modesty, but as a precaution in the event anyone was watching. "Well, Majid. What's so urgent?"

"I just talked with colleagues in Virginia. Zaha was killed during a police raid in Paris the other day. Steve Randall discovered her location from the National Gendarmerie. He and Hans Jensen accompanied a French SWAT team and broke into her hotel room. She'd stayed in Paris longer than planned and was having a romantic liaison with some young salesman when the Gendarmerie arrived. Zaha killed Hans and a few of the SWAT team, but Steve shot her."

"Major Steve Randall" Dana almost spat the name, "he's the bastard who killed John Paul Moore."

"Are you forgetting Moore was a traitor who sold out his country for half a million dollars?"

She laughed. "I'm not forgetting. But he was *our* traitor. His information was essential in obtaining the general's briefcase. Without him, we wouldn't have acquired the suitcase nukes."

Dana's thoughts returned to her time in bed with the lusty commander. If he'd been half as good a lover with his wife as he had been with her, their marriage would never have fallen apart.

At that moment, the full import of Zaha's death struck her.

Her feelings toward her lost follower were a complex mixture of motherly affection and envy for Zaha's sexual openness. She was acutely conscious she and Majid would find it difficult to replace yet another devoted comrade.

Her emotions quickly found an outlet. "Jolene Martin and Alex Werth are the ones to blame. Their team has been dogging our footsteps since we left Virginia. They'll be searching for us now that we're in the States."

Majid stared at Dana, as if amazed to hear her stating the obvious with such vehemence.

"I'm tired of being pursued," Dana said. "I still can't believe they guessed we were going to meet the Russians in Nuremberg. They almost captured us in Volkspark Marienberg. If we eliminate those two, Frank Mansfield won't be able to field another crew with such keen instincts for tracking us down. My next step will be to take out Martin and Werth."

In her private thoughts, Dana qualified that pledge. More precisely, her next step was to obtain five million dollars from rich friends of her mother. For that, it was necessary to travel to New York City.

CHAPTER 56

The rain ended shortly after Dana and Majid drove into New York. Surviving forty-five minutes of weaving through congested and borderline-insane midmorning Manhattan traffic, Dana was relieved to be back in a familiar neighborhood of Queens. She directed Majid to let her out of the Sequoia two blocks from the Jamaica station of the Long Island Railroad.

During the drive, she had discussed with him two assignments once he returned to the Washington area. First, and most important, he must finalize plans for using a suitcase nuke to blow up the Pentagon. Second, and vital, he must recruit three additional members to their cell to help with scenarios for planting the two nuclear bombs.

She knew Majid was always on the lookout for recruits. He'd mentioned a few terrorist wannabes. But he hadn't been convinced they measured up. With the loss of other members of their cell, the recruitment bench was beginning to look stronger.

After saying farewell to her closest, and for now only, follower, she walked toward the Jamaica station, managing her suitcase and handbag. Jamaica was a major transit hub from which she could travel virtually anywhere in Queens or greater New York City. She felt a twinge of remorse at being unwilling to disclose her residence even to someone as close as Majid. *What is wrong with me that I hold even trusted comrades at arm's length?* she wondered. Only with Joffrey Gobert had she felt free to be totally open. That made his loss more hurtful.

Once off the subway, she hailed a taxi and traveled to an area populated with midrise apartment buildings. She dismissed the taxi driver on a busy thoroughfare and strolled the final two blocks to her home, glancing around to confirm she'd eluded any pursuers. She favored the anonymity of apartment living in New York. Apartments provided the illusion of having neighbors, without the necessity of becoming acquainted with anyone.

Upon entering the lobby, she checked the mailbox for Mr. and Mrs. Jacques Michel. There was the usual collection of trivia. Since she was fluent in French from her days as a student at the Sorbonne in Paris, she had no difficulty posing as the wife of a Frenchman.

Her cover story to the building superintendent—whom she bribed liberally to look the other way if he had questions about her lifestyle—was that she and her spouse were often away because of their jobs. She claimed to be a flight attendant for Air France and said Jacques worked for the Renault-Nissan Alliance, which explained why they often traveled abroad.

To add credence to the notion Jacques really existed, from time to time, she hired the services of a male escort. After dinner at a nearby restaurant, she brought the man to her apartment. The sex, although enjoyable, was a fringe benefit. The real purpose was to validate her cover story in the minds of the curious, especially the building superintendent and the maid whom he hired to clean her apartment. Evidence in the bed and bathroom left no doubt she shared the quarters with a real man.

Apart from the escort, the superintendent, and the maid, no one knew she lived in the apartment building. Her hideout guaranteed total anonymity. A perfect base for conducting business with the tycoons with whom she had an appointment tomorrow afternoon.

Most of her mother's business friends knew of other residences owned by Dorothea Hamilton Di-Longhi: a palatial condo on Fifth Avenue with a beautiful terrace view of Central Park; an estate on the Gold Coast of Northern Long Island; a villa outside Florence,

Italy; and an apartment in Paris, which Dana insisted her mother buy when she was a student at the Sorbonne, and which she refused all family entreaties to sell. The wealthy liked to flaunt their properties, and Dana found the many residences relaxing and often convenient to her secret life. She also owned a condo in Fairfax City, near George Mason University, where she lived daily when working as a professor. The family home in Vienna had been sold long ago.

She regretted not suggesting to Zaha that she stay at her old apartment in the Latin Quarter near the Sorbonne. The Gendarmerie would not have found Zaha there. Habitual caution at not linking her public persona with her actions as a terrorist gave her pause. She felt a twinge of guilt, realizing her obsessive caution may have been the ultimate cause of Zaha's death.

Upon awakening at six, Dana began preparing her mindset for the noon meeting with four business tycoons who had the power to decide her financial future. The meeting, perhaps inevitably, was at the Harvard Club in midtown Manhattan. From years of coaching by her mother, she knew such men—and they would all be men—scheduled meetings at high noon, not because they intended to combine business with lunch, but to make it convenient for the cronies to dine together afterward.

She wondered idly whether the men knew, or would care, that her master's and PhD degrees from Harvard entitled her to membership. God knows her mother was rich enough and sufficiently well-connected, she could have arranged for Dana to join the most exclusive university club in the United States. Women had been granted full membership since 1973. She chuckled as she recalled Groucho Marx's famous quote: "I'm resigning. I refuse to belong to any club that would have me as a member."

Getting serious, she considered how to dress and prepare herself for the high-stakes meeting. Anxious to avoid any hint of looking provocative—these men undoubtedly had an immunity to beautiful women flaunting their attractiveness—she selected a light blue wool pant suit, complemented by an ivory blouse with pearl buttons that climbed to her neck. The blouse triggered a jolt of memory about the incident in Geneva where she had sliced her stomach to convince the Saudi delegation she was worthy of receiving their funds.

She decided on no jewelry, except for a Patek Philippe watch in Rose Gold studded with diamonds. The ensemble was understated but guaranteed to showcase she was her mother's daughter.

After taking her customary travel precautions, she strode into the Harvard Club five minutes early. Prompt, but not overly anxious. She was escorted to a private meeting room on an upper floor. As she entered the room, three of the men rose to greet her. The fourth, a portly gentleman with a cane leaning against his wine-red leather chair, nodded formally. She eyed the ashtrays, which showed they'd been smoking cigars and cigarettes, the butts extinguished on her arrival. The pungent aroma of smoke lingered in the room.

Offered coffee or tea, she chose a cup of coffee with two sugars, emulating her mother's preference on the off chance any of the men would recognize the choice.

There were no introductions. After a portentous silence, one of the men, whom she knew to be Wayne Durwood, Chairman and CEO of a family-owned manufacturing conglomerate, spoke. "We're reliably informed you're the leader of a secret political movement with the goal of reforming American society. A revolutionary of sorts. It all sounds rather romantic, bordering on fanciful. Some of us are skeptical. We'd like to know if you're serious?"

Dana met his cold look with one of her own.

"As serious as a heart attack. Sufficiently so, I accept as followers only men or women who are willing to sacrifice their lives for the cause."

Taken aback by the stark response, Durwood said, "We understand you're asking for our support with a donation of five million dollars. Is that correct?"

"Yes. Although I wouldn't hesitate to accept more if you chose to offer it."

"The amount aside, why should we support your cause, when we know so little of the specifics?"

"You mentioned that ours is a *secret* movement. We don't disclose our activities to anyone."

"Not even for the chance to obtain a donation of millions?" Durwood said.

"Not for any reason."

She picked up her cup and took a sip of coffee, weighing the reaction to her refusal on the faces of the four men. Astonishment was the way she interpreted the universal expression. These men rarely or never encountered anyone who would not bend to their will when an important sum of money was on the line.

"I'll tell you this, however. What you wish for is a society and body politic that is drastically different from what exists today. We share common goals. Moreover, we are on the cusp of a truly revolutionary coup. While I can't reveal the details, I can promise you, when it happens, our movement will make front page headlines in the *New York Times* and the *Wall Street Journal*."

Impressed by her words and demeanor, Durwood turned to his companions. Each of the other tycoons gave a barely perceptible nod of agreement.

"Ms. Di-Longhi, you shall have our support. We will make an initial donation of ten million dollars. Contact us if you need more."

CHAPTER 57

Majid strolled into the Starbucks at the corner of Beulah Road and Route 123 in Vienna. He knew the area because it was only four miles from the Northern Virginia house he'd shared with other cell members in the past. But the town lacked the anonymity prized by terrorists.

He was accustomed to the hustle and bustle of anywhere in the vicinity of Tysons where Muslims shopped freely in the ubiquitous stores, without having to endure second glances. None of that here. Vienna was a small town. People said "hello" to each other on the street, an act Majid found threatening. No one was anonymous.

He relaxed a bit when he glimpsed a table of Muslim teenagers, sipping concoctions that resembled soda fountain drinks more than variations on coffee. Scanning the room, he spotted the young woman he was scheduled to meet, seated alone in a far corner.

On the way to join her, he ordered a black coffee *grande*—whatever that meant—from the barista. Carrying his overly full coffee as cautiously as he would a Molotov cocktail, he approached the table and sat in the chair opposite the woman where he could face her and keep an eye on the front entrance.

"Reema?"

She smiled. "You must be Mr. Black."

Her saucy smile, just a bit coquettish, reminded him of Zaha, and he struggled to suppress memories of his lost colleague. Recognition of the need to recruit replacement members of their terrorist cell, including females, was coupled with guilt they would be risking their lives, just as Zaha had given up hers in Paris. He was resigned to his morally ambiguous quest, believing it essential if they were to help Dana defeat the Great Satan.

Reema was tall—a couple of inches taller than Majid himself—and willowy, with rich black hair falling to her shoulders. Her skirt was hiked up and long, shapely legs protruded under the edge of the table.

She was striking but not quite beautiful, and she seemed older than the twenty-two years she'd told him at their first meeting in the Barnes and Noble at Tysons. There was something about the way she looked at him that day, as though she could penetrate his pose of normality and see the terrorist within. That look emboldened him to risk striking up a conversation with her and, as a result, scheduling this meeting.

"You know my name is not Black."

"Of course not. It's Mohammad . . . or perhaps Osama." Her lips twitched mischievously.

Anxious to test her capacity to conceal her true feelings, he said, "How would you hide the knowledge that I'm a terrorist?"

A hint flickered in her eyes that his outrageous statement shocked her equanimity, then her face recovered a bland stare.

"Was that a test? What do I need to say or do to convince you I'm capable of being discreet when circumstances call for it?"

"Tell me about yourself."

"My name is Reema Hussain. I'm a college student. In my senior year at George Mason University, majoring in economics. Bored stiff with spending my time studying stuff that may help me find a job, but will be useless in the future. My parents came here from Iraq, and I was born in Virginia. I'm an American citizen. My parents are naturalized citizens, and boringly upper middle class. So, we're not subject to scrutiny by the FBI or other agencies of the federal government. I lost my virginity when I was sixteen, and I've been sexually active ever since. While I prefer men, I have no objection to having sex with a woman."

He raised his eyebrows at the last revelation. Was she trying to provoke him? To seduce him?

"What are your political views?"

"I've been self-radicalized following news about the Islamic State. ISIS is the only hope for the future of the Middle East, perhaps of the world. But I have no intention of engaging in the ridiculous 'lone wolf' terrorism that's fashionable today. It accomplishes nothing."

Majid kept his face expressionless. His goal was to learn about her. Not to give her clues to the "correct" response.

She forced a grim smile, as though belatedly conscious of the seriousness of today's encounter.

"When I saw you in the bookstore, somehow I knew you were involved in something more meaningful. That you arranged to meet me here is further proof. Either you're really a terrorist, or you're part of an FBI entrapment sting. Are you going to give me a fake bomb and direct me to blow up the Vienna metro? Don't keep me in suspense."

"Are you always this outspoken? Being indiscreet can get you a one-way ticket to prison or to an early grave."

"I can be as discreet as a cardinal saying mass to a church full of whores when I choose to be. Right now, I'm trying to audition as a fellow terrorist."

Majid snorted. "What you're trying is my patience. I want you to be serious."

"Give me a task. My actions will prove to you what my words have not."

"Come with me," he said and got up to leave Starbucks. He walked Reema outside and led her to the Sequoia, opening the passenger door. "Get in."

Without a word, she climbed into the SUV. He slammed the door and got in the driver's side. He drove out Beulah Road to Wolf Trap Park for the Performing Arts. He stopped the car in a cordoned off area and followed a path into the woods adjoining the open-air theatre that hosted performances from world class entertainers.

Reema hurried to keep pace. When she tried to ask a question or start a conversation, he shushed her with a wave.

After they'd walked a half mile from the nearest humanity, deep into the woods, he gestured for her to sit on a large rock. He stood before her. A lonely hawk circled overhead, keeping watch.

"Terrorism is not a game. A month ago, I was part of a terrorist cell with five members and a leader. Today, the leader and I are the only survivors. You saw news reports of the suicide bombings that killed and wounded hundreds in the Washington area. Our cell was responsible. In those incidents, five suicide bombers—men and women—died."

Reema blanched and held her hand to her mouth. Tears began to leak down her cheeks and she rubbed her eyes dry. She breathed heavily.

Both kept silent for several minutes, staring at each other.

At length, she spoke haltingly, "I'm not afraid to die. But I refuse to be a suicide bomber. Is there some other role I can play?"

"At this stage, we don't need suicide bombers. We have much bigger targets in mind. But they call for great skill and involve considerable risk."

"Risk of being killed?" she asked.

"That. Or of going to prison for life."

"Would I have to do anything you command?" she said.

"I might be the one to give you directions, or they could come from our leader, whom you will meet soon. You must obey without question. You're an extremely strong-willed woman. Are you willing to subject yourself to our discipline?"

"Gladly. I'm only rebellious when I can't identify with a meaningful cause. I promise to devote myself to your goals. Do you believe me?"

"*Inshallah.*

CHAPTER 58

In the early morning hours, Jolene and Alex's plane touched down at Andrews Air Force Base. She turned to Alex in the adjoining seat.

"I'd like to ask a favor."

"Ask away. If it's in my power, I'll grant it."

"I'm wasted. Since we lost Dana in Nuremberg, I haven't been able to think straight. I know the hunt for the bombs is urgent, but, as things are now, I'm useless. Give me a couple of days to rest and regroup at my farm near Leesburg."

"Makes sense. Today's Tuesday. I'll see you back at NCTC first thing Thursday morning. Will that work?"

"More than generous." Jolene felt foolish as they stumbled through the formalities of the exchange. They'd just shared and survived life-threatening experiences that should foster enduring closeness. Beyond that, she'd felt many moments when the urge to embrace Alex was virtually overwhelming. Even now, as she listened to the pilot's voice droning on about final steps in their landing, her yearning to touch and be touched returned with a surge of sexual excitement.

She was unable to fathom why these feelings were blocked by fears of once again getting involved in a relationship headed into an abyss of disappointment. Her time with George Southern in Geneva, rather than serving to rekindle strong feelings of attraction, was a reminder their romance was a thing of the past, a distant, and not altogether sad, memory of what might have been had fate not intervened with Rick Birmingham's attempted rape and the ensuing scandal.

• • •

Nearing home, at the entrance to the farm, her first sight was Stephanie who, in response to her telephone alert, had ridden Regret to form a welcoming committee of two. The teenager waved her signature straw cowboy hat and shouted "hooray."

Stephanie raced the Beemer back to the stable, winning the contest easily because she wasn't constrained by having to follow the road.

Jolene leapt out of the car, embraced the teenager, and turned her attention to Regret. Caressing the thoroughbred's forelock, she said, "You're a beautiful filly. I've missed you like crazy."

She began to cry with happiness, hugging Regret. She tossed her key fob to Stephanie and mounted her pride and joy.

"I'll be back in an hour," she yelled and galloped toward the trail through the woods.

Jolene spent the rest of the day getting reacquainted with Regret. Back in the stable, she rubbed down the filly and led her to her stall.

Then she took time to pay her respects to King—formally dubbed White King—the snow-white stallion in the adjoining stall. Once her favorite thoroughbred, before Regret stole her affections, she still loved King and missed spending time with both horses while away in Europe.

That night, she crawled wearily into bed. In a moment of maudlin sentiment, she pondered how much lost happiness weighed in the balance with attempts to save the world. She was embarrassed by her foolish turn of mind.

She wondered if her dad, the hardheaded intelligence guru Richard Martin, ever experienced instances of weakness and second thoughts. Her dad was often on her mind when she visited the farm. It was here he'd taught her to ride, and, more importantly, to understand horseflesh. It seemed their only moments of real closeness were associated with horses, racing, and the farm.

Jolene loved her mom Camille Karami Martin, but she never felt the special relationship she sometimes had with her dad. Perhaps her mom's emotional coolness came with being a world-class brain surgeon. Jolene knew her mom's medical colleagues called her the "Ice Queen." More likely, a pattern of standoffishness stemmed from the experience of being the only child of French and Lebanese professors of science. Her mom grew up partly in France, Lebanon, and the Manhattan environs of New York University, where Jolene's grandparents taught in the years before both died in a senseless auto accident only days after her mom graduated with highest honors from the Bronx High School of Science.

Fingering the locket at her neck, she resolved to work harder to stay in touch with her parents. As a first step, she began planning to pay a surprise visit to her mom once the crisis with Dana was resolved.

Her fraternal grandparents, dead more than five years, inspired her love and gratitude, notably for leaving her the farm in their will. But had it not been for her dad, she would have failed to appreciate the legacy. Unfortunately, her dad's frequent absences, and their mutual hardheadedness, often led to arguments, clashes of will, and lingering resentments.

CHAPTER 59

Alex drove west on Route 7 headed for Leesburg. He'd memorized the directions to Jo's farm, but just to be on the safe side, he activated the navigation app on his car. He glanced at his watch, 5:45 a.m. Right on time to arrive in the half hour interval before sunrise, when he surmised Jo would be heading for the stable.

A few minutes later, he pulled into the entrance to the farm and spotted a teenager climbing out of an older Grand Cherokee. From Jo's description when she waxed nostalgic about her time at the farm, he recognized Stephanie, who looked after Regret and King. He pulled his Range Rover next to the Jeep, jumped out, and introduced himself.

Eyeballing Alex as if to check whether he measured up, Stephanie said, "So you work with Jolene?"

"I do. We just flew back from Germany together."

Fishing for information, she said, "Jolene never talks about what she does for the government. What do you do?"

Seeing through the gambit, he laughed. "I do the same things Jo does."

Jarred by his shortened form of the name, Stephanie saw her employer and idol hurrying toward them from the farmhouse. "Here comes *Jolene* now."

Recognizing the put down, Alex avoided signaling any reaction. He waved to Jo, noting the flash of surprise cross her face, quickly masked by a smile that looked only partly insincere.

Jo walked up and, with unaccustomed formality, shook Alex's

hand. He resisted the temptation to offer a welcoming hug. After all, he was on her home territory, where house rules applied.

"I see you two have met. Stephanie, Alex is my boss, at least for the duration of our current assignment. Alex, Stephanie is a godsend who runs this farm, takes care of two thoroughbreds, and enables me to sleep nights when I'm on travel. She's also a good friend whom I would trust with my life."

Stephanie blushed in reaction to the praise. "Excuse me. I've got things to do in the stable. Pleased to meet you Alex."

He watched the teenager depart, wondering whether her last comment was a flat-out lie, a meaningless pleasantry, or a true sentiment. He decided Stephanie had an adult's adroitness at social ambiguity.

• • •

Jolene confronted Alex and said, "What are you doing here? I told you I was wasted, and I needed time to rest and regroup at the farm."

"You had yesterday by yourself. I hoped today we could spend time together and find ways to dispel both of our demons."

She turned away and wandered toward the training racetrack, unable to face the implications of what Alex had just said, but unwilling to ignore the hope it might turn out to be true.

He hurried after Jo and reached for her hand as they walked.

"Do you ride?" she asked, surprising them both by the question. *Where did that come from?*

"Yes. During summer break, in college I worked on my uncle's ranch in Montana. Every day I spent several hours in the saddle."

Deciding to add to the challenge, she said, "Do you have any experience with a racing saddle or English saddle?"

"Absolutely none. It won't surprise you to learn they use western saddles in Montana."

"Don't be a wiseass. I'm asking serious questions for a reason. Have you ever ridden a thoroughbred racehorse?"

"No. But I've ridden quarter horses that have been in races. And I competed in a rodeo once, although, truth in advertising, I ended up landing on my ass, which bruised my pride more than my body."

She looked him up and down, fighting conflicting emotions. She wanted Alex to stay and spend the day with her, but the only common activity that came to mind ran the risk of proving fatal to him.

"Frank Mansfield would be pissed if he knew I asked you, but would you be willing to go riding with me? I must caution you, even recreational riding on a thoroughbred will be different from anything you've ever experienced. Handled wrong, my horses will kill you."

Alex tried and failed to look humble.

She laughed at the pretense.

"Okay. You're determined to show you can rise to any challenge. Far be it from me to keep a man from his destiny. I'll race you to the stable."

Having given him fair warning, she took off like a rabbit.

He reacted quickly, but she'd already gained a three-step lead.

By the time they arrived at the stables, the runners were neck and neck.

Stephanie stepped out into the sunshine, looking at the panting racers like they were fugitives from a nearby movie set.

Once she caught her breath, Jolene said, "Stephanie, what I say next will convince you I've lost my mind. Don't ask questions. Just do it."

"Oookay," the teenager said hesitantly.

"Alex is an experienced rider. However, he's only ridden quarter horses with a western saddle. In the next fifteen minutes, I want you to introduce him to King, show him how to use an English saddle, and teach him everything he needs to know to ride a thoroughbred around the training racetrack and on the path through the woods."

Jolene watched the teenager, who was never at a loss for words, standing openmouthed, staring at her in disbelief.

After a long pause, the girl considered the request, shaking her head. Digesting the prefatory comments, she shrugged her shoulders.

Turning to Alex, she said, “Follow me, and try not to step in the horseshit. I have a feeling there’ll be a whole lot more before this day is over.”

• • •

Out of the corner of her eye, Jolene observed Alex’s riding style, while King and Regret trotted side by side. For the first time she could recall, Alex had a tentative, almost nervous, look on his face.

She sighed to herself. “At least he hasn’t fallen off *yet*.”

She felt a twinge of conscience risking Alex’s life to put him in his place for presuming to show up uninvited at the farm. She tried to be honest with herself. Wasn’t she secretly glad he came? Hadn’t she fantasized about spending time alone with him? Making passionate love with him?

Whoa. She was letting her fantasies move faster than the horses. In a victory of emotion over reason, she decided there’d be no more reining in her feelings. Today was the day for making new dreams.

“Alex,” she barked, using a louder and more commanding voice than intended.

He glanced over, clearly uncomfortable not keeping his gaze locked securely on the back of King’s head.

“Watch how my body moves in rhythm with Regret’s strides. That’s how King expects you to ride. Try to mimic my motion.”

After a bit of trial and error—quite a lot of error—Alex began to learn how to emulate proper horsemanship while riding a thoroughbred. She continued the exercise until it looked as though he was getting into the routine.

“Now we’re going to move from the training racetrack to the woods. We’ll see how you handle King in a more bucolic setting.”

After riding a half-hour in the woods, glancing at summer wildflowers and an occasional deer startled by the horses, they came to a shallow creek. A massive oak tree had fallen across the water.

The tree provided a bridge for the nimble of foot, but protruding branches allowed no passage for the horses.

Jolene turned in the saddle and faced Alex.

"This oak wasn't down the last time I rode this way. Stephanie told me there'd been a bad storm. We'll need to turn back."

"Okay."

"By the way, your horsemanship is getting respectable. It's entirely possible you may ride all the way to the stable without falling off King."

"Is that what's known as damning with faint praise?"

"No. It's what's referred to in polite society as a compliment. I'm impressed. I've never seen a novice rider catch on to riding a thoroughbred so quickly."

Alex nodded, conscious this was the closest they'd come to having a personal conversation that wasn't fraught with tension and unspoken thoughts.

"In honor of your accomplishments, I'd like you to join me for dinner tonight." She'd blurted out the invitation without thinking. The implications of asking Alex to stay late sent her pulse racing. Was she ready to take their professional relationship to a personal level? And did personal necessarily lead to sexual intimacy?

"Can you cook as well as you ride?"

She relaxed a bit at his willingness to break the tension with a joke.

"If worst comes to worst, we can share a pizza that's in the freezer. In the refrigerator, there's a bottle of prize-winning Virginia cabernet from a nearby vineyard."

"You're on."

After dinner, they sat in front of the fireplace finishing off the bottle of wine.

"How'd you happen to end up on this farm with two world-class thoroughbreds?" he asked.

She told the story of how she'd inherited the farm from her

grandparents and how she'd bonded with her dad over their mutual love of horses and racing.

Afterwards, they sat in companionable silence. Gradually, the sexual tension began to intrude on the quiet.

Jolene rose from her chair and walked toward Alex. She leaned over and kissed him gently on the lips. He gripped her shoulders and pulled her onto his lap. They embraced, feeling no need for conversation.

She stroked his hair. "All day, I've wanted to touch you and be touched by you. I've tried to avoid it, but it's no use. I want you, and I'm not ashamed to admit it."

"And I want you." He stood and gathered her in his arms. "Which way is your bedroom?"

CHAPTER 60

Mickey Walsh parked the black Ford Expedition on the side of the access road to Jolene's farm. The car was a quarter mile from the farmhouse and a brisk wind was blowing toward them. He was confident any noise they made at that distance would not be heard by the occupants. Mickey, code name Bulldog, was the assassin in charge of the trio whose assignment was to terminate with extreme prejudice Jolene Martin and anyone else on the property. After the killings, they were to burn down every structure.

Bulldog's partners in crime—code named Dane and Husky—climbed out of the vehicle and stood, waiting for instructions.

Each of the assassins was named after a dog breed that, in the mind of their superior, fit either their personality, appearance, or both. Mickey was Bulldog because that was his typical demeanor. Dane (short for Great Dane) was noted for his height and golden blond hair, marking him as a stereotypical Scandinavian in the eyes of his colleagues. Husky (short for Siberian Husky) was a stout 250-pounder who kept bragging about his Russian relatives in Brighton Beach, Brooklyn, New York.

"Listen up," Bulldog said. "Leave your weapons in the SUV."

He opened a black briefcase and pulled out three older model revolvers in poor condition. "We'll use these." He handed each of the men one of the guns and stuck the third in his belt.

"What the fuck?" Dane said. "This revolver's no better than a Saturday night special."

Husky said, "Yeah, and my Russian grandmother keeps a better gun than this under her pillow at night. What the hell's going on, Bulldog? This gal, Jolene, is supposed to be an ace intelligence operative and a crack shot. If I'm going up against her, I want a weapon I can depend on to put her down with one bullet."

"I've got a rule," Dane said. "I never go into a gunfight unless I'm familiar with the weapon. We can't try these out here."

"Shut up. Both of you. The gun in your hand is the one you'll use. I know they look like junk, but I've fired them both and they work."

"Why do we have to use these pieces of shit?" Husky said, not about to be intimidated, even by Bulldog.

"Because we have orders to make her killing look like the work of a home invasion by inexperienced crooks. We'll take anything worth stealing. Also, I'm going to 'lose' my gun during the shootout. The cops will find it in the debris after the fire's put out. That'll clinch the evidence about who did the murders. Your guns we'll toss in the Potomac."

"Who thought up this cockamamie idea?" Husky said.

"File a complaint tomorrow. But don't give me any more crap tonight."

"Okay, okay. Let's get this over with. How do you want to work it?"

Bulldog decided the two were through griping and were ready to get down to business. He shared their view that the plan was one of the dumber ones he'd been involved in. But he wasn't about to let on in front of these jerks.

"We'll walk from here to the farmhouse. Dane, you cut the power and knock out the lights. The connection is in the rear. Once you've done that, enter through the back door and clear the downstairs and cellar. Husky and I will enter through the front door and head upstairs. Whoever sees Jolene first should put her down, three shots in her torso. Empty the revolver randomly around the room. Be careful not to make it look like a professional job. Pretend you're twenty years old, high on drugs, and scared out of your mind."

"What if we find anyone else in the house?" Husky said.

"Kill them the same way. No survivors. A burned crime scene will be all that's left to tell the story."

Husky and Dane nodded. They understood the logic of total annihilation.

• • •

Jolene awoke to the sound of a quiet buzzing and saw a tiny bright red bulb blinking in the far corner of her bedroom ceiling nearest the door. Her alarm system, which her dad had cautioned her to install, was working. A backup generator was one of many modifications to make the farmhouse into a fortress. She poked Alex who was asleep beside her.

He propped himself up on one elbow. "What's going on?"

"The electricity to the house just died. Either we're under attack or it's a genuine power outage. And I haven't seen or heard any sign of a storm."

She swung her feet to the floor, picked up the gray T-shirt beside the bed and pulled it on. From the bedside table, she slipped on the shoulder holster and drew her Glock 19. There was no need to rack the slide. She always kept the weapon locked and loaded, ready to fire.

At that moment, she heard two crashes.

"Intruders have breached the front and back doors."

She switched on the tactical flashlight she kept next to the pistol on the table and lit up the chair where Alex left his clothes and weapon prior to their lovemaking early in the evening. He jumped off the bed, pulled on his trousers, and grabbed his weapon.

Once she saw Alex was armed, she opened the closet and removed a Winchester 1100 semi-automatic shotgun.

"Is that loaded?" he asked.

"With twelve-gauge buckshot." She flicked off the safety.

She pulled on a pair of jeans, jammed her cell phone in a rear pocket, removed some extra shells from a drawer, and stuffed them in her other pockets.

She could hear pounding on the stairs. Moving quickly to the bedroom door, she reached for a large bolt and locked the door.

"Help me with this dresser."

Together they wedged the heavy dresser in front of the door.

She pointed to the window from which stray glimmers of moonlight were leaking through dark clouds.

"Follow me onto the roof. We'll go down the ladder and circle around behind the attackers."

She crept quickly and quietly through the window and traversed the walkway to the ladder, with Alex on her heels.

Once on the ground, Jolene pulled out her cell and called Stephanie.

"Steph. Intruders are attacking the farmhouse. Stay at your home; they're not likely to come there. But arm yourself, just in case.

"Call the county police and alert them. My guess is these guys are trained assassins who are probably carrying military style weapons. The cops should exercise extreme caution. Remind them not to shoot the homeowner. Alex and I are armed."

Jolene could hear loud crashes coming from the vicinity of her bedroom, which she attributed to the intruders breaking down the door and forcing their way past the furniture she and Alex used as a barrier. Then she heard two shots fired, which she attributed to one of the attackers unleashing nervous energy by firing blindly around the bedroom.

She looked right and left before asking Alex. "What's your best guess which door they'll come out when they've finished searching the house and realize we went out the window? Front or back?"

He pointed to the roof. "That way."

She aimed the shotgun at the attackers who were taking the rungs of the ladder two at a time. She fired and the first man screamed as he dove toward the ground. The second man reversed direction and started to climb toward the supposed sanctuary of the roof. A blast of nine buckshot pellets caught him in the back. He dropped in his tracks.

Her peripheral vision glimpsed a third man running from the rear of the farmhouse toward the access road.

Alex yelled, "Stop or I'll shoot."

The intruder spun around and began firing his revolver. He was over one hundred feet away and his shots went wild.

Alex emptied his pistol and Jolene fired her remaining shotgun shells.

The fleeing attacker grabbed his leg, limped a few steps, and fell to the ground.

Alex turned to Jolene. "We've nailed three intruders. Is that it?"

"That's my guess. After we look at that guy and see how badly he's hurt, we'll check the house carefully."

She reached in her pockets and began reloading the shotgun.

Alex said, "Let me borrow your pistol. I didn't take time to grab a backup magazine."

She withdrew her pistol from its holster and handed it to him.

Still experiencing an adrenaline rush, she tried to calm down as she walked side by side with Alex, keeping a cautious eye on the prone assailant. She'd seen him throw away his revolver after firing his last cartridge, so she wasn't worried. But at The Farm she'd absorbed the combat lessons of seasoned instructors who'd preached: "Never assume anything about the enemy."

Alex rolled the body over. The attacker was dead.

They returned to the farmhouse and searched carefully for a fourth intruder. They found no one.

Jolene called Stephanie to inform her the attack had been repulsed.

"Call the police and let them know the homeowners are the only ones alive on the farm."

Soon after she ended the call, she heard sirens in the distance.

CHAPTER 61

Amal al-Askari pulled her FBI special agent credentials and showed them to Detective Mark Rogers. She gestured to her fellow agent Randy Colfax who casually flipped open his credential case.

"We're here about last night's shootout at the Martin farm. Jolene Martin and Alex Werth both hold sensitive positions in the intelligence community. This case involves national security, and the FBI is assuming jurisdiction."

"I'm not so sure about that," the detective said. "This is Loudoun County. We take charge of our own criminal activity. If you have any information to share, I'll be glad to listen."

"I understand your position," Amal said, dialing her cell phone.

"Let me speak to Director Robinson please." When the FBI director answered, she handed the phone to Detective Rogers.

Annoyed at the theatrics, Rogers grudgingly accepted the phone. "Who's this?" He listened a few moments, then turned pale.

"Yes sir . . . I understand sir . . . I'm passing her the phone now." He handed the mobile back to Amal.

She held the phone to her ear. "Thank you, sir. Sorry to trouble you. We'll take charge at this end. If you'd tell the SAC we could use a couple more agents and the Evidence Response van, I'd appreciate it."

Ignoring the detective, she said to Randy, "Robinson will direct the special agent in charge in Richmond to send reinforcements. He believes help is already on the way."

Detective Rogers scurried back to the interrogation room to

bring his partner detective up to speed on the recent developments that removed the case from the county's jurisdiction and put the FBI in charge.

Freed from the never-ending stream of questions pursuant to deaths resulting from a shooting by an official, Jolene and Alex walked up the hall. She and Amal hugged. Alex shook hands with Randy, welcoming him to the team charged with tracking down Dana Hussein al-Sadi.

Amal briefed Jolene on the latest turn of events, while the two men went off to sit in chairs at the side of the detective squad room.

"Detective Rogers was being a hardass. I had to call Director Robinson to set him straight. The FBI has sole jurisdiction regarding the incident at your farm. Richmond is sending more agents and the Evidence Response van. They'll conduct a thorough search of the farmhouse, the surrounding area, and the Expedition the would-be assassins parked just down the road. Their remains will be transported to Quantico, where the autopsies will be performed, not that we expect to learn much. Rogers put their fingerprints in the system, so we'll see if the CIA connection shows up."

Jolene said, "My guess is it won't. Rick Birmingham is behind this, but he's too smart to allow any direct link between the Agency and the assassins. We'll probably learn they're former Special Forces, with no record of what they've been doing in the recent past."

Amal nodded. She opened her briefcase and pulled out a pair of jeans and a sweatshirt with NEW ORLEANS emblazoned on the front. "Use these to change from the jail garb the local cops gave you when they checked your clothes for GSR."

"Yeah," Jolene said. "Big surprise when CSI 'discovers' gunshot residue after I told the detectives I'd discharged a shotgun several times and killed two men, maybe three, depending on whether Alex or I nailed the third assassin."

By the time Jolene returned from the ladies' room after changing clothes, Amal was holding out her shoulder holster. "I convinced

Rogers he didn't need this for their evidence kit. Especially since they'll have to turn everything over to the FBI Evidence Response Team anyhow."

Jolene slipped on the holster. "You don't happen to have a spare Glock 19 in your magic briefcase?"

Pulling out the weapon, Amal said, "How'd you guess?" She walked over to Alex and handed him a second pistol.

Having watched the interplay between the two women with some amusement, Alex said, "Don't you have a change of clothes for me in that briefcase?"

Amal showed him the empty case. "Sorry. Besides, jail garb looks good on you, boss."

Jolene retrieved her cell phone and Alex's, which had been taken by the Loudoun detectives. She noticed an urgent voice message from George Southern, who was responsible for liaising with the Nuremberg *polizei* and the GSG 9 Counterterrorism unit of the German federal police.

She returned the call and listened briefly. "Oh my god." She gestured frantically to her fellow team members. "You've got to hear this."

CHAPTER 62

Jolene triggered the speaker button on her cell phone, informing Alex and Amal about the voicemail she'd just received. "George says the German anti-terrorist police have a lead on the suitcase nukes. Listen up." She beckoned the others to gather around. "George—Alex and Amal are here with me. So's Randy Colfax, Amal's FBI colleague, who's joined our team."

She glanced up as Detective Rogers entered the room, seeing him gape at the group huddled around Jolene. "Be aware, George, we're in a police station in Loudoun County—never mind why—so tailor your remarks accordingly."

Rogers, the only detective in the squad room, took a seat at his desk. He looked intrigued by the unexpected turn of events.

George's voice seemed to fill the room. "I'm in Hamburg, working with the GSG 9 Counterterrorism police. They've been investigating a Dr. Klostermann, who's suspected of smuggling contraband into the US, mingled with legitimate shipments of medical devices."

"We hear you, George."

"It's nearly certain Klostermann met with Dana Hussein al-Sadi and a confederate two weeks ago. According to an informant in the doctor's organization, Klostermann was paid one hundred thousand dollars to ship two boxes to the Port of New York. The boxes each weighed nearly one hundred pounds and were packaged to conceal radioactivity."

Alex interrupted. "When were the boxes scheduled to arrive in New York?"

"Last night."

"Get all the information you can from George. I've got to call Mansfield," he yelled to Jolene, as he ran toward the detective's desk.

"Rogers, keep other cops out of this room, and forget everything you've heard. We're on a classified mission for President Scofield. The nation is at risk of a terrorist strike many times worse than 9/11. Two nuclear bombs have been smuggled into New York."

Picking up the detective's phone, he said, "How do I get an outside line?"

After a few minutes, he was connected to Director of National Intelligence Frank Mansfield.

"Frank, Jo just learned from George Southern that the nukes were shipped from Hamburg two weeks ago. The cargo ship arrived in the Port of New York last night."

He listened to Frank's response and jumped to his feet with an angry expression and a red face.

"Fuck the CIA. Those bastards tried to kill Jo and me yesterday. Rick Birmingham is the devil incarnate. We've got to work through the FBI and other intelligence agencies. You don't have to *lie* to the CIA. Just don't tell them anything. Following the nukes is the best lead to track down Dana. According to the president, that's still *our* role."

CHAPTER 63

The midmorning traffic didn't bother Dana as she and Majid drove out of the Port Authority terminal with the crates containing the suitcase nukes stored in the rear of the Sequoia. She was thrilled Klostermann's shipment was part of the "green lane" program in which trusted shippers had fewer containers inspected and hence were cleared for faster pickup.

"Klostermann may be a greedy bastard," she said, "but he knows how to run a smuggling operation. Our cargo got through New York's convoluted bureaucracy of international shipping in record time. That was the best hundred thousand dollars any terrorist ever spent."

Weaving through a bewildering maze of trucks, cab drivers, and other cars, Majid said, "We can't relax until we're out of New York City and on the New Jersey Turnpike headed for DC. How long will it take us to get to the George Washington Bridge?"

"On a good day, anything from a half hour to an hour." As a frequent visitor to, and occasional resident of, New York City, Dana had learned not to be optimistic about traffic patterns.

• • •

Jo, Amal, Randy, and Alex were in Randy's Lexus driving at top speed—accompanied by a police escort, courtesy of Detective Rogers—headed for Leesburg Executive Airport. Director Robinson had arranged for an FBI helicopter to pick them up at Godfrey Field and fly them to New York as the quickest way to connect with FBI special agents at the Port Authority.

Alex interrupted his telephone call with Gordon Berghardt, the FBI special agent in charge in New York City. He asked the SAC to hold on and muted his call.

"Shit. Berghardt says we missed them. Two crates shipped from Dr. Klostermann were picked up by a woman matching Dana Hussein al-Sadi's description and a man who looked Middle Eastern."

Jo said, "By now, Dana's partway to Washington with the bombs. See if the FBI can locate video footage of her vehicle. We can ask the New Jersey State Police and other jurisdictions along the route to put out a BOLO for terrorists and give them photos and other information we have about Dana and her vehicle."

"I'll pass that on to Berghardt and ask him to coordinate it," Alex said.

Amal said, "Remind him to include in the Be On the Lookout anything they pick up from surveillance videos about the man accompanying Dana."

CHAPTER 64

After Majid crossed the Rubicon of the George Washington Bridge, Dana briefed him on the next bit of deception to shake the Feds off their trail.

"Take the turnoff to downtown Newark. I'll direct you once we get near the area I'm looking for."

They drove in silence for a few minutes. Dana alternated between elation at having finally achieved her goal of obtaining two nuclear weapons and brainstorming how to ensure her prize would reach its destination in the Washington area.

She guided him past the Prudential Center indoor sports arena toward Route 21, a haven for used car dealerships. She spotted one that fit the profile she had in mind where she could purchase a vehicle on short notice with no questions asked if the buyer put up sufficient ready cash. She pointed to a spot on the street a short distance from a dealer that boasted *Best Deals in New Jersey on Certified Pre-Owned Cars.*

"Let me out here. I'm going to buy a replacement vehicle. We'll dispose of the Sequoia later. In the meantime, find a vacant lot and remove the suitcase nukes from the shipping crates and dispose of the crates. The crates are heavy, can you handle them by yourself?"

"Of course." Majid looked indignant, as though his manhood had been questioned.

Unfazed, Dana continued. "If it's feasible, keep the packing material Klostermann used to shield radiation; otherwise, dispose of that too. Pick up carryout coffee and sandwiches for both of us.

Meet me at this location in an hour."

She could tell from a raised eyebrow and the shrug of a shoulder, Majid was mildly annoyed to have the latest chapter of their getaway plan sprung on him without advance notice. But, knowing her propensity for keeping secrets, she was confident he would accept events without complaining. Once again, she berated herself for failing to be totally open with her most trusted subordinate.

Ignoring the salesman who rushed toward her when she sauntered onto the dealership lot, Dana roamed throughout the property, eyeing each SUV critically. Finally, she saw a Black man with an air of authority notice what was going on and hurry out.

"I'm the manager. Name's Danny Washington. How can I help you? I hate to see a pretty lady like you walking around in the hot sunshine. Let me show you our best deals. What kinda car you lookin' for?"

Dana pointed to a dark blue Chevy Suburban that had seen better days, but had no obvious defects. "Tell me about this Suburban."

Putting on an enthusiastic face, he said, "Good choice. Only four years old, with just a tad under two hundred thousand miles on her. But she was well kept up. As you can see, we've put on some almost new tires. I can let you have her for eighteen thousand dollars."

Not confident of her aptitude for judging the mechanical condition of a used car, she decided to rely on her astute ability to judge men. She believed Washington was telling an approximation of what he imagined to be the truth. As used car dealers go, he was probably no more dishonest than average.

"I'll give you fifteen thousand in cash if you can have the car gassed and ready for me to drive out of here in less than one hour."

He looked her over carefully and nodded, sensing from her attitude he wasn't likely to strike a better bargain.

"You got yourself a deal, honey. Give my mechanics forty-five minutes and we'll have her ready to go. You can wait in my office."

Unwilling to be holed up in the same room with a man she could tell fancied himself a Don Juan, she said, "Thanks for the hospitality, but I'll get some exercise by walking around the neighborhood." She gave Washington her fake driver's license.

"I'll hand over the cash just before I leave."

• • •

When Majid returned, she joined him in the Sequoia. Over lunch in the vehicle, she briefed him on purchase of the Suburban.

"The car's ready now. We'll drive it a couple of blocks away to avoid the spying eyes of the car salesmen and switch everything to the Chevy. Then you can follow me to the neighborhood where we'll ditch the Toyota."

After exchanging the cash for the keys with Danny, Dana drove up Route 21, circled past Newark Penn Station, and headed for one of the poorest sections of the city. Unlike Northern Virginia, where multi-ethnic diversity was the norm, poverty-stricken Black neighborhoods were still predominantly Black, with a sprinkling of Hispanics and other ethnicities.

Majid parked in the center of the public housing neighborhood, stepped out of the Sequoia, and after transferring the cargo, deposited the keys in a cup holder, left the doors unlocked, walked over to the Suburban, and climbed in. Dana immediately drove off. They both knew to beware of residents who were prone to take out their frustrations with daily living on outsiders invading *their* territory.

"That car will be stolen before we get out of sight," she predicted. In the rear-view mirror, she could see several young men crowding around the Sequoia like wolves circling a crippled deer.

CHAPTER 65

Felix pocketed his cell phone, having learned from Alex that he, Jolene, Amal, and Randy were returning to the National Counterterrorism Center.

Alex explained why the action was moving from New York to Arlington, Virginia, location of the Pentagon—which he and Jo were convinced was Dana Hussein al-Sadi's primary target—with somewhere in the DC area a likely secondary target.

Felix summoned Courtney Gonzalez, Steve Randall, Mike Sato, and the Navy SEALs to the conference room.

He briefed the NCTC team on the latest developments and current frustrations he'd heard from Alex. Then he asked what progress they were making in their investigations. "For the past few days, you've been working with the FBI, trying to help them track down potential terrorist cell members Dana might have recruited. Any leads?"

Courtney glanced at her teammates and got a go-ahead signal they were comfortable with her as spokesperson.

"So far, the FBI has struck out," she said. "There's no evidence any of the main suspects in their files have been contacted by anyone linked to Dana. Nor have they heard tips about plans for a major operation of the type the suitcase nukes would require."

Felix shrugged. He was not the sort to deny the obvious. "So we're nowhere. Alex and his crew are nowhere."

Courtney continued. "Alex believes Dana and the guy in the video the FBI sent us earlier today are heading from New York to this vicinity. Of course, they may switch cars. Alex wants us to brainstorm what the terrorists might do next and take appropriate action until he and Jolene arrive, which should be soon because they're traveling on an FBI helicopter."

The normally taciturn Luke was the first to speak up. "A few years ago, I was assigned to the Pentagon. The nature of my job enabled me to explore virtually everywhere in that building. If Dana could get a suitcase nuke inside, there are innumerable places to hide a bomb until she's ready to set it off. "The trick is getting the device through security, which is unbelievably tight."

Shifting excitedly in his chair, Steve interrupted. "I also worked at the Pentagon. She doesn't need to get the bomb *inside* the Pentagon. Even a small nuke has incredible destructive power, the bomb just needs to be *close enough* to ensure widespread death and destruction."

Luke continued. "A delivery truck would work. Even if it's stopped at security, it would be close enough. The impact of the explosion would be devastating."

Eager to join in, Mike said, "Anyone with a parking permit could gain access to the grounds. That might be near enough to set off the bomb and cause considerable damage. Hell, it doesn't have to be anyone with a connection to the Pentagon. Don't forget, the Blue and Yellow metro lines stop at the Pentagon Transit Center. A suicide bomber could set off a nuke in the subway station. The media would report the explosion as having occurred at the Pentagon.

Courtney stood and began to take notes on a whiteboard in the small conference room, listing the options mentioned so far:

SECURITY TO ENTER PENTAGON

DELIVERY TRUCK

PARKING PERMIT

PENTAGON TRANSIT CENTER

She summed up. "We've highlighted a lot of the obvious tactics. Felix, maybe we should recommend that Amal and Randy propose a joint FBI-Pentagon task force to identify possible ways of deploying a nuke in or near the Pentagon and countermeasures to stop them."

Felix nodded. “These are all good ideas. We’ll pass them on. Unfortunately, none of this brainstorming brings us any closer to tracking down Dana and other terrorists in her cell.”

Courtney yelled. “Hold on. I think that’s the helicopter.”

They all hurried out of the conference room and ran for the window to watch it land.

CHAPTER 66

Once the group returned from the helipad to the conference room, Jolene stood and addressed the team.

"I just got off the phone with FBI headquarters. They located the Sequoia Dana was driving."

"Where?" Courtney asked.

"It was abandoned in a low-income public housing neighborhood in Newark with the keys inside. A gang of teenagers took it and were caught by police a few miles away after they crashed into another car while running a red light. They'd been drinking and smoking marijuana. When questioned, they fessed up, bragging about their joy ride.

Alex said, "Following up on that lead, the FBI located a used car dealer who remembered having sold Dana a Chevy Suburban for fifteen thousand dollars."

"Great," Courtney said. "Did they put out a BOLO on the Suburban?"

"Yes," Jolene said.

"Thirty minutes ago, the Suburban was located in Fairfax. Same MO. The Chevy was left in the Bailey's Crossroads area, near Culmore Park. A group of MS-13 gang members stole it, drove it while under the influence, and smashed into a telephone pole. A sixteen-year-old Hispanic who was driving was caught trying to escape, hobbling away on a crippled leg. His gang left him behind and ran."

Alex said, "The *good news* is, Dana's back."

"The *bad news* is, Dana's back," Jolene said.

CHAPTER 67

Majid assembled one woman and two men, the three Muslims he'd recruited to join Dana's cell. All four were waiting for her arrival in the living room of the house they had purchased in Pimmit Hills.

Their new hideout was near Tysons and only five miles from the Dar Al-Hijrah Islamic Center, which was not far from where they'd stayed before Jaber and Omar were captured by the authorities. Majid shared Dana's bias for living in areas with high concentrations of Muslims. Hiding in plain sight was working for them.

Dana surprised the group by swooping into the living room from what would, in a normal household, have been the dining room. Her hand was in her purse and her expression failed to convey how glad she was to meet the newcomers. Majid knew she was secretly grasping her Glock G43, which replaced her beloved Baby Glock, but was even more deadly and almost as concealable.

He guessed from her aggressive stance that Dana was aware of a threat in the room, and it could only come from one of the new recruits. When she pulled out the Glock and pointed it at the newcomers, Majid's hunch was confirmed.

He drew his pistol and commanded, "Reema, Abdullah, and Fajer lie down on floor. Put your hands behind your head. Don't move."

Terrified, the three complied, stretching out prone.

Reema screamed. "Why are you doing this? We came here to serve you. Not to be treated like criminals."

"Shut up," Majid yelled, getting caught up in the tension of the situation.

Dana spoke for the first time. "I was informed one of you is a traitor. You're working for the FBI."

The air was filled with confused shouts.

"NO."

"NOT ME."

"HELP."

"QUIET," Dana thundered. "I'll shoot to kill the next person who speaks."

A grim silence descended.

"I'm going to interrogate you, one at a time," she said in a calm voice, which was even more frightening than shouting.

She prodded Reema with her foot, while looking at Majid. "What's this one's name?"

"Reema."

"Reema, get up slowly and come with me."

She glanced at Majid. "Keep the others here."

Reema rose shakily to her feet, tried for a defiant look, then began to cry. "I swore to Majid I'd be loyal to you and do whatever you commanded. How could you think I'm a traitor?"

"We'll talk upstairs. Head for your bedroom." Dana knew from an earlier phone conversation with Majid the girl had slept in the house the previous night.

Reema trudged up the stairs, followed by Dana, who kept the Glock leveled dead center on her back.

When they entered the girl's room, Dana pointed to the bed.

"Lie on your back on the bed and don't move." She glanced around the room and spied a fleece robe thrown carelessly on a wooden chair. Keeping a watchful eye on Reema, she removed the robe's belt and tossed it to the girl.

"Tie this securely around your left wrist."

Puzzled, but anxious to do anything that would win her captor's trust, Reema complied.

"Now, pull the end of the belt through the wooden slat at the head of the bed."

Once that was done, Dana said, "Wrap the belt around your right wrist two times."

Satisfied Reema was in no position to resist, Dana hurriedly thrust the Glock in her purse, jumped onto the bed, and straddled the girl's waist. She grabbed the end of the belt that was loosely wrapped around her captive's right wrist, pulled it tight, and tied it securely.

She climbed off the bed, tossed the robe into a corner of the room, pulled the chair near the bed, and sat on it.

Gazing into Reema's eyes, she said, "Now we can talk. Tell me why I shouldn't believe you're a traitor."

Reema opened her mouth to speak, and Dana placed two fingers on her lips.

"Before you say anything, know this . . . if you confess to being a traitor, I'll shoot you between those beautiful eyes and you'll die instantly. But if you lie, I'll discover the truth. Then you'll suffer for days and pray for death before I kill you."

Reema stared back terrified.

"First, I'll cut out your tongue so you can't scream. The next day, I'll gouge out those dark brown eyes, so you can only listen to the ticking of the clock and wonder about the next step in your torment. Will I cut off your fingers first, one at a time, or your toes? Perhaps it would be better to start with your breasts, or maybe just the nipples. Did you know there are two hundred and six bones in the human body? Most of them can be broken and still allow a person to live."

Tears were streaming down Reema's cheek. She moaned softly as she listened to the litany of tortures being recited in a hypnotic voice.

"Now you may speak," Dana said.

Overcome with emotion, Reema thrust her head to one side and vomited on the floor beside the bed. She choked, coughed, tried to speak, and emitted indecipherable mumbles.

Dana picked up the robe and gently wiped Reema's mouth. She

untied the belt and held the girl tenderly in her arms.

Reema buried her face between Dana's breasts and sobbed.

"Don't cry, my dear. I know you're loyal. I'm sorry to put you through that, but I had to be sure. Come with me. I'll take you to my bedroom. You can rest there while I question the men."

• • •

When Dana returned to the living room, Majid nodded to the two men who sat with their backs to the wall leading to the kitchen. Their hands and feet were bound with durable climbing rope.

Fajer glared at Dana, desperate to prove he was not afraid. He was a small man, but his shoulders and upper arms were large. A scraggly black beard that looked like he shaved only once a week decorated an angular face and square jaw. He wore a faded Washington Commanders sweatshirt over too-tight jeans that telegraphed the bulge in his crotch. Despite elaborate efforts to stand out, something about his personality made him fade into the background.

Abdullah Khauli was younger, midtwenties, and he made no attempt to conceal his terror. He was still sobbing from the aftermath of being interrogated by Majid. He was tall and thin, almost handsome in a pretty-boy fashion. He wore a long-sleeve dark-blue checkered shirt that buttoned in front, but the top three buttons were undone. Head and chin were closely shaved. Majid told Dana he recruited the young man despite his flamboyant appearance, because Abdullah had an impressive knowledge of engineering and science. The cell needed a second member who could minister to the suitcase nukes.

Pointing to the men as he mentioned their names, Majid said, "I've questioned Fajer and Abdullah. In my opinion, either of them could be the traitor."

He paused to allow the suspects time to react. Both men visibly shuddered. Abdullah's wailing grew louder.

"But I also thought it possible both could be loyal, and your source, for whatever reason, was lying. You should question them yourself."

Dana stared first at one man, then the other, saying nothing for several minutes. The silence was more intimidating than any words or actions on her part would have been.

At length, she opened her purse and removed a hand exercise squeeze ball. She pointed to a roll of green duct tape resting on the coffee table. "Use the duct tape to secure this ball in Abdullah's mouth. If he continues to wail, you have my permission to cut out his tongue."

Hearing Dana discuss his fate so dispassionately, Abdullah fought to keep quiet, gasping for air like a goldfish dropped on the carpet.

She bent down by Fajer's feet and untied the climbing rope. Gesturing with her Glock, she beckoned him to stand. "Go ahead of me and climb the stairs."

On the second-floor landing, she directed him to the master bathroom, opened the entry from the hall, and pointed for him to go inside. To ensure Reema didn't interrupt Fajer's interrogation, she locked the far door that led into the bedroom where she'd left the girl.

"Climb into the tub.

Looking defiant, he said, "Why should I?"

"Because I'll shoot you between the eyes if you don't."

Without further protest, he scrambled into the tub.

"Lie down on your back."

He obeyed instantly. Even though he was short, his feet still stuck up on the back of the tub.

Dana repeated the threats she'd made to Reema to prompt her to tell the truth.

Shaken to the core as he listened to the menu of tortures if he didn't confess, Fajer's pretense of courage evaporated.

"I beg you, don't kill me. It's true, I was approached by FBI counterterrorism special agents and asked to be a paid informant. But I refused. They had nothing on me, so they let me go. I don't know what you were told, but that's the truth. I lied to Majid when he recruited me, because I thought there was no way the FBI would find out what I was doing."

"I believe you," she said. "No one would make up such a stupid story if it weren't true. Unfortunately, the story proves you're a fool. And I can't have a fool in my cell, even one who wants to combat the Great Satan. In time, the FBI would have found us by tracking you. So far, there's no indication they've done so."

Fajer babbled, "Spare me."

"I hate to kill a well-meaning fool. Let's make a deal. First, do you have any family or other ties in the Washington area or anyplace else in the Eastern United States?"

"No. I live in an apartment in Fairfax and have some belongings there. But I have no relatives, no personal ties, and no car."

Dana nodded approvingly. "Here's what I propose. I'll give you two thousand dollars. Pay cash for everything until the money runs out. Do not return to your apartment. Take the Silver Line metro from Tysons. Go to Union Station and buy a ticket for the next express train to California."

When Fajer started to speak, she held up her hand to demand silence.

"Don't tell me where you're going. Change your name and live as an illegal immigrant for one year. Get a job. Live as normal a life as possible. Commit no crimes. Forget you ever knew Majid or me. If you promise to do that, I won't kill you."

Dana removed a switchblade from her purse and cut the rope binding her captive's wrists.

Excitedly, Fajer said, "I promise. You can trust me. May Allah bless you for not killing me."

She followed him down the stairs and gestured to Majid all is well.

"Fajer is leaving us. We'll never see or hear from him again. I'll explain later."

She bent over Abdullah, yanked off the duct tape from his mouth, and removed the ball. To Majid, she said. "Untie Abdullah. He's loyal."

When the young man rose shakily to his feet, still trembling, Dana embraced him warmly.

"Welcome to our cell. We'll make history together."

Majid whispered, "*Allahu Akbar*."

CHAPTER 68

Jolene and Alex were cloistered in his office discussing next steps to stop Dana from deploying the nuclear weapons.

Jolene said, "We're reasonably certain Dana's principal target is the Pentagon. We have no way of knowing her second target, though."

Alex nodded in agreement. "It's essential to include the FBI on the task force. Dana's in the States. From now on, everything's *domestic terrorism.* The FBI has primary jurisdiction. In theory, the CIA is barred from operating within the US. But that's not going to stop Rick Birmingham and whoever is helping him."

"Nothing we can do about the CIA," she said. "Let's focus on *our* operation. Amal is FBI and she has the best all-around knowledge of terrorism of anyone on our team. Randy is new to our group, but he's familiar with FBI counterterrorism operations."

"Okay. FBI liaison is covered," he said.

"Courtney should be part of the task force," Jolene said. "She's the most creative person I know in the nuts and bolts of terrorist operations. What I can't figure out is how we should deploy the attack dogs . . . Steve, Mike, and the Navy SEALs." She'd begun to adopt Alex's shorthand for the military members of their team whose primary role was killing the enemy, either on defense or offense. Our problem is we don't have enough brain trusters . . ." she paused, aware of what she'd just said. She looked pointedly at Alex and saw him trying to hide the hint of a smile. "Okay. Come right out with it. Say 'I told you so.'"

"The thought never crossed my mind," he said, stifling a laugh.

More seriously, he added, "We should team Luke and Steve with Courtney, Amal, and Randy. Both guys served in the Pentagon and could make a valuable contribution. They've been close to our investigation from the beginning."

She said, "We still have to decide how to use the remaining members of our team. Apart from you and me, we have Felix, who's Mossad and a brilliant scientist."

"How's this for an idea," he said. "We form two teams operating independently. You head one team with Mike and Bob. Felix heads the other team, backed up by Fred. I'll stay at NCTC with communication support from Tommy Lee and Sally."

"That could work, but that leaves Felix shorthanded. George Southern is spinning his wheels since the action has moved to the States. He's a trained CIA operative, and he works well with our team. He's probably the only person from the CIA we can trust. Get him transferred to the task force."

"You're right. George would be a big help. We need anyone who's up to speed on what we're doing and how we function. I'll call and ask Mansfield to make it happen ASAP."

Alex looked at her closely. She'd told him about her sexual history with George while both were in training at the Farm. "Are you sure you want George teamed with Felix and not with you."

Her eyes twinkled. "George is a cherished part of my history. My romantic future lies elsewhere."

CHAPTER 69

Reema awoke as if from a drugged sleep. Her last memory was of Dana bringing her into the master bedroom, removing her clothes, giving her a short nightgown to wear, and tucking her tenderly under the sheet.

As she came fully alert, awareness grew that Dana was asleep in an easy chair placed between the bed and a window through which an early morning sun was shining.

Her first impulse was to panic. What should she do? Get out of bed quietly so as not to awaken her boss? Pretend to go back to sleep? Carefully nudge Dana awake and try to learn about her assignment?

At that moment, Dana awoke. She held out her arms and Reema came into her embrace. She stroked her hair, kissed her forehead, and began to whisper.

"You say you're loyal."

Reema lifted her head to look Dana in the eyes, responding in a hushed voice. "Yes, I'd give my life for you."

"You told Majid you will devote yourself to our goals."

"Without question."

"I have a mission for you. You must learn to seduce a woman."

Surprised, Reema jumped to her feet.

Despite her taunting Majid that she had no objection to having sex with a woman, she'd never had a lesbian relationship. Although, she had come close with her freshman roommate one night until mutual embarrassment overcame libido and they both lost their nerve.

"What?" she exclaimed, as if she failed to understand what Dana had just said.

"You heard me. Our mission requires the cooperation of a professional woman who will do what we need her to do only if she has a powerful incentive. Your assignment is to become an object of sexual desire so intense, the woman will do anything to make you want her as much as she will come to covet you."

"There's more to developing a close relationship between two people than sex," Reema protested primly. "There's friendship, mutual admiration, and many other feelings."

"Those other things become important if you're taking a psychology course. But love and intimacy take time to develop, while sexual desire can be stimulated in the moment. The only thing that should matter to you, Reema, is that I want you to seduce a professional woman in your first encounter. Will you do it? Are you willing to learn how?"

"Yes, if you'll teach me."

"I'll teach you."

Reema waited breathlessly, wondering what would happen next.

Dana began to explain.

"Your target is a high-ranking civilian in the Pentagon. She's about my age, good-looking, although by no means drop dead gorgeous. I tried to seduce her myself. She invited me to join her for drinks and dinner at a fancy restaurant in Georgetown. However, when I observed her looking over patrons at nearby tables, I realized she was more intrigued by attractive women in their twenties than she was by me."

Reema listened, fascinated by the surprising anecdote.

"After dinner, I made a lame excuse not to accompany her home and never saw her again. Since Majid described you as saucy and sexy, I decided you would be the one to seduce her."

Reema was intrigued by the challenge of seducing a woman Dana had been unable to beguile.

Dana said, "After the seduction, once the target has fallen into a deep sleep, it will be time for you to undertake the important part of your mission."

"What?" Reema asked, startled, assuming the seduction would be the goal that was expected of her.

"You must open the target's purse and remove her car keys. Call Majid on your cell and tell him you're ready. He'll send Abdullah to the door. When he arrives, he'll rap very quietly. Open the door and give him the keys. In about a half hour, Abdullah will return with the keys. Put them back in the target's purse."

"And then what should I do?"

"Enjoy the rest of the night and the next morning in whatever way pleases you and the target. Sleep. A sexual encore. Anything. So long as it does nothing to arouse the target's suspicion."

"I understand."

"She'll send you away when she goes to work. After you leave, head for Tysons and shop. Buy yourself a beautiful outfit—I'll give you five hundred dollars for spending money. When you finish shopping, return to your apartment in Reston. By then you should be very tired. Stay home tomorrow night. I'll contact you the next day and tell you what I need you to do."

"What will Majid and Abdullah do with her car?"

"That, my dear, is nothing to concern you."

CHAPTER 70

Reema awoke to sunshine pouring in through the bay window on the east side of the building. She rolled over on one elbow and watched Barbara Willoughby sleep. Since accomplishing her seduction, she'd learned more than the woman's name. Once her lust had been satiated, Barbara had confided her innermost secrets to the lover who shared her bed.

"I shoplifted jewelry compulsively when I was sixteen . . . My master's degree in political science at a prestigious university—I won't embarrass by naming—was earned by virtue of liberally plagiarizing my thesis . . . When I travel on the Pentagon's dime, I always pad my expense account . . . I never have an orgasm during sex with a man."

The seduction was a mind-blowing experience, but Reema quickly tired of Barbara's confessions. Although the story she told about one man's frenetic efforts trying to bring her to a climax was hilarious.

• • •

Ever the gracious hostess, Barbara fed Reema a sumptuous breakfast. After which, they showered together, and she dressed for work. When ready to depart, she kissed her lover and offered her a ride. Reema declined. They left together. Saying goodbye reluctantly, Barbara took the elevator to the garage, climbed in her car, and drove to work.

She parked in her customary spot in the Pentagon lot, beeped the car locked, and strolled toward the nearest entrance. Memories of loving embraces the previous night occupied her thoughts. Unaware the name and phone number Reema gave her were phony, she resolved to call Reema later in the day and see if they could get together that evening for another romp.

CHAPTER 71

Amal escaped the Pentagon meeting room and fled to the restroom with Courtney. "If I have to endure another five minutes of Rick Birmingham spouting off about how the CIA should have a monopoly of the search for the suitcase nukes, I'll shoot the bastard."

"Not if I get a crack at him first," Courtney said. "Or I may just have Luke and Steve follow him into a bar tonight."

They continued joking while making their ablutions side by side.

"Yeah," Amal said. "Did you hear the one about three men who walked into a bar and only two came out?"

They both had a laugh, mostly at themselves for the clumsy attempt to relieve the tension of a half-day spent in another boring and largely fruitless multi-agency task force meeting.

"It could be worse," Courtney said. "If Frank Mansfield hadn't intervened with the president, Birmingham and Farnsworth would have convinced Pentagon officials to throw us off the task force this morning on the grounds the CIA has the ball in tracking the nukes while we're limited to catching Dana and company."

"Yeah," Amal said. "Then I'd be home taking a nice nap, instead of going back to the meeting room to endure another four hours of bullshit."

Courtney got serious for a moment as they strolled back to the room. "So far, we haven't learned any tactics for deploying the nuke other than those we brainstormed at NCTC."

Stopping in midstride in the corridor, Amal mentally reviewed the tactics Courtney had summarized on the whiteboard. A virtually eidetic memory enabled her to visualize them:

SECURITY TO ENTER PENTAGON

DELIVERY TRUCK

PARKING PERMIT

PENTAGON TRANSIT CENTER

"You're right. We've spent half a day covering the same ground. And no one at the Pentagon has a clue which tactic the terrorists are most likely to use."

Courtney said, "The only progress we've made is the agreement to have a bomb disposal squad with training in disarming nuclear weapons on constant standby. If we get an alert to the location of the suitcase nuke, the squad can be deployed at a moment's notice."

"The FBI is taking the same precautions in the District," Amal said. "The FBI's bomb disposal techs have formed a joint team with ATF and the Metropolitan Police Department's bomb squad."

Just before they entered the meeting room, Amal's cell phone vibrated. She glanced at the screen and recognized the call from one of her contacts in the FBI Counterterrorism Division. "I've got to take this. Let's walk back to the restroom."

Moving aside for a couple of squared-away junior officers hurrying down the hall, she slipped the phone in a jacket pocket, removing it when the coast was clear.

Speaking in a hushed voice into the phone, she said, "What do you have for me?" She knew the FBI's counterterrorism offices were staffed with a sprinkling of CIA officers. She'd cautioned her colleagues to be careful what sensitive intelligence they shared and how, so no information leaked to Birmingham or Farnsworth.

Her contact said, "A few days ago, the FBI got a lead on a guy named Fajer Karim. We'd heard stories he'd been self-radicalized by watching ISIS propaganda on the internet. Two special agents tried to recruit him as a paid informant. He declined the offer. But they decided to have him followed. Day before yesterday, he entered a house in Pimmit Hills, Virginia, near Tysons."

"I know the area," Amal interrupted.

Her contact continued. "Later, he left the house and walked to the Silver Line Tysons Corner Station. He was tailed, but we lost him after metro travel was disrupted in an accident, and all passengers were supposed to catch a bus. He skipped the bus and disappeared."

"Why am I just hearing about this?" Amal demanded angrily.

"Unfortunately, the special agents were called away on another emergency and only just got around to reporting the fiasco of losing Karim."

"Give me the address in Pimmit Hills."

After she got the information, she hung up and called Alex. She summarized what she'd been told.

"I'll send Jolene's team to Pimmit Hills."

Amal cut him off. "She just has Mike and Bob to back her up. That's a lot of fire power, but we don't know if Dana is in the house, and, if she is, how many terrorists are with her."

"Don't worry," Alex said. "I'm only ten minutes away. I can get there before Jolene's team. If the situation looks hairy, I'll have Felix and his guys join us before we breach the house."

"Guys . . . that would be Fred and George Southern. Has George arrived from Germany already?"

"He flew in this morning. Claims he's ready for action, even though he still looks jet lagged."

Amal said, "Courtney and I will soldier on in our task force meeting. So far, no one has come up with new ideas about where the terrorists might attempt to strike with the bomb or any significant changes in ways to defend against an attack. But the good news is we now have a Pentagon bomb squad on standby."

CHAPTER 72

Dana's cell was in the process of regrouping after she decided it was too risky to remain in the house in Pimmit Hills, despite Fajer's assertions he'd not compromised their security. She wasn't willing to take chances at this stage of their operation.

Since they'd disposed of the SUVs, the suitcase nukes had been stored in the trunks of two roomy sedans: a Mercedes-Benz 2015 C-Class and a 2014 BMW. The Benz was used to convey one of the bombs to the trunk of the Pentagon woman's vehicle after Reema "borrowed" her keys in the aftermath of seducing her the previous night.

Dana had Majid move the BMW from the garage in Pimmit Hills to the parking garage at Union Station. The Beemer would have little chance of being discovered there, and the nuke would be available anytime, day or night. He also parked his getaway vehicle, a 2013 Hyundai Elantra, at Union Station.

Abdullah registered at a motel in Arlington, not far from Arlington Cemetery, within walking distance of the Pentagon. Majid was staying at a modest hotel in the District, from which he could take the metro to Union Station.

Dana's first thought was that she would sleep in her office at George Mason University, taking for granted her condo in Fairfax City was not an option. The office had once been the domain of the head of the history department before he retired. It boasted a small bathroom with a shower, a comfortable couch, a refrigerator, and a microwave—during crunch projects, she'd stayed there in the past. No sooner had she entertained that thought than the absurdity of it struck her. She suspected the authorities had learned her real name, and her GMU office would be staked out as well as her condo residence.

She opted for the Four Seasons Hotel in Georgetown, a mere ten-minute drive in the Benz to the motel near Arlington Cemetery where she and Abdullah were scheduled to meet. Once again, she followed the principle of hiding in plain sight as most likely to confound her pursuers.

Remembering her last conversation with Reema, she smiled when she imagined the young woman's consternation when it dawned on her the directive to shop at Tysons and then go home and wait for Dana's call was a simple case of misdirection. Dana had no intention of contacting her anytime in the future. She was anxious only for Reema to be in a location where she would be safe when two nuclear bombs exploded in the Washington area. Life was her reward for an interlude of sexual instruction, as pleasant for the teacher as for the pupil.

Taking into account the diminished number of members in her cell and growing concerns about pressure from the NCTC, FBI, CIA, and other intelligence agencies, Dana decided her second nuclear bomb would be unleashed in the District. The Capitol loomed as the favored target, the choice governed in part by expediency. Time was running out, and no further changes in strategy could be entertained.

Assisted by Abdullah in the event of any technical glitches, her plan was to use her cell phone to detonate the bomb parked at the Pentagon in the trunk of the target Barbara Willoughby's sedan. Majid would detonate the second bomb in the BMW parked on a street near the Capitol. Both weapons were scheduled to explode at four that afternoon. At four o'clock, the Washington area was guaranteed to be clogged with rush hour traffic. Emergency vehicles would be trapped in gridlock. The carnage would be absolute.

At the moment of the historic explosions, the terrorists planned to be driving safely out of town, Abdullah and Dana in the Benz and

Majid in the Hyundai. Dana's instruction was to regroup in New York City, where they would be lost among millions. She had no intention of traveling to New York. En route, she would dispose of Abdullah—hopefully without finding it necessary to kill him—and launch her escape plan to the destination of her retirement.

Each evening since acquiring the nukes at the Port of New York, she'd spent a few moments thinking about where she would go and how she would spend the millions stashed in her savings accounts in Switzerland and the Cayman Islands. She revisited her fantasy of spending time on a topless beach on the French Riviera—each replay growing more elaborate. The fantasy culminated in a fancy bedroom in a hotel in Saint-Tropez on the Côte d'Azur, where a man who bore a distinct resemblance to Joffrey Gobert made passionate love with her throughout the night.

CHAPTER 73

Alex approached the address Amal was given by her FBI contact. He drove slowly by, eyeballing the nearly brand-new custom home. Nothing unusual in the style for the revamped Pimmit Hills community: gray cement-board siding, two stories, three to four bedrooms, with a welcoming front porch and a two-car garage. Undoubtedly listed for just over one million dollars. An upscale, multiethnic neighborhood, typical of the Vienna-Tysons area for the past decade.

Circling the block, he decided to park and walk in from the opposite street, cutting through the adjoining backyards, to approach the house from the rear. There were no fences hindering access. Lawns were green and neatly mowed, either by the resident owners or the ubiquitous lawn services that roamed Northern Virginia.

Looking around the neighborhood on a sunny midday, he spotted no nosy neighbors. This was an area where, in the typical household, both men and women commuted to their jobs. Children went to school or, in the summer, to childcare or organized sports. By local ordinances, which were strictly enforced, dogs were kept on a leash or inside the house. He heard no barking.

While waiting for Jo, Mike, and Bob to arrive, Alex checked the garage. Peering in through a side window, he confirmed both bays of the two-car garage were empty. He walked around to the rear door and turned the knob. Unlocked. Entering, he marveled at the orderly interior and mentally compared it to his cluttered garage where various categories of junk (which he rationalized were all essential for some unspecified future purpose) filled one bay, barely leaving room for his Range Rover. Looking down, he confirmed the garage floor was clean and clear of defacing oil spots. He sniffed, and, apart from a lingering odor of gasoline, could smell nothing.

Any cars that had been garaged here were new and in good condition. He suspected they were also long gone. The only tools hanging on the walls were a broom and a lawn rake. An old-fashioned power lawnmower was shoved in a corner. Several black garbage bags were neatly folded and lying on a near-vacant shelf.

He mumbled to himself, "If the garage is any indication, the terrorists have already fled to parts unknown."

Scowling, he exited the rear door and quietly closed it.

Motion across the expanse of the two yards caught his eye. Jo's Beemer was parking behind his Range Rover. Mike Sato climbed out of the passenger seat. Bob Xavier exited the rear door. Neither man tried overly hard to conceal the MP5 submachine gun strapped under his blue blazer.

Alex smiled. The attack dogs have arrived, ready to rock and roll.

He waved them over, and they clustered at the rear of the garage.

"As far as I can tell, there are no nosy neighbors watching. The garage is empty and looks like it's barely been used. It appears Dana's cell has flown the coop. We'll be cautious going in, just in case."

His comment was met with quiet nods. No one was gung-ho.

Alex glanced at his watch, 1:05 p.m.

"Jo, you and Mike take the rear door and clear the downstairs and basement. Bob and I will take the front door and clear upstairs. We go in sixty seconds."

The entry and search was accomplished without incident. The place was cleaned out, and the terrorists' departure confirmed.

Alex called the team together in the living room.

Jo said, "The coffee maker in the kitchen still contains a cup of lukewarm coffee. Looks like they left this morning."

Bob ran down the stairs and hurried into the room. "I may have something. This scrap of paper was discarded on the floor of one of the smaller bedrooms."

He handed the note to Alex, who held it up to the light and read it aloud. It contained the name and address of a motel.

"Motel 1, Arlington."

"Dana was shorthanded," Jo said. "One of her new members hasn't had time to be trained to her usual standard."

"Let's roll," Alex said. "Jo, you ride with me. Give your keys to Mike."

They hurried outside, slamming the rear door closed.

Alex started the Range Rover and peeled out of the parking space. "Call Felix and tell him to bring his team and meet us at the motel in Arlington. Call Amal and have her alert the FBI to what's going down. If a forensic team scrubs the Pimmit Hills house, they may find something we missed.

As Jo opened the door and climbed in the Range Rover, Alex said, "Phone Amal. Tell her to burn rubber and meet us at the motel. We may need her ability to speak to the terrorists, assuming any of them can't or won't speak to us in English. Ask Courtney to take charge of developments at the Pentagon."

CHAPTER 74

Coming from the Pentagon, Amal was the first to arrive at Motel 1. She brought Luke in case the situation evolved into a firefight. She hesitated before getting out of the car.

"We'll wait until Alex and Jolene get here. At this point, we don't know whether we're dealing with one terrorist or the entire cell, however many that might be."

"Let's talk to the desk clerk," Luke said. "He may be able to tell us what room the guests are in and how many there are."

"Good idea." She exited the car, drew her pistol, and concealed it under her jacket.

The man at the desk appeared to be in his fifties and had spent too much time catering to patrons at third-rate establishments. His white shirt was wrinkled. A garish tie with a small stain that could be mustard did nothing to improve his appearance. A five o'clock shadow was more than two hours early. He looked ready for a nap.

He scowled at the unwanted patrons and uttered a perfunctory greeting. "How can I help you?"

Luke stepped forward and leaned on the desk, towering over the clerk.

In a voice loaded with menace, he said, "This morning you rented one or more rooms to terrorists. Unless you want to spend the rest of your few remaining years in prison, you'll tell this lady anything she wants to know."

Terrified, the man looked first at Amal, next at Luke, then back to Amal. He was afraid he'd guess wrong about whom to address.

Near babbling, he said, "I'll tell you everything. Actually, I don't know anything. Some young Muslim-looking guy came in alone early this morning and rented a room for three nights, starting last night so he could have immediate access to the room. Some woman made a reservation for him over the phone yesterday with a credit card, so I thought he was legit. He's in room 203 in the back. You can use my master key if you want."

Amal held out her hand. "Give."

He fumbled to remove the key from his chain and passed it to her.

"What else do you know?" she demanded.

"He didn't have a car, but that didn't seem suspicious. Lots of people who stay here for a few nights don't have cars. The woman didn't come with him. This place may not look fancy, but it's not a hot-sheet motel." The man tried to look indignant at the idea he'd be a party to anything sordid, drawing himself up to his full height of five feet seven inches.

"Show me a floor plan of the second floor."

The man opened a drawer in the front desk and handed her the floor plan for the motel.

The sound of Alex and Jolene charging through the door caused Amal to react by whirling and pointing her pistol at Alex, who was in the lead. "Sorry. Next time, don't forget to knock."

Strictly business, Alex frowned. "What have you learned so far?"

"A young Muslim guy checked in early this morning. A woman reserved the room for him, starting last night for three nights. He's alone in room 203 in the back."

She showed the floor plan to Alex and Jolene.

Alex pointed to Luke. "Stay here and keep our friend company. Phone us if any of the other terrorists show up. The three of us will head for room 203."

He put his phone on mute and gestured to Jo and Amal to do the same.

Once outside room 203, he held his finger to his lips. He eased the master key into the door, turned the knob, and quietly entered the room. He spied the young man lying on the room's only bed, sound asleep on his stomach and snoring loudly enough to serenade the neighbors if any were around.

• • •

Jolene whispered to Amal, "Handcuff him and give me the key."

Amal holstered her pistol, opened her purse, and removed a set of handcuffs. She sidled up to the bed, grabbed the terrorist by the left wrist, and fastened the cuff. When the man awoke, he struggled to escape. She seized his right wrist, torqued it behind his back, and chained both hands together.

Dragging a desk chair next to the bed, Alex lifted the man and forced him to sit in the chair.

Dazed and terrified, the subject stared at his captors. "Why are you hassling me? I didn't do anything. Are you cops? Am I under arrest?" His eyes fixed on Amal, who leveled her pistol at him. "Don't shoot."

Not saying a word, Amal stepped forward and pressed the weapon against his forehead.

Jolene pushed the pistol aside and moved in front of Amal.

"We won't have to kill him. I'm sure he'll cooperate." Jolene played *good cop* in the *good cop/bad cop* scenario. She leaned over the young man, as though they were partners in crime, and spoke in a quiet voice. "To answer your question, no, we're not cops. We're your worst nightmare."

Amal continued to look threatening.

Jolene said, "What's your name?"

"Abdullah . . . Abdullah Khauli."

"See, I told you he'd cooperate. There's no need to kill him," Jolene said triumphantly, looking over her shoulder at Alex and Amal, as though she'd just won an argument. "How old are you?"

"Twenty-five." By this point, Abdullah had the message loud and clear. To survive, he had to cooperate.

"Stand up," Jolene said. When he complied, she added, "Turn

around."

She unlocked the handcuffs and handed them to Amal, along with the key.

"He won't need these. Abdullah has proven he's eager to cooperate."

Pushing gently on Abdullah's chest, she eased him back into the chair.

"Now, listen carefully to what I have to say and don't interrupt. We know you're a terrorist. And we know you're helping Dana Hussein al-Sadi who plans to explode two nuclear weapons in the Washington area."

"NO," he screamed.

She shushed him. "Please, you were winning points for cooperating. Don't blow it. If I'm convinced you're working with me and telling the truth, I'll find a way to shorten your stay in prison."

Abdullah gasped.

"Yes. You *will* spend time in prison. But how long and how severely you're treated can be determined by those of us in this room. I'm with the Feds." She pulled out her credentials and flashed them in front of Abdullah, too rapidly for him to take in her agency. "I have the power to influence whether you'll serve time at a supermax prison where the felons are alone in a cell twenty-three hours a day, and the other hour they live in fear of being beaten up or stabbed with a shiv. Or you could be sent to a country club prison where all the white-collar criminals go. I can determine whether you'll be sentenced to life in prison or only a few years."

She pulled her pistol and pointed it between his eyes. "If you refuse to cooperate, I will shoot you right here, right now."

Abdullah shuddered, reacting as though he feared death was only seconds away.

"You choose your destiny. Tell me the truth, the whole truth right now, and I'll be merciful. Lie or continue to deny, and this will be your last moments on earth. Or you may experience time in prison that'll feel like an eternity in hell."

Shaken to the core by the threats from the one person in the room he believed to be his salvation, Abdullah was sobbing. His shoulders were shaking.

"I'll give you one last chance to cooperate, Abdullah. What are Dana's plans?"

He wiped away the tears, with the air of having decided to gamble on his female captor's mercy.

Startling everyone, the alarm on Abdullah's cell phone began buzzing.

"Don't shoot," he screamed, holding up his hands to ward off the expected attack. "That's my wake-up call. Dana's meeting me here in twenty minutes, at three o'clock. We'll leave here, headed for New York. Dana needs me."

When Jolene raised her eyebrows skeptically, he said, "I may look like a kid, but I'm a trained scientist." He threw his chest out proudly as if to prove the boast. "I know how to activate the suitcase nuke, or to troubleshoot if there's a problem. The bomb was okay when Majid and I examined it last night after we placed it in the trunk of the car of the woman Reema seduced. She called me to hand off the woman's car keys. I gave them back after we hid the bomb."

Near babbling, he stared at Jolene to see how his words were being received. Reassured she took no aggressive action, he continued, speaking somewhat more confidently. "The woman was expected to drive to her job at the Pentagon. Dana only needs me if something goes wrong with the bomb, but nothing can go wrong. She'll detonate the nuke at four o'clock sharp while we're driving out of town."

Jolene stared at her teammates, presenting a calm facade, but astonished at the matter-of-fact revelations of the young terrorist.

Abdullah continued to talk, the floodgates now open. His voice was filled with pride at his role in the historic attack to come. "The bomb can only be detonated from Dana's cell phone. She dials a certain number and enters the code. Majid and Dana are the only ones who know the codes. Unless someone goes through the correct procedure, the bombs are safe."

Jolene cleared her throat, trying to hide how shaken she was by the thought of a nuclear weapon exploding at the Pentagon, less than two miles away. "You're doing very well, Abdullah. I'm proud of you. Tell me the name of the woman Reema seduced."

"Barbara Willoughby."

"And Barbara works for the Pentagon?"

"Of course. The whole point is that her parking place is close enough to the building to ensure a lot of casualties and maximum damage."

Jolene glanced at Amal who pulled out her cell phone as she ran from the room.

"Of course. That's good to know. You're racking up a lot of points on the board, Abdullah. If you keep going this way, your future will look much brighter."

Abdullah relaxed slightly.

"Tell me. What are the plans for the second suitcase nuke?"

"I have nothing to do with that. It's entirely Majid's responsibility."

Jolene nodded. "I see. And where is that bomb?"

"Majid keeps it in the trunk of a BMW in the parking garage at Union Station. He plans to park the BMW near Congress. He'll call from his cell phone and enter the code number to trigger the bomb at 4:00 p.m., while driving out of town in a green Hyundai Elantra."

"What's the color and model of the BMW?"

"Red. A 2014 BMW 3 sedan." Abdullah was preening at being able to show off his knowledge of vehicle models.

Jolene gestured to Alex, who quickly exited the room.

She knew at this juncture both the bomb squad on standby at the Pentagon and the one in the District would be alerted. She breathed a sigh of relief. They weren't out of the woods, but, at long last, things were beginning to look up.

Abdullah had fed them the targets of the two suitcase nukes—

the Pentagon, which they'd long suspected was Dana's primary objective—and Congress. She tried to think what further information she could pry from the pliable youth.

"Where is Reema, and what's her role at this point, since she succeeded in seducing Barbara Willoughby and getting you her car keys?"

"Her only job was to seduce Barbara. She was a huge success. I last saw her at Willoughby's condo when she gave me the keys to Barbara's car so we could put the nuke in the trunk. Dana never told us what Reema was to do next or where she was going. She's a nice girl, very sexy. I wish her next job were to seduce me." Abdullah blushed. "I hope she'll be okay when the bombs explode."

"We need you to tell us the names and assignments of other members of your cell."

"There are no other members. Majid told us everyone else was killed. When I was recruited, another Muslim, named Fajer, was rejected. He had attracted the attention of the FBI, so Dana sent him away."

"What kind of car is Dana driving?"

"A Mercedes-Benz 2015 C-Class sedan," he said.

Jolene concluded she'd gotten all the information possible from Abdullah. The most crucial action was to forestall the bomb explosions, which was up to the bomb squads.

At that moment, Amal and Alex returned.

"I alerted the bomb squad at the Pentagon," Amal said. "They'll pinpoint where Barbara Willoughby's car is parked and begin disarming the nuke."

Jolene threw Alex a questioning look.

He gave her a grim smile. "The MPD Bomb Squad is deploying near the Capitol. Within minutes, they'll have dozens of cops, FBI special agents, ATF, and Capitol Police searching for a red Beemer."

"So far, so good," Jolene said. "There's nothing more *we* can do about the two nukes. *Our* priority is to apprehend Dana and any of her cell members who are still at large."

Alex asked Jolene, "What more have we learned from Abdullah?"

"He's been extremely cooperative. We know the only terrorists from that cell still at large are Dana, Majid, and Reema. The others are dead or captured."

"It only takes one to detonate two suitcase nukes," Alex muttered.

"No, two," Jolene said. "Dana is scheduled to pick up Abdullah here at Motel 1 at three o'clock. She's driving a Mercedes-Benz 2015 C-Class sedan. At four o'clock sharp, she'll detonate the nuke parked at the Pentagon in the trunk of Barbara Willoughby's car. Dana and Abdullah will leave here headed for New York City where they plan to meet up with Majid."

Alex looked puzzled.

Jolene clarified what she'd learned from Abdullah.

"Majid's job is to detonate the nuke in the trunk of a red Beemer parked near Congress. That explosion is also scheduled to occur at four o'clock. Then he'll travel to the New York rendezvous."

"What about Reema?"

"Reema's whereabouts are unknown. She left Barbara Willoughby this morning. Abdullah said Dana never told the others in the cell where Reema would be going or what she would be doing. We can ask Courtney to question Willoughby to see if she can shed any light on what Reema is up to."

Amal said, "I'll call Courtney and ask her to quiz Willoughby."

CHAPTER 75

Participants fled the meeting room when word leaked the Pentagon's bomb disposal squad would be searching for a suitcase nuke hidden in the trunk of Barbara Willoughby's car. Wearing protective gear—not that it would prolong their life if a nuclear bomb exploded near them—the bomb squad technicians rushed out to disarm the device.

Rick Birmingham stood next to Elmer Farnsworth outside the Pentagon meeting room. "The president gave the CIA the primary responsibility for finding the nukes," Rick said. "Alex and Jolene exceeded their authority."

Elmer looked at his partner in conspiracy as though he'd lost his mind. "Do you think President Scofield or anyone else will give a rat's ass about that? Alex and his team won the game. Jolene scored the winning touchdown. She got the young terrorist to tell us their plans to bomb the Pentagon and the Congress. Every one of those NCTC bastards is a hero. In this town," he and Rick had it in common to think of the Pentagon as an integral part of Washington, "success is the only currency that spends. Today, you and I represent failure. We'll be lucky if we keep our jobs."

"I won't stand for being branded a failure. I'll find a way to blame the outcome on Jolene."

Shaking his head, Elmer said, "Rick, I say this to you as the closest thing you have to a friend. You're full of shit. We lost." Watching Rick's face redden with uncontrolled anger, he said, "If you continue to push it, Jolene will retaliate by reopening the attempted rape charge against you. You need to face it. Everyone, including me, knows you're guilty. Jolene's mistake was to accuse you lacking evidence. Her dad has been working quietly behind the scenes to set the stage for her to reopen the case." Elmer laughed nervously, "Now that she's the queen of Alex's merry band of heroes, she won't need proof. All she'll have to do is repeat the accusation. She's untouchable. If she ran for sheriff in Dogpatch against Li'l Abner, Jolene would win in a landslide."

CHAPTER 76

Dana pulled under the portico at Motel 1 and scanned up and down the street for any sign of the Feds. Seeing no evidence she was in danger, she parked the Benz facing out in the event she needed to make a quick getaway. Why wasn't Abdullah out front waiting for her to pick him up? She glanced at her watch and confirmed the time was three o'clock.

She mentally reviewed the instructions she'd given her recruit. There was no possibility of a misunderstanding. She was scheduled to arrive at three. She and Abdullah would head out of town, toward Baltimore on I-95, ultimate destination supposedly New York.

The prudent thing would be to kill Abdullah en route, and then activate her escape plan. But her conscience rebelled. She would have no hesitation in taking the young man's life if he betrayed her. Only a bit less if he posed an obvious threat. But, in his short time with the cell, Abdullah had been loyal. According to Majid, he'd been a helpful partner in obtaining the keys from Reema after she had seduced Barbara Willoughby. He'd assisted in placing the suitcase nuke in Barbara's trunk. He stood ready to provide technical support in activating the Pentagon nuke in the unlikely event his assistance was required. In short, Abdullah did everything expected of him and did it capably.

The verdict, if she were to remain true to her own values: Abdullah earned the right to live. She decided he would accompany her to Baltimore. There, she would see him safely on the Acela Express train to New York where he could meet Majid, if Amtrak was still operating. The two men could work out their future together. She would travel alone to her destiny.

Having stood motionless by the front door of the motel while she resolved the moral dilemma regarding her new recruit's life, Dana took a hard look inside the lobby. Why was no one at the front desk?

No Abdullah. No clerk. No one in the empty lobby.

Were it not for her preoccupation with Abdullah's fate, her spidey sense would have alerted her to danger sooner.

She eased back to the Benz, quietly opened the door, and slipped behind the wheel. Wasting no motion, she peeled rubber and had the car racing toward the entrance to Route 66, the fastest road out of the Washington area.

Abdullah betrayed her.

Given the opportunity, she would kill him without further thought.

He must have told the authorities of her plans to meet Majid in New York. That she never had any intention of traveling to New York was irrelevant. She knew all roads toward Baltimore and points north would be subject to the tightest scrutiny in history.

In an instant, her itinerary changed. She was no longer headed north.

She'd flee south and west.

The kernel of a once abandoned plan began to grow in her brain. *Now was the time to kill Jolene,* the woman who, more than anyone, sought to foil her plans to destroy the Great Satan.

One final question remained: should she detonate the bomb at the Pentagon the second she got out of range or wait until the appointed hour of four o'clock?

CHAPTER 77

Jolene looked around at the sound of the door banging as Luke came charging into Room 203. She wondered what prompted him to desert his post guarding the front desk.

"What happened, Luke?"

"Dana arrived and got spooked. The guy at the desk was having a seizure. I was trying to settle him down in the adjoining office. By the time I decided it wasn't necessary to call 911 and checked what was going on outside, Dana was peeling out of the parking lot. My guess is she's heading for Route 66."

Amal said, "I'll alert the FBI to reactivate the BOLO for terrorists and follow up with state police and local cops. She's probably guessed Abdullah spilled the beans. New York is the last place she'll go."

"Let's hope she sticks to her timetable," Alex said. "If she detonates the nuke at the Pentagon before the bomb squad has time to defuse it, we're all screwed."

Jolene glanced at her watch: 3:03 p.m. "Whatever motivates Dana, she's not suicidal. She's a survivor. Her goal is to avenge her brother Jake by destroying the Pentagon. She'll give herself another half hour to get out of range at the earliest."

She fixed Alex with a questioning stare. "Should we alert the bomb squads at the Pentagon and the Capitol of the need to work faster, just in case?"

He took a moment to decide.

"No. They're going to be doing their best against what they were told is the timetable. No point in distracting them and wasting precious seconds or minutes when we're only guessing."

CHAPTER 78

Felicia Pepperdine—daughter of a cop and sister of two, with eight years on the District of Columbia Metropolitan Police Department, the last three on the Bomb Squad, six months in charge of the unit—was inevitably nicknamed Pepper. With flowing honey-blond hair and of medium height, she not only resembled Angie Dickinson in her TV role of *Police Woman* as "Pepper," but her quick, hot temper made the moniker fit.

However, when Pepper was on the job, her personality was transformed. She became as cold as ice. She was well below zero today, jogging the streets around the Capitol area, searching for a red Beemer.

"Over here, Pepper," her partner Stan Ralston yelled, pointing to a red sedan parked half a block from the Hart Senate Office Building.

The two cops hustled to the suspect vehicle. Neither was wearing a protective suit, even though others in the squad were required to, even today. Pepper and Stan had the primary responsibility for defusing the nuke, and, when minutes and seconds were crucial, they gave priority to freedom of movement. Also, being realists, they knew the extra safety was illusory when inches from a nuclear weapon, however small.

Pepper waved to the MPD Bomb Squad truck, trailing them up the street, to pull forward.

Two technicians, decked out in the full array of bomb squad protective gear, hurried to the rear of the BMW. They had their instructions from Pepper: "Open the fucking trunk and get your asses out of the way."

"Holy shit," Stan said. "It looks like the real deal."

Pepper nodded solemnly "Our information says it is."

She reached in the trunk and felt around the casing holding the nuke. She could detect no obvious booby traps.

"Give me a hand getting this sucker out of the trunk."

For a brief time, before he injured the ACL in his right knee in a game against the Cowboys, Stan had been a two-hundred-forty-pound tight end for the Washington Redskins in their years before they became known as the Commanders. The powerful man could have manhandled the bomb by himself. But he followed Pepper's lead, and gave her a hand.

Pepper removed the casing and examined the triggering mechanism. She glanced at her watch.

"We have thirteen minutes to disarm this bomb," she muttered.

Stan gave a mirthless chuckle. "Let's hope the goddamned terrorists set their watches accurately. If four o'clock comes too soon, we're screwed."

One of the Bomb Squad crew ran up smiling. "*I got good news.* The Pentagon Bomb Squad successfully defused their suitcase nuke. They said, 'Just follow normal procedures.'"

Pepper looked up, scowling. "That's *bad* news. They had twenty minutes head start working on their bomb before we located ours. If we follow normal procedures, we're dead."

Stan nodded. "So, find a shortcut."

The two made a good team. Stan's equanimity in all situations nicely balanced Pepper's volatile temperament. For the most part, they kept their relationship strictly professional. The sole exception had occurred after a particularly hairy assignment when they'd gotten drunk to let off steam. The partners retired to Stan's tony condo in Adams Morgan and began playfully fooling around in his living room. A frolicking dance number led to a tender embrace, which ended with them sharing Stan's bed. The next morning, they'd agreed the sexual encounter could never be repeated since it would compromise their dangerous work environment.

After six minutes of manipulating the nuke's firing mechanism with her sensitive fingers, Pepper glanced at her watch.

"Seven minutes left. We can't afford to follow normal procedures."

Both technicians knew normal procedures involved taking careful step followed by careful step until the bomb was disarmed. Each step was designed to ensure the technician a ninety-plus percent safety margin before proceeding to the next move.

"I'm going to speed up the procedures," she said. Once I reach a fifty percent safety margin, I'm moving to the next step. Is that okay with you?"

"Roll the dice, partner," Stan replied calmly.

He kept a careful eye on her fingers caressing the mechanism, while monitoring the time.

"Two-minute warning."

"Fuck the confidence threshold," she muttered.

Now, he could barely follow the movement of her fingers.

At last, she leaned back and sighed with satisfaction and relief.

"Done. The nuke's safe."

"Piece of cake. You had thirty seconds to spare."

"That's thirty seconds extra you need to hold me in bed tonight."

CHAPTER 79

Majid drove out of the District on Interstate 95, headed for Baltimore, and pointed north to New York. He was proud of the role he'd played as Dana's second in command, confident their mission was coming to a successful end.

With Abdullah's help, he'd secured one of the suitcase nukes in the trunk of Barbara Willoughby's car. That morning, the target of Reema's seduction would have unwittingly driven her car to work and left it in her Pentagon parking space.

He glanced at his watch. In ten minutes, Dana would detonate the nuke at the Pentagon. Simultaneously, he would detonate the second nuke, which he'd parked on First Street, SE, between the Hart Senate Office Building and the Capitol building.

At the time of the explosions, he expected to be on the outskirts of Baltimore. He doubted he would hear the bombs being detonated or see the mushroom clouds. Should he turn the radio to WTOP so he could monitor the broadcasts of the horror in the Washington area? No. He wasn't sure he could handle the excitement of the moment and drive safely at the same time.

Without realizing what he was doing, he said aloud, "I'll wait until tonight when I'm in my hotel room in New York. Then I'll watch the spectacle on TV. They'll play it over and over for hours, just like 9/11, only worse."

His thoughts went back to the day when he heard the military spokesperson describing his Sunni father's death, along with fourteen other medical personnel, in a hospital, far from the nearest

ISIS battlefield, as an unfortunate incident of "collateral damage." He only regretted that the spokesperson would not be in the vicinity of the Capitol when the bomb destroyed the neighborhood with a blast and the ensuing nuclear fallout.

Majid's remembrances were interrupted by the distant sound of a police siren. Glancing in his rear-view mirror, he could see the tell-tale flashing lights of a police cruiser climbing the rim of the hill behind him in the distance. He had no doubt something had gone wrong, and the Maryland State Police were after him. Possibly Abdullah had been captured and told the authorities he was driving a Hyundai Elantra.

There was no way his car could outrun a police cruiser. Moreover, the Maryland State Police would simply call ahead to have other cruisers cut him off.

He saw the turnoff to Baltimore Washington International Airport. From past efforts to economize on air travel, he'd taken flights into BWI. The airport was only a short distance from I-95. Perhaps he could get lost in the confusion of the terminal and steal a car or escape in a taxi.

He made a quick decision and spun the wheel to head for BWI. The cruiser didn't keep him in suspense for long. In his rear view he could see the cruiser attempting the turn to follow him. The trooper must have lost control at high speed, and he veered into a ditch and crashed.

Majid put the pedal to the metal. The Hyundai surged forward. He calculated that with any luck at all, he would make it to BWI before being overtaken by other troopers who were tailing him. With the reprieve of losing the closest police car, he was confident he would arrive at the airport in time to arrange his escape.

Nervous tension mounted as the moments ticked away. He glanced at the clock on the dashboard. Four o'clock. It was time!

His fingers trembled as he dialed the number on his cell phone and entered the code that would command the explosion. Taking a deep breath, he pressed the green send button.

CHAPTER 80

Dana realized she was racing away from Motel 1 in a panic. Her first instinct was to head for Route 66 West as the quickest way to escape.

No. It was the quickest way to get caught. Because that's just what Jolene Martin would assume she'd do. If she had any hope of surviving long enough to end Jolene's life, much less enjoy a luxurious retirement, her first imperative was to dispose of the Benz.

She turned left at the next corner and headed in the direction of the Ballston metro. Her search focused on finding a large parking garage in the building complex clustered around the metro.

Once she spotted the parking entrance, she pulled in, took her ticket, drove to the highest floor, and searched for the darkest and most remote spot.

She parked and sat in the front seat, taking inventory of her possessions. She decided to abandon her suitcases in the trunk, concluding the only essentials were in her purse: her cell phone, her Glock, and two sets of phony ID.

She locked the Benz and carried the keys with her to be deposited in a convenient storm drain in the street.

Careful not to appear rushed, she hurried to the Ballston metro and boarded the first Silver Line train to Tysons.

On reaching the Hyatt Regency Tysons Hotel—where her adventure had begun with General Winston's assassination—she jumped in a taxi and directed the driver to take her to a nearby car rental office she remembered was a few blocks away.

The bellman who witnessed the comings and goings through the lobby on the night General Winston was killed was working days. By chance, around three thirty, he saw a woman climbing into a taxi whom he would swear was the spitting image of the female assassin. He fished in his billfold for the card Alex Werth had given him that fateful night with instructions to call if he thought of anything else. He dialed the number on his cell phone. Someone answered, "Alex Werth's office" and said he would pass on the urgent message to Alex.

CHAPTER 81

Keyed up by the excitement of believing he'd just detonated the bomb in the trunk of the red Beemer parked by the Hart Senate Office Building, Majid almost missed the sign for the consolidated BWI Car Rental Facility. He entered the facility and headed for Hertz.

Approaching the area where cars were returned, he parked away from Hertz attendants busy checking in two lanes of vehicles. Abandoning his luggage, he approached the office until he spotted the sign for Gold card customers indicating the spot where their cars were parked, unlocked, with the keys inside. He saw a smartly dressed woman in her thirties slinging a suitcase into the rear seat of a metallic blue Toyota Lexus.

"Pardon me, ma'am."

The woman's glossy blond hair tilted toward him as though questioning whether she'd really heard herself addressed as "ma'am."

By the time she realized what was happening, Majid had moved close enough that she noticed he was pointing a pistol at the midsection of her tailored silk pant suit. She opened her mouth as if to yell for help.

"Don't scream. If you do, I'll have to shoot you, and neither of us wants that."

A terrified look froze on her face, but no sound passed her lips.

"Good. I see you're being reasonable. I promise you will come to no harm if you do what I say."

More silence. Then a quick nod of her head signifying a willingness to obey.

"I'm going to escort you to the passenger door and you're going to get in and fasten your seat belt. Do you understand?"

"Yes. I won't give you any trouble. Just don't hurt me."

Majid took her by the arm, caught her when she stumbled, and guided her to the other side of the car. He opened the door and helped her inside.

Once she was strapped into the security of the car seat, she held her face in her hands and began to weep. Since she posed no immediate danger, Majid ignored her while he familiarized himself with the controls on the latest model Lexus. As he hoped, the key fob was lying on the console, and the vehicle was fully gassed and ready to operate.

He gently pried the woman's purse from her hands and rifled through her billfold until he found her driver's license. Since the car was rented in her name, it was necessary to show her license to the attendant at the gate to complete the contract and secure the car's release.

The only alternatives were for her to drive, which he knew to be unworkable for any number of reasons, or for him to assume the role of designated driver. Just to be on the safe side, he kept his license handy in case the attendant asked to see it as well.

Confident she'd cried herself out for the moment, he handed her a Kleenex from her purse. "Can you hold it together until we're safely out on the highway?"

She nodded and appeared resigned to her fate.

CHAPTER 82

Tommy Lee repeated the telephone message. "That's what the bellman told me. He was the same guy who was on duty the night of the general's assassination. You gave him your card and said to call." He shook his head in disbelief.

"Incredible coincidence. The bellman spotted Dana getting into a taxi at the Tysons Hyatt."

Alex couldn't believe America's number one terrorist had showed up only two miles from their headquarters at the National Counterterrorism Center.

Once he grasped the import of the news, Alex said, "Tommy, contact the bellman and ask him to try and identify the taxi that picked up Dana. We're heading back to NCTC."

He called Jo and Amal who were still at Motel 1 questioning Abdullah.

After briefing them on what he'd learned from Tommy Lee about Dana coming to the Hyatt, he said to Amal, "Notify the FBI and the Fairfax police that Dana was seen leaving Tysons in a taxi about five minutes ago. Ask them to saturate the area."

She said, "Okay. I'll also have the cops contact the major taxi companies that service the Hyatt. Maybe the driver can pinpoint Dana's location."

When Amal stepped out of the room to make her calls, Jo said, "From Tysons, Dana has lots of choices of main highways: Route 66 (probably west), 495 (north toward Maryland or south toward Alexandria or Richmond), or the Dulles Toll Road (toward the airport, Leesburg, or points south and west). That's not to mention a labyrinth of local roads leading all over the place. But she's not going to do all that in a taxi. Where's she heading right now?"

Looking puzzled, Luke said, "Is there any chance she has another hideout in the area. Her house in Pimmit Hills was near Tysons and not far from their place near Dar al-Hijrah Mosque. Maybe there's a spare car parked in a garage someplace."

Shaking her head, Jo said, "Possible, I suppose, but doubtful. According to Abdullah, all the signs point to Dana and her cell getting out of Dodge, expecting to blow up the Pentagon and Congress. What would be the point of a third hideout?"

Luke shrugged his shoulders and kept silent.

"I agree she's trying to flee," Alex said. "In order to do that, she needs another vehicle. What are the ways to get a car?"

Luke perked up. "Steal one. If she were going to do that, Tysons would be the obvious place. But she took a taxi *away* from Tysons, so that's not it."

"Buy one, new or used," Jo said. That's what she's done before. There are probably a dozen car dealerships near Tysons. The problem with buying a car is, it takes too much time. She's almost used up the clock before her four o'clock timetable for detonating the suitcase nuke she believes is ready to explode at the Pentagon. Just twenty minutes left. She needs transportation to start out of the area immediately."

"Rental," Alex and Luke shouted together.

Alex turned to Amal, who'd just come back into the room. "Have the Fairfax cops check car rental locations near Tysons. She's probably renting a car as we speak. Have the FBI put out a BOLO."

The issue of Dana's whereabouts resolved to the extent possible for the moment, Alex addressed Luke.

"Stay at the motel with Abdullah. Try to pry more information from him. I'll have Mansfield send a couple of agents to pick him up. We'll leave Amal's car for you with the keys under the mat. When they've taken Abdullah into custody, join us at NCTC. We'll leave word with Tommy Lee if we get any indication where Dana has gone, and you can join us in the hunt."

Jo poked Alex on the shoulder, "Where are the other members of our team at this point? We need to mobilize as many as possible in the search for Dana."

"Courtney and Randy were questioning Barbara Willoughby at the Pentagon to see if she knows anything about where Reema might be. They're available to head for Tysons to work with the Fairfax cops."

"I sent Mike and Bob back to NCTC to stand by until we knew where we stood with the suitcase nukes. Now that the bombs are being defused, they're free to spearhead the search for Dana, since they're the closest to Tysons.

"Felix, George, and Fred have almost caught up with the Maryland State Police who are chasing Majid who's fleeing near BWI. They need to keep after Majid."

CHAPTER 83

Dana steered the gray Chevy Malibu into the beginnings of Route 7 rush hour traffic and sped west. For the dozen miles from the Avis car rental to Sterling, she drove ten miles over the posted speed limit—hardly a strain for the turbocharged V-6 engine in the Premier model she'd chosen. Passing from Fairfax into Loudoun County, she heaved a small sigh of relief. To an unknown extent, the police in Loudoun would be less attuned to her pursuit than the Fairfax cops, who would be aware of her many footprints living, teaching, and killing in their county.

Monitoring the time without being aware of doing so, she counted the seconds ticking away to four o'clock. She pulled into a shopping area and parked to give the ceremony of destroying the Pentagon the attention it deserved. She meticulously dialed the number for the bomb, entered the code, and pressed the green button. Her only sensation at that moment was satisfaction she had finally avenged Jake. She expected to hear a faint sound of the explosion and witness the telltale mushroom cloud. However, there was neither sound nor sight. No more was there any sign of the Capitol bomb detonating. Perhaps she was too far from ground zero or the winds were blowing the wrong way.

Spotting the parking garage she remembered from an outing to Sterling some months earlier, she drove to the top floor. She parked next to a nondescript sedan in a badly lit corner and proceeded to switch license plates. Having gained a modicum of invisibility from the maneuver, she exited the garage and headed west toward

Leesburg. At the first intersection with a country road, she veered off, intending to take back roads that roughly paralleled Route 7 to Point of Rocks, where she would cross the bridge, following Route 15 into Maryland.

Beginning to relax as she increased the distance from Fairfax County, she toyed with the idea of listening to news of the bombings on WTOP. Ultimately, she decided to wait until she could witness the destruction on TV.

Her destination in Maryland was Deep Creek Lake in the westernmost corner of the state, as far as possible from the Baltimore heading Abdullah would have reported without ending up in West Virginia. As a college student, when she sought to drop off her mother's radar, Deep Creek Lake was one of her favorite hideouts. No records linked her to the locale, and no friends or family members knew of her connection to the lake. In the heart of summer, Deep Creek Lake was a highly popular vacation destination. She would be one stranger among a horde of strangers.

Using a false ID, Dana checked into a remote cabin whose rustic log exterior and the flashing neon sign promising NO TV argued for a laid-back clientele who wouldn't disturb her rest. Exhausted, she stripped off her clothes and climbed into bed. She was too tired to face up to next steps, much less to plan. She couldn't even bring herself to visit a local bar to watch TV images of the destruction of the Pentagon and Congress she and Majid had wrought. There'd be time enough for that tomorrow.

Before she dozed off, she remembered that today was Wednesday.

It was essential to disappear for three days. By Sunday, the manhunt for the terrorists responsible for the devastation in the Washington area should take on elements of routine. Alex and Jolene's team, who'd been working in a pressure cooker for several weeks, would need a break. Dana's best guess was Jolene would spend time at the farm with her beloved thoroughbreds over the weekend. No way would the pursuer expect to be pursued on her home territory.

CHAPTER 84

Majid eyed his unwilling passenger as he drove out of the Hertz garage.

"What's your name, ma'am?" he said, trying to dispel the obvious terror paralyzing her. He succeeded better than he intended.

"Dammit, stop calling me ma'am. My name's Bernadette. You can call me Dr. B."

"Dr. B?" Majid echoed, intrigued, despite himself.

"Yes. I'm a scientist. Not some floozy you can just kidnap and take as a sex slave."

"A scientist?"

"Stop repeating everything I say. It's most annoying. Why did you kidnap me?"

"I have no intention of kidnapping you. I just needed a car. Any car. And you were the only one getting into a vehicle when I came by."

"You mean you didn't target me as a candidate for White slavery?"

"Dr. B, I can assure you my intentions are honorable. I'm interested in your car, not your body."

Majid had the sensation their conversation was taking on the elements of farce, when he caught a glimpse of three police cars racing toward BWI just as he was turning back onto Interstate 95, once again headed for Baltimore.

He estimated the cops would mill around for at least a half hour before they caught on to his ploy of carjacking a Hertz Gold card customer. By then, he would be in the heart of Baltimore, well on his way to once again switching cars. Before then, he had to decide what to do with the obstreperous Dr. B.

Having concluded neither her life nor her virtue was under immediate threat, Majid could see Dr. B was girding her loins to go on the attack.

"If you're only interested in my car, take it and let me out at once."

"I can't do that. I'm wanted by the authorities. If I stop to let you out, that will put me at risk. When we get to Baltimore, I'll set you free."

Anxious to change the subject, he said, "You say you're a scientist. What's your field?"

"I'm a chemist. Also, I'm a biologist. My field is cancer research. You wouldn't understand."

"I might understand more than you think. A few weeks ago, I heard Huda Khousraf speak on cancer research at the Library of Congress. I knew her for a brief period."

He neglected to elaborate he had been Huda's lover and the one who persuaded her to don a suicide bomb vest and blow-up Metro Center.

"You knew Huda Khousraf?" The question was asked in much the tone one might marvel he'd been a next-door neighbor of God's Messenger Muhammad. "I heard she died."

Majid nodded. "I heard the news also. She was a great loss in the battle against cancer." He risked a glance at Dr. B. She was clearly flabbergasted, not knowing how to relate to this unexpected dimension of her kidnapper.

Motion in the rear-view mirror caught his eye. A black SUV was speeding toward him in the distance, rapidly closing the gap. He stared at the speedometer to confirm what he knew to be the case. The needle hovered just under eighty miles per hour. He'd pushed beyond the 10 mph margin most cops were inclined to overlook. But speeds near 80 were not unusual in this section of I-95.

The SUV to his rear must be racing well over 100 mph. Majid was no believer in coincidence. He was being pursued. Despite having eluded three Maryland State Police cruisers by his gambit at Hertz car rental, he'd picked up other pursuers, perhaps FBI.

Almost of its own volition, his foot rammed the accelerator to the floorboard. The Lexus's V-6 responded with a quick burst of power.

His engineer's brain made a hasty calculation. Could he make it to downtown Baltimore before being overtaken by the SUV? Not a chance.

The turnoff to I-695 headed for Towson, however, was within reach. He swerved into the left lane, cutting off an eighteen-wheeler semi, and receiving an angry blast from its horn in return.

Swooping onto I-695, Majid found himself in the thick of Baltimore's rush hour. While it couldn't compete with Washington area traffic's propensity to creep along, and sometimes grind to a halt, anytime from three in the afternoon to seven or later at night, Baltimore drivers suffered their own traffic nightmares, often hurtling bumper to bumper near the speed limit.

When his rear view confirmed the black SUV had followed him down the ramp to the Baltimore Beltway, he saw no alternative to competing in the road race. The Lexus darted from lane to lane at the slightest opening. The screeching of brakes and honking of horns warned Majid he was pushing the envelope of driving exploits.

Except for one time when he'd gotten lost driving home from Oriole Park at Camden Yards, he'd never been on I-695. He had no idea where the Beltway went or how to get off. None of that mattered. He just had to outpace the SUV monster pursuing him.

Unfortunately, that wasn't happening. The SUV driver must have won the Indianapolis 500. Bit by bit, he was gaining.

Dr. B's screams finally penetrated Majid's consciousness. "Stop. You're going to kill us if you keep driving like this."

"Shut up so I can concentrate. We're being chased. For me, it's escape or die."

Near panic, Majid concluded only one option remained that held any hope of getting away. He'd read about the maneuver and seen it in the movies, but he'd never dreamed it would work in the real world.

He'd been driving in the fastest lane on the left, weaving in and out as necessary to forge ahead. He slowed and pulled the right front of the Lexus even with the rear of the Ford sedan in the next lane. Without warning, he swerved the wheel to the right and struck the Ford in the left rear panel covering the tire. The sound of the crash reverberated over the roar of the wind. He fought the steering wheel to bring the Lexus under control.

The Ford spun crazily and smashed into a pickup truck in the lane to the right. What followed was a crescendo of violence as vehicles began colliding. The pile up escalated.

Once he regained control of the Lexus, he stared at the rear-view mirror, trying to detect any sign of the black SUV. He saw none in the mélange of wrecked cars, and immediately slowed to the speed limit.

Despite a worrying thumping sound coming from the right front fender, he could detect no problem with the Lexus's steering.

He turned to Dr. B.

"Talk now if you wish. We've lost our tail. At least for the moment."

CHAPTER 85

Felix called Alex on his cell phone to report that Fred was the one who had spotted Majid, accompanied by an unidentified woman, barreling away from BWI.

"We'd been following the troopers as they took the turnoff toward the airport. They would have no way of knowing the terrorist eluded their dragnet. Inform them Majid somehow got a car and gave them the slip. He was last seen driving a late model blue Lexus heading toward Baltimore on I-95. He's accompanied by a white female."

George, who was driving the SUV, lost no time reversing direction and following Majid.

Sitting in the front passenger seat, Felix watched with admiration George's skill as he piloted the SUV in pursuit of the Lexus. The speedometer climbed to 90, 100, 110 . . .

The SUV was on the brink of overtaking the Lexus when Majid must have noticed the pursuit, sped up, and abruptly veered toward the down ramp to the Baltimore Beltway. By some miracle, George was able to avoid crashing into the eighteen-wheeler Majid nearly ran off the highway.

Despite the Lexus's frantic maneuvers, George was gradually closing the gap. It was only a matter of time before the pursuers would be near enough to force the smaller car off the road.

Unexpectedly, Majid resorted to tactical ramming, sometimes used by police to force a second vehicle into an uncontrolled spin. The result was numerous cars slamming together, blocking the highway. Only George's creative driving enabled their SUV to skid onto the shoulder. Although the SUV experienced numerous dents, it was still drivable, which was more than could be said for most of the cars in the smash up. There was no way to forge ahead past the barricade of wrecked autos.

George shoved the SUV into reverse and began careening backwards on the shoulder until he came to an opening in the center barricade that would enable him to drive through to traffic heading the other direction. He switched on emergency flashers and sped toward the oncoming traffic.

Felix tightened his seat belt, lacking faith the maneuver would be sufficient to save his life in the event of a head-on collision.

CHAPTER 86

Believing he'd shaken the black SUV following him, Majid began considering how to get away from I-695 toward more familiar territory. He saw the sign for Exit 16 to Route 70 headed East to Baltimore and began moving to the rightmost lane. He eased down the ramp and entered the community of Woodlawn, Maryland.

Anxious to appear inconspicuous, he adhered to the speed limit and stayed in the slow lane of traffic. Gradually relaxing, he turned his attention to Dr. B, who'd withdrawn into a shell of angry silence.

"I promised when we got to Baltimore, I'd let you go. But how do I know you won't notify the police as soon as you're released?"

"You don't. In fact, you should assume I'll call the authorities at the first opportunity."

"Honesty is not the best policy under these circumstances. It could get you killed."

"Is your word worth nothing?"

"Dr. B, you would be wise not to provoke me. In case it hasn't dawned on you, I'm a terrorist fleeing for my life. I've no time for social niceties."

Majid was having difficulty comprehending why he'd started this conversation. He was responsible for the deaths of hundreds, perhaps thousands. Why this reluctance at snuffing out the life of one woman? Then it dawned on him.

He'd sacrificed Huda Khousraf in the battle against the Great Satan. At the time, he felt he had no choice; he followed the dictates of necessity. But Dr. B was another matter. He had a choice. No grand mission was at stake. Was his life intrinsically worth more than hers? Perhaps, in a small way, letting her live to carry on cancer research could compensate for taking Huda's life.

He noticed they were driving out of the residential area into a stretch of open highway. If he drove a few miles and released Dr. B, there would be little risk. By the time she could get to a phone, he'd be well into the heart of Baltimore.

"In five minutes, I'll stop the car and you can get out. Leave your cell phone. Feel free to notify the police whenever you can. I do not wish harm to come to you."

Tears of relief trickled down Dr. B's cheeks.

CHAPTER 87

Playing chicken with oncoming traffic, George alternated between the so-called slow lane, which was stampeding toward them at a combined speed of over 150 mph, and the shoulder of the road, when there was more than a few feet of shoulder. Barrels placed on the shoulder often took up the usable space, marking the ubiquitous road construction. The SUV sent more than a few barrels flying.

Felix pointed to the right of the front window and yelled, "Majid just took Exit 16 onto Route 70."

George slammed on the brakes and did a skidding U-turn left, barely making the Route 70 exit.

Fred said, "I'll alert Alex."

He passed on the message.

They all heard Alex's reply on the speakerphone. "The dumb son of a bitch just drove into Woodlawn. That's the Baltimore headquarters of the FBI. Amal will alert the Feebies. Maybe they can head him off."

Counting on getting a pass from the FBI if they were stopped by the local police, George sped through Woodlawn. Heading out of the community to open highway without incident, he gunned the vehicle.

A few miles up the road, Felix yelled, "There's a woman ahead hitchhiking toward Woodlawn."

Fred said, "She's the one Majid kidnapped. Pick her up. Maybe she knows where our fugitive is heading."

George pumped the brakes, bringing the SUV to a skidding halt thirty yards past the woman on the opposite side of the road.

Felix leapt out of the SUV and ran toward the woman. Her bewildered expression telegraphed she didn't know whether to be relieved she'd been saved or terrified at an unexpected new threat.

"Don't be alarmed. You're safe now." Felix held up his credentials. "We're Federal officials chasing the terrorist who kidnapped you."

"Thank God," she said, bursting into tears of relief.

He held her while she sobbed, gently but hurriedly guiding her toward the SUV.

At that moment, Fred jumped out of the vehicle and began waving at a black sedan racing toward them, siren screaming, and lights flashing in the grill. The FBI arrived with a flourish.

Felix eased the woman into the back seat of the SUV and set about trying to calm her.

"You're safe now," he repeated. "What's your name?"

"Call me Dr. B," she choked out, between sobs.

After Dr. B calmed down, he learned she had no information of value to share, other than the fugitive told her he was headed to Baltimore. Given where they were and what was up the highway, that was a foregone conclusion.

CHAPTER 88

The blue Lexus raced toward Baltimore. Majid racked his brain trying to think how to abandon this car, which was attracting pursuers like a magnet, and find another, hopefully anonymous, form of transportation.

Perhaps he should forget about cars and take the train? No, that wouldn't work. After the explosion at the Pentagon and the Capitol—which he was confident he and Dana had pulled off—Amtrak travel along the Eastern Seaboard will be halted by the authorities, just as train travel was curtailed after 9/11.

The bus? No, nobody relies on the bus.

Perhaps he should hijack a truck, or semi like he'd almost driven off the road when cutting onto I-695? Nobody fucks with an eighteen-wheeler. He could shoot the driver and hide him in the sleeping compartment all those big rigs have in the back of the cab. He laughed out loud at the absurdity of the idea. He'd never driven *any* truck, much less one of those monsters. The very idea terrified him.

Cars were the only option. The Lexus would be the target of a BOLO scrutinized by every local, state, and federal law enforcement agency in Maryland and surrounding states. A parking garage was the best bet for trading the BOLO magnet for an anonymous vehicle.

He considered his options. Where to find a suitable parking garage? A downtown business center or Camden Yards?

He chose Camden Yards, believing any police around the ballpark would not be on the lookout for terrorists.

• • •

Lieutenant Marguerite "Maggie" Flanagan swung the Baltimore Police Department's helicopter, FOXTROT 1, around for another pass. She instructed her copilot, Alberto Himenez, to get a picture of the blue Lexus's license plate.

"We don't want any mistakes, Al. If we flag this guy as a wanted terrorist, holy hell will rain on him in the next few minutes."

Al dutifully began recording the scene.

"No question about it," he said. "That's the car described in the FBI's BOLO."

Maggie called dispatch who, per standing orders, patched her through to Captain Wilkerson.

The captain said, "Where's the Lexus now, Lieutenant?"

"The terrorist's on Green Street about six blocks from Camden Yards."

"Here's what I want you to do. Climb to a higher altitude so he doesn't notice you're following him. But stay low enough you can monitor the action. Notify Sergeant Perry to apprehend the suspect, using whatever force he deems necessary."

"Darnell Perry of the Special Operations Section?"

"Yes. You know Darnell?"

"He and my dad were partners when both were patrolmen. Do you want me to deal directly with him, sir? Wouldn't you rather give him the orders yourself?"

"You have the visual overview. And you know Darnell. Don't waste any more time. Over and out."

Maggie tuned her radio to the Special Ops channel.

"Sergeant Perry, I'm relaying an urgent order for you from Captain Wilkerson. Come in."

"That you, Pigtails Flanagan?"

"This is priority business, Sergeant. And we're being recorded. The blue Lexus flagged in the FBI BOLO as being driven by an armed and dangerous terrorist is approaching Camden Yards on Green Street. The captain says apprehend the suspect using whatever force you deem necessary. Come in."

"I see the damn Lexus approaching the intersection where I'm parked. I'm going to ram him."

Maggie could hear the roar as the police cruiser's engine fired up, followed by the squeal of tires peeling out from a dead stop.

She spied Darnell T-boning the Lexus a split second before she heard the ear-splitting crash.

No longer concerned about concealment, she dropped the helicopter like a rock to the lowest altitude consistent with safety. She yelled at her copilot, "Record this. We'll be testifying about today's events for hours in court."

She saw the Lexus door being forced open and a dark-skinned male stagger out. He turned toward the police cruiser just as the burly sergeant extricated himself from the airbag in his steering wheel that would have slammed into his face from the impact of the crash.

Sergeant Perry banged the driver's side door a couple of times and shoved his way onto the street.

Both men drew their pistols and, groggy from the wreck, fought to keep their balance.

Maggie activated the loudspeaker.

"Throw down your weapon or we'll be forced to shoot you from the helicopter.

She eyed her copilot to confirm he'd armed himself with the sniper rifle carried in the cockpit for just such a contingency.

The sergeant and the terrorist faced off at less than twenty feet and commenced firing. Within seconds, Al directed three aimed shots from the rifle.

The terrorist lurched when hit, dropped his weapon, spun in place, and fell to the road.

Concerned, Maggie checked Darnell and realized he'd also been shot. Even at this distance, she could see blood spurting from his left arm and covering the sergeant stripes on his dark blue shirt.

Fighting panic, she barked into her radio, "Officer down. Officer down. Send a bus. Camden Yards on Green Street. The suspected terrorist in the FBI BOLO was also shot multiple times. Both men's gunshot wounds are serious."

Having done all she could in light of the situation, Maggie flew the helicopter to a slightly higher and safer altitude.

She glanced at Al and saw he was laughing.

"What?"

"*Pigtails* Flanagan?" he chortled.

Her cheeks burning, she said, "For fucks sake, I was fourteen years old, and I had a helluva crush on Perry."

CHAPTER 89

Waking from a deep sleep, Dana was glad she'd remembered to place the *DO NOT DISTURB* sign outside her cabin door. The last thing she wanted to face this morning was housekeeping arriving to clean her temporary domicile. She intended to offer the staff a generous tip if they would ignore the cabin for the remainder of her stay.

She glanced at her watch—nine o'clock. This was the latest she'd allowed herself to sleep in months. Her internal alarm was usually ringing by six. The full weight of her exhaustion, physical and emotional, struck home.

Lost momentarily in her fantasy, she imagined the next few days at Deep Creek Lake would be devoted to the Three R's: recreation, relaxation, and reading. Swimming was one of her favorite sports and had been ever since Jake had rescued her from drowning. Although there were attractive beaches and designated swimming areas at the lake, she missed the challenge of swimming in open water at the Gold Coast in New York where dodging sailboats piloted by novice sailors was part of the sport.

Springing out of bed, she paused before the mirror to admire her nude body—shapely legs, slim waist, rounded breasts, and powerful shoulders. *Not bad for thirty-two,* she thought. Luxuriating in the shower, she began planning ways to assassinate her nemesis, Jolene.

Her priority, after a hearty breakfast at the diner, was to get to the nearest sporting goods store and stock up on clothing and outdoor equipment. If possible, she wanted to obtain a rifle or shotgun, which could be easier to do in Virginia—especially at a gun show—than here in Maryland.

In a worst-case scenario, she was willing to rely on her Glock G43, with which she was proficient. But she was reluctant to test her skill in a firefight with any handgun beyond twenty-five yards. There was little doubt Jolene had long guns ready at hand on the farm. Dana believed the stories in the media that virtually any home in rural America had weapons.

She was not hesitant to risk close combat. She was unwilling, however, to be outmatched in fire power. She resolved to depart Deep Creek Lake Saturday morning and to spend the day shopping for firearms.

She dressed and drove to Oakland, Maryland where there were several breakfast options and a nearby Teddy's Great Outdoors. Teddy's stocked any clothing and equipment she would need, including night stalking. Walking from her car to the diner, she stopped by the drug store and picked up copies of the *Washington Post, Baltimore Sun,* and the *Loudoun Times-Mirror.* Surprised not to see blaring headlines about the explosions at the Pentagon and the Capitol, she resisted the temptation to study the papers on the spot, deferring a close reading until she'd been fortified by her morning coffee.

She slid into a booth where greater privacy was assured and ordered a hearty breakfast, including pancakes, eggs, and bacon. Only after taking a swig of coffee did she work up the courage to examine the *Post.*

Feeding her worst fears, there was a total absence of news about the explosions of nuclear weapons destroying the Washington landmarks. At the bottom of page one, she spotted an article headlined RUMOR DENIED PENTAGON TARGETED BY BOMBER. She skimmed the front-page coverage and turned to page four where the story continued. Reporters cited unnamed sources who leaked widespread rumors a bomb was found in a Pentagon official's car trunk. The bomb had been defused before exploding.

Pentagon spokeswoman Captain Danielle Davis told the *Post* there was no basis for the rumor.

Dana frantically turned pages, searching for any mention of a threat to the Capitol. Nothing.

The bastards covered up both attacks. Surprisingly, the Metropolitan Police Department—famous for leaks—threw a blanket of silence over the attempted bombing of Congress. Too many people must have been aware of the attempt at the Pentagon to put a kibosh on rumors, but they got away with an official denial.

She angrily threw the newspaper into the booth seat opposite her. It took all her resolve not to burst into tears. Months of planning. Lives sacrificed. All for naught. Jake remained unavenged.

She held Jolene responsible for the debacle. The indomitable Fed frustrated Dana's moves at every turn. She was the architect of the report in the general's briefcase, and she blocked the terrorists from capitalizing on the secret blueprint. Jolene anticipated the exchange of bombs for dollars with Kasayeva in Nuremberg. Although not directly responsible for Nour and Joffrey being killed in the gunfight with the Russian mafia, Jolene was somehow part of the problem. Jolene's team killed Zaha in Paris. Her team captured Jaber and Omar at the safe house in Pimmit Hills and Abdullah at Motel 1.

In the throes of Dana's emotional collapse, Jolene was culpable not only for her own but the world's woes, including global warming and world hunger.

She drained her coffee cup and waved frantically at the waitress for a refill. *Get a grip*, she told herself, but no one was listening.

When her pancakes and all the trimmings arrived, she stared at the mountain of food, having lost her appetite. What was the point?

She was used to striving for important goals throughout her life. She'd bested other competitors, even Kasayeva. Attaining a PhD from Harvard was no small accomplishment. Nor was leading a terrorist cell responsible for killing more Americans than any group since 9/11. Why then was she overwhelmed by a feeling of abject failure?

She'd done her best to blow up the Pentagon and the Capitol. But fate had intervened. No. It wasn't fate. *Jolene Martin* was the omnipresent stumbling block. Well, Sunday, Jolene would be taken off the board.

Then she would rebuild a terrorist cell whose sole purpose would be to level the Pentagon and the Capitol. Jake would be avenged. Her pride and self-confidence would be rehabilitated. Her nemesis would be dead.

CHAPTER 90

Cantering on Regret around the training racetrack, Jolene kept up a steady stream of narrative designed to convince Alex, riding next to her on White King, of the differences between racing thoroughbreds and working on a ranch with quarter horses.

"I know it gets hot in Montana, and you have to take care to cool down a working quarter horse at the end of the day. But heat in Virginia in August can be life threatening for people. It's equally or more dangerous for horses, particularly thoroughbreds.

"Look at us, we're soaked with sweat because the temperature has been in the upper nineties. Sure, we cooled down with a bit of skinny dip in the creek by the fallen oak tree. King and Regret had their own cool down then. But that's not enough."

She glanced at Alex to try to figure out whether his silent listening meant he was really paying attention, or whether it was a sign of patronizing a lover to get her into the sack at the end of the day. *Damn his tendency to be inscrutable.*

Deciding any more lecturing would be counterproductive, she reined in Regret and dismounted, swinging her legs free and landing balanced on both feet. She was secretly pleased a somewhat surprised Alex mimicked her behavior.

Walking without talking, she held the reins and led Regret toward the stable. After securing the filly inside her stall, she removed the English saddle and carried it to the rack in the tack room. Her lover mirrored her every movement, following her lead in avoiding dialogue.

She returned to Regret and began rubbing her down.

"Good girl," she said, stroking the horse's forelock.

"Did you miss me? The world is a mess, and I was trying to do my bit to make it better. But being away from you for so long was a big part of the sacrifice. Hopefully, we did some things right. We'll have to wait and see how it comes out. At least, I have this weekend to spend time with you."

She decided not to bore the filly with the details of what she'd done in Europe and since returning to the States to try to save the world.

When the horses were looked after, Jolene heard Stephanie's jeep approaching the farm. It was the teen's practice to make sure everything was in order as part of her afternoon's routine. She never accepted Jolene's assurance that the farm's mistress had things under control.

Listening to the welcome sounds of Stephanie's arrival, Alex silently prayed the girl's presence would be the catalyst needed for Jo to settle down. While he refrained from voicing his thoughts, he'd grown increasingly concerned about his lover's state of mind since they'd left Northern Virginia for a supposedly relaxing weekend at the farm in Loudoun County.

Far from relaxing, Jo exhibited uncharacteristic behaviors—like lecturing about the importance of the cool-down phase of riding—that bordered on the bizarre. Only during the lovemaking while skinny dipping at the creek had she loosened up.

He knew what was bothering Jo, because the same problem was lurking at the back of his mind. What was Dana Hussein al-Sadi plotting now that her attempts to detonate two suitcase nukes had been frustrated? And where was Dana at this moment?

He mentally replayed the last NCTC debriefing when the team had brainstormed those two questions. There were as many viewpoints as there were people in the meeting room.

Courtney started the discussion. "Dana will abandon terrorism. The risks are too great. Her background and description, complete with videos when she was posing as various personalities, have been shared with US intelligence and law enforcement agencies, albeit with a heavily sanitized version of what crimes she committed to earn a description as a 'most wanted' terrorist."

A few heads nodded in agreement.

Courtney continued. "She'll retreat to the life of privilege she's enjoyed since birth. Right now, Dana's sunbathing on a nude beach in front of a luxury hotel in some haven for criminals and tax dodgers where the authorities refuse to grant the US extradition rights."

Felix and Amal argued for a contrary point of view.

Felix reminded everyone of Mossad's Operation Wrath of God in which the Black September terrorists who massacred eleven Jewish athletes during the 1972 Olympics in Munich were eliminated one by one over a period of two decades.

"In the Middle East, revenge is often conflated with justice. Dana believes our NCTC team is responsible for her failure in what she saw as a just cause. She *will* find a way to strike back against us as a group or as individuals. Alex and Jolene are at particular risk."

Amal nodded. "The main emotion driving Dana is hatred of the Pentagon brass whom she holds accountable for betraying her brother. In her mind, that guilt extends to those of us in this room and, in a way, to all of America. Her identification with ISIS is just a pretext. If there were no ISIS, her behavior wouldn't change."

Courtney looked up in surprise at the last comment.

"I agree with Felix that Jolene and Alex will bear the brunt of her anger," Amal said. "The attempt to kill them will be her next move. But even if she's successful, that won't be the end of her rampage. She'll recruit another terrorist cell, seek to acquire more nukes from Russia, and redouble her efforts to blow up the Pentagon. She's obsessed. Nothing short of death will stop her."

On that bleak note, the team broke up.

On reflection, Alex was convinced by Amal's prediction of Dana's behavior. He whispered, "The bitch is stalking Jo this very minute."

CHAPTER 91

Dana parked the rented Chevy Malibu behind an abandoned gas station store two miles away and hiked cross country to within sight of Jolene's farm. The sliver of a moon peeking through dark clouds was fighting a losing battle with the leafy overhang of dense woods. The night vision stalking equipment she'd bought at Teddy's Great Outdoors was proving to be worth its weight in gold.

A teenage enthusiasm for orienteering was paying off. She couldn't have done a better job zeroing in on her target if she were marching across fields and along a woodland path in broad daylight with signposts every hundred yards.

In addition to the Glock, ready at hand in the top of her backpack, she carried a SIG Sauer AR-15 style rifle in her left hand. She'd chosen the rifle as the best of the best at a widely advertised gun show near Dulles airport. The easy maneuverability afforded by the sixteen-inch barrel, pistol grip, and adjustable shoulder stock made it suitable either for close combat or medium-range sniping. With a thirty-round magazine, it boasted more firepower at short range than a pistol and greater accuracy at longer distances than a shotgun.

At four o'clock, she noticed a slight rise of the land by the side of the path she was certain the horses would follow into the woods. It was an ideal spot to construct a blind of bushes and tree branches. She would be able to see Jolene without being seen. The element of surprise made her even more confident of her ability to kill her nemesis.

No action would be expected at the stable before sunrise. The vegetation at the edge of the woods was thick enough to mask the blind, concealing her movements. She settled down to pass the time, resting her back against a fallen tree trunk near her sniping position.

The aroma of coffee wafting near her pillow brought Jolene awake. She opened her eyes to Alex holding out her favorite mug filled with the life-giving liquid. She took a swig of coffee and set the mug on the bedside table next to her ready-to-fire pistol. A glance at the window confirmed dawn had not yet arrived.

Throwing off the sheet, she yawned and stretched. Her nude body trembled with anticipation as she watched Alex eying her with desire. After a night of lovemaking, she felt relaxed and content. While she didn't entirely dismiss Alex's warnings that Dana was stalking her, she was determined not to let those thoughts disturb her enjoyment of this interlude with her lover.

Sunday was a day with no agenda. She could entice Alex to join her in bed and enjoy another amorous frolic. Or they could ride to the creek and skinny dip, fool around, and take a nap listening to the sound of the running water. In the unlikely event sex grew boring, she subscribed to the *Washington Post* and the *New York Times*.

The humor of the situation dawned on her, and she laughed out loud.

"Hungry?" he asked, sharing a grin.

"Now that you mention it, I'm starved."

"That's good because I made enough pancake batter to feed a small army. My first thought when I saw you lying there looking so enticing was that the batter might go to waste."

"Not a chance, and we'll have to stay active today to ensure it doesn't go to *waist*."

They both chuckled at the corny joke as she jumped off the bed, stumbling on a boot she'd left on the floor last night when hurriedly disrobing. He caught her and pulled her to him, first as a gesture of protection, then the warmth of her body triggered other impulses. His lips brushed hers and she responded. The kiss deepened.

Her fingers began to undo the buttons on his shirt, first one, then when there was no objection, all of them. Seemingly impatient with the tempo, he unfastened his belt and pulled off his jeans. He kicked off shoes and removed T-shirt and shorts, tossing them into the corner.

The electricity of their bodies touching stimulated more touching, stroking, caressing. Eager for deeper intimacy, they fell into bed. In the past few weeks, their relationship had moved beyond simple physical attraction to an emotional closeness. But physical desire remained a driving factor. Sex and love were intertwined in ways Jolene couldn't fully grasp and was hesitant to examine too closely. For the moment, she was content to lose herself in Alex's touch.

• • •

After making love and falling asleep in each other's arms, they were awakened by a shout, "Hello the house. I need to talk with you right now."

"Stephanie's arrived," Jolene said.

The lovers dressed and rushed downstairs, toting their pistols at the ready.

"What's going on? Jolene said, resonating to the urgency in Stephanie's voice.

"I was out with King on the training track when I thought I spied someone lurking behind the bushes at the edge of the woods by the path to the creek. I couldn't be certain, and I was afraid to be too obvious about staring. I didn't want to spook the intruder if it was an intruder."

Knowing the teenager's eyesight to be acute, having watched her follow the movements of a hawk she herself couldn't see in the distance, Jolene took the warning seriously.

"What'd you do?"

"I cut King's workout short and rode back to the stable, put him safely away in his stall, and hustled here to alert you and Alex. It may be nothing. But since you've had some serious *somethings* in the past, it'd be dumb to take a chance."

"You did the right thing," Alex said.

He glanced at Jolene and said, "It seems Amal was right. Unlike Courtney's prediction, there are no nude beaches around here."

Stephanie lifted her eyebrows at the odd comment. But she shrugged, as if she were growing accustomed to odd occurrences.

"We should alert the team to the likelihood Dana is stalking us," Jolene said.

Alex nodded. He took out his cell phone and dialed NCTC.

When Tommy Lee answered, he explained that Dana Hussein al-Sadi was suspected of lurking at Jolene's farm in Loudoun County. He repeated the location of the farm even though he knew the communications chief had contact information for all members of the antiterrorist team at his fingertips.

"Notify the team and direct them to get here ASAP. They should park their vehicles a mile away and hike to the farmhouse from the far side. Enter through the cellar door, which is on the opposite side of where we believe Dana is hiding to ambush us. Come armed for combat. We'll try to take Dana alive. Caution the team not to risk their lives to do so."

Jolene believed Alex's plan was to wait to confront Dana until all of the team was assembled, overwhelming force being the favored offensive strategy whenever possible. In this instance, she questioned the strategy. Dana had proven adept at anticipating her opponent's actions, much as Jolene herself was gifted in that regard.

When Alex concluded his call, she tapped him on the shoulder. "We can't afford to stall until the team arrives. Dana has outguessed us in the past, as she did Kasayeva in Nuremberg. If we fail to show outside, she'll assume something is up. She'll slip away, and we may never get another chance to capture or kill her."

He looked thoughtful and turned to Stephanie.

"How long ago was it you first glimpsed the terrorist we know as Dana?"

"Five to ten minutes, more or less."

"And you've been in the house about five minutes. We don't know how much information she may have about our weekend routine . . . actually, we haven't been doing this long enough to have a routine . . ."

Stephanie tied to hide a grin, doubtless reacting to Alex's description of a weekend love nest as a "routine."

Jolene intervened. "In any case, if a half hour or more goes by and she sees no one show their face outside, she'll suspect something is wrong. She'll disappear, and we'll have wasted a golden opportunity."

She squared her shoulders. "I'm going to the stable. I can find things to do with the horses that will lead her to believe we're getting ready to go riding together.'

Alex protested. "Don't be a fool. That's too dangerous. Catching her is not worth putting your life on the line."

"Give me a little credit. I can swing in and out of her line of sight, without allowing an opening for a sniper shot with a rifle. The distance is great enough she'd have a hard time hitting me with a shotgun, and a pistol shot would be impossibly difficult."

"You can't do it," Alex insisted loudly. "As your team leader, I forbid it."

This time Stephanie didn't bother trying to hide her grin. She knew Jolene well enough to anticipate her reaction to being told what to do in that tone of voice.

Jolene didn't bother answering. She snatched the western straw hat off the teenager's head and hurried out the door, headed for the stable. Her pistol was tucked in the belt at her back.

CHAPTER 92

The sight of Jolene hurrying out the farmhouse door startled Dana, even though she'd been waiting for just such action for nearly a half hour. By the time she got in sniper position, her target had disappeared into the entrance to the stable.

Wait a minute. Was that Jolene she saw? The western straw hat on the figure's head was the same as the one the teenager wore who was riding the white stallion around the track earlier this morning.

Could she be sure the figure glimpsed for scant seconds was Jolene and not the teenager? She replayed the images in her mind, focusing her trained artist's eye. Her art history professors at Harvard often commented on her astonishing visual memory. As a sniper, her memory trick was invaluable.

Yes. She was certain. *The figure was Jolene.*

Then why the hat? She imagined everyone riding in the country around here might wear western hats. Why not? The style was practical for keeping the sun out of their eyes, as well as shading them from Virginia's searing summer heat.

What else would riders be expected to wear, a baseball cap? Those ridiculous helmets which were supposed to protect riders from brain injury in the event they fall off the horse?

No. A western style hat is natural—even to be expected. But *the same hat* as the teenager was wearing? Was it the same hat? A moment's reflection convinced Dana it was. What kind of game was Jolene playing?

Was her prey trying to fool her into thinking the teenager was the one coming to the stable? To cause her to doubt her own eyes?

No. The bitch was too smart and knew her too well to pull that.

At once, the explanation struck Dana. *The teenager saw her.* She had told Jolene.

If so, why the charade? The sensible thing to do would be to hole up in the farmhouse and call for help. No way Dana would try to attack the house. It's old-style, built like a fortress.

Only one reason Jolene would let herself be seen coming to the stable: to keep her would-be assassin in the vicinity with the hope of a sniping shot. The stalemate would go on until the cavalry arrived. *Jolene will show herself—offer a tantalizing glimpse. Like a burlesque striptease, never reveal enough to offer a clean shot.*

At that moment, Jolene led a different horse—not the white stallion—out of the stable, turned and ducked back inside, leaving the horse standing partially in the open, taking care not to offer herself as a vulnerable target.

"Now I know her game," Dana whispered aloud. "She imagines she's safe in the stable, while I lurk in the woods hoping for a workable sniper shot that will never come. "But she doesn't know mine. My best gambit is to trap her in the stable and kill her there."

CHAPTER 93

Talking quietly to Regret while stroking her flank, Jolene said, "Don't be upset if you hear some loud banging noises. That's just people working off their frustrations. Nothing for you to be concerned about."

She then turned her attention to King, still in his stall, and uttered more meaningless calming sentiments of the sort humans often impart to animals, more to cope with their own inner disquiet than to have the desired effect in dispelling the anxiety that permeated the shared atmosphere.

As was her wont, she sought to analyze the scene at the stable from Dana's perspective. Were her brief appearances outside the stable believable? Or was the charade transparent, likely to inspire the terrorist to alter her tactics?

She glanced at her watch. Only ten minutes since she'd darted from the farmhouse to the stable. But that was enough time for Tommy Lee to alert the team to head for the farm. At best, it would take nearly an hour for them to arrive and assemble inside the farmhouse. More time to mount an encircling maneuver to sneak up on Dana. Was it credible the terrorist would prove gullible and wait for her game plan to play out for that length of time?

Not a chance. Dana was bound to figure out she was being mousetrapped. If so, what action would she take? Would she retreat?

No. She'd mount an attack on the stable.

Jolene stepped outside, took a quick look around and ducked back in. She'd seen nothing out of order. The sun was still hot. The sky was filled with white pillowy clouds sailing across a blue backdrop. The breeze, such as it was, blew warm air from the woods toward the farmhouse.

She knew what had to be done, just as she knew Alex would be pissed once he found out she'd done it. Removing the western straw hat, she placed it carefully on a shelf in the tack room. Stephanie loved that hat and would be upset if any holes were shot in it.

Her one disappointment was not leaving a cache of arms in the stable when she'd placed rifles and shotguns at strategic locations in the farmhouse. No matter. She had her pistol, and that would have to do. Checking the weapon, she satisfied herself it was ready to fire.

She slipped quietly out the back door of the stable and dropped to her knees, crawling through tall weeds toward the woods that circled the property. Taking care, it was possible to sneak up on Dana's location without being seen. If she were lucky, she'd surprise Dana lying in ambush staring at the stable, waiting for her target to reappear. If she were unlucky . . . well, she wasn't prepared to consider that alternative.

• • •

Alex's mood transitioned from irritation at Jo *ignoring*—no, make that *defying*—him, by charging impetuously out to the stable to bait Dana with glimpses of her body, to serious concern for his lover's safety.

He mumbled to himself, "Moreover, there's not a damn thing I can do about it."

To his surprise, Stephanie interrupted his soliloquy. "But there is."

He blinked at her. "What?"

"I said, of course there's *something* you can do to protect Jolene. There's no reason for you to stand around like a bump on a log waiting for reinforcements to arrive. Deputize me to do the waiting."

Stephanie's expression telegraphed he was too dense to see the obvious.

"You go out. Find Dana. Kill her. Then Jolene—or *Jo*, as you prefer to think of her—is rescued. You're the hero. The two of you can resume your 'weekend routine.' Things can get back to normal around here."

Alex stared wide-eyed at the seventeen-year-old who'd just articulated one of the most cold-blooded summaries of battlefield tactics, replete with irony and humor, he'd ever heard.

"If I followed your suggestion," he began hesitantly, "that would leave you here alone and unprotected."

Stephanie laughed. "Alone, maybe. But this house is a damn arsenal. Every pantry, closet, and storage area is stocked with a rifle or shotgun and enough ammo to fight World War III. I'm an excellent shot. This farmhouse is a fortress. I can protect myself. Tell me what instructions to give the cavalry when they arrive. Then get your ass out there and kill Dana."

Responding to the teenager's assurances she could take care of herself, Alex prepared for the hunt. He selected a semi-auto shotgun as optimal for close-quarters combat, the pistol grip giving the advantage of one-handed fire, if necessary. He stuffed his pack with 12-gauge shells, mixing buckshot and slugs. He added extra magazines for his pistol and a bottle of water. Once armed, he slipped out the back door and began the process of encircling his prey.

Choosing a passage through the woods roughly parallel to the road, he calculated it would bring him to the opposite side of the riding path to the creek from where Stephanie had spotted Dana.

He jogged the first half of the route, confident distance and a wind blowing from Dana in his direction would diminish the likelihood she could hear him approach. Once he drew closer, he slowed his pace and crept cautiously, thankful the summer underbrush would cushion his footsteps. When the opening from the riding path to the creek came in sight, he dropped to his knees and began crawling, cradling the shotgun in the crook of his arms.

Once in position behind a clump of bushes that would serve as a blind, he searched the foliage on the other side of the path. Nothing. No sign of Dana. No movement at all.

He agonized over how long he should wait for some hint of his target. Once he exposed himself by crossing the opening of the path, he'd be a sitting duck, vulnerable to an easy shot from Dana's weapon.

On the other hand, if she'd already begun moving toward the stable to surprise Jo, there would be nothing to stop her. He decided to take the known risk to rush to his lover's protection. If he guessed wrong, at least Jo would have the sound of gunfire to alert her to what was happening.

He assumed a sprinter's stance, calculating a quick rush would allow for the minimum time of exposure. If Dana spotted him charging toward her, there was a slight possibility she would be so startled it would give him an equal chance of getting off the first shot. In this game, whoever shoots first is the winner. No one could survive a blast from his shotgun. And, if his assumption was correct that Dana was armed with a rapid-fire rifle, a quick burst would put him down for good.

A former sprinter on his high school track team, he waited for the imaginary sound of the starter pistol. When the pistol fired, he exploded across the path to the other side. As soon as he was safely in the underbrush, so far unscathed, he dove for cover behind a dead tree limb.

A tad surprised to be alive, he scrutinized the area where he calculated Dana had lurked in wait. Sure enough, he could see signs someone had hidden there, and recently. He checked out the tree limb he'd used for cover and spotted an indentation such as a body would have made by resting there for a time.

Stephanie was right. She'd spotted Dana hiding in ambush. Were it not for the teenager's alertness, both he and Jolene would be dead by now, assassinated by a revenge-seeking terrorist.

As it was, Dana had moved on, undoubtedly creeping toward the stable, having seen through Jo's charade of playing hide and seek.

There were no options. He needed to overtake the assassin and take her off the board before she reached the stable and terminated his lover.

Throwing caution to the wind, he began running full-out in the direction of the stable. He knew this action put him at extreme risk. If Dana heard him before he saw her, there was no doubt she would shoot the moment he appeared in her sights. At best, he would have a split second to dive for cover.

• • •

The sound of running feet pounding through the underbrush to her rear alerted Dana to trouble. She'd been guilty of the cardinal sin of any combatant trying to stalk an opposing force. All her attention was focused to her front. She'd forgotten the field of combat encompassed 360 degrees, and the enemy's position could be high or low. The opposing force could be in one location or separated in two or more.

Her instinctive reaction was to spin toward the approaching footfalls. She fired two bursts from the rifle, held hip high without consciously aiming. After firing, she dropped prone and listened. The explosive blasts were followed by an ominous silence.

No more footfalls. No cry of pain. Did that mean she'd succeeded in killing her opponent? Had she missed and blasted nothing more than tree limbs and bushes? Were one or more aggressors lying wounded and invisible in the underbrush between her current location and the entrance to the riding path through the woods where she'd commenced her stalking maneuver?

Now she faced a real dilemma. Her rifle fire was a warning signal to Jolene, undoubtedly inviting a counterattack. Dana could no longer hope to sneak up on an unsuspecting prey in the stable, if that had ever been realistic. The prey was now the hunter. Dana knew she had to face up to the possibility of attack from two fronts.

Briefly, she considered the option of leaving the field of battle. At present, she could see none of her enemies, which meant she was similarly invisible to them. Why not steer a path at right angles to the one she'd been following? She could escape through the woods before anyone knew she was gone. While Jolene and her other opponents (if any were still alive) wasted time on a fruitless search of the woods, she could retrieve her car from the abandoned gas station and flee.

Her fortune, coupled with her skills at eluding the authorities, offered the promise of a safe and luxurious retirement in the destination of her choice. She was beautiful and desirable. Other lovers—men or, if she chose, women—would be there for the taking. There would be time and money to pursue her love of art. This was the life she'd fantasized about when playing a female Midas with the millions she'd saved in the aftermath of Kasayeva's death, to which was added the ten-million-dollar contribution at the Harvard Club.

Shrugging, she knew she would do none of those things. Her fate was written in the sand on a Long Island beach when she was saved by her brother. She'd dedicated a life of terrorism to honoring Jake and avenging the dishonor the Pentagon brass had showered on his memory.

No choice.

Her destiny demanded she assassinate Jolene and any others impeding her mission. The Pentagon would fall, and the event would be publicized as payback for the perfidy of Pentagon potentates. There'd be time enough for an idyllic retirement *if* she survived all that.

The rifle fire prompted Jolene to freeze. The instructor in small-unit combat tactics at The Farm emphasized the importance of avoiding movement whenever possible. He was fond of repeating the principal clue to survival on the battlefield: "The human eye is attracted to motion, especially unexpected or unusual motion."

Still as a statue, she remained immobile behind a dense bush. Her eyes scanned the woods in the direction of the gunfire. Memory rehearsed what she'd heard, recognizing the characteristic blasts of a semi-auto rifle firing powerful ammunition.

She couldn't resist the temptation to glance at the pistol in her right hand. Not normally prone to waste emotional energy on water under the bridge, she couldn't avoid another moment of remorse at not placing a rifle and shotgun in the stable.

"Suck it up," she mumbled. "Be thankful for the pistol and warning shots alerting me to the threat, since it's headed my way."

She dropped to her knees and began to crawl forward, a spider scurrying across a web. Coming to a depression in the ground, she crept in and decided to make a stand at what passed for a trench, offering a smidgen of protection from oncoming fire. To better blend into the terrain, she smeared dirt on her face and hands and stuck weeds in her hair.

As ready as she could be, she lay still and waited for Dana to come to her. When worries about who might have been the recipient of the rifle fire competed for her thoughts, she pushed the concern to the back of her mind.

After several minutes, movement in the brush about forty feet to her front captured her attention. She waited for confirmation a human was the cause. Rabbits and squirrels scurried through the woods, as well as foxes and larger animals. She'd been mistaken before.

Then she made out a sneaker, sticking out from behind a clump of wildflowers. Staring intently, the outline of part of a leg attached to the sneaker was dimly visible. The body was bound to be connected to the leg in a predictable location. Forty feet was a viable distance for a pistol shot. At the shooting range, she could place several rounds in a silhouette target's center body mass from forty feet.

But she reminded herself, combat is different from the controlled environment of the range. Even if she hit Dana's prone body, she couldn't be sure any wounds would be fatal. An injured Dana, with a semi-auto rifle and sufficient ammo, could rain deadly fire on Jolene's shallow trench. A wiser course would be to hold off and wait for her attacker to advance to within easy range of a kill shot.

After a brief hiatus, she rejoiced at having been patient. The figure began to move, slithering forward through the wildflowers toward a cluster of holly bushes. For a moment, Dana was partially exposed and within pistol range.

Jolene took careful aim and fired three shots, the first a head shot and the next two into her target's torso. Dana's body jerked as the bullets impacted. Then she slumped forward with her face in the dirt, blanketing the rifle she'd been cradling in her arms.

Cautiously approaching the motionless body, Jolene pressed her pistol against the back of Dana's head while she felt for a pulse. After confirming the terrorist was dead, she confiscated the rifle, turned her back on the corpse, and began jogging in the direction from which she'd earlier heard the rifle bursts.

Her breath choked to a stop when she spied Alex sprawled across a log, blood still leaking from wounds in his arm, side, and scalp. Forcing herself to act, she hurried to his prone body and frantically searched for vital signs. Breath returned when she detected heartbeats, albeit faint.

She slipped out her cell phone, turned off the mute button, and dialed the farmhouse.

"Stephanie, Dana is dead. The threat is over, but Alex is severely wounded."

"What can I do to help?" the teenager asked.

"Call 911 and have them send an ambulance to the farmhouse. Then saddle Regret. Bring an extra blanket and straps or rope so we can carry Alex on the filly. You and I will bring him back to the house. I'm afraid he might bleed out if we wait until the paramedics come to him in the woods."

"Where are you?"

"Remember all those holly bushes when we walked from the back of the stable toward the entrance to the riding path to the creek?"

"Yeah."

"Alex and I are about one hundred yards east of the holly."

"I'll be there in less than five minutes."

CHAPTER 94

Listening to the doctor, Jolene learned Alex's wounds were not as serious as she'd feared when first coming upon him bleeding in the woods. Alex was sleeping in the recovery room, waiting to come out of the anesthesia, while she received a report on his condition.

"He's young, strong, and healthy, so we can expect a quick recovery," Dr. Indira Prakash said, in a tone that led Jolene to believe she was attracted to her patient by more than professional regard. "The wound to his arm will heal with no aftereffects. The bone was not fractured. The gunshot to his spleen was more serious. However, the operation was successful. To my surprise, I was able to save the spleen." The surgeon smiled modestly at her skill. "A lower rib guarding the spleen was fractured. That will cause him pain for some time. Not much today's medicine can do for a cracked rib." The information was imparted with an air of blatant self-satisfaction.

Dr. Prakash was slim but shapely, regal in her white coat. Her black hair was done in a twisted bun that set off an aquiline face. Jolene was as impressed with the young doctor's beauty as she was by her physician's skills. She experienced a twinge of jealousy at the idea of the doctor lingering over Alex's care, fearing her bedside manner might involve more than guiding the patient toward a speedy recovery.

"Thank you, doctor. I'll pass on your good news to Alex's colleagues. How long before he can be discharged?"

"Today's Sunday. He could go home Wednesday, maybe even Tuesday."

Jolene nodded, indicating that was about when she expected. "And how long before he can resume normal activities?"

Dr. Prakash shook her head. "That's hard to say. Best case scenario, avoiding undue physical strain, he should be able to get around and do most things in a couple of weeks. I'll need to see him regularly during that period to monitor his progress. He should be fully recovered in six weeks to two months."

As the doctor left the room, Jolene mentally resolved to accompany Alex during those "regular" visits. She trusted Dr. Prakash's medical skills, but she was unwilling to trust her as a woman.

During her Monday morning visit, Jolene saw that Alex was past the stage of being groggy. He seemed anxious to talk.

"Tell me what happened after I was shot."

She related the sequence of events: Dana leaving him for dead, or at least out of action, and stalking toward the stable.

"She knew I would hear the gunshots and be alerted. Apparently, she believed it was realistic to surprise me or, at least, prevail in a gunfight, since she had a high-end rifle with plenty of ammunition. As luck would have it, I set up in a good location. She had the disadvantage of having to crawl through an open area, leaving her vulnerable to an easy shot with my pistol. I hit her with three rounds, any of which would have been fatal. To be honest, I had no intention of taking her alive."

"If she lived, she would have remained a threat," he said, shaking his head resignedly. "Fortunately for humanity, Dana and Majid are both dead. How's the sergeant who shot Majid outside Camden Yards?"

"Felix stayed in Baltimore until he got word Sergeant Perry was going to be okay. He'll be laid up for a month or so, but he's expected to make a full recovery. Perry is slated to receive a Medal of Honor from the Baltimore Police. The helicopter crew who identified Majid's car and guided the sergeant to the terrorist have been recommended for Bronze Stars."

"What about the bomb squads at the Pentagon and the Capitol?

Their actions involved the highest level of personal risk, and they probably saved more lives than anyone in history."

She shook her head sadly.

"That's a sticky wicket. Both nuclear bomb threats are part of an official cover-up. There's some talk behind the scenes of secret recognition. I'm not optimistic it will ever happen. The same is true of our team. We're being disbanded; no one getting any attaboys." She smiled resignedly. "Not that the bureaucratic jockeying matters to our guys, who are satisfied having succeeded against all odds."

Alex nodded in agreement and leaned forward, flinching from the pain in his side.

"Does that clean the slate for Dana and her terrorist cell?"

"Yes, except for the mysterious Reema, whose role was to seduce Barbara Willoughby to smuggle the suitcase nuke to the Pentagon in the trunk of her car. We have fingerprints and some vague descriptions, but she seems to have disappeared without a trace."

Jolene was beginning to get bored at recapping the culmination of a month filled with life-threatening tension. She was anxious to bring up their personal relationship, but she wasn't sure how. Also, she was plagued by jealous uncertainty that Alex might prove tempted by the romantic overtures she expected Indira Prakash to lavish on him in the guise of medical care.

Alex said, "I've been talking with Dr. Prakash about my treatment over the next couple of months."

"Oh?" Jolene flinched visibly, but she was grateful Alex was staring off into space and could not have noticed.

"She emphasized I needed to rest and gradually increase my exercise, while avoiding stress. I called Frank Mansfield and explained the situation to him. He told me Rick Birmingham and Elmer Farnsworth were being investigated for their recent activities. Then, he approved two months sick leave in advance."

She pretended to ignore the news about Birmingham.

"That's the least he could do, since you led the effort that prevented an epic disaster."

"I asked him if he could use his influence to get you a sabbatical for two months so you could look after me. Would you be willing to have me stay at your farm? Stephanie could help us make sure an extended 'weekend routine' was not too stressful."

Jolene gave a surprised laugh. Unconsciously, she fingered the gold locket on her neck.

"Yes, on one condition."

Alex raised an eyebrow. "What's the condition."

"After you've recovered a bit, I want you to accompany me to New York to meet my mom. Then we'll begin the process of tracking down my dad, so you can meet him."

In response to Alex's smile, Jolene jumped on the hospital bed and embraced the patient.

ACKNOWLEDGMENTS

A book is the product of many hands over a prolonged period of time. First, I would like to thank John Koehler and the accomplished team he and Joe Coccaro have assembled. My editor Becky Hilliker deserves special mention for taking the draft of my inaugural manuscript and turning it into a finished novel. Danielle Koehler has accomplished miracles both in the design of my author website and making a believer of a devout skeptic about the value of social media in promoting literature. My daughter Nori Jones has played a pivotal role in many areas of working with the Koehler Books team.

While there is a world of difference between fiction and nonfiction, numerous editors and coauthors have assisted in my forays over the years writing about public policy and controversial current events.

I would like to underscore the contributions to my all-too-slow acquisition of writing skills of presenters and participants at numerous conferences organized by the Mystery Writers of America, International Thriller Writers, Virginia Writers Club, and others.

All writers draw upon a lifetime of experience and such is my case. I'm indebted to relatives, friends, neighbors, teachers, and colleagues in the many places I've lived, worked, soldiered, and traveled, spanning fifty states and several countries in Asia and Europe.